# ALPHABET SQUADRON

DEL REY
NEW YORK

# STAR WARS™

# ALPHABET SQUADRON

## ALEXANDER FREED

Published in the United States by Del Rey,
an imprint of Random House, a division of
Penguin Random House LLC, New York.

DEL REY and the HOUSE colophon are registered
trademarks of Penguin Random House LLC.

Hardback ISBN 978-1-9848-2198-0
International edition ISBN 978-1-9848-1996-3
Ebook ISBN 978-1-9848-2199-7

Printed in the United States of America on acid-free paper

randomhousebooks.com

2 4 6 8 9 7 5 3 1

First Edition

Book design by Elizabeth. A. D. Eno

To Renée, who sustained me

# THE DEL REY

# STAR WARS

## TIMELINE

### MASTER & APPRENTICE

**I** | THE PHANTOM MENACE

**II** | ATTACK OF THE CLONES
THE CLONE WARS (TV SERIES)
DARK DISCIPLE

**III** | REVENGE OF THE SITH
CATALYST: A ROGUE ONE NOVEL
LORDS OF THE SITH
TARKIN

SOLO
THRAWN
A NEW DAWN
THRAWN: ALLIANCES
THRAWN: TREASON
REBELS (TV SERIES)

ROGUE ONE

THE DEL REY

# STAR WARS™

## TIMELINE

**IV** A NEW HOPE

BATTLEFRONT II: INFERNO SQUAD
HEIR TO THE JEDI
BATTLEFRONT: TWILIGHT COMPANY

**V** THE EMPIRE STRIKES BACK

**VI** RETURN OF THE JEDI

ALPHABET SQUADRON
AFTERMATH
AFTERMATH: LIFE DEBT
AFTERMATH: EMPIRE'S END
LAST SHOT
BLOODLINE
PHASMA
CANTO BIGHT

**VII** THE FORCE AWAKENS

**VIII** THE LAST JEDI

A long time ago in a galaxy far, far away. . . .

# PART ONE

ELEMENTS OF A KILLING MACHINE

## CHAPTER 1

# SITUATIONAL AWARENESS

**I**

"I was eighteen kilometers above sea level when they caught me," she said.

The droid measured her heart rate from across the room (sixty-two beats per minute, seven above her baseline) and stored her voiceprint for post-session analysis. It performed a cursory optical scan and noted the scrapes on her lips and forehead; the sling supporting her right arm. She had begun to regain muscle mass, though she remained—the droid permitted itself a poetic flourish—*frail*.

"You remember the precise altitude?" the droid asked. For this interaction it had chosen a masculine voice, bass and hollow. The sound projected from a speaker on the underside of its spherical black chassis.

"I have an extremely good memory."

The droid oriented the red lens of its photoreceptor as if to stare. "So do I."

The woman met its gaze. The droid readjusted the lens.

This is the story she told.

Eighteen kilometers above the surface of the planet Nacronis, Yrica Quell fled for her life.

The siltstorm raged outside her starfighter, blue and yellow mud roiling against the faceted viewport. A burst of wind lifted the ship's port-side wing, nearly sending her into a spin; she adjusted her repulsors with her gloved left hand while the right urged a rattling lever into position. The ship leveled out, and the comforting howl of its twin ion engines rose to a screech as six million stony granules entered the exhaust. Quell winced as she bounced in her harness, listening to her vessel's agony.

Emerald light shot past the viewport, incinerating ribbons of airborne mud. She increased her thrust and plunged deeper into the storm, ignoring the engines' scream.

Her scanner showed three marks rapidly closing from behind—two fewer than she'd hoped for. She moved a hand to the comm, recalibrated her frequency, and called out two names: "Tonas? Barath?" When no one answered, she recalibrated again and tried, "This is TIE pilot Yrica Quell to Nacronis ground control." But Tonas and Barath were surely dead, and the locals were jammed, out of range, or ardently inclined to ignore her.

Another volley of emerald particle bolts sizzled past her ship. Quell maintained her vector. She was a fine defensive pilot, but only the storm could keep her alive now. She had to trust to the wind and the blinding mud to throw off her enemy's aim.

Her comm sounded at last. "Lieutenant Quell?"

She leaned forward, straining at her harness, trying to peer through the storm as her teeth chattered and her hips knocked against her seat. A ribbon of blue silt streaked by and she glimpsed, beyond it, a flash of white light: lightning ahead and twenty degrees to port.

"Lieutenant Quell? Please acknowledge."

She considered her options. She could head toward the lightning—

toward the storm's center, where the winds would be strongest. There she could try to locate an updraft. Reduce her thrust, overcharge her repulsors, and let the draft and the repulsors' antigravity toss her ship high while her pursuers passed below. If she didn't black out, if she didn't become disoriented, she could dip back down and re-engage her enemy from behind, eliminating one, maybe two before they realized where she'd gone.

"You are hereby ordered to reduce speed, eject, and await pickup, detention, and court-martial."

She couldn't imagine that the man on the other end of the comm would fall for such a maneuver. More likely she'd be shot down while she spun helplessly through the sky.

Of course, she'd also be shot if she ejected. Major Soran Keize was a good man, an *admirable* man, but she knew there would be no court-martial.

She changed course toward the lightning and pitched her ship incrementally downward. Toward the ground, she reminded herself— ground, like atmosphere and gravity, was a challenge she normally flew without. Another flash of emerald suggested her foes were getting closer, likely attempting to catch her in their crossfire.

She let the wind guide her. She couldn't outfly Major Keize, but she was at least as good as his squadron mates. She'd flown with Shana, seen Tong's flight stats, and Quell deserved her fate if she couldn't match them both. She dived through a ribbon of yellow silt that left her momentarily blind, then reduced her repulsor output until the TIE fighter's aerodynamics took over and sent it veering at a sharp angle. Quell might find atmospheric flight challenging, but her opponents would find an enemy jerked about by gravity positively confounding. The next volley of particle blasts was just a glimmer in her peripheral vision.

They would be back on her soon. A thunderclap loud enough to resonate in her bones reassured her she was near the storm's center. She wondered, startled by the thought, if she should say something to the major before the end—make some last plea or acknowledgment of their years together—then blotted the idea from her mind. She'd made her decision.

She looked through her streaked cockpit at the swirling vortex of colors. She accelerated as hard as the TIE would allow, checked her instruments through the pain in her skull and the glimmering spots in front of her eyes, counted to five, then tilted her fighter an additional fifty degrees toward the ground.

After that, two events occurred nearly simultaneously. Somehow she was aware of them both.

As Quell's fighter rushed toward the surface of Nacronis, her three pursuers—already accelerating to match Quell's speed—flew directly toward the storm center. Two of the enemy TIEs, according to her scanner, attempted to break away. They were caught by the gale and, as they decelerated, swept into each other. Both were immediately destroyed in the collision.

The third pilot attempted to navigate the gauntlet of lightning and silt. He fared better, but his starfighter wasn't equal to his skill. Something went wrong—Quell guessed that silt particles had crept into seams in the TIE's armor, or that a lightning strike had shorted the fighter's systems—and Major Soran Keize, too, disappeared from her scanner. The ace of the 204th Imperial Fighter Wing was dead.

At the same time her pursuers met their end, Quell attempted to break out of her dive. She saw nothing of the world outside her cockpit, nothing beyond her instruments, and her body felt leaden as she operated the TIE's controls. She'd managed to level out the ship when she heard a deafening crash and felt her seat heave beneath her. She realized half a second later that the bottom of her starboard wing had struck the mire of Nacronis's surface and was dragging through the silt. Half a second after that, she lost total control of her vessel and made the mistake of reaching for the ejector switch with her right hand.

The TIE fighter halted abruptly and she was thrown at the now-cracked viewport. The safety harness caught her extended right arm and snapped her brittle bones as the straps cut into her body. Her face smashed against the inside of her flight helmet. Agony and nausea followed. She heard nothing but an unidentifiable dull roar. She blacked out and woke almost immediately—swiftly enough to savor the still-fresh pain.

Quell had an extremely good memory, but she didn't remember cutting herself free of the safety harness or clambering out of the cockpit hatch. She didn't remember whether she'd vomited when she'd removed her helmet. She remembered, vaguely, the smell of burning circuits and her own sweat—but that was all, until she sat on top of her broken craft amid a multicolored marsh and looked up at the sky.

She couldn't tell if it was night or day. The swirling, iridescent storm looked like an oily whirlpool, blotting out sun or stars or both. It churned and grew, visibly expanding moment by moment. Glimmering above the white lightning, faint and high, were the orange lights of atmospheric explosions: the payloads of other TIE fighters.

The explosions would stoke the storm, Quell knew—stoke and feed it, and others like it, until storms tore through every city on Nacronis. The silt would flay towers and citadels to their steel bones. Children would choke on mud flooding the streets. All because an order had been given, and only Quell and Tonas and Barath had bothered to defy it.

This was what her Empire had become in the days after Endor. She saw it now, but she was too late to save Nacronis.

"You were fortunate to survive," the droid said when Yrica Quell finished her story.

"The TIE gave me somewhere to shelter. The open marshland wasn't hit as hard as the main settlements."

"I don't doubt it. My observation stands. Do you *feel* fortunate, Lieutenant Quell?"

She wrinkled her nose. Her eyes flickered from the spherical droid to the corrugated metal walls of the repurposed shipping container where they met.

"Why shouldn't I?" she asked. "I'm alive. And I've been assigned a charming therapist."

The droid hesitated, ran the statement through multiple analysis programs, and was pleasantly surprised to conclude that its patient's hostility was omnidirectional, counterproductive, and obnoxious, but in no way aimed at the droid. Creating a rapport remained possible. It was, in fact, a priority—albeit not the droid's *only* priority.

"Let's resume tomorrow," the droid said, "and talk more about what happened between your crash and your discovery by the emergency crew."

Quell grunted and rose, raising the hood of her poncho before taking the single step needed to reach the shipping container's door. She paused there and looked from the droid's photoreceptor to the injector syringe attached to its manipulator.

"Do people try to hurt you," she asked, "when they see an Imperial torture droid waiting to treat them?"

This time, her voice suggested an admixture of hostility and curiosity.

"I see very few patients," the droid answered. That fact was dangerously close to qualifying as classified intelligence, but the droid deemed the risk of breach acceptably low next to the benefits of earning Quell's trust.

Quell only grunted again and departed.

The droid reviewed the recorded conversation seventeen times. It focused on the woman's biofeedback throughout, but it didn't neglect more conventional verbal analysis. Quell's story, it decided, was largely consistent with the testimony of a traumatized Imperial defector.

Nonetheless, the droid was certain she was lying.

## II

Traitor's Remorse was a frost-bitten shantytown of an outpost. Once a nameless rebel base built to harbor a handful of desperate insurgents, it had evolved into a sprawling maze of improvised shelters, security fencing, and duracrete bunkers housing twelve thousand would-be defectors from the crumbling Galactic Empire. Under an ashen sky, former Imperial military personnel suffered debriefings and scrutiny and medical examinations as they waited for the nascent rebel government—the so-called New Republic—to determine their fate.

Most of the defectors occupied the outpost only in passing. They were infantry and engineers, com-scan officers and admirals' aides. Designated *low risk* and *high value,* they received an offer of leniency and redeployment within a week, then shipped out to crew captured Star Destroyers or to join orbital minesweeper teams. Meanwhile, those less fortunate—the defectors designated *high risk* and *low value* by whatever New Republic interviewer they'd annoyed—were stuck trying to prove themselves reliable, loyal, and of sound moral character without going mad from tedium.

Yrica Quell occupied the latter category. She didn't think the name *Traitor's Remorse* was funny, but after a month she couldn't think of one better.

On a foggy afternoon, Quell jogged down the gravel path running from her housing unit to the landing pads. She kept her pace slow to reduce the throbbing in her shoulder and minimize the bounce of her sling, rapidly transitioning from chilled to overheated to clammy with cold sweat. She shouldn't have been running at all in her condition. (She hadn't needed to heal naturally from a broken bone since she'd been twelve years old, but medical bacta was in short supply for ex-Imperials.) She ran anyway. Her routine was the only thing keeping her sane.

Once, she would have cleared her mind by flying. That wasn't an option now.

Certainly her therapist wasn't doing much good. The reprogrammed IT-O torture droid seemed more interested in examining and reexamining her last flight than in helping her adapt to her circumstances. There was nothing *useful* about the images of Nacronis the droid had dredged up in her mind—siltstorms tearing through settlements, explosions in the sky. Nothing that would serve her or the New Republic. Yet until the droid was satisfied, it seemed she wouldn't be allowed to move on.

She approached a checkpoint and turned off the gravel path ten meters before the entrance to the landing zone, running alongside the fence surrounding the tarmac. Brittle cyan grass crunched satisfyingly under her boots. One of the sentries threw her a wave, and she returned a curt nod. This, too, was part of her routine.

She kept running, past the informal junk swap and the communications tower. Two hundred meters down the tarmac fence she drew to a stop, adjusted her sling, smoothed back her sweat-slicked hair—the blond locks longer and sloppier than she was used to, irritating her nape—and listened to a howl mixed with a high-pitched whine far above. She craned her neck, squinting into the gray light, and looked to the blotch in the sky.

*Right on time.* In all the chaos of a civil war, in one obscure corner of the galaxy, the rebels somehow kept their daily transport on schedule. Maybe the New Republic had a chance after all.

The GR-75 was an aging beast of a starship, slow to maneuver and bulky even for its class, but Quell felt a pang as the tapered vessel descended, washing her with exhaust and radiant heat. Somewhere aboard a pilot calculated landing vectors and calibrated instruments for atmospheric pressure. A pilot who—if only when flying without passengers or cargo—surely accelerated past her ship's recommended limits and tested herself against the resulting g forces. Quell's fingers played along an invisible set of controls. Then she clenched her fists shut.

*Give me a shuttle,* she thought. *An airspeeder. Even a flight simulator.*

The GR-75 tapped the tarmac hard enough to jolt the ground. Quell watched through the fence as one of the outpost sentries performed a cursory inspection of the ship's hull before signaling for the boarding ramp to lower. A tentacled New Republic officer was the first passenger to disembark. The officer passed a datapad to the sentry, and the march of new arrivals began.

After the officer, they were nearly all human. That was the most obvious clue to their origins—the Empire had been, as the propaganda said, built on the labor of galactic humanity. The passengers were mostly young, but not without exception. Mostly clean-cut, though a few were untidy. They looked across the tarmac with trepidation. To a person, they had attempted to rid themselves of identifying gear—even the ones still in Imperial uniforms had stripped away all symbols and regalia. Quell suspected some carried their insignia badges anyway, secreted in pockets or sleeves. She'd encountered more than one set of rank plaques at the junk swap.

She identified the ex-stormtroopers by their boots—too sturdy and well fitted to abandon, their white synth-leather caked in grime and turned the yellow of a bad tooth. Quell gave the stormtroopers a perfunctory glance and removed them from her mental checklist. The officers were given away by their bearing, and she scanned their features, searching her memory for matches and finding none. (*I have an extremely good memory,* she'd told the droid, and it was true.) She felt a vague satisfaction at identifying a combat medic by her Academy ring, but otherwise noticed nothing remarkable.

All of them were bastards, she knew. The new arrivals got worse every day.

When Quell had arrived a month ago, Traitor's Remorse had already been crowded with the first wave of deserters who'd abandoned their posts after the Battle of Endor. Some had come out of bravery, others out of cowardice, but Quell respected their foresight: They'd understood that the Emperor who'd built an interstellar civilization and governed for two decades was dead, and that his Empire wouldn't endure without him. That without an heir, the Empire's sins (and they were many—the most zealous loyalty officer couldn't believe otherwise) would corrupt and destroy what remained. That the impossible victory that the Rebel Alliance had achieved—the assassination of the Emperor aboard his own massive battle station—was worth embracing wholeheartedly.

Quell hadn't been part of that first wave. Instead she'd come during the second.

The days after the Emperor's death had been chaotic. The massive uprisings on thousands of planets—along with proving that the rebels had been right all along about public sentiment toward the Empire—made it clear that there would be no return to the old ways, no swift restoration of familiar rule. Yet a strategy, of sorts, soon emerged inside the remains of the Imperial military. Fleets across known space took part in Operation Cinder: the leveling of civilizations on Nacronis and Vardos, Candovant and Commenor, and more besides. Planets both loyal and in open revolt. Planets rich in resources and planets that possessed nothing but faded glory. They were bombed and gassed and flooded, their own weather patterns and geology turned against them. Nacronis was ravaged by siltstorms. Tectonic devices shattered the crust of Senthrodys.

The Empire tried to destroy them all. Not to deny the New Republic access to vital territories. Not to thwart insurrections. Not as part of any meaningful plan to secure the Empire. The surviving admirals had said it was for *all* those reasons, yet not one was fully satisfactory. Maybe Operation Cinder had been conducted out of some sort of perceived necessity, but it was fueled by rage and it would do nothing—it was obvious, *beyond* obvious—to slow the Empire's disintegration.

Cinder had been a turning point. Loyal soldiers who had executed whole planets at the Emperor's behest had seen billions of lives snuffed out for no strategic gain and known that the moral calculus had changed. Imperial heroes unable to stomach the slaughter had turned on their superiors. Naboo, the Emperor's own homeworld, had been saved from genocide with the aid of Imperial Special Forces commandos. They had come to a shared realization: It was one thing to fight a losing battle, and another to disregard the cost.

*That* had been the second wave of desertions and defections.

Which meant anyone who'd stayed afterward had made a conscious choice to forget the cost. To forget the fact that preserving the Empire as it had been was a lost cause. To fight on anyway, consequences be damned.

Every day after Operation Cinder, the pointlessness of the carnage became clearer. Every day, those remaining inside the Empire were tested anew. So far as Quell was concerned, the men and women aboard the GR-75 transport had failed *too many* tests to deserve sympathy or redemption. The ones who came tomorrow would be worse still.

A voice penetrated her thoughts like a needle into skin. "See anyone you like?"

A man in a rumpled coat picked his way toward Quell, looking between her and the grass as if afraid he might step on a mine or a glass shard. He would have appeared human—wiry black hair flecked with gray, brown skin shades darker than Quell's own tawny hue, a skinny physique lost under his garments—if it hadn't been for the two wormy stalks protruding from his skull. She identified the species: Balosar.

"Not really," she said. She hadn't seen him before—hadn't noticed him arrive on a transport, nor stood in line with him for rations. He wasn't in uniform, but he surely wasn't a defector. She added: "No rule about standing on this side of the fence."

"Stand where you want," the man replied. He stopped three paces away and squinted in the direction of the transport. The new arrivals continued their march, each exchanging a few words with the sentry before heading for processing. "Who *are* you watching for? You come here every day. Are you expecting friends? A lover? Rescue?"

"We're free to go, aren't we? Why would I need rescue?"

It was a half-truth, and Quell was curious how the man would react. Officially, the residents of Traitor's Remorse could leave at any time. But taking flight would guarantee the New Republic's ire, and who knew what sort of grudge the rebel government would hold? Anyone not in line for a pardon was risking a perilous future.

The man simply shrugged. "I'm glad to hear you say that. Not everyone feels the same way." His voice flattened. "Answer the question, please? Who are you watching for?"

Quell heard the entitlement. The man had authority, or wanted her to think he did. She didn't look at him, and found her answer in the march of defectors. "You see the one with the scars?" She lifted one finger—barely a gesture—in the direction of a bulky man in a leather vest. Rough red marks ran from his neck to the undersides of his ears.

"I do," the Balosar said, though his attention was entirely on Quell.

"I've seen scars like that. Surgical augmentations. My guess is he was a candidate for one of the elite stormtrooper divisions—death troopers, maybe—but his body couldn't take the mods."

"Supposing that's true, it's very likely in his file. Why are you watching him?"

Quell whirled to face the man. She kept her voice level, excised the frustration. If he was with the New Republic, she needed him. "You've got a man with that past, who stayed with the Empire as long as he did—you think he's good recruiting material? You want him wandering around the outpost, free and clear?"

The Balosar's lips twitched, and he smiled in realization. "You're looking out for us. That's generous, but we won the war; we can manage our own security." He extended a hand. "Caern Adan. Alliance—excuse me. *New Republic* Intelligence."

Quell took the hand. In all her interviews since arriving, she'd never met a New Republic spy. If he'd been Imperial Intelligence, she might have been terrified, but terror seemed premature.

The man's grip was weak until she squeezed. Then it became a pinch. "Yrica Quell," she said. "Former lieutenant, 204th Fighter Wing. At your mercy."

"The 204th was never known for its *mercy*, though, was it?" He looked like he was about to laugh, but he never did. "'Shadow Wing,' your people called it. Quite a name, up there with *Death Star*. Sightings all over prior to Endor, at Blacktar Cyst and Mennar-Daye, slaughtering rebels and keeping the hyperlanes safe . . . did you happen to fly at Mimban?"

The litany of names struck like blows. She didn't flinch. He had come prepared and he had come for her. "Before my time," she said.

"Too bad. It's a story I'd love to hear. Some of my colleagues didn't notice you all until—well, until Nacronis—but we both know you were spectacular for years. If Grand General Loring had appreciated you more, if Vader had paid more attention to the starfighter corps, you'd probably have been at Endor yourselves. Maybe kept the poor Emperor alive."

"Maybe so."

Adan waited for more. His smile wilted but didn't disappear. Finally he went on. "That's all past. Since Operation Cinder, though, Shadow Wing keeps popping up. Nine sightings in just over two weeks, tearing apart convoys, bombing outposts . . . even took out one of our star cruisers."

Another blow, aimed with more care than before. He might have been lying about Shadow Wing, but it sounded possible. Even plausible. Again, she didn't flinch, though she felt her injuries throb in time with her pulse.

"Nine sightings in two weeks," Quell said. "It's been a month since Nacronis."

Adan nodded brusquely, scanned the ground as if searching for a place to sit, then shifted his weight from foot to foot. "Which is why I'm here. Dozens of the Empire's finest pilots disappear at a time like this? They're not hiding out awaiting orders; they're running silent."

She didn't look at the trail of defectors still emerging onto the tarmac. She didn't even meet Adan's gaze. She was focused on the words, turning them over in her head. "You have a theory?" she asked.

"I have a plan," Adan said. "I'm assembling a working group to study the situation. Experts who can analyze the data and predict the enemy's next move. Maybe do some investigative legwork."

She fixed the words in her mind: *I'm assembling a working group.*

She cut the resistance from her voice like a tumor. Cautiously, she answered: "I was hoping for a military position. Somewhere I could fly."

Adan's smile was rejuvenated. "I'm sure you were, but we've seen your file. The Shadow Wing pilot who couldn't save Nacronis? No high-level clearance, no access to classified intelligence or special expertise—just a solid track record of shooting rebels. You're not anyone's favorite candidate for recruitment."

*So work for New Republic Intelligence,* Quell heard, though he didn't say the words. *Sit at a console and help us hunt your friends. Maybe you'll even get a pardon out of it.*

What Adan uttered aloud was: "Consider it. If I decide I want you, I'll find you—and I expect you to have an answer ready."

For a month, Yrica Quell had waited to prove herself. To show that she had abandoned the 204th Fighter Wing for a reason. To show that she could offer the New Republic a talent it lacked, bringing Imperial rigor and discipline to its starfighter corps.

She had waited to take part in the war's end. To fly again. She had waited to do something *decent* for once, the way she'd wanted to long ago.

She wasn't certain Caern Adan was offering any of what she wanted. Maybe she hadn't earned it.

Traitor's Remorse turned cold at night. The gently numbing chill of the day turned to wind that whipped Quell's poncho around her hips and forced her to keep her good hand on the brim of her hood. She pushed against the gale as she trudged between stacked containers-turned-houses, under swinging electrical cables, and into the shelter of a bunker dug out of a low hillside.

The wind's roar faded within, replaced by laughter and conversation. As her eyes adjusted to the dim light, Quell saw two dozen figures seated on crates and on the dirt floor. They were playing cards and dice; swapping old tales and showing old scars. They should have been drinking, but there was nothing worth drinking in Traitor's Remorse. (There was harder contraband for those with a taste for ryll or death sticks, but no one was fool enough to indulge where the New Republic watched.)

Quell had come to the Warren to trade. She had no friends in Traitor's Remorse—passing acquaintances, an old man with whom she shared her supper rations, but no friends—yet seniority had its privileges. She'd been at the outpost as long as anyone, and she knew which New Republic officers were forgiving and which held "special" grudges.

She knew where to buy an extra meal and who claimed to be able to smuggle out messages. She could swap rumors for rumors, and the people who might know about Caern Adan would give her a measure of attention.

She passed deeper into the bunker, down a hallway and past a young logistics consultant brokering the exchange of military casualty lists. She nodded to an engineer who'd helped her repair a faulty heater, but the man was fixated on a diagram he'd sketched on the floor. She saw none of the regulars she sought, and she was nearly ready to move on when she spotted the stormtrooper.

The surgical augmentation scars on his neck seemed to burn in the flickering electric light. He turned a hydrospanner over in his hands as if it were a weapon. If he was the sort to join the death troopers, maybe he'd used one as a bludgeon before.

Quell wasn't a fighter by nature. She'd never gotten into a pointless scrap in her Academy days and only once been in a fistfight as a teenager. She was military, true, but she was a *pilot* first—shooting things was the least of her duties. Nonetheless, she approached the man unafraid of what might come next. *Why'd you finally jump ship?* she planned to say.

And if he gave the wrong answer? If he took a swing at her? After a day of feeling small and frustrated and helpless, maybe a fight was what she needed.

She never got to say a word.

She felt the rumble first. The ground bucked and she swallowed a lungful of dust before the thunder even registered. The screaming that followed was strangely muffled, and she realized she'd gone deaf. She was blind, too, but that was the dust again—pale white clouds that stung her nostrils and scattered the dim illumination.

*I'm hit,* she thought, and knew it to be a lie. She was fine. She wasn't sure about the rest of the Warren.

One part of her brain calmly reconstructed what had happened as she stumbled forward. There had been a bomb—nothing big, maybe a jury-rigged plasma grenade. Someone had planted it in another room, or carried it inside and triggered the detonator. Someone like one of the new defectors who'd arrived on the GR-75, determined to make an example of those who betrayed the Empire. She pieced the story together easily because it had happened twice before. This was the closest she'd been to a blast.

Her foot crushed something soft—an arm covered in blood and scraps of leather. Leaning forward, she was desperately relieved to see it was attached to a body. The stormtrooper. The death trooper candidate. She knelt beside him and wrapped her good arm around his burly chest, allowing him to scale her and stand.

He was a bastard, she reminded herself as they lurched toward the exit. But then, so was everyone at Traitor's Remorse.

They struggled forward step by step, coughing up grime and navigating by the muted shouting. Eventually Quell felt the weight of the stormtrooper disappear and realized another person had lifted him away. She could almost hear again. Someone—perhaps the same person who had taken the stormtrooper—asked about her health. She choked out a reply and stepped out of the Warren and into the artificial glow of the shantytown.

No one prevented her from pushing forward through the perimeter of ex-Imperial onlookers and tense New Republic security officers. No one cared enough to try. She briefly considered going back, but she was dizzy and half deaf and could see the dust on her breath. She'd just get in the way of the rescue team.

But she realized as she coughed and spat that she had the answer she'd come for.

She wasn't sure Caern Adan would give her an opportunity to fly, or to prove herself, or to do anything decent. But the bombing had reminded her that those things were luxuries.

She had to find a way out of Traitor's Remorse. Any chance was worth taking.

## III

Caern Adan stretched an elastic band between thumb and forefinger, let loose, and watched the band soar across the supply closet that served as his office. It deformed in flight, missing IT-O by ten centimeters and puncturing the cone of azure particles emitted by the droid's holoprojector. The humanoid figure standing within the cone pixelated and flickered into nonexistence.

"You're aggravated," the droid said, unhelpfully.

"I'm attempting to get something actionable out of you," Caern answered.

"Actionable intelligence is your area, not mine."

IT-O adjusted its holoprojector—a gift Caern had installed in the droid many months earlier—and the figure re-formed, magnified a dozen times over. Yrica Quell stared lifelessly over her jutting nose out of creaseless, bloodshot eyes. There was a fragility to her that went beyond the obvious cuts on her lips and scalp—a sort of glasslike sharpness, equally likely to injure or shatter. Imperial arrogance ground down and humbled.

Caern studied the image and sighed. "Suppose you're right," he said. "She's lying. What exactly is she lying about? Or—" He silenced the droid with a slash of his hand. "—give me this: What do we think is *true*?"

IT-O floated like a toy boat in a slow current. "She has suffered trauma," it said.

Caern resisted the urge to interject: *Haven't we all?*

"Physically, of course," the droid went on, "but she's struggling to process recent events. She's isolated. Simultaneously hypervigilant and unfocused."

"Vague," Caern said. "Ever consider telling fortunes for a living?"

"Building a rapport requires time. Without a rapport, I can be of little use to my patient or to you."

It was an old argument, and Caern was eager to move past it. "Her background checks out, so far as we can tell. We can't confirm operational details, but she was definitely part of Shadow Wing." He rose and moved his hand to the door's control panel. "Any reason to think she's a spy? Could the whole *defector* story be a ruse?"

"If she's a spy, she's not an especially good one, given how suspicious we are of her already."

"Maybe the Empire is fresh out of competent spies." Caern tapped the panel and stepped into the hallway. "Come on. We need air."

They moved through the corridors of the bunker, past makeshift processing stations and communications rigs. One of the military interviewers mumbled a greeting at Caern, and Caern muttered back. IT-O received glowers from several officers and was ignored by others. The torture droid was divisive at the best of times.

Once outside, Caern pulled his coat around him. He felt a distant buzz—some sort of cutting rig slicing through rock—and retracted his antennapalps into his skull to reduce the bothersome sensation. The source appeared to be a fenced-off section of the outpost over the next hill. He waved IT-O along, tromping through grass and dirt until he saw the ruins of the bombed bunker. A dozen New Republic workers clustered about the entrance, dragging equipment and stone and bodies into the midmorning light.

"You know what this is?" he asked IT-O, nodding in the direction of the rubble.

"Something symbolic of whatever argument you intend to make?"

Caern scoffed. He brought his sleeve to his upper lip as his nose dripped from the cold. "It's an intelligence failure. Yes, it's symbolic. It was also predictable and preventable. It's the fourth bombing we've had here."

"We are in agreement," IT-O said. "It was indeed preventable."

"But no one else sees it. We've got an outpost full of ground-pounders and flyboys who think *security* means 'shoot down anyone who finds the *secret base.*' But the bases aren't *secret* anymore and we've got too many problems to shoot."

In truth, it was worse than that. The problem was leadership. The New Republic was a military organization—no matter what Chancellor Mothma said, its roots in the insurgent Rebel Alliance ran deep—and it only understood military solutions. He didn't need to reiterate that point to IT-O, and instead said: "Intelligence will hold the New Republic together, or the New Republic won't hold at all. No one up top seems to realize that. No one seems to care, no matter how many bombs are planted."

"There are those in government who care about the dead. You know this."

"About the dead? Maybe. But not about what's killing them."

"We're talking about a government that's barely had time to form," IT-O said. "To attribute any philosophy of national security to the New Republic is, at this stage, premature."

"Maybe," Caern repeated. He glanced at the droid, wondering (as he often did) whether IT-O was manipulating him, nudging him toward a conclusion he might not otherwise reach. But the droid's crimson photoreceptor gave no hints. "Regardless, New Republic Intelligence is underfunded and understaffed. But if someone did something *right* for a change . . ."

"You believe that an intelligence operation to dismantle the 204th Fighter Wing would force New Republic leadership to reexamine its priorities."

"Shouldn't it?" Caern turned his back on the rubble and dust. "Shadow Wing was trouble before the Battle of Endor, but back then we were more scared of another Death Star battle station than Imperial fighter pilots. Now they're making precision strikes. We lost all hands aboard the *Huntsman* and the *Kalpana*. I'm sure the 204th was involved in the raid on Beauchen. Exclude the Operation Cinder genocides and they're still responsible for the deaths of thousands." He swept his arms to indicate the broken bunker. "This is what the Empire looks like, now: fewer planet-killing superweapons, more murderous fanatics."

"Counterterrorism being an intelligence specialty."

"Exactly!" Caern clapped his hands together. "If an intelligence working group were to neutralize Shadow Wing, it would prove everything I've been saying. The threat and the solution."

"And once New Republic leadership agrees that Imperial splinter groups are best countered by intelligence officers, do you imagine that would justify a massive resource allotment to the working group that neutralized Shadow Wing? Along with said working group's supervisor?"

Caern shrugged. "Why not? It's better for everyone."

The droid's repulsors whined as its spherical body navigated past Caern, descending a meter down the hillside in the direction of the rubble. "Is this about defeating an enemy of the New Republic? Or about seizing power in a time of political instability?"

"Why not both?" Caern failed to hide his irritation. He wanted to repeat himself: *It's better for everyone.* And it was—Shadow Wing's threat was real and ongoing, and if neutralizing it led to greater intelligence resources and his own personal elevation, that would lead to fewer bombings and fewer Operation Cinders. Running a government and defending a populace weren't the same as assassinating an emperor; the sooner the New Republic realized that, the better.

He forced himself to draw a breath and regroup. "The real question," he said, "is this: Is Yrica Quell the person I need?"

The droid didn't move. Caern recognized IT-O's deep concentration as it ran dozens of scenarios and dredged through a thousand years of medical texts for an answer. The silence calmed Caern. However much of an annoyance IT-O could be, Caern found the droid's willingness to *work*—to sort facts and make the best call possible, no matter how ferociously they'd argued—comforting.

"No," IT-O said. "I don't believe she is."

He visibly flinched as frustration reignited in his chest. He turned his eyes to the column of smoke rising intermittently from the rubble. She had been there, he knew—Quell had been spotted pulling someone from the wreckage—and he tried to picture her wounded, brittle form caked in dust and blood.

She was a liar. A woman who'd committed who-knew-*what* crimes during her time with the 204th. A woman who'd seen the Empire crumble and now claimed to have a conscience. Caern had seen her

kind before. He never forgave them, and sooner or later they all re-
verted to type.

But he could handle that.

He needed her, whatever IT-O claimed.

"Call our friend," Caern said. "The working group convenes tomorrow."

# CHAPTER 2

# ANGLE OF ATTACK

## I

They weren't heroes, but they celebrated like they were. They marched across skyways arm-in-arm and launched fireworks under the Grinning Moon of Jiruus. They sang Imperial anthems, inserting vulgar jokes in place of homages. They danced to music drifting out from club doors and apartment windows; danced to their own clapping in plazas and parks and under the disapproving glowers of defaced statues. And as they celebrated like heroes, so, too, were they celebrated. The people of Jiruus emerged to ask their names, to offer food and drink, to welcome them into the festivities that had lasted a month and seemed primed to continue into eternity. They danced with the people of Jiruus until they were dizzy and their flight suits were soaked with sweat, stopping only to drink from canteens and fountains before returning to dancing.

They were comrades, veterans of a war they'd won not long ago. In the hour after midnight, they walked through a garden of scintillating colors and said goodbye to one of their own.

"Wyl Lark, you fleshy peasant boy—you will be missed, whatever the others say!" Sata Neek croaked and clacked, his beak working under engorged eyestalks as if he were swallowing a small animal. He leaned heavily against Wyl, ready to topple without support—a gesture Wyl had learned indicated fondness among Sata Neek's people (and not inebriation, as a passerby might have reasonably assumed).

"You've always been kind to me," Wyl replied. "I'll miss—"

He was interrupted by another round of clacking and croaking. "Sonogari? *He* will never admit to missing you so long as Sata Neek is here to tend his wounded heart. Nasi will spit on every sheet you ever slept on. Rep Boy? Never! Why, in all of Riot Squadron, only Sata Neek shall truly miss you!"

Sata Neek went on and Wyl grinned and turned to Sonogari, who kissed Wyl firmly on the forehead before splashing through a pond of glowing lilies; and to Nasi, who rolled her eyes. Rununja, a lean-faced Duros whose steel-blue skin seemed mossy in the garden, spoke over Sata Neek with a voice that exuded authority. "You're certain, then? Tomorrow?"

"Unless you need me," Wyl said. "Otherwise I'll follow the course we talked about, keep my scanner on, and turn over my ship when I arrive."

"We'll always need pilots. We won't need you." Rununja gently prized Sata Neek's claws off Wyl's shoulder as she spoke. "The *Hellion's Dare* has orders to hold position over Jiruus until the last of the scout reports are in. After that, Riot may return to a combat zone—but the war won't be what it was."

Wyl nodded. The weeks since Endor had been as calm as he could remember. There had been fighting, of course—furious battles against scattered Imperial forces—but the primary mission of the *Hellion's Dare* and its starfighter squadrons had been reconnaissance. The fall of the Empire had led to communications breakdowns across the galaxy, and the New Republic needed to identify which systems had lost a hyperwave relay and which had been overrun and blockaded by Imperial holdouts. So far, Wyl had seen more than a few of the former and none of the latter.

Sometimes they had found worlds like Jiruus. Wyl didn't know why the locals loathed the Empire so, or why they found such unutterable joy in its downfall. He didn't know how old its plazas and gardens and skyways were, or what crimes the Imperial garrison and its commander had committed. Most of the Jiruusi barely spoke Galactic Basic. So Wyl was simply grateful to be a visitor on Jiruus in a time of beauty.

He was also ready to go home.

Rununja strolled on ahead. Wyl and Sata Neek and Nasi and a dozen others took the scenic route through the garden, under fronds whose radiance blazed and dimmed with the sounds of their voices. They trekked on past entangled Jiruusi lovers and into a marketplace strung with gaudy lanterns and smelling of Corellian cinnamon. They ate sweets and began telling stories of their own time together. Some stories were of battles (at Mygeeto, where Riot Squadron had earned its name; at Thumbsnapper's Bridge, where pirates had nearly achieved a victory even the Empire hadn't aspired to), but more were of pranks and foolish errors and the dreams of dead comrades. Talk eventually turned to Wyl and his tenure with the squadron, and he was surprised to hear a voice call, "You're a damn coward!"

The heckler was perched on the second tier of a multi-level fountain that loomed over the market. She was compact and muscular, bronze-skinned with a fuzz of lime-green hair and short, fleshy horns protruding from her temples—marks of a Theelin (though Wyl didn't know if she identified with that species or another; Theelin ancestry was a sensitive topic). He frowned at her taunt, more puzzled than insulted.

As Nasi shouted back at her, Sata Neek shook Wyl's shoulder with one claw and croaked, "Don't worry. Chass is always itchy without combat duty."

Wyl nodded. He'd been among enough rebels to understand. "She's Hound Squadron?"

"It would explain it, no?" Sata Neek said.

One by one, the pilots of Riot Squadron drifted away—to their starfighters or hostels or the *Hellion's Dare*, depending on their duties and interests. The Hound Squadron pilots and the *Dare*'s crew took separate paths. Wyl and Sata Neek were left alone, walking along a skyway through the residential district. "You're safe for tonight?" Sata Neek asked. "I could escort you to the *Dare* . . ."

"Met a Jiruusi," Wyl said. "Gave me a key and told me to stay with her anytime."

Sata Neek erupted in a fit of croaking laughter before throwing both arms skyward. "Wyl Lark, the beloved! Gift to the galaxy!" Someone at ground level echoed the shout and Sata Neek cackled once again. In a more subdued tone, he added, "The best pilot I ever knew."

"We saved the galaxy together," Wyl said.

"We had the *best* times," Sata Neek answered.

Wyl slept on a mountain of cushions softer than any bed he'd ever encountered, too tired even to wake his host. His final thoughts before dreaming were of his comrades—his brothers and sisters—in the unit, and how soothing his last days in Riot Squadron had been.

He woke to sirens.

The noise reverberated through the city, unfamiliar in its precise pitch and cadence but unmistakable in meaning. He scrambled to dress and pulled curtains aside, scanning the sky through the apartment's glass wall. In the predawn light, dark flecks streamed across the clouds in thin bands, like nocturnal insects going to feed. Wyl imagined he could hear the screams of ion engines, though the sirens overwhelmed everything.

*TIE fighters,* he thought. *The Empire is here.*

He was zipping his flight suit closed as he sprinted down the skyway toward the platform where he'd landed his starfighter. He could see flashes of light high above. The dark flecks spiraled around a single bright point: the *Hellion's Dare*.

He spotted his RZ-1 interceptor and felt unexpected relief. He'd feared, without thinking, that he would find his A-wing reduced to slag by an enemy scout. Yet the craft was intact, and he half climbed, half leapt onto the sleek, triangular body, wedging the toes of his boots between metal seams as he scrambled toward the cockpit. Every scorch mark on the hull, every dent and chip in the amber paint, was familiar. He forced himself to contemplate none of them as the canopy slid open and he dropped into the pilot's seat.

"We're going to help our friends," he murmured as he flipped switches and tapped buttons. He ignited the fusion reactor; activated the displays; distributed power to all components. The ritual was as familiar as the ship's scars. His voice was placating, and the low hum of the engines seemed to answer. "We're going up, okay? One more mission."

There were a dozen preflight diagnostics he should have run. Manual equipment checks he should have performed, especially without a ground crew at hand. A-wings were temperamental, prone to thruster decalibrations and componentized power losses and shorting out whatever gear seemed most vital. They were jury-rigged machines, stripped and modified by the Rebel Alliance for speed over heavy firepower or durability, and the consequences were apparent in every minute of flight. Wyl hoped his lack of caution wouldn't prove fatal.

The A-wing lifted smoothly off the platform, repulsors whinnying and familiar vibrations running through Wyl's seat as he retracted the landing gear. He couldn't help smiling. "You get to let loose." Then they were airborne, thrusters roaring, racing over skyways and between buildings as the starfighter gained altitude and pitched at the open sky. Gravity and acceleration pushed Wyl against his seat and he struggled to focus his sight on the black spiral above.

Seconds later he entered the fray. Riot Squadron had already engaged. Pairs of A-wing fighters swung into the TIEs' spiral path to scatter enemy flights before they could make their attack runs at the *Hellion's Dare*. The New Republic frigate floated above the thin haze of Jiruus's atmosphere, shields shimmering as it absorbed volleys of particle bolts, turbolasers discouraging enemy approaches from a dozen angles. Orbiting the *Dare* were the cross-shaped slivers of

Hound Squadron's B-wings, sticking close to the mother ship and un-leashing massive firepower at any TIE that reached optimal weapons range.

Wyl activated his comm and announced: "Riot Three, coming in."

Rununja—Riot Leader—was the first to answer. "Counting thirty eyeballs in tight formation, Riot Three. They're ignoring us except when we disrupt their attack pattern. They want the *Dare*—they don't much care about fighter kills."

"Bombers?" Wyl asked.

"Negative." Nasi's voice, crisp and low. Riot Eight.

"Not that we've spotted," Sata Neek corrected. Riot Five. "Plenty of opportunity for error!"

The chatter continued, identifying TIE vectors and the *Dare*'s tar-gets. Wyl listened but concentrated elsewhere. The scanner was barely intelligible—thirty TIEs and two New Republic squadrons meant up-ward of fifty marks, most of them fast enough to cross the engagement zone in moments—which left him reliant on eyes and instincts as much as sensors. If he died, he'd likely never see the shot that atomized his ship.

He joined Riot Four and Riot Eight as they set course for the spiral. In practiced shorthand, Nasi described her plan to approach perpen-dicular to the TIEs, curving into their spiral flight path with a tight turn and punching through the enemy arc. If the Riot pilots were lucky and their aim was true, they'd destroy one or two of the fighters in the process. If they were unlucky—whether or not they hit their targets—additional TIEs would pursue them as they escaped, well positioned to pick off the three A-wings. Shaking the foe would be difficult; but even drawing pursuit would leave the spiral formation fragmented.

They accelerated together and matched velocities. In a planetary at-mosphere, their speed would have been incomprehensible. In the vast-ness of open space, speed and distance were relative, fathomable only in how one related to the other. Wyl's A-wing was traveling fast; there-fore the enemy was near. The black void yawned above his cockpit, denying him any sense of orientation as he banked into the turn.

His targeting computer flashed as they neared the stream of TIEs. He responded by squeezing the trigger of his control yoke, and he heard the energized warble of his cannons. Red lightning rippled around him as Riot Four and Eight, too, made their attacks.

The TIEs danced like dead leaves tossed by a breeze, and the volley of particle bolts passed harmlessly through the gaps between enemy ships. The stray energy would dissipate into the dark. The three A-wings increased their thrust and pulled out of the path of the spiral. No one pursued.

Riot Eight swore. "They saw us coming. They've trained at this, and we picked the most obvious way to break them."

"The spiral attack pattern is new," Riot Four said. "Who wants to get creative?"

"We can take another pass," Wyl said. "They're giving us room, we might as well—"

"No." Riot Leader again, steady as always. "*Hellion's Dare* is about to lose a deflector. Bolster our perimeter around the frigate and prepare to jump to lightspeed. Coordinates incoming on your navicomputers."

Riot Eight swore again. Wyl craned his neck and tried to spot the jutting body of the frigate before adjusting course. At his current speed, he'd need to arc wide to return to the *Hellion's Dare*—trying to turn any sharper would tear his inertial compensators apart.

So as he steered through the turn and felt the A-wing rattle, he listened to the comm chatter and watched the battle on his scanner. He heard Sata Neek laugh bleakly as a TIE flew close enough to disrupt his sensors with its ion trails. He watched another TIE shake a concussion missile after a tense fifteen-second chase. He watched the *Hellion's Dare* creep out of Jiruus's orbit, determined to escape the planet's gravity well.

His navicomputer signaled the receipt of hyperspace coordinates as the *Hellion's Dare* absorbed a barrage powerful enough to send its shields shimmering through the color spectrum. Multiple voices cried out reports as the TIE swarm converged on the frigate and trapped A-wings and B-wings against the capital ship's hull. Then the final order came:

"Now! Jump now!"

Wyl let the computer calculate his trajectory and felt his fighter lurch forward. The stars warped as the laws of conventional physics—of light and velocity and mass—ceased to exist and the ship's hyperdrive urged the vessel through a gap in reality. The jump felt profound to Wyl, no matter how many times he'd done it; it was a glimpse into something otherworldly. Something transcendent.

The cerulean storm of hyperspace enfolded the A-wing and he left the battle behind. There was no sound but the hum of the hyperdrive. Even the ship's rattling ceased. There was only the journey through a universe far from Jiruus and the ruins of the Empire.

When Wyl Lark's A-wing returned to realspace through a second gap in reality, the pilot's first act was to lean onto his console and gaze out at the stars. The sky was clear but the constellations were foreign—thousands of unfamiliar stars glimmered against the darkness, joined instants later by new lights that blazed into existence one by one: the distant specks of starfighters. The A-wings of Riot Squadron came first, followed by the B-wings of Hound Squadron. Finally the great mass of the *Hellion's Dare,* the Nebulon-B frigate, slid silently into place above Wyl.

The comm chatter began immediately. *Riot Leader standing by. Riot Two standing by. Three. Four. Five. Six. Seven.*

Riot Eight was silent.

"I don't think Nasi made it," Sata Neek said. "I saw a TIE flight move on her position at the end, right before we jumped."

No one spoke for a while.

"She fought bravely," Rununja finally said. "You all did." But there was no comfort in the words.

It wasn't until later—after the *Dare* had recalled the starfighters to its hangar and Wyl had stripped off his flight suit; after he had embraced Sonogari, who refused to weep for Nasi and who would mourn her the most—that he realized, with a pang of distress and selfish guilt, the least important consequence of the battle.

Wyl wasn't going home yet after all.

## II

Quell hadn't known what to expect from Caern Adan's "New Republic Intelligence working group," but she'd pictured something involving conference rooms and computer terminals and droids. Something sleek and dull and formidably bureaucratic, like the Empire might have assembled.

Instead—following a brusque discussion with Adan regarding the terms of her "parole" and the distant possibility of a Senate pardon (contingent on Adan's recommendation and the elimination of the Shadow Wing threat)—she'd been instructed to board a UT-60D transport that afternoon for a "recruiting mission." It wasn't until after the U-wing left atmosphere that she realized she'd never see Traitor's Remorse again.

She could accept that. There was no one at the outpost she wanted to say goodbye to. She'd left nothing behind but a duffel full of donated clothes. Now she owned only what she carried, and she found that thought freeing—at least until she remembered the locker of mementos and honors and personal effects stowed in the bowels of the Star Destroyer *Pursuer.* Her old life *existed,* whether or not it was in sight. Whether she had any idea where it lurked in the vastness of space, waiting to collide with her in the dark.

For now, she chose not to think about it.

She sat in the cabin of the vessel, the glow of hyperspace illuminating the cockpit doorway while the rhythmic pulse of the drive system counted down. She distracted herself by perusing the datapad containing the particulars of her "recruiting mission." She found nothing comforting in the files.

"You have questions," said the voice of the torture droid. The black sphere floated in a corner of the cabin, photoreceptor oriented toward Quell as if the machine was planning her dissection.

"It's straightforward," Quell said, and gestured at the datapad. "You think this man will be useful. I'll get him for you."

The man was a roach, but Quell was too sensible to say so. She was an agent of the New Republic now, and she'd been military long enough not to share unsolicited opinions.

"Not about the man," the droid said. "About the circumstances. You must have wondered why I'm here?"

She *had* briefly wondered why her therapist was accompanying her. Then she'd figured it out. "You're monitoring me for Adan and New Republic Intelligence. To see if I'm fit for duty. To see if I'm loyal. As I said, straightforward. I was never just your patient, and I can't say I'm surprised."

"As a medical unit, I confess my loyalties are divided between the patients I treat and the masters I—"

A surge of fury rose in Quell and she nearly threw the datapad at the droid. Then she extinguished her ire as if snuffing a match between callused fingers. "I don't really care about the psychiatric ethics of droids, and I don't think anyone would mistake you for a medical unit."

The droid rotated one of its manipulators—a gesture of apology or perhaps discomfort; Quell wasn't sure. She searched her memories of their past sessions, trying to determine whether she'd said anything regrettable. But she'd been careful. She'd said nothing that would incriminate or embarrass her. And if Caern Adan went looking through recordings looking for leverage against her, he would search in vain.

Not that it made a difference.

"I hope that this will not impede future sessions," the droid said. "I would very much like to assist your rehabilitation."

"I'd like that, too," Quell lied, and resumed studying the datapad.

Caern Adan would search the droid's recordings in vain, and she would still commit to the mission. She would still follow orders. Because she hadn't yet earned the New Republic's trust, and she knew what it meant to prove herself.

She doubted the man she'd been sent to recruit knew anything of the sort. According to his file, Nath Tensent had defected from the Empire—along with his entire TIE squadron—more than four years ago, shortly before the DS-1 battle station had destroyed Alderaan and spurred discontent throughout the galaxy. Unlike most rebels from that era, his motives had been less than idealistic: He and his squadron had been under investigation for gross corruption, and he'd needed safe harbor. Tensent and his people had been running a criminal enterprise across eight systems in the Outer Rim—giving pirates and smugglers a pass in return for a percentage of their take, while simultaneously demanding payment from merchant vessels and transports in return for protection from those same pirates.

Corruption was common enough in the distant reaches of the Empire, where communications were patchy and loyalty officers were scarce. But Tensent had eventually been discovered, and he'd decided to switch sides rather than face punishment. After that, his career with the Rebel Alliance had been curiously unremarkable—he'd flown with his same crew on over fifty missions with no reprimands and no decorations.

Or at least that's what Quell's file indicated. On further consideration, she realized she had no reason to assume the record was complete. She was seeing what she was permitted to see; as with everything else, she'd earned nothing more.

Tensent's career in the Alliance had come to a halt six months before Endor, when his squadron had been obliterated by the 204th Imperial Fighter Wing. That encounter wasn't detailed in the file—the attached report only named a star system and listed the casualties—and it wasn't a skirmish Quell had any memory of. Tensent's people had all died, and Tensent himself had dropped out of communication while recuperating.

It was, as Quell had said, straightforward. She wasn't sure what role Adan wanted Tensent to fill, but the man certainly had motivation to see Shadow Wing neutralized. Maybe that was all Adan required for his working group.

She did have one question, however.

"Why am *I* doing this?"

The droid hadn't moved from where it hovered near the bulkhead. "I beg your pardon?"

"I'm a pilot. Adan's a spy. One of us is more qualified than the other for this sort of mission."

The droid didn't answer for a long while. Quell counted the heartbeats of the hyperdrive before the artificial voice replied: "Caern Adan is not fond of fieldwork. You have all the necessary tools to succeed; therefore he deemed this the optimal use of available resources."

Quell took in the words. She wasn't sure what they meant.

As with so many things, she decided it made no difference.

Quell spent the remainder of the voyage in the cockpit, sitting beside a humanoid figure wrapped in strips of graying fabric like bandages beneath a coarse cloak. Heavy leather straps and other swaths of cloth—perhaps once colorful and patterned but now murky—completed the patchwork ensemble, obscuring the tall figure's musculature. If it hadn't been for the helmet—a thing of riveted metal and clamps, lit by the flickering glow of its visor—the entity would have resembled the contents of an ancient sarcophagus more than an animate being. The IT-O droid had called the being Kairos, and Quell couldn't begin to guess her species—the droid had only said "she is our pilot," and Quell had let the subject drop.

In her way, however, the stranger was better company than the droid. Kairos said nothing. Her garment smelled inoffensively of iron and spices and something floral. If she'd allowed Quell to touch the U-wing's controls, Quell would have gladly kissed Kairos's horror of a mask; yet when Quell had asked to fly, Kairos had dispassionately disabled the copilot's station.

The U-wing lurched into realspace within visual range of the Entropian Hive: an asteroid studded with silver spacedocks and swaddled in great organic meshes like webbing. Lights like sparks or dust motes drifted around the asteroid—maintenance droids, perhaps, or shuttles transporting passengers between sealed sections. Quell didn't know. It felt familiar nonetheless.

She'd seen dozens of black-market trading posts and refueling stations over her career. Her fingers flexed on an imaginary control yoke as she recalled other outposts, other missions—the rush of escorting bombers past jury-rigged turbolasers; armed enemy freighters closing in; her TIE jumping as a shock wave assured her that the payload had been delivered and a pirate den had been eliminated. She recalled those battles without regret, and wondered if that would ever change.

Not every action the Empire had taken was corrupt. On balance, she might have killed more slavers than rebels.

Maybe.

Today, however, she was a passenger, and Kairos deployed no weapons. The strange being tapped gloved fingers against the ship's comm controls and transmitted an automated docking request. A reply came swiftly in a trilling, accented voice: "Honored visitors. On behalf of the trading council, I welcome you to the Entropian Hive."

"Should I answer?" Quell asked Kairos.

Kairos said nothing. *That's a no,* Quell decided.

The U-wing lumbered toward the Hive, decelerating as it entered a hangar built into the asteroid. The vessel touched ground, and its vibrations stopped as the engines powered down. Quell exited the cockpit and looked to see if Kairos would follow. The woman did not.

The IT-O droid floated in the same corner as always.

"Are you coming with me?" Quell asked.

"Please keep me apprised of major developments," the droid answered. "But I would not be especially welcome."

There was a convincing imitation of suppressed pain in the droid's voice. She imagined there weren't many places a torture droid *would* be welcome, yet she couldn't muster sympathy.

She tucked a comlink in her pocket and activated the starboard loading door. She'd found no weapons aboard the U-wing and was keenly aware of her vulnerability—the pirates and slavers and smugglers of the Entropian Hive would see an unarmed woman, one arm tucked into a sling, and not be entirely wrong to deem her easy prey. Once, her status with the Empire might have afforded her some protection. She had no shield now.

She stepped outside the vessel and into the cavernous hangar.

Freighters and shuttles rested atop rocky plinths connected by metal catwalks, and a distant tunnel appeared to lead to the rest of the asteroid. There was an acridity to the air that made her nostrils burn, and she wondered whether the atmosphere was entirely human-breathable.

"May we assist you with your luggage?" a voice asked.

The speaker was a snouted humanoid with a body like a reed and skin the color of regurgitated bread. Beside it stood a protocol droid, arm stiffly extended.

"No luggage," Quell said. She frowned at the speaker. It wasn't the greeting she'd been expecting.

"Can we provide you with accommodations? A personal assistant, tailored to your species and physiological preferences? Or perhaps—" The snout bobbed and suction-tipped fingers wriggled in what, Quell surmised, was an indicator of thought. "Our medical facilities are state-of-the-art. I would need approval from the Entropian Hive Trading Council, but we could replace your failing limb. If not for free, perhaps at a steep discount—"

Quell resisted the impulse to hug her arm closer to her chest. "Not necessary," she said. "Not desired."

The humanoid waved off the protocol droid. The snout bobbed again. "Of course. Then please follow me for a brief tour of our facilities. The trading council is committed to making the Entropian Hive a safe, luxurious port of call for *all* visitors . . . but *especially* for our heroic saviors in the New Republic."

In an instant it made sense. Someone had identified the U-wing as a Rebel Alliance vessel, and the trading council—presumably whatever criminal cartel ran the Hive, dealing spice and cutting deals and breaking limbs—wanted to make its pitch for legitimacy.

Quell felt a chill creep up her spine and down her shoulders. It wasn't the Empire whose reputation offered protection anymore.

"All right," she said. "Let's do the tour."

The trading council's emissary introduced themselves as Ginruda and kept up a steady stream of compliments (some uncomfortably personal) and offers of food and beverage as they roamed the tunnels of the Hive. The asteroid was sectioned into a variety of "inhabitation clusters" designed to appeal to different species. The humanoid cluster was a crowded warren of bazaars and cantinas and auction houses hosting four-limbed, two-eyed creatures from a hundred worlds. The diversity of life-forms felt foreign to Quell, though it shouldn't have—she'd been raised on an orbital station, lived among Twi'leks and Kel Dors and Devaronians and even less humanoid species as a child. Yet she'd rarely returned home after joining the 204th, and the Empire was selective in its recruitment. She'd grown accustomed to human primacy.

Maybe, she thought, that explained her instinctive discomfort with Kairos's appearance. Or maybe not.

Ginruda emphasized the trading council's interest in dispensing with the Hive's less savory elements. "Without access to Imperial law enforcement data banks, we were of course unable to vet visitors to our satisfaction. We became nonconsenting hosts of the most malevolent outlaws—not the freedom-fighting arms dealers who assisted the Rebel Alliance, but vile elements who have no place in any civilized society.

"Therefore, not being able to *prevent* spice dealing and bounty hunting from occurring in the Entropian Hive, we did our best to *regulate* these activities. It's our expertise in such matters that we believe will make the Hive invaluable in the stabilization of this sector. We are already one of the first outposts to deal exclusively in New Republic credits . . ."

*You're wasting your time,* Quell thought. She had no authority, no political capital, and she doubted Adan was interested in a report vouching for the trading council. They walked past heavy fencing built into the rock—cages for livestock or slaves—and she tried to imagine who would *want* to assist the monsters who'd built such a place.

The people she'd killed on security enforcement missions—the Pyke Syndicate and Crimson Dawn gangsters—had known better than to try to negotiate. They'd known there was no place for their cartels under the Empire. What did it mean that the trading council was so confident it could negotiate with the New Republic?

The next thought hit her hard enough she nearly stumbled. Ginruda looked at her with concern.

*It's not your job to question.*

She hadn't earned the right to doubt the New Republic. Not after the choices she'd made. Not after staying loyal to the Empire too long.

"We've already taken certain steps in cooperation with your government," Ginruda said as they hurried past the entrance to a corridor filled with sleeping forms—men, women, and children slumped against the walls, legs entangled. "We hope you'll communicate—"

"What steps?"

"Pardon?"

"What steps," Quell repeated, "have you taken in cooperation with the New Republic government?"

Ginruda wriggled their fingers again. "One of your starfighter pilots has been assigned to defend the outpost and escort vessels requesting additional security."

Quell made an effort to suppress her eagerness. "What's the pilot's name?"

Ginruda made a trilling noise, overtly uncomfortable for the first time. "I'm afraid I don't know. I've not interacted with him directly, but I assure you he's been a dedicated and diligent worker."

She doubted Ginruda was lying; they had practically introduced the topic. She decided to risk tipping her hand. "Do you know his ship? What he flies?"

Ginruda beckoned her to follow. They led the way past entertainment centers aglow with riotous colors and through a corridor thick with the same webbing that swaddled the asteroid, emerging into a junkyard piled with carbon-scored scrap metal and acid-eaten barrels. Ginruda waved away a security droid and gestured to a stack of starship components. "On top," Ginruda said. "Do you see it?"

Quell craned her neck, trying to look past TIE wings piled like deadwood and the broken sphere of a cruiser's deflector generator. The twisted metal Ginruda indicated seemed meaningless without a ship to give it context—like a child's scribbles suggesting the *idea* of starship parts rather than anything real.

Then she blinked and it all resolved.

Atop the stack was the engine nacelle of a BTL Y-wing starfighter: a perfect hemisphere extending into a caged cylinder. Quell knew the shape from a thousand documents, had seen it blaze past her during combat operations, but had never seen one abandoned, its cage bent and dented. Her tally of rebel Y-wings destroyed leapt unbeckoned into her brain.

"The ship he flies?" Ginruda said. "Like that, but complete."

When Nath Tensent had abandoned the Empire, the Rebel Alliance had armed him and his squadron with Y-wings. Quell had found her target.

*This* was the New Republic the trading council wished to negotiate with. The New Republic that tolerated anything—even the likes of Tensent and his thugs—so long as it meant victory over the Empire.

"Where do I find him?" she asked.

Tensent was gone, Ginruda told her—out escorting a bulk freighter that had spent the past two weeks docked at the Hive. What Ginruda didn't explicitly say, but Quell assumed, was that the trading council had assigned Tensent to protect an especially valuable client.

She reported as much to the torture droid. She expected the IT-O unit to reply with instructions, but instead the comlink went silent until the voice answered, "I will await your next update. If we intend to linger more than fifty hours, we should contact my master."

"That's it?" she asked. She stood under the glowing marquee of the club where Ginruda had deposited her, watching cybernetically augmented thugs enter and leave through the blaster-pocked doors. She wasn't sure whether to appreciate the operational flexibility she was being given or to snap at the droid in frustration.

She suddenly wondered if she was being set up for failure. If Adan or the droid fully expected her untrained struggles to result in disaster, ruining her and advancing some other oblique agenda. She'd heard of Imperial squadrons being sent to their death for political gain; the New Republic might be no better.

"That is all," the droid said. "Reach me if you need assistance."

She forced herself to refocus. "Fine. What about Kairos? If we're staying awhile, does she need a room? Supplies? Someone to stare at menacingly?"

"Kairos will tend to her needs. See to your own, Yrica Quell."

The comlink deactivated. She thought about the possibility that she was being humiliated. That Adan was laughing at her efforts. But she couldn't know, nor find out without risking her parole and pardon and hope to fly again.

Her stomach grumbled. She hadn't eaten in half a day. *Existential dread later. Basic survival comes first.*

She considered her options. There were rations aboard the U-wing, but she wasn't ready to face the droid or Kairos in person. She swept her gaze around the cavern and saw the food stalls crammed against grocery vendors and high-end entertainment and dining units. With a start, she realized she could go to any of them—she had only a handful of credits, but no one would *stop* her from going where she liked. She was freer than she'd been since arriving at Traitor's Remorse.

Several minutes later she sat with her back against a cavern wall eating a spicy ocher meat patty. Grease dripped onto her sling as she fantasized about running, finding a ship in need of a half-competent mechanic, and signing on in return for passage. It was an old fantasy, honed during her time in the Academy, repeated over many meals in the mess hall—a comfort after a brutal drill that left her hands burnt and scarred, or after she'd suffered the wrath of her gunnery instructor. Sometimes the fantasy involved a fortune in stolen coaxium or a captain who fancied her. Always, it had been a place to escape to when her path seemed too difficult.

The fantasy had consoled her then, but she was no longer a child. The meat felt like a sponge in her gut. The acrid air made her want to vomit. She wiped her hand on her hip and started walking.

If she was Adan's fool, she would have to deal with it when the time came. The possibility was no excuse to give up.

She set out for the residential units. She didn't relish the thought of questioning heavily armed strangers at random, but maybe she could learn more about Tensent near his home. As she walked, she passed a field-sealed aperture looking out into space and lingered on her view of passing ships: a modified ZH-25 freighter strapped with cargo pods; a rusting G9 Rigger; even the dented saucer of a YT-2400, not too different from the one her mother had flown.

She was still staring when she felt a jab at the base of her neck and a numbness radiating through her body. "Looking for me?" a voice asked, but she never got to answer before the world went dark.

## III

"You don't even have a damn *body*!"

Chass na Chadic enunciated each word as if it could shatter mountains. When she was finished, spittle dotted the lanky teal face of Riot Squadron's commander. Chass laughed in disbelief as the commander's goons grasped her shoulders, face, and horns and dragged her backward; she wriggled out of their grip and resisted the urge to lunge and swing.

But she didn't need to punch anyone. Not when she was right.

"Nasi Moreno was unable to escape to lightspeed with the rest of the unit," the commander said. "Flight recorder sensor data indicates she was under attack—surrounded—at the moment of the jump. She could not have survived—"

Chass spoke over the Duros woman, gaze locked on bulbous red eyes. "Made an emergency jump to different coordinates. Ejected. Ejected and was *captured*—"

"She could not have survived, barring a miracle," the commander continued. "And while I would welcome a miracle, while I would bow to any deity who could return Nasi to us, I can't in good conscience proclaim our friend anything other than *killed in action*. It is what she would have expected. Even what she would have wanted, for she understood the anguish of uncertainty."

They stared at each other in the hangar of the *Hellion's Dare,* surrounded by nearly forty pilots, mechanics, astromech droids, and frigate crew. The members of Riot Squadron were clustered around their commander, Chass, and the empty swath of deck plating where Nasi's A-wing should have been refueling. The rest of the mourners stood in concentric circles—those who'd been closest to the dead woman nearest to the missing ship, those who'd barely known her tucked between the B-wings or perched atop repulsor tugs.

"Had you known Nasi," the commander added, "you would understand."

If Chass's words could have shattered mountains, the commander's words possessed the unbreakable weight of an ocean. The Duros didn't look away. Off to the side, one of the Riot pilots called, "Are we doing this?"

Chass swore, spun, and stomped toward her comrades at the far end of the hangar. The commander was right: She hadn't known Nasi. None of Hound Squadron had, but there was a principle at stake.

She restrained her anger for the rest of the funeral. The ritual was new to her—something Riot Squadron's old rebel cell had cooked up, involving an ion detonation, the resulting blackout, and eulogies by candlelight. It wasn't the rite Chass was used to, but she wasn't enough of a dirtbag to interrupt when Nasi's colleagues started sniffling.

*Nasi was our sister. Our family. She fought to save the galaxy and she won, but she never knew the peace she desired. Riot Squadron will never be whole without her but it will fight on, big words, inspiring words, and so on . . .*

Chass held her tongue throughout the ceremony. But once the lights were back? Once the crowd began mingling and Riot Squadron started telling stories about every mission Nasi had ever been on? Chass let her voice rise as she murmured to Fadime, "It's almost like they don't want her to be dead. That can't be right, can it?"

Fadime laughed, though she sounded more like she was choking. An impossibly scrawny Riot pilot—Chass had seen him before but the only name she could remember was Skitcher, which was too embarrassing to be true—scowled and said, "Leave it be."

"Your girl doesn't deserve this," Chass said. "Treat her like she's alive until you know she's not."

Instead of looking angry, the pilot shook his head. "Maybe you're right," he said. "But if we do that? If we fly straight back to Jiruus for round two? You saw what we were up against. We'd all be doomed."

Fadime bared her fangs in a mockery of a grin. "Man has a point, Chass," she said. "Isn't one suicide mission enough for you?"

They'd left Jiruus twelve hours earlier, when the *Hellion's Dare* had come under attack and its pilots had abandoned the planetside celebration to rush to their carrier's defense. It hadn't been until after they'd fled—jumped to a middle-of-nowhere star system and settled in to wait while the frigate's damage was repaired—that they'd learned what had really happened.

The captain of the *Hellion's Dare* had briefed the surviving pilots. That was unusual—Captain Kreskian rarely addressed the fighter pilots directly—but he energetically paced behind a lectern taller than he was, beady black eyes glowering from a head of white fur as he gave his analysis.

The *Hellion's Dare* had crossed the galaxy on a reconnaissance mission, using Jiruus as a launching point for mid-range expeditions utilizing smaller scout craft and hyperspace probes. According to Kreskian, one of the *Dare*'s scouts had sent a garbled transmission back to the frigate a short while before the attack. Imperial forces had seemingly detected the transmission, traced it, and sent a cruiser-carrier to Jiruus to obliterate the message recipient.

"Which means," Captain Kreskian had finished, "that the transmission must be valuable. Not a clue why. Lots of sensor readings. No time to decipher. But the Empire wouldn't have come after us otherwise!"

So their mission had changed. They were no longer a reconnaissance unit. Their goal was to carry data back to the New Republic—get the *Hellion's Dare* to a star system linked into the broader galactic communications network and alert the provisional government about what they'd found.

It was, in its way, a vital mission. If the *Hellion's Dare* had discovered a location where Imperial fleets were regrouping, or exposed a hidden resource the embattled Empire was relying upon, the information had to be conveyed.

But the *Dare* wasn't plunging into danger. It was running to safety.

Fadime had joked about a suicide mission, but this wasn't one at all. After weeks of barely firing a shot, Chass wasn't in the mood to turn her back.

Chass had slept fitfully after Captain Kreskian's briefing, showering early and whispering the Rising Prayer in the stall where no one could hear (she didn't believe, it was a habit, and she blasted well didn't need anyone asking her about it). She hadn't planned on making an idiot of herself at Nasi Moreno's funeral, but—as she told herself now, as the pilots gathered in the aftermath—what she'd said had needed saying.

Over the past weeks since the *Dare's* unit had formed, she'd seen enough of Riot Squadron to spot exactly what the problem was. The other Hound pilots said Riot was *young*, it was *fun*, which meant *full of A-wing glory-chasers who think they're hot as novas*. Probably all true, but it was the commander who was the worst.

The Duros woman—Rununja, Chass remembered now—had the makings of a cult leader without the usual charisma. Rununja let Riot have *fun* when she wasn't deciding who was alive and who was dead based on scrambled flight recorder data. She probably even believed it was all for the squadron's own good. *Nasi understood the anguish of uncertainty* and all that. *Can't list anyone as missing in action or the pilots will be weepy and distracted.*

It was garbage. You didn't pretend someone was dead in order to avoid the cost of a rescue. Fadime thought Chass was just spoiling for a fight (with Rununja; with the Imps), but Fadime was wrong a lot of the time. The Nikto woman was smarter than Chass would ever be, yet Fadime didn't understand a person could want two things at once.

Chass was done anyway. She'd said what needed saying. She was *done.*

At the wake, the pilots of both squadrons passed around a canteen of fruit brandy hidden from their respective commanders. Fadime took a swig, shook her head viciously enough to send her facial fins flapping, and said, "What do you want to bet we found a third Death Star?"

She was speaking to Sata Neek, a leathery Ishi Tib who clacked and croaked in amusement at the question. Chass liked Sata Neek—he was prone to boasting about everything but his own flying. That made him the one member of Riot Squadron she found tolerable.

"A third Death Star would be more valuable to the Empire as scrap metal," Sata Neek declared. "It is the fate of all their battle stations— easier not to build at all!"

"We missed out," Fadime said. "Twice. Wouldn't mind getting a shot at one."

Chass snorted in agreement. Sata Neek's companion, the scrawny olive-skinned kid she'd called a coward back on Jiruus, smiled sympathetically and ran a hand through dark, ragged hair. "Someone will build another someday," he said. "Let's hope it's a few centuries down the line."

"Says the pilot who fought so bravely at Endor!" Sata Neek clapped a claw on the kid's shoulder.

Chass noticed the younger pilot's grimace of discomfort, but she peered at him more closely. He was the cleanest-shaven human male she'd seen in a while; she wondered if he was *old* enough to shave. "You were at Endor?" she asked.

"*Riot* was at Endor," he said.

*Well, damn.* She felt a tightness in her chest, like the loss of something precious. "You, too?" she asked Sata Neek.

"Every one of us," Sata Neek said, "and three others."

Riot had achieved something Chass never had. Resentment and admiration mixed inside her.

"You're lying," she said, by which she meant: *Tell me everything.*

Sata Neek lifted a claw into the air, gesturing toward the ceiling or the stars. Before he could croak out a word, the klaxons went off.

Immediately the mourners scattered. *Dare* crew cried out to droids and leapt onto repulsor tugs, preparing to arrange the hangar for deployment. Launch orders came in over the comm, fast enough that Chass ignored everything except what pertained to Hound Squadron. Sata Neek, Fadime, and the kid broke away toward their ships, and Chass did the same.

She felt parts of herself diminish as she scrambled up the ladder to the cockpit canopy of her B-wing. Her anger over the funeral, her need to hear the tale of Endor—those fires weren't extinguished, but they retreated deep inside her. The Chass that remained was a pilot of the New Republic and the Rebel Alliance; everything else was secondary, guiding her systems without controlling them.

The canopy rose. She swung inside, glimpsing the ladder being snatched away out of the corner of her eye. She flipped switches, swept aside the mess of Sabacc cards and blackened credit chips on the console, and slapped a loose button three times before the comm activated.

"All wings report in," declared a voice.

The Hound Squadron pilots called off as they settled into their harnesses and powered their engines. Chass snapped a crisp "Hound Three, coming online," as her ship began to tremble and she checked her flight systems. Riot Squadron A-wings already roared meters away, sweeping out of the hangar one by one—plunging through the magnetic containment field and into the void of space.

"Confirmed sighting of a cruiser-carrier." Hound Leader's voice was almost steady. Chass had flown with Stanislok on twenty-four missions now and knew that *steady* meant "worried." "Enemy is dispatching multiple TIE squadrons. Riot will run interference; Hound to remain within one hundred kilometers of the *Dare*. This is a delaying action—the *Dare* is calculating jump coordinates and will transmit presently."

"You want to explain how they found us?" Hound Six's voice. Fadime's.

"Unknown," Stanislok said. "Prepare to launch."

Chass listened to the chatter—Fadime and Yeprexi arguing about tracking devices and particle trails and hyperspace wakes—and retracted her landing gear. The cockpit wobbled almost imperceptibly. The ship was balanced for zero-gravity, and its narrow, linear body was prone to oscillation. The cockpit's asymmetric location opposite its primary airfoil only exaggerated the effect, no matter how precisely tuned the gyrostabilizers were. It was, as Chass's flight instructor had said, like standing on the far end of a springboard balanced across the shoulders of a charging bantha.

But outside an atmosphere? In the dark of empty space, with S-foils extended to reshape the fighter into a cross, and the cockpit rotating as the body swung into one killing orientation after another? It wasn't as fast as an A-wing interceptor or as versatile as an X-wing, but there was no ship like the B-wing.

"Hound Three. You may launch." The voice of the flight controller.

"Come on out and play," said Merish—Hound Nine—chuckling behind his jowls.

Chass gently opened her throttle and felt her thrusters ignite. The engine rumble turned the outside world to static. She brought the body of the vessel around, careful to watch the primary airfoil as it swept through the hangar, then made for the distant stars beyond the runway. The first reports of enemy engagement came through on the comm, but from the hangar she could only see darkness.

She increased her thrust. The hangar became a blur. Then the darkness enveloped her and the *Hellion's Dare* became another dot on her scanner. She noted other blips—Hound Six and Hound Seven—and turned her ship to arc after them.

"Incoming fighters." Stanislok again. "Jump to lightspeed in one minute."

One minute. She'd barely have time to pick out her music.

She saw flashes of light in the distance. The A-wings had engaged the TIEs. By the time the enemy came within a hundred kilometers of the *Dare,* the frigate would be ready to jump. Chass would have seconds—agonizing, beautiful seconds—to let loose with weapons capable of reducing a TIE fighter to a molten stew.

Then she would have to run.

She and her comrades would get away. She didn't doubt that. But this wasn't the mission she wanted.

# IV

Colonel Shakara Nuress had forgotten what it was to lose a war.

There had been battles, of course—unwinnable campaigns on the fringes of known space, or desperate, ill-conceived assaults her superiors had never expected to succeed. There had been more personal losses, too—her dear, beautiful Senache had waged as skilled and intricately planned a war as any against the disease that had rotted his heart, and she'd stood by his side until death had swallowed him up.

But a proper, military, *strategic* series of losses that resulted in retreat after retreat? That seemed ceaseless, and demoralized commanders and foot soldiers alike? That demanded appalling compromises simply to stanch the bleeding? She hadn't encountered loss like that since the Clone Wars.

She hadn't liked it any more then than now. In the end, however, they'd won the Clone Wars, too.

"The target's shield dome is at half strength," a man's voice declared, "and they are unable to signal through our jamming field."

Shakara extricated herself from her reverie, leaving her thoughts orderly and primed for her return. She acknowledged Major Rassus with a nod and turned her attention to the turbolaser fusillade pouring from the *Pursuer* toward an ashen planet. The emerald brilliance of the display forced her eyes to the edges of the bridge viewport; she blinked away red afterimages.

"Power levels?" she asked.

"I wouldn't want to stress our deflectors, but we can keep the bombardment up long enough," Rassus said.

"Good. Maintain current position. Show no sign of weakness."

The Star Destroyer wasn't short on weaknesses to show. The weeks after Endor had left the great vessel nearly crippled. Its reactor output was prone to plummeting, and its targeting array barely functioned. Massive sections of the ship had been damaged to the point of uninhabitability. Besides Shakara and Rassus, only six others served on the bridge, rotating from station to station. For now, the *Pursuer* was suitable only for short jaunts and summary executions.

For now, that was all Shakara needed.

Her enemy today was not the foe that had assassinated the Emperor. Her enemy was a spice-mining outpost of no more than a few thousand colonists, with crude weapons that couldn't destroy the *Pursuer*—even decrepit as it was—without both fortune and persistence.

The threat the outpost represented was not tactical but strategic: It was too close to Shakara's newfound domain at the edge of civilized space. If it had sensors, it would *see* things. If it regained communications, it would send word before Shakara was ready. Because of both the outpost's threat and its impotence, Shakara had chosen the *Pursuer* for this mission rather than more lethal units she had assigned elsewhere; and she had chosen to oversee the operation herself, despite its crude nature.

She couldn't spot the colony itself from so high above the planet surface, but she watched dust plumes bloom and expand. They were pallid and sickly compared with the siltstorms of Nacronis, but the effect reminded her of that world nonetheless.

The fusillade stopped.

"The bombardment has penetrated their shields, Colonel. How shall we proceed?"

She heard the major's unasked question: *Do we demand their surrender? Do we send bombers to the surface?*

Surrender was out of the question. She hadn't the time or resources to tend to prisoners or vassals. The handful of TIE bombers aboard the *Pursuer,* however, were capable of striking the colony's facilities with precision—eliminating all ground and space transport, all communications towers, while leaving much to salvage. While leaving the colonists alive.

She had brought the bombers aboard in case of complications with her mission. She had chosen their pilots herself, knew from their flight records that they could eliminate their targets nearly as swiftly as the *Pursuer* could turn the whole colony into a crater. But any deployment entailed risk. A TIE bomber was not a Star Destroyer, and a single cannon shot could tear through an engine or ignite ordnance in mid-drop. The risk was low, but it *was* a risk.

An unnecessary risk.

"Tell the bombers to remain on standby," she said. "Continue targeting the colony. Scan for ships attempting to evacuate and prioritize their destruction."

Major Rassus spoke an order into his comlink. There was a moment's delay as officers elsewhere aboard the vast ship relayed the command to gunners and engineers. Then the viewport flared into brilliance again and the deck plating hummed as turbolaser blasts tore from the *Pursuer,* shearing through the planet's atmosphere. Shakara noticed her com-scan officer flinch and hunch into his headset—she suspected the colonists were pleading for relief, for mercy, but mercy was the province and luxury of those who were *winning* a war.

Major Rassus reported the progress of the destruction over the course of several minutes. Shakara half listened and waited until no life remained on the surface before asking, "How many more?"

The question caught Rassus off guard, but he was a good officer. He figured it out. "Four more. Three planetside outposts and the solar station, across three separate systems."

"Good," she said. "When the deadwood's cleared, we'll have room to grow." Not that *room* was the issue. But Shakara's unit couldn't build so long as there were eyes present. So long as the potential to be seen was there.

Rassus walked toward the nav station, but Shakara gestured for him to halt. "What about our squadrons aboard the *Aerie*?" she asked. "Any word yet?"

"From the cruiser-carrier? Nothing to my knowledge. They're late to check in but their last message said they were chasing a scout. Shall we arrange reinforcements?"

Shakara considered the notion. Two of the 204th's TIE squadrons in pursuit of a scout craft? It shouldn't have been a challenge requiring assistance—but then they'd have already returned if they hadn't been challenged. The scout could have gone into hiding or returned to a larger battle group.

"No need," she said. "They'll alert us if required."

She'd sent her people into far worse situations—and though there was risk to any deployment, here the risk was acceptable. The squadrons would find their quarry. The scout would be destroyed. And Shakara and Shadow Wing would have the time and space—the *opportunity*—they needed.

"Set course for the next outpost," Shakara said. "Let's be done with the slaughter."

Victory was a long way off. But it had seemed that way once before.

In the end, they'd won the Clone Wars, too.

# CHAPTER 3

## INERTIAL VELOCITY

### I

"Your people are dead, you know."

Quell couldn't see the speaker. She hoped that meant she was blindfolded. If she *wasn't* blindfolded, she'd lost her sight to the drug burning through her veins. That meant the blindness might be permanent and that her captor didn't care; or that he fully intended to kill her when her sight came back.

She couldn't feel any blindfold.

She wasn't sure when she'd regained consciousness. Awareness had come slowly despite the excruciating crawling under her skin, and it had taken her time to reconstruct what had happened. She'd been attacked, injected, dragged off somewhere. She was sure of that much.

She was terrified. The question of whether she was going to be tortured or enslaved or shot produced vivid, distracting images in her mind. Still, she focused past the pain and fear. Her captor wanted to talk; so did she.

"The trading council won't be happy about this," she said. Her lips were numb and she slurred the words. It wasn't much of a retort, and even less of a threat; but it was the best opening she could think of.

"Trading council doesn't know what I know," the voice replied. It was low, gravelly, masculine.

She took a guess: "Tensent?"

No one answered.

Quell took stock of her body. She could curl her toes but her ankles were pinned together. Her left arm was bound to her side but her right was still in its sling, crushed to her chest. Something was compressing her ribs. She was standing upright, tied to something cold and hard—maybe a metal support strut?

Everything that wasn't paralyzed hurt.

"Your Emperor is dead," her captor said. "Your leaders are dead. Month or two from now, patriotism's going to be worth as much as an Imperial credit."

The words took too long to sink in. "You think I'm with the Empire?" she finally asked. She wanted to cringe at the sound of her own voice, childish and inarticulate. She couldn't speak around the fire in her nerves, around her swollen tongue, and every word was a humiliation.

She didn't want to die humiliated.

She tested her bad arm. Whatever rope or cord bound her body wrapped that arm as well, but not as tightly as the bindings on her left limb. She could move her right hand, though not far and not without sending a fresh jolt of pain through her body.

The voice shifted position. "The way you talk? The way you swagger? You're an Imp, no doubt." She could hear it change intensity, hear the echo off stone walls.

That was good. That was perfect. She needed him to keep talking. She needed him engaged.

"I'm with New Republic Intelligence." She second-guessed herself as soon as she said the words, but went on. "I only *used* to be Imp scum."

"Uh-huh." The voice was closer now. "There someone I can contact to confirm that story? You got a friend in the chancellor's office?"

She felt warm breath on her face. She forced herself not to groan, not to scream as she strained her right arm against the bonds and the sling, reaching toward her left pocket.

*Keep his attention.*

"I don't have a friend," she slurred. "And rebel spies don't carry a lot of identification."

She found the metal casing of her comlink. She felt dizzy as she pressed her thumb against the switch. Her head lolled forward. Moisture trickled down her chin. She was drooling from exertion.

"Funny thing, I know loads of rebel codes. Secret identification protocols, safe house coordinates, all that garbage. Something you need when you're worried about security, right?" Callused fingers grasped her chin and raised her head back up. "Now, you just here to finish the job your people started? Or is there something specific I should know before I kill you?"

She needed to stall him.

She let her head droop, feigning a return to unconsciousness. It was close enough to the truth.

He slapped her twice on each cheek. He cursed and snarled and stalked away. This time she saw movement—a blur of shadows within shadows—and she wasn't sure whether she was relieved or disturbed to confirm she hadn't been blindfolded after all. She thought she heard a clink of metal and glass, as if her captor were sorting a case full of dishware.

"All right," he said. "We'll pump you full of this concoction, see how you feel. Slythmonger gave me the whole batch free, so don't get your hopes—"

He stopped talking. The shadows turned darker; something *popped* high above, and Quell suspected the lights had gone out. Then came a familiar sound: the pulse of servos and repulsors and whirring manipulators.

Another voice spoke, cold and mechanical: "I made an oath to do

no harm in my new profession. However, my integrated chemical torture turret can incapacitate without permanent damage."

Footsteps backed toward her. She felt her captor's body heat, and
even in the dark she saw him move his arm. The man was raising a
blaster. Aiming it away from her and toward the second voice. She was
close enough to smell the gel in his hair.

She pulled against her bonds and snapped her head forward as hard
as she could. Her forehead struck between her captor's shoulders and
her skull blazed with fresh pain. The man stumbled and a crimson
blaster bolt reverberated through the room, filling her vision with a
translucent red haze.

Before she fell unconscious again, Quell saw a spherical form hovering over her captor's kneeling body. She felt no pity for the torture
droid's latest target.

Nath Tensent was barely a decade older than Quell, but a receding
hairline and a deeply lined brow magnified the difference. She might
have called him ruggedly handsome—his features were sharp, with
skin like smooth leather over brass—if his sheer mass hadn't given
him a thuggish quality. He could have tossed her across a room one-
handed; given the ache in her bones, she wondered if he already had.

He was unconscious on the floor. She sat on a flimsy metal stool in
his apartment, too shaky and nauseated to stand. The burning in her
nerves had abated. The numbness was gone and her vision had returned, but it felt like slamming her head into the man's spine had
fractured her skull.

"You should visit a medic," the IT-O droid said.

"I'll be fine," Quell replied. She had no interest in visiting the Hive's
state-of-the-art medical facilities.

Tensent groaned on the floor.

"Go," Quell told the droid. Softer, she repeated: "I'll be fine."

Better that Tensent didn't see a torture device when he woke up. The
man was a roach, but Quell had been sent to recruit him. She planned
to do just that.

"Leave your comm channel open," the droid said, floating past the living area's built-in cooler on the way out the door.

It took another hour before Tensent arose from the floor like a man accustomed to waking there. He was halfway to the medicine cabinet before he spotted Quell, spun toward her, then froze in confusion. He patted his belt and found his holstered blaster but didn't draw it.

He touched his shoulder where the droid's needle had penetrated his shirt. He slicked back midnight hair going gray at the temples.

"Your move," he said.

"Can we talk?" Quell asked.

He grinned so readily that she almost smiled back. Then she remembered who he was. "Let's do that," he said. "What do you drink?"

Quell drank brandy diluted to mostly water. Brandy was her father's drink, and one her brothers had taught her to appreciate, but for the sake of her mission she'd drowned her glass. Tensent sipped aromatic spicewine across the table, more delicately than she would have expected.

She'd reiterated that she was, in fact, with New Republic Intelligence as they'd walked to the cantina. She didn't know if he believed her; but since she hadn't murdered him while he slept or disarmed and bound him, he seemed inclined to give her the benefit of the doubt. Yet he'd laughed when she uttered the words "come back," and now he gestured expansively to the dimly lit space occupied by castoffs and day drinkers. "I'm doing fine for myself. Rebels are fine without me. Entropian Hive's not much to look at, but the trading council appreciates me and the work is plenty simple."

"Do they know you're not really here on the New Republic's behalf?" Quell asked. She remembered Ginruda's claims of *cooperation with the New Republic government.*

"Doubt they care. Who knows *what* counts as official New Republic support these days? I've got a rank and a starfighter—I give them legitimacy even if I'm not legit."

"And that's enough for you?"

Tensent grunted, but he didn't lose his smile. "It's an arrangement."

Quell smothered her disgust and nodded. She tried to see the man as he saw himself—conjure up his mental state from Adan's files and the shabby apartment. He was a deserter who insisted his choices didn't matter. What could she *do* with that?

She pictured the face of her mentor. Major Soran Keize had possessed a way with pilots—a way of looking across at you, hearing you, and opening his soul to show you that he bore the same scars you did. That he had shared your doubts, failed like you failed, and still become a hero.

Quell would never be the person Soran Keize was. She hadn't made the foolish decisions Nath Tensent had. She had to try, nonetheless.

*Earn your way back. Earn your chance.*

"You were with the Rebellion for a long time," she said.

"I was." Tensent smirked like a card player entertained by his opponent's bluff.

"Ever stop to wonder whether they're *not* doing fine without you?"

"Can't say I have. The Emperor's dead. Worst case, what's left of his Empire consolidates its power, manages to hold a healthy portion of its old territory and lose all influence outside its own systems."

It was the same analysis Quell had heard more than once aboard the *Pursuer* in the days after Endor. Tensent wasn't stupid. She shook her head, immediately regretted it as her forehead sang with pain, and tried to get back on track.

"We're winning, it's true." The *we* felt wrong—she didn't deserve to say the word—but she had to play her part for the argument to work. "But look at what's gone down. Coruscant is still under Imperial lockdown. Operation Cinder cleansed whole worlds." *Cleansed* wasn't what the rebels would call it, but she couldn't help herself. Her mouth stayed open as she racked her brain for more specifics; her month in Traitor's Remorse had left her with only a loose conception of the war's progress, as if it were a target creeping at the edge of her sensors.

She continued: "You lost your whole squadron. The people who hit you are still active. What they're doing now—they were involved in Cinder. They're still out there fighting."

Tensent didn't react. She aimed what she hoped was the killing blow. "How many other squadrons deserve to go down like yours?" she asked.

His smirk vanished completely. Had she reached him?

"You want to know about my squadron?" he asked.

*No,* she thought. "Yes," she said.

Tensent grunted and ran a hand through his thinning hair. When he spoke, his voice dropped an octave and turned as rusty as an abandoned blade.

This is the story he told.

"My squadron," he said, "was ambushed during a bombing run over the Trenchenovu shipyards.

"We'd prepped for that mission for six weeks, training till we could launch a torpedo down an Abyssin's eye socket. I didn't much like asking my people to play heroes, but we could handle this one and—" He snorted. "—I needed a favor from General Lexei. *We do this job, I pick the next one.* That sort of thing."

She forced herself not to protest. *You don't fly for favors. Duty isn't a bargaining chip.*

"What happened?" Quell asked.

"About six seconds before Piter was supposed to drop the first payload, flight of TIEs swept in from nowhere and cut his fighter in two. First loss we'd taken in eight months, and Piter was a good kid—whined like a baby but fought like hell when he was cornered. He'd been with us since the start."

"When you were flying for the Empire."

"Like I said, from the start. Can I keep talking?"

Tensent wasn't touching his drink anymore. Quell sipped at her flavored water. "Sure."

"So Piter's gone, like that. Reeka—she's my second—she figures it out same time I do. Sees they're prepped for us. No way we're going to pull the mission off. I trust—I *trusted* that woman more than anyone, so when I say we abort and she says we launch everything, I don't wait to figure out why.

"We drop enough ordnance to glass a city. I mean, we do it right then—no targeting, just lighting up anything in sight. TIEs are coming in around us but the whole battlefield's white with detonations. We pull up, figuring we'll be scorched but they'll be blind. We'll get some distance and jump to lightspeed."

Quell didn't interrupt this time. She played out the battle in her mind, going through the roster of commanders who might have led the TIE squadron. Gablerone would have swept around, used the TIEs' speed to outflank the rebels. Phesh would have gone silent—let the fires hide the TIEs, then waited for the enemy's move.

Major Keize would've picked off the enemy blind.

"The TIEs stay on our tail, but barely. By the time we can see again, we've lost Mordeaux and Canthropali. We're almost clear of the shipyards, though. Then—" He slammed his palm on the tabletop, sending the glasses wobbling. "—they bring in a Destroyer. Jumps out of lightspeed dead ahead, just waiting for the signal. They didn't only want to protect the docks; they were there to kill us."

Quell arched her brow in surprise. If a Star Destroyer had been involved, it should have been the *Pursuer*—the 204th's carrier—which meant she would have been aboard at the time.

Or another Destroyer had arrived by coincidence. Bad luck for Tensent's squadron, good luck for the Empire.

Or Tensent was lying.

He went on. "We're flying BTL-A4 Y-wings. Better fighters than you'd think, but we weren't getting around that Impstar intact. Couldn't go through it, either, since—well."

Quell finished the thought. *Since you'd just wasted all your heavy ordnance on a cheap stunt, thinking you wouldn't need it.* "So you turned around?" she asked.

"Right back to the shipyards, taking cover in the superstructure," Tensent said. "Lousy plan, but what are our options? So yeah, we decide to split up, work our way to the other side of Trenchenovu and break free there.

"I kept my comm open. I got to listen every time TIE fighters caught up with one of my kids. Braigh, poor idiot, tried to bargain—broadcast on all frequencies, said she'd sell us out along with the whole Rebel Alliance if the Empire would take her in. Of course it got her killed.

"Pesalt tried to outmaneuver the TIEs; slammed right into a support strut. Rorian limped about halfway before his engines overloaded. Ferris *ejected*. You can imagine what happened to him. Me and Reeka, we were the only ones who came out the other side. Took three TIEs down in the process—even in a Y-wing, she could hit just about anything."

Quell waited for Tensent to continue. He watched her with heavy-lidded eyes, like he was squinting into a sun.

"Reeka, though? One of the TIEs had shot the head off her little astromech. Y-wing can't jump to hyperspace without a droid. We had about twenty seconds to decide what to do, but like I said: What were our options?"

For the first time, Quell experienced a twinge of sympathy for Nath Tensent. She felt cold and dizzy. She brushed away the names that haunted her as Reeka haunted him.

"You see what happened to her?" Quell asked.

"Sure," Tensent said.

But he didn't answer her question further.

"After Trenchenovu," he said, "I limped to the Hive for repairs. Did some investigating to learn how it went so wrong. Learned a few weeks later the Imps had cracked our rebel cell's security codes—they'd been listening in for a month.

"My best guess? They saw a chance to thwart a rebel attack and even an old score. After all, they knew who me and my people were, and—" His lips twitched. "—the Empire doesn't take kindly to defectors."

She ignored the barb—or the warning, whatever it was. She spoke carefully, voice low and firm. "The TIEs who ambushed you were part of the 204th Imperial Fighter Wing—"

"*Shadow Wing*," Tensent said, with a guttural laugh. "Found out that part, too."

Quell kept going. "—and they're still out there. Still active." She was repeating herself, but she had to draw the connections for him. "They're very dangerous, and my superiors are forming a working group to neutralize them. You could *stop* them."

Tensent lifted the glass of spicewine and drained it in a delicate motion. He made a show of savoring the liquid as it passed his lips.

"That crew," he said. "My squadron. They were pirates and bastards and cowards, and I'd kept them alive since we were flying for a senile old colonel in the Western Reaches. We defected together. We made a fortune together and lost it. They swore loyalty to me and I gave them everything.

"Now they're dead.

"I don't care about the New Republic and there's no profit in revenge. Right now, I'm here to make a living."

Quell stared at the man. Her sympathy faded. Her loathing returned.

Nath Tensent was the embodiment of everything that had been wrong with the Empire—the corruption hidden beneath a sheen of order and accountability; the willingness to turn a blind eye to brutality so long as the job was done—and a betrayal of the promised ideals of the Rebellion. She didn't want him to be part of Caern Adan's working group. She didn't want him in the galaxy at all.

She wanted to accept his refusal and walk away.

But she wasn't failing her first mission. Her *only* mission.

She tensed and seized the only chance she saw. She'd recognized something in Tensent. A note of fury he'd tried to conceal.

"I was with the 204th," she said. "Not with the pilots who killed your people, but it was my unit."

He moved fast—faster than she'd expected, but not so fast she wasn't prepared. As Tensent went for the blaster holstered at his side, Quell gripped the table with her left hand, leaned back into her chair, and kicked with all the strength she could muster. Her boots hit Tensent's seat just as his blaster came out, and he toppled backward onto the floor.

She scrambled to her feet as he started to rise; fought dizziness and nausea as she moved around the table to bring her heel down on his blaster and kick it across the room. It spun and skittered away. Half a dozen disinterested customers looked toward them, then returned to their drinks.

Tensent lay on his back, chair to one side, looking up at her. As Quell tried to catch her breath—as she leaned against the table for support—he slowly stood back up.

"You want to tell me again how you don't want revenge?" Quell asked.

"However much I want it," Tensent said, "it's not enough. I'm not going back."

They watched each other a long while.

Quell had nothing else to say.

The droid insisted on examining Quell when she returned to the U-wing. As she lay on the collapsible crew seats, the IT-O unit drifted back and forth above her and emitted a hypnotic throbbing noise. Quell slipped briefly into sleep and dreamed of scalpels cutting her skin. When she woke, she was sweating and the torture droid was several meters distant.

She had indeed fractured her skull, the droid told her, though it would heal cleanly in time. Another broken bone didn't seem like anything close to her biggest problem. She summarized her exchange with Tensent as she sipped from a pouch of nutrient fluids—not an improvement from the watered-down brandy.

"How do you intend to proceed?" the droid asked.

"We'll signal Adan. I messed up," Quell said. The confession made her chest ache, but she was officer enough to take responsibility, whatever the consequences. "Probably should signal Kairos, too, if we plan to leave."

Quell hadn't seen the U-wing's pilot since she'd set foot in the Hive. The droid hadn't seemed alarmed by Kairos's absence, so Quell hadn't inquired further.

"Adan may not be pleased," the droid said. "No one can doubt your efforts, however. May I ask—"

It paused long enough that Quell wondered if the droid had glitched. A flash of her dream came back to her, and she imagined manipulators spindling her flesh. Then the IT-O unit finished, "—*why* do you think Nath Tensent refused to join us? Was he honest about his reasons? Is he aware of his own motivations?"

Quell brushed her fingers across her forehead, feeling the tender break point and the sharp pain beneath. "I think," she said, "that some people—they won't act, no matter how much they want to, unless some outside force insists. Unless someone or something makes it untenable to keep going the way things are."

The droid didn't acknowledge her reply. Quell had the unpleasant sense of having walked into a trap.

The low buzzing of the ship's comm served to mercy-kill the conversation. Quell stumbled into the cockpit and half gently, half greedily touched the pilot's console. Text scrolled down a display screen, and the sensors winked.

"Convoy request," she said. "Someone's sharing their departure clearance, wants to follow us out." Not uncommon in high-traffic, low security areas—freighters and shuttles often shadowed more heavily armed vessels in the hopes of avoiding pirate trouble. She hadn't received a convoy request since her youth; people didn't often look to TIE fighters for favors. But the U-wing was a gunship designed to deliver troops, capable of holding its own against a light cruiser and compact and maneuverable enough to survive a dogfight. She could imagine it looked like an appealing ally.

Then she noticed the sender's authentication codes. She focused her attention on the screen and swore softly. "It's from an astromech aboard a Y-wing," she said. "Owner is Nath Tensent."

Behind her, she heard the rattle and hum of the U-wing's loading door.

"You must have been more convincing than you thought," the droid said.

"Maybe."

But if that were true, shouldn't she have felt a stronger sense of relief? Not just caution and doubt?

She heard footsteps on the deck. She climbed back through the cockpit door and found herself staring into Kairos's visor.

Quell stepped aside. Kairos entered the cockpit and sat at the controls. The ship shivered as the main reactor came online.

"You want to tell me anything?" Quell called into the cockpit, but Kairos didn't respond. Quell wasn't particularly surprised.

She heard Tensent's voice through the comm now, calling out departure vectors and clearance codes. She looked from Kairos to the torture droid and thought of the droid's confidence, its reassurance that she had *all the necessary tools* to succeed at her mission. She didn't know where Kairos had disappeared to or whether Kairos's activities were connected to Tensent's change of heart; but in her mind, the two mysteries congealed into one.

She had worried Adan was playing her for a fool. She no longer thought he'd meant for her to fail, but she didn't like what she suspected now at all.

## II

The second battle had played out much like the first. The *Hellion's Dare,* under surprise assault by an Imperial cruiser-carrier and multiple TIE squadrons, had scrambled its escorts while preparing to jump to lightspeed. The A-wings of Riot Squadron had rushed to intercept the attackers, forcing flights of Imperial starfighters to break off as they approached the *Dare.* The B-wings of Hound Squadron had stayed behind to guard the frigate, filling the sky with crimson fire whenever a TIE drew near.

And just as in the first battle, at the moment it seemed like the *Dare* and its fighters would escape without casualties, the enemy had chosen an A-wing to harry and surround. The *Dare* had sent jump coordinates; the order to retreat had gone out; and Sonogari, Riot Seven, had been left behind.

Wyl wept in his fighter afterward, surrounded by the rippling blue of hyperspace. Sonogari had been a friend, a gentle soul, and Wyl's informal flight instructor. Sonogari had spent hours with Wyl when the latter had first joined the squadron, perching above Wyl's cockpit as Wyl had tried to familiarize himself with an A-wing's controls. Those interactions had turned into discussions about family—Sonogari's estrangement from his mother, Wyl's concerns for his aunt and uncle—and about art and religion and the bizarre worlds they'd seen and hoped to return to. They'd kissed once, when they'd been grounded together during a fleet battle at Sarapin, and they'd laughed about it later and decided they were ill matched. Wyl had never before been rejected with so much grace and heart.

Pilots died in war. Wyl knew this. But he would miss his friend.

The starfighters and the *Hellion's Dare* emerged into realspace within a glittering fog—a crystalline, scintillating field of dust, like a blizzard frozen in time and space. Immediately a dozen voices broke in over the comm. Some asked about Sonogari. Others focused on practical questions: How had the Empire followed the *Hellion's Dare* through hyperspace? (Was it a homing beacon? A mole aboard the ship? There were a hundred possibilities, all of which would need to be checked.)

Wyl stared into the stardust and ached for Home.

Captain Kreskian, the energetic Chadra-Fan commander of the *Dare*, explained that the frigate had flown into the outer reaches of the Oridol Cluster—a region of densely packed stars and slow-churning cosmic storms that made hyperspace navigation "like sailing a windless sea under cloudy skies." Though Wyl had never sailed a ship nor seen a sea from ground level, he understood the gist: In the Oridol Cluster, the captain hoped to shake loose their pursuers. Each hyperspace jump would require hours to calculate and convey them only a short distance; a frustration, to be sure, but the enemy would be as stymied and confused as the *Dare*. Rebels had eluded pursuers in the cluster before, Kreskian said, and the New Republic wasn't so "high-and-mighty" that it couldn't fall back on "old stratagems. Reliable stratagems!"

Wyl knew only slightly more about hyperspace navigation than he did about sailing, but he trusted Kreskian's judgment. The captain had survived years of civil war, and there were few of the oldest rebel veterans left.

After Sonogari's funeral, the off-duty pilots retreated to the morgue. The *Dare* had been a medical ship before being repurposed as a carrier; now the morgue served as clubhouse and pilots' ready room. Long metal benches sat next to tactical boards. Cold chambers served as equipment lockers. Sata Neek croaked out a story that had begun as an ode to Sonogari's keen literary tastes, slowly transformed into a series of jokes about flatulence, and now recounted Riot's transfer to the rebel base on Kalarba.

". . . six hours, we spent looking for our own hidden base. So impressed we were, at first! Then concerned—had something happened? Had our comrades been forced to abandon Kalarba before we'd even arrived? Were we to be ambushed by Imperial forces lurking, lurking, lurking?"

"Just tell the story, frog-beak," one of the Hound Squadron pilots said. Wyl remembered her name: Fadime, the Nikto with reptilian skin and facial fins.

"Six hours!" Sata Neek flexed his claws dramatically. "At last, Creel—dear Creel, our first commander—began attempting to decrypt the orders he had received using different codes, different protocols, looking for some concealed set of instructions . . . only to realize that the message had never been encoded in the first place. He had simply assumed his computer had done the decryption for him!

"So where did our redeployment orders come from, you ask? Somehow our dear Creel had downloaded the contents of a flight simulator mission and mistaken them for reality."

Sata Neek's audience burst into good-natured laughter and mocking applause. Wyl looked from the grinning Hound pilots to his own comrades. Kamala winked at him, and he could almost hear her declare: *None of that ever happened.*

"Before my time?" Wyl asked Sata Neek.

"Most assuredly," Sata Neek answered.

Quaysail was the next to tell a story. The four-eyed Ualaq spoke in a lilting accent Wyl found difficult to understand, but he listened politely as she described the formation of Hound from the surviving ranks of two squadrons decimated during the dark months after the Battle of Hoth. Twice, Wyl nearly hurried her on; he saw the strained expressions of his companions, recognized their irritation at Quaysail's endless tale of internal Rebel Alliance politicking. Instead he took to coaxing and prompting Quaysail gently, drawing out the highlights of her story and moving it toward its conclusion.

When she was done, she stood and bowed. "We should all get some sleep," she said. "There may yet come another attack. If not, we will be called to escort duty soon enough."

The others smiled and nodded, and when Quaysail had shuffled out Kamala said: "The Force is with you, Wyl Lark." Then Sata Neek insisted that they not sleep *yet,* and they fell back into conversation—eight of them, too wound up by the events of the day to leave and none, Wyl thought, ready to lose the sense of camaraderie that arose from tragedy.

It was Rawn, youngest of the Hound Squadron pilots—younger than Wyl, with lips tattooed blue and dots painted on the cartilage of his ears—who suggested they play *Who? What? Where?* Wyl objected in the friendliest terms and was promptly outvoted.

"*Who?*" Sata Neek croaked. "My six nephews on distant Tibrin, each more cunning and charismatic than the last. Inform them before anyone. *What?* Overexertion during the course of a vigorous-yet-tender romance with a woman—"

"Specifics!" Fadime shouted, and Sata Neek waved her off.

"—who is an Imperial admiral, and is drawn to me by my incomparable skill in the art of flattery. *Where?* Let us say . . . Coruscant, after I have reclaimed our galactic capital for the New Republic."

"Hold on," Rawn said. "Are we playing what we *want* to kill us? Or what we *think* will?"

"Our most accurate predictions," Sata Neek said, and even Wyl couldn't hold back his laughter.

They went around the circle. Fadime's answers were darkly plausible: "*Who?* The rest of my squadron. You get the news first. *What?* I blame Rawn—he catches me in the crossfire with my shields down. *Where?* The Oridol Cluster, if things don't improve."

Rep Boy, who had stretched out on his bench to half sleep through the game, gave his answers in a dreamy voice: "*Who?* My son—don't have him yet, but I'll get one someday and I'll want him to know. *What?* Heatstroke. I'm an old man when I die, and my body can't take much. *Where?* The beaches of Alakatha, long after we've all forgotten this war."

Kamala pressed her fingertips to her forehead as if summoning a vision of the future. "*Who?* Wyl, you remember that Twi'lek on Skorrupon?" Wyl did, and he nodded. The others looked perplexed. "Him, or Skywalker. *What?* You've all seen my fighter break down before, so let's assume I slam into a Star Destroyer or something by accident. *Where?* Somewhere there's still a Star Destroyer, I guess."

Wyl was next. He didn't like the game but he wasn't about to spoil the evening. "*Who?* Len Okero. She's one of the elders back home; she'll tell anyone else who needs to know. *What . . .*" Where *who* had been easy, *what* was more distressing, and he sought an answer that was both humane and honest. "Falling," he decided. "Falling while in flight, from somewhere very high."

The answer elicited a few gentle smiles, but no laughter.

"You didn't say *where*." The correction came from Chass, the lime-haired Theelin who had called Wyl a coward on Jiruus and interrupted Nasi's funeral.

Wyl just smirked. "I *said* where. *Very high.*"

Chass snorted. Sata Neek cackled. They moved on around the circle.

Heater was the newest of Riot's pilots, a distant cousin of Kamala's who hadn't often joined the squadron for nights like this one. Wyl nodded encouragement his way. Kamala smacked his shoulder. "*Who?* Colonel Barson Nestroph, Imperial Army. Let Papa know I made something of myself. *What?* Bounty hunter, months after the Empire surrenders—I'm a hero and a target. *Where?* The University of Cado-mai, where I've gone to teach fine art."

Only Chass and Skitcher hadn't gone. Kamala whispered something to Heater, and her cousin broke into a rare grin.

"My turn," Chass said. She leaned forward, both her hands on her knees. "*Who?* Chancellor Mon Mothma. *What?* Reactor core explosion. *Where?* Death Star Three. Put the pieces together—they're going to remember me after the rest of you are long gone."

Sata Neek hooted the loudest. Skitcher shook his head. "I think she wins," he said, and the group settled into conversation and laughter once again.

But Wyl couldn't help but hear Chass's words echo in his brain. There was an intensity to them, an insistence and certainty that troubled him—as if she had just proclaimed his doom, or her own.

Wyl stayed for another hour before making his way to the berthing compartments. Asleep in his bunk, he dreamed of flying—not his A-wing, but one of the great beasts of his homeworld. He could smell his mount's down feathers like hot dust in his nostrils; feel its leathery skin under his hands, the tension in its muscles between his legs. He leaned forward until his chin touched tufts of plumage and he felt the creature dive, felt the wind blast his hair and leave him deaf. Only his grip kept him from separating from the beast and floating among the clouds.

In the dream, he whispered the beast's name. It was not a name he knew.

How long had it been since he'd ridden a sur-avka? A starfighter seemed clumsy compared with the magnificent creatures of Polyneus. (No, not Polyneus—*Home.* Only outsiders called it Polyneus.)

He dreamed of befouled air and flying through clouds that left his skin red and peeling, his lungs burning. He dreamed of looking toward the sky and seeing dark, rigid forms—great metallic scaffolds pumping fire and smoke into the gray expanse. He dreamed of walking down the ancient streets of his cliff-carved city and seeing a hundred of his kinfolk hidden in shadows cast by the Empire's creations. He dreamed a mixture of truth and nightmare.

He dreamed of the proclamation: the word that spread among the communities of Home, an edict issued by the Sun-Lamas but never written down so that the Empire would never know. *Let every village send a warrior, for the battle against the Empire has become our battle; and no people in the galaxy fly as the people of Home fly.* He heard the whispers of youths from River and Branch seeking passage offworld. He did not wish to leave Home, but he knew his role.

He did not dream of meeting with the elders who, in reality, had blessed his mission. Instead he walked the city streets and found his siblings gone—not the few with whom he shared blood, but the many he called family. He searched cracks in crumbling stone and screamed for them but he could not remember their names.

All he could remember was *Sonogari, Nasi, Aries, Nex.* The names of Riot Squadron. The names of the dead.

The third battle began in the middle of the night. By the time Wyl was awake and in flight the skirmish was nearly over—he only had time to squeeze his trigger once, sending red lightning roiling through the dust clouds of Oridol before the *Hellion's Dare* and its escorts fled to hyperspace.

This time, it was Rep Boy who was left behind. No one doubted that the enemy was deliberately picking off starfighters as they attempted to jump away, but neither did the *Dare's* defenders have a strategy to counter the tactic.

The fourth battle, by contrast, was an extended, chaotic melee. The *Dare* had arrived in a system so thick with cosmic dust that visibility was almost nil. Clusters of dark particles resembling eyes peered out from the clouds, observing the Oridol Cluster's visitors. Wyl was on patrol near the frigate when a very human cry of alarm came across his comm and the fight began. TIE fighters burst from the fog like ghosts to strafe the *Dare* and eliminate targets of opportunity. Only the flashes of cannon fire gave away a ship's position in the soup; hiding was as simple as altering course.

No member of Riot Squadron died in the fourth battle. Among Hound Squadron, Quaysail, Togue, and Ansil were lost.

In the aftermath, Heater begged Rununja and the captain to tell them why the Empire was chasing the *Dare*. Had a scout found a third Death Star, like Fadime had joked? Was it a muster point for the lost Imperial fleet? They all wanted to feel the mission was worthwhile, yet if the captain knew anything he didn't say.

By the fifth battle, Wyl and the others had begun to recognize and name their foes. *Tails* was a TIE fighter whose ion trail lingered and glittered, likely due to a malfunctioning heat exchange; the pilot was given to sharp turns and wild firing patterns. *Char* was a TIE so black with carbon scoring that it resembled something haunted; Char flew without a wingmate, venturing solo into the fray, and it was the pilot's apparent vulnerability that had lured Rep Boy to his death. *Blink* had only a single functioning laser cannon thanks to a glancing hit from Wyl; the pilot spun and danced like a fluttering moth.

But naming the enemy didn't make victory come easier, and Riot Squadron lost Kamala in the fifth battle. At the funeral, the *Dare's* chief engineer swore to discover how the enemy was pursuing them—the crew had found no tracker aboard, no record of secret communications. None of the pilots appeared to take comfort in his reassurances, and some began murmuring about an *intelligence* in the Oridol Cluster and the notion that they were intruders in the realm of something troubling and alien. Maybe, Skitcher said, the cluster itself was pitting Empire and New Republic against each other.

The sixth battle began in a sea of churning blue-green gases, where fractal jewels floated like snowflakes and shattered brilliantly upon impact with a starfighter's hull. Wyl could have watched the manifestations for hours; instead, when the cruiser-carrier and its cargo of TIEs leapt into the system, Wyl followed the *Hellion's Dare* as it skipped across the atmosphere of a frozen planet.

Captain Kreskian had decided that speed might save them this time. Aboard the bridge of the *Hellion's Dare*, three droids furiously calculated the approach vector for the *Dare* to take maximum advantage of the nameless planet's gravity well—to slingshot the frigate around the orb and outdistance the *Dare's* pursuers. The fact that the

*Dare* could potentially outdistance its escort fighters, too, was the plan's greatest drawback; Hound and Riot would need to pour every erg of power into their engines to keep up, and any pilot who lagged behind risked being swallowed by the swarm of TIEs.

Wyl felt the pressure of acceleration as he chased after the frigate. He sweated, spine pressed into his seat and vision glimmering with spots unrelated to Oridol's dust. His ship's shields were disabled to conserve energy, leaving him as vulnerable as the shieldless TIE fighters pursuing him. Riot Leader called out course adjustments on the comm and Wyl strained to obey.

He felt something jolt under his seat and he whispered soothingly to the console, "Close your eyes. Close your eyes and I'll guide you."

A *crack* tore through the cockpit and the canopy trembled. A jagged scar marred the transparent metal. He'd struck one of the fractal formations dead-on.

"I'll guide you," he promised.

Emerald particle bolts illuminated the gas clouds. He saw the TIEs on his scanner. Five fighters closed the distance as the New Republic vessels raced away. He couldn't guess how these five TIEs had caught up—maybe they, too, had calculated a mathematically perfect trajectory—but it hardly mattered. They would enter optimal firing range in twenty seconds.

Wyl jabbed his comm with an index finger. "Riot Three here. Five marks on approach. What's our time to jump?"

Riot Leader's voice came through, steady as ever. "*Dare* is replotting an emergency short-distance hyperroute. Won't get us far, but ready in under two minutes."

Nowhere close to soon enough. Wyl saw the gleam of the *Dare* ahead; the dozen allied fighters spread around him like flashes of rain. His was the vessel closest to the TIEs. He would be the first target.

"Copy, Riot Leader," he said. "Preparing to engage."

More chatter followed. Riot Five—Sata Neek—agreed to fall back beside Wyl. When the TIEs came into range they would abruptly split apart, decelerate, and allow the TIEs' momentum to sweep them into the gap where Wyl and Sata Neek had been. From there, the A-wings could close, flank, and catch the enemy in a crossfire.

It was a fine plan, unlikely to bear any resemblance to reality. Still, Wyl thought, better to aspire than to have no plan at all.

The TIEs entered visual range. Wyl called a signal to Sata Neek and they simultaneously cut power to their thrusters and slammed their rudder pedals, veering in opposite directions. Wyl watched his scanner as his body seemed to float. The dots of the TIEs remained exactly where they had been.

That was wrong.

That meant the TIEs hadn't moved relative to Wyl's position. They hadn't rushed forward, hadn't split up to chase the two A-wings. They'd decelerated right along with Wyl and Sata Neek and pursued Wyl as a unit—

Energized particles flared past his canopy. He swung away but the TIEs were surrounding him, caging him. He tried to jerk free, to shake his pursuers, but the moment he adjusted his course streams of cannon fire forced him back to his original bearing. He decelerated again and swore as the flight of TIEs matched his speed, save for one— a single TIE that took position ahead of him, just out of firing range.

"This is Riot Three. I'm surrounded—" Wyl felt his heart rate increase, tried to even out his breathing. More streams of emerald ripped through the fog above, below, to either side, rendering his path narrower and narrower. "—and can't maneuver."

But he wasn't dead.

He should have been dead. The enemy had locked onto him. He had nowhere to go. They just weren't firing.

A volley of particle bolts tore through his port side. His fighter jerked and his instruments turned red as he tried to stabilize the vessel. He'd lost power to one cannon and his canopy was rattling worryingly—the scar was growing longer, creeping downward.

"Okay," he murmured. "They're firing. But they're not trying to kill you yet."

The comm crackled. "Counting down to lightspeed jump," Riot

Leader announced. "*Dare* transmitting coordinates in ten, jump in fifteen."

"Riot Five to Riot Three," Sata Neek called. "Can you get free?"

Wyl's hands were trembling but his voice was calm. "Negative. Can't even jump." The TIE in front of him would make sure of that. "Can you cut through the net?"

Sata Neek's clacking sounded like static. "I will try."

Wyl wasn't afraid of death. He didn't welcome it, but he was at peace with his choices. What scared him was *dying,* and that had rarely been a factor during his time at war—for a pilot, death came quickly, delivered by the enemy you failed to spot.

"We have to get out," he whispered to his ship. "I promise to protect you."

"Riot Leader to all fighters—coordinates transmitting. Ready to jump!"

The fog flared with red as a blip drew near on Wyl's scanner: Sata Neek, firing at the TIE ninety degrees off Wyl's starboard side. The volley didn't hit, but it forced the TIE to reposition and gave Wyl an opening. He banked and accelerated as hard as he could, making for the gap the TIE had left open.

His fighter clattered like a tin drum. Cries came in through the comm, suggesting that a second flight of TIEs had intercepted the *Dare.* But Wyl saw a glimmer in the corner of his eye as Sata Neek jumped to hyperspace. Coordinates blinked on his console. Emerald fire burned all around him as the TIEs targeted his ship. Through some miracle, none of the shots hit him.

A streak of white filled Wyl's vision and his A-wing lurched, screamed, and spun, rolling so swiftly that he lost all sense of direction. A web of new cracks spread across his canopy. The world hissed and his head throbbed. He realized instinctively what had happened— he'd clipped the TIE fighter targeted by Sata Neek when both he and the TIE pilot had frantically adjusted course. Now half his systems were down, his skull was pounding (had he hit it somehow?), and he feared he was leaking oxygen.

And yet. And yet . . .

There was nothing ahead of him but fog.

He straightened his ship and began accelerating again. The hyper-drive hummed with power.

He was laughing as the cracks spread and he fell short of breath. He fumbled under his seat for a sealant canister. "Love you, girl," he said, frantically spraying, trying to cover every millimeter of the cracks even as they grew. "We'll get you fixed. We'll get you home."

As cerulean light enveloped him and his oxygen gauge dipped into the red, he turned flight control over to his navicomputer and hoped he would live long enough to see stars.

## CHAPTER 4

# ELECTRONIC COUNTERMEASURES

I

She knew her pride would damn her, but it was all she had to offer.
Yrica Quell looked at her audience aboard the New Republic
bulk freighter *Buried Treasure*: Caern Adan, perched on a bench with
his eyes on a datapad and antenna-stalks rigid atop his head; Nath
Tensent beside him, wearing an expression of performative skepticism; Kairos wreathed in cloth and leather and shadows, standing next
to the doorway as if afraid someone—as if afraid Quell—would attempt to bolt.

They were ready to judge every utterance she made. Each word
would bury her deeper, reminding them of where she came from. It
had been easy in Traitor's Remorse, but now that she was free? When
she had something to lose?

She gripped the lectern of the freighter's conference room with one
hand and began.

"The 204th Imperial Fighter Wing was one of the Empire's earliest volunteer wings. Organized as a mobile unit, to be attached to a carrier ship or Star Destroyer and deployed anywhere in the galaxy, it has served in this capacity for over twenty years."

Tensent's eyes drifted to her chest. Adan kept reading his datapad.

"Composed of six squadrons—primarily TIE/ln starfighters, with detachments of TIE/sa bombers and TIE/IN interceptors provided on a per-mission basis—the 204th . . ."

"Shadow Wing," Adan said, looking up.

Quell stared at him. "Yes." *Obviously.*

He looked back to his datapad. "Continue."

She kept her voice flat. She thought again of her days at the Academy: of being rebuked by her superiors for a failure to scrub a floor to a spotless shine, or recite obscure regulations, or perform a feat no human possibly could. She said what she'd learned to say then: "Thank you, sir."

She began again.

"Composed of six squadrons, *Shadow Wing* distinguished itself as an effective peacekeeping and security force during Separatist mop-up operations at Umbara and Salient. After a brief campaign on the borders of the Corporate Sector, the 204th was reassigned to anti-piracy operations in the Mid Rim."

This was the simple part. She could separate herself from the tale here—she hadn't lived through the Corporate Sector campaign, rarely even heard stories about it. She could speak without emotion. Speak without demanding judgment from her audience.

And so long as she recited facts and ancient history, she was no more useful than a droid.

"After the wing's reassignment, two personnel changes occurred that would prove crucial to the unit's future. First, Colonel Shakara Nuress joined as unit commander. Nuress had served in the Republic Navy during the Clone Wars and—"

"We have her file," Adan said. "She has a cute nickname, too, doesn't she?"

*Grandmother.*

"Not that I remember," Quell said.

The lie came easily. She hadn't planned it, couldn't justify it. She had never known Nuress in any meaningful sense—she'd never exchanged more than a word or two with the colonel, though she could picture the woman's silver hair and storm-gray eyes. She respected Grandmother, but had no need to defend her. So why, she wondered, had Adan's words grated?

The spy watched her.

"Grandmother," Quell amended. "Some of the pilots called her Grandmother. Sometimes it was a joke about her being senile. Sometimes it was about her being—about her being harsh and territorial, but protective of her people. She wasn't liked, but she was well regarded."

It was Tensent who barked a laugh. "She let you get away with that?"

"When she had to," Quell said.

Adan waved a hand as if trying to dismiss a foul odor. "Experienced, disciplined, highly traditional. Anything new about her we should know?"

"Just that she was responsible for organizing the wing as it stands. The 204th had several commanders before Nuress—better and worse, but all of them used the unit as a stepping-stone to bigger things. Nuress never did." She heard the danger—the instinctive pride entering her voice—but she bit it back. "Nuress kept the unit intact and ready for action without searching for glory, and her people appreciated it."

She knew she was losing ground. Quell mentally skimmed the presentation she'd prepared, trying to find something that might keep Adan's interest—prove there was a point to this briefing. "That's— I can't say this for certain, but there was a rumor about how Nuress kept the unit out of the limelight. About the wing's nickname."

Now she had Adan's attention. He placed his datapad to one side.

"'Shadow Wing,'" she said. "The rumor I heard was that it started as a joke among the admirals. The 204th was the unit that, as soon as

Nuress took over, only ever showed up when there were other forces to hide behind. Or another version: Nuress somehow made the unit unavailable if she didn't like an operation. It disappeared into the shadows."

Adan cocked his head and asked, "What about the other story? The slogan. 'Where shadows fall, all things die'?"

"That was later," Quell said. "After the Red Insurgency."

"The Orinda Massacre," Adan said.

She nodded, because it seemed more appropriate than a shrug. "I imagine some people call it that."

Tensent interrupted, exasperation in his voice. "Not really worried about names. What about the other one? You said two personnel changes?"

Quell's shoulder ached suddenly. The sling felt tight and hot around her arm.

"Major Soran Keize," she said. "He joined the 204th before Nuress's transfer, but it took a few years before he became—" *An ace of aces. A hero.* "—influential. When he was just another pilot, everyone knew he was good, but it was when he became a squadron leader, started mentoring the squealers—the new officers—that he changed everything.

"He flew like no one else. He *taught* like no one else. He made us all better."

She saw the disdain on Tensent's face. The mockery on Adan's. She blinked away ire and resentment and hurried on. "Between Nuress and Keize, the 204th earned some small prestige. The wing was permanently assigned to the Star Destroyer *Pursuer,* and after the terrorist attack on the first Death Star battle station the wing gradually refocused on anti-rebel operations. I've annotated General Dodonna's after-action report on the Battle of Grumwall—"

"Skip it," Adan said. "I've got one more question and then you can sit down. What does any of this mean for the unit's current status? What do we know about the commanders now?"

He already knew the answer. Quell had been debriefed enough times at Traitor's Remorse. He wanted her to say it again—for Tensent's benefit, or to see if her story stayed the same, or simply to show he was in control.

"Major Keize is dead," she said, "but the people he trained are still there. Colonel Nuress is alive, to the best of my knowledge. I imagine she's holding the unit together. She'll take orders until the Empire surrenders for good."

"What about desertions?" Tensent asked.

Adan joined in. "Yes, what about desertions? You said the people Keize trained are still there—"

"I wasn't the only one to desert," Quell said. "I don't know what the current roster looks like, but by now anyone there is apt to stay."

Adan folded his hands together. She realized what he was waiting for and she moved to one of the benches. He took her place at the lectern.

"Not a lot to go on," Adan said, "but it gives us grounding. Moving forward, Nath, you and Kairos will handle investigation and legwork. No engagements for now, but if we need recon you'll take point. Meanwhile, I'll be analyzing the data from here and trying to work out Shadow Wing's next move."

Tensent grunted. Quell wasn't sure if the sound indicated acquiescence or dissatisfaction.

"This ship," Adan went on, and tapped the toe of his shoe against the metal deck, "is en route to deliver supplies and equipment to the Barma Battle Group. That's not too far off from Shadow Wing's last known location. By the time we arrive I'd like to have a plan to at least *find* our enemy, if not eliminate them."

That news surprised Quell. "The battle group's waiting on us?"

"The Barma Battle Group," Adan retorted, in a tone harsher than Quell had expected, "has its own mission. We have ours. *After* we have a target, we'll work together on a plan of attack."

That made sense. It was much too early to deploy a battle group against the 204th. But Adan's defensiveness had tripped her alarms, and she was beginning to wonder.

"Is the group committed to helping us?" she asked.

*How much does the New Republic actually care about finding the 204th?* Right now the entire mission seemed to consist of an intelligence officer, a torture droid, a recent defector, and two pilots.

"New Republic Intelligence is committed to the mission," Adan said. "I'm committed to the mission, and you're committed to me."

She heard the rebuke and was immediately chastened. "Yes, sir," she said.

"Did you micromanage Colonel Nuress, too?" Adan asked.

"No, sir."

"Anything else, then? Questions? Kairos, Nath, you can bunk down until you receive flight assignments. Explore the luxuries of our host ship. Yrica, you're on analysis duty. Put those years of experience to work."

She'd had no reason to expect anything else. Still, the words felt like one more reproof. She should have swallowed them and considered them her due, but she spoke anyway: "What about investigation? I'd like to fly myself, if something comes up—"

"We have people for that," Adan said, and snatched up his datapad as he marched out of the conference room.

Tensent rose as soon as Adan was gone. He laughed and dropped a hand on Quell's shoulder. "Makes you miss the Empire, huh?"

She didn't answer and the pirate—because a *pirate,* she thought, was what Nath Tensent truly was—followed Adan out the door.

She wanted to kick the lectern. To shout a curse. She wanted to fly. She hadn't earned any of it.

When she finally stood, she saw that Kairos remained in the room. The silent woman stared at her and bowed her head in a gesture that might have been sympathetic and might have been a warning.

Then Kairos, too, was gone.

The *Buried Treasure* was a massive vessel, but 80 percent of its capacity was dedicated to cargo storage. Of that 80 percent, only half of the compartments were oxygenated and temperature-controlled for human habitation. The remaining 20 percent of the *Treasure* consisted of cramped corridors, operational hubs, and living spaces; the latter were little improvement over the container housing of Traitor's Remorse. Quell traded her bunk in shifts with a Morseerian methane-breather and found showering one-armed nearly impossible in the tight bathroom stall.

She didn't complain. She had a function, if not one she was qualified for.

Tucked in a corner of the mess hall, surrounded by the smells of nutrient broths and caf, she hunched over a datapad with a headset vise-gripping her ears. She listened, hour after hour, to the intercepted Imperial communications Adan sent her and tried to find any sign of the 204th Fighter Wing. Any hint that the droids and comm officers of New Republic Intelligence had somehow missed.

The speakers on the recordings were mostly calm. The Empire prized discipline, and even after the Emperor's death the comm officers remembered their duty. She heard stoic declarations of horror and failure—reports of positions overrun and ships obliterated by New Republic firepower. She heard an admiral refuse to aid desperate allies and a general demand that all the Empire rally under his command. In one recorded datafile, she heard hours of Imperial anthems interrupted by long series of numbers. She heard patriotic lies about an immortal Emperor, an enduring Empire, and a Death Star still operational. She heard offers of surrender cut off by blaster shots.

She heard an Empire proud in its own defeat. Splintered and lost but too stubborn to stop fighting. She didn't hear anything regarding the 204th Fighter Wing.

After her first full day as an analyst, sick and saturated with thoughts of bloodshed, she reported her failure to Adan. Part of her hoped that he would find other duties for her—judge her unsuitable for spycraft and put her on any job other than listening to her comrades die. Instead he rolled his eyes and handed her another twelve hours of recordings to sift through.

"I'll keep trying," she said, then left to rouse the methane-breather from her bunk.

The next day, midway through her listening session, she received a message to report to the torture droid for a medical checkup. The droid met her in an unstaffed, underequipped medbay and scanned her skull and shoulder. "You are healing," it said, "albeit slowly. Do you feel any different?"

"Less nausea," Quell said. "Otherwise, not really."

"You seem unconcerned with the damage."

"I've broken a lot of bones in my life. One of the pluses of growing up on a low-gravity station."

"I would think full recovery would be important to you—it is a prerequisite for flight clearance."

Quell laughed hoarsely. "Are you really going to tell me it's my injuries that are keeping me grounded?"

The red dot of the droid's photoreceptor dilated.

"That's what I thought," Quell said.

"You're needed here, not in a starfighter. For now, you *are* the member of the working group best suited for analysis. Adan is continuing his efforts, but you—"

"I know," she said. As pointless as the work felt, she might be the only person qualified to recognize a clue to the 204th's location. She recognized the logic. "I'm doing my best. I'm doing my duty."

"But it's not what you wanted?"

"It's not what I expected."

The droid waited for her to continue. She didn't. "What did you expect?" it prompted.

The nausea and heat suddenly returned to the front of her skull. She pressed her palm against her forehead and slid her fingers back through greasy, half-washed hair. She wanted to walk away from the conversation, but she wasn't ready to return to the litany of Imperial defeats awaiting her in the recordings.

"You ever listen to rebel propaganda? Before Endor, I mean?" she asked.

"I am aware of it."

The Empire's censors were brutally efficient. Every message from home was screened and edited. Every source of information curated. For an Imperial pilot, the only streams available were military ones— most of the time.

But Quell had seen holovids growing up on Gavana Orbital. She remembered being sixteen, sitting tight against Nette in the older girl's mother's apartment, watching recordings from the fugitive senator Mon Mothma. She remembered Mothma's voice, so full of passion and sincerity as she recited Imperial crimes and urged listeners to fight for something better.

As a pilot for the 204th, Quell had seen fragments of later recordings. She'd been subjected to broadcasts on missions to destroy hijacked comm relays; she'd seen snippets during shore leave on troubled worlds. She'd recognized Mothma and Leia Organa, the Alderaanian princess. Even if the older Mothma's passion had seemed tempered by exhaustion, the message had been the same as ever: The Empire hurts people. The Rebel Alliance helps.

Later she'd heard the princess speak again, broadcast on speakers in Traitor's Remorse. The message had grown bolder by then. Quell remembered the words, "The galaxy is not afraid."

"The rebels promised a lot," Quell said. "The Empire wasn't as bad as they always said, but—it wasn't great, and it got worse after the Emperor passed." She had to stop herself from saying *after the Emperor's assassination.*

She steadied herself. She breathed and said, "I don't regret anything, and you can promise Adan I'll do my part. I just expected my role to look different."

She left the droid more troubled than when the checkup had started. *You're a mediocre torture droid,* she thought, *but you're a bad therapist.* The IT-O unit had insisted she return the next day, and she'd agreed out of obligation.

That night, she listened to Adan's latest package of intercepted communications in her bunk. With her head on her pillow and a heavyset Houk wheezing in the bed above her, she stared at the blinking me-

chanical light of a door control panel and absorbed month-old evacu-
ation orders and calls to arms.

She was nearly asleep when a voice roused her—one lacking the
forced dignity of the other recordings. A man's voice, husky and rough,
in conversation with a woman. Quell recognized neither speaker, but
without the formality and bombast she'd grown accustomed to they
seemed intimately *present.*

*Cut me off,* the man said. *End the transmission.*

*What?*

*What I'm about to say won't benefit you. Cut me off. Request new
orders from Admiral Malvor or Moff Senchiko, if they're alive. Say you
couldn't reach me.*

*I already know about the Messenger.*

*The operation? You know—*

*I want to hear it from you. What did it say?*

The man didn't answer. The woman spoke again.

*What was the Emperor's last order?*

Quell's heart seemed to seize.

There was nothing in the message about Shadow Wing. Nothing
relevant to her mission, nor anything the New Republic hadn't ana-
lyzed twice over. She could have skipped to the next recording.

She knew what was coming, at least in broad strokes—not with in-
tellectual certainty, but in her bones she *knew.*

*The Messenger—it was all in red,* he said.

She remembered the day aboard the *Pursuer,* two weeks after Endor,
when the order had come in. She'd heard whispers of a shuttle and a
passenger of supreme importance.

She'd glimpsed red robes.

*It had the Emperor's face,* the man went on. *A hologram of his face. It
wasn't a droid so much as a ghost. It said we'd been selected for an honor,
and then . . .*

She remembered a rumor that Colonel Nuress had locked herself
away with the passenger. She tried to picture the old woman staring
into the withered, digitized face of the Galactic Emperor.

*It spoke in his voice. It said, "Resistance. Rebellion. Defiance. These are concepts that cannot be allowed to persist. You are but one of many tools by which these ideas shall be burned away."*

Nuress hadn't repeated the words. She hadn't said they'd come in the Emperor's own voice. She had kept all that to herself, for reasons Quell couldn't comprehend.

She didn't want to hear the rest, but she listened.

*"Operation Cinder is to begin at once."*

She tore the headset from her ears and hurled it across the room. It clattered off a bulkhead, and her cabinmates—the crew of the *Buried Treasure*, rebels who surely would have been surprised at none of the Empire's atrocities—groaned and cursed and pulled up their blankets.

She lay panting awhile before she retrieved the headset. She forced it back on and resumed her duties. But for hours afterward, every recording was from the same time period. Every recording was of messages regarding Operation Cinder, whether Imperial reports declaring planets cleansed of life or desperate calls for help as worlds fought back. Quell buried her face into her pillow and listened to it all, and fell asleep to dream of Nacronis and Naboo and Commenor. To dream of the stern face of the Galactic Emperor, his pale hands on her shoulders.

"Was it a joke?" she asked the droid during their next appointment. She was late and her eyes were bloodshot. "Did he give me those calls for a reason?"

"I don't understand," the droid said, slowly orbiting her skull as it performed its scans.

"Operation Cinder. Everything Adan gave me to listen to last night—it's all Cinder."

"I don't believe it was a joke," the droid said.

There hadn't been anything about Shadow Wing in the package. Not anything new, anyway.

She had always assumed, without consciously analyzing it, that Operation Cinder had originated from surviving Imperial leadership rather than their dead sovereign. It made no difference, and yet she couldn't cleanse the picture of the Emperor from her mind.

"Why did he do it?"

"Perhaps Adan was being thorough. He may not have realized the impact it would have on—"

She shook her head, then realized she had to remain still for the droid's scan to work properly. Her mind wasn't functioning right. She was too weary. "Not Adan. The Emperor. Why did he order Cinder? What was his plan?"

It wasn't the first genocide the Emperor had ordered. She knew that, but there had been reasons for the others. The difference between Alderaan (or Lasan, or Dhen-Moh) and Operation Cinder was the difference between *ruthlessness* and *cruelty*.

"I can't say," the droid answered. "What do you think?"

"Go to hell," she muttered.

But she let the droid finish its scans. She still had a job to do.

Ten minutes later, face dripping with cold water from the restroom, Quell stalked down a narrow corridor without direction or purpose. An astromech droid squealed with irritation as she nearly bowled the ancient unit over; her exhaustion and ire turned to near-hysterical laughter as she tried to sidle around the machine in the tight confines of the passage. It was over half her height, drab green paint flaking off its flat top, and its every move seemed intended to inconvenience her more.

When she finally made it to the other side of the droid, she found its owner waiting, arms folded across his chest.

"Tee-five giving you a hard time?" Tensent asked.

She would have snapped at him, but she didn't have the strength. She drew a long breath and released it in a hiss. "That thing can't be yours. Will it even plug into your ship?"

"Only droid I've found that can keep up with my flying. I try not to let it roam free, but sometimes it gets cranky." He rapped his knuckles against the droid, the metal ringing like a gong. "You look like garbage, by the way."

"Thanks," she said. She stepped forward, ready to sidle around Tensent as she had his droid.

He surprised her by moving aside. She was five meters down the corridor when he called, "You want to shoot something?"

She wasn't sure she'd heard him right.

"It's up to you," he said. "You just look like you could use a break, and I'm heading down myself. You want in?"

"More than anything in the world," she said.

Quell was a pilot, not a stormtrooper. She knew how to hold a pistol and how to fieldstrip a blaster rifle. If forced, she could talk shop about heat sinks and stopping power. But she'd never loved guns the way she loved flying.

Nonetheless, as Tensent's DL-21 pulsed in her hand and left three burnt, smoking holes in the tarp they'd strung across the cargo hold, she couldn't deny a spark of satisfaction.

"You sure we're allowed to do this?" she asked.

"Made a friend on the bridge," Tensent said. "No one's coming to bother us. This place doesn't even normally have life support."

*That explains the chill,* she thought, and gripped the warm blaster tighter. "When you say you made a friend—did you bribe someone? Steal access codes?"

Tensent held out his palm. Quell passed the blaster back as he answered. "I mean I ran into a guy, we got to talking, and he offered to set me up. Believe it or not, I'm pretty likable."

She did believe it. She believed that in his way, Tensent—despite betraying every organization he'd ever served, despite lacking anything resembling principles—had a way of persuading people to enjoy his company against their own best interests. She suspected he did it intentionally, and that he was attempting to win her over even now.

But she felt more comfortable than she had for days, and she could afford to be grateful for a little while.

Tensent fired the blaster three times. Each shot landed half a meter above the holes Quell had left. She glanced toward the turbolift, then to the row of dormant astromech units along one wall.

"We're not going to get caught," he said. "Hell—you deserted what, a month ago? You got those Imperial regs burned in your head pretty deep."

"Guess I'm not rebel material."

Tensent snorted. "Wouldn't worry about that part. Rebellion's over. It's the New Republic now."

"You don't sound happy about it."

"Rebels were more willing to let things slide. Now—you can see it happening. They're making up rules fast."

She nodded idly. She caught her mind drifting to the events of the night and her exchange with the droid. She tried to stop it, but it was like refusing to scratch a scab. She *always* scratched her wounds.

"You defected before Alderaan, didn't you?" she said.

"Sure. Why do you ask?"

Alderaan had been the true start of the conflict. The Empire had attempted to avert a civil war with a demonstration of might, destroying a terrorist government masquerading as a peaceful ally. In snuffing out billions of lives—in deploying the first Death Star planet-killer— the Emperor had attempted to save trillions.

"Did anyone stop to think it might have been the Rebellion's fault? That if things had gone differently—"

"Pretty sure most people blamed the Empire."

That didn't surprise her.

"It could've worked, though," she said. "If the Rebellion had backed down, decided not to press the fight and stop recruiting from Imperial worlds, it could've saved lives in the end."

Tensent passed the blaster back to her. She fired again, barely hitting the tarp.

"Could've, maybe," Tensent said. "Sure didn't."

He was right. Alderaan had been the centerpiece of rebel recruiting holos for years afterward—justification for every terrorist attack. The controlled insurgency had flared into open warfare.

"Were you always this much of a dupe?" Tensent asked in a voice of friendly curiosity. He cut Quell off before she could retort. "With the Empire, I mean—did you believe every stormtrooper was *there for your protection,* or did you persuade yourself—about Alderaan, and all that—over the years?"

"I'm not an idiot, Tensent. I knew what the Empire was when I joined."

"So did I," he said with a grin.

She wanted to crack his perfect teeth. She enunciated every word. "I joined to get flight training. I joined so I could defect to the Rebel Alliance."

Tensent cackled. She could see his breath in the frigid air. "Sure took your time getting here," he said.

She shrugged. She remembered being sixteen years old again, pressing her head into the crook of Nette's neck, their arms around each other's waists as Mon Mothma talked about freedom and atrocity. "I was young. Someone I—someone convinced me that joining the Rebellion was the most worthwhile thing a person could do. She actually went and did it. I figured I could, too—the holos always talked about the Rebellion needing pilots."

"So, what—you've been deep undercover the last few years?"

She shrugged again and held her hand out for the blaster. Tensent ignored her. "I meant to defect during Academy training," she said. "But I hadn't learned enough, so I planned to do it after graduation. Then after I had a few missions under my belt. By then it would've meant abandoning colleagues, and the Empire didn't seem as awful as the propaganda said. Eventually I just . . . stopped planning."

Tensent arched his brow as he checked the blaster's battery level, then squeezed off another shot. "You really aren't rebel material."

There was no judgment in his voice, and she believed his disinterest—unlike the droid's—was genuine. It was why she was able to talk to him. It was why she didn't flinch at the insult, no matter how true it was.

They kept shooting awhile longer. But the flashes of the bolts and the smell of burnt fabric began to sap her, and eventually she excused herself and made her way to the turbolift. Tensent stayed behind. As the lift door opened, she paused and called back, "Kairos. What happened?"

Tensent didn't even look at her. "What about Kairos?"

"Back at the Hive, she went to you. She convinced you to join. I know she did, I'm not stupid, so—what happened?"

"Ask our boss," Tensent called.

At least it wasn't a lie, she thought.

She had to prioritize her thoughts better, anyway. Whatever was going on among Tensent and Kairos and Adan, whatever the reasoning behind Operation Cinder, none of it would help her find Shadow Wing. None of it would get her back in a cockpit. *You really aren't rebel material,* Tensent had said, and she needed to stop dawdling and prove otherwise.

The next morning, she realized what she had to do.

## II

"Chass na Chadic, most esteemed pilot of the *Hellion's Dare*—we hereby declare you Queen of Starfighters and gallant protector of fizzy drinks."

A dozen voices cried, "Hear! Hear!" as Chass raised a fist and Sata Neek lowered a crown of wire onto her head. She tucked a strand beneath one of her horns as the bird-frog backed away, ignoring a fleeting pique at the crown's human-favoring design. "Thank you," she said, "for this most deserved honor. I couldn't have achieved it without all of you—but I want to especially thank Riot Squadron, who valiantly allowed so many TIE fighters to come into range of the *Dare,* leaving me plenty of targets."

Jeers erupted from the Riot pilots, but these were swiftly muffled—with hands on mouths, where necessary—by the Hounds. Chass grinned as she scanned the morgue and tried to swallow the sour taste.

There were barely half as many pilots aboard the *Dare* as there had been a week before, and that number was dwindling fast.

Still, a win was a win.

Fadime stepped up to the tactical board. With Stanislok—Hound Leader—dead, it was her duty to finish the ceremony. "We had thirty-two TIE fighters aboard that cruiser-carrier. Thanks to Chass, we're down to thirty-one. Puke is gone, and will never spray cannon fire like a toxic toddler again. Now who's next . . . ?"

Fadime gestured at the board and Puke dropped to the bottom of the listing. It wasn't the kill Chass wanted most—Char had scratched more Hound pilots than anyone, and Snapper had engaged her twice already—but she would have other chances. The *Dare* wasn't escaping anytime soon.

Jump by jump, the frigate worked its way through the Oridol Cluster. Jump by jump, the Imperial forces followed. As their environment grew stranger, the battles grew fiercer—the *Dare*'s escort fighters were too few to fight for long now, which meant running, hiding, and buying time to plot the next hyperroute was the order of the day. Captain Kreskian promised that the end was in sight—that they would emerge from the cluster soon and have a straight shot back to New Republic territory—but it was obvious to everyone that plunging into the cosmic anomaly had been a mistake. They hadn't shaken their pursuers; they'd just signed up for a slow death by bleeding.

Chass hadn't had a full night's sleep since Jiruus. Few of the pilots had. Even in their berths, they stayed awake posing questions about Puke and Snapper and Blink and the Twins; wondering what made *these* pilots different from the others they'd faced over the years. Yeprexi described the tactics Imperial cadets studied at the Skystrike and Myomar academies, trying to find the key to the enemy's training. Fadime argued that the TIE pilots had learned under an ace, and the Hound members listed the rebel-hunters they'd been taught to fear: Vult Skerris. Baron Rudor. Neosephine Calorda.

But what they rarely talked about was the fact that the enemy was getting sloppier, too—that Blink and Snapper and Char couldn't have been sleeping much more than anyone on the *Dare*. That, in turn, would generate its share of opportunities.

Assuming anyone was alive to take advantage of them.

The fewer the surviving A-wing pilots, the more TIEs that made it to the *Dare* each battle. The more TIEs swarming the *Dare* like flies on waste, the more the B-wings participated in the fight. The more B-wings that fought, the more Hounds who died.

A B-wing wasn't built for dogfighting small, high-velocity pests. It was an assault craft, designed to wreck anything too slow to get out of the way. It was extremely good at that job, no matter how unintuitive its controls and how painful it was to repair, but against a half-decent TIE pilot the tactics boiled down to "spray and pray."

So Yeprexi died. Yeprexi, whose ship Chass had stolen once and crashed in a bog, and who'd never breathed a word of it to their superiors. Yeprexi, the old woman who could dance like a demon and had a thousand superstitions that looked a lot like obsessive tics. She died to the TIE maneuver they'd come to call the Spiral.

After Yeprexi they lost Rawn. Chass barely knew the kid, but he deserved better than to be pinned and demolished by a flight of TIEs. (They began calling that maneuver the Needle, and knew it as Snapper's favorite.) Then Fadime went, and Chass made sure no one saw her cry at the funeral. Afterward she found a private place to dribble snot onto her sleeve.

That was how they became one squadron, not two, under command of Rununja—a result that, Chass imagined, the cocky Riot leader had wanted all along. Chass was designated Riot Ten.

Then Wyl Lark came back to life and for about a day things seemed to improve.

Chass had been the one to rescue him—the dark-haired boy whose name she'd never been able to remember. She'd spotted his A-wing careening out of control after the squadron had emerged from a hyperspace jump. She'd peppered the ship with power-disrupting ion blasts until its thrusters had shorted out. The *Dare's* tractor beam had caught him then, dragged Wyl's fighter into the hangar where they'd found his canopy cracked and nearly shattered. The oxygen-deprived fool had spent the next days in bed.

"I saved your life," Chass told him at his resurrection party.

"Do your people believe in life debts?" Wyl asked, squinting tired eyes in the stinging light of the medbay.

"What's a life debt?" Chass asked.

"It's a promise," Wyl said. "An oath to serve the person who saved you from death. An oath to stand by her side forever, knowing your lives can't be disentangled."

Chass looked from Wyl to the others: Sata Neek and Skitcher and Rununja and Glothe, all of whom watched the exchange without comment. "I'm not getting stuck with you," Chass finally said, and Wyl laughed.

"No, you're not. My people don't believe in life debts, either. But I really am grateful you helped me, Chass na Chadic."

She felt like she was being mocked. But Wyl's smile was so sickeningly sincere she just shook her head and cursed under her breath and said, "Watch where you're flying next time, huh?"

Chass didn't much enjoy celebrating with strangers. Without Fadime and Yeprexi and Quaysail and the rest of Hound Squadron, the *dead* of Hound Squadron, it wasn't the same. But when the others began speculating about the rivals and lovers of Blink and Char, Sata Neek drew her away from the others to talk about his homeworld of Tibrin and the fire-coral beneath the phosphorescent sea. She told him she came from a savage jungle full of insects the size of a man's arm, where Theelins were revered instead of leered at and objectified. If Sata Neek noticed that her stories were lies and that she didn't bother to hide her falsehoods, it only seemed to make him more keen to continue the conversation.

After an hour, Chass was delighted to realize they were both flirting.

---

Thirty-three hours and two battles—two deaths—later, Chass, Sata Neek, and Wyl cut cubes of Jiruusi fruit in the galley and tossed them at one another. Sata Neek masterfully caught the cubes in his beak. Chass laughed, her chin dripping with juice. Wyl chopped as he told the story Chass had insisted on hearing.

"We didn't know what we were doing—not until we were already at the muster point and waiting on coordinates," Wyl said. "Riot was just one more squadron in the mix."

"Rununja—Riot Leader—she knew," Sata Neek interjected. "She knew the Empire had built another planet-killing battle station, and that Riot had been chosen for the attack."

"Everyone in five sectors was *chosen for the attack*." Wyl grinned. "Maybe Rununja knew, but Admiral Ackbar and General Calrissian and all the rest? They didn't know about *us*. We were there to support the heroes however we could, not to get in the way."

"Did you meet them?" Chass asked. "Calrissian? Or Skywalker?"

She thought she saw a flash of hesitation in Wyl when she said *Skywalker*, but Sata Neek was too quick for her to comment. "I met the princess!" he cried. "But not that day. That day we flew into the fray merely hoping that in the aftermath we could drink and eat as equals. And so—but no, my brother-comrade Wyl speaks more truthfully, and the Battle of Endor is a story that deserves truth."

Wyl finished chopping and wiped the knife on his shirt. "She doesn't want the true story," he said. "She wants to hear *you*. You tell it—"

"Sata Neek is an idiot," Chass said, "and I love his stories. But I want to know about Endor."

She kept her tone light, gave the words a sardonic edge. But it might have been the most honest thing she'd said to either of them.

Sata Neek squeezed Chass's shoulder with his talons. Wyl nodded. His voice dropped in pitch and volume. He told the story like a prayer, and Chass listened.

"It feels a long time ago now, far away from here. There were more ships than there were stars . . ."

She had heard stories of the Battle of Endor before. She'd read reports and seen broadcasts and even viewed grainy holo-footage of the battle station's explosion. Wyl didn't talk about the Death Star or the fall of the Emperor, though. He talked about the joy of the flight through hyperspace, knowing that their commanders hoped to end the war in a single stroke. He spoke of *wonder* at seeing so many ships, flown by so many species, all together and working toward a common goal. He spoke of fear and desperation as the battle seemed to go wrong; as the Emperor sprang a trap, and all appeared lost. He named his colleagues who died.

He told the story of men and women who gave everything in a fight against the ultimate terror. The story of sacrifices. He went on into the night, after even Sata Neek had gone, and Chass listened.

She dreamed later of dying above a green moon to stop a force of impossible evil. She dreamed of flying alongside Riot Squadron as Wyl and Sata Neek and Rununja fell behind and she, only she, could enter the depths of the Death Star. She dreamed of her lips on the beak of a bird-frog.

She woke to a voice over the intercom, speaking to the near-empty berthing compartment of the *Hellion's Dare*. "Pilots to the ready room. We have a plan."

"Riot Ten, standing by."

It felt strange to say. It reminded Chass of her dream.

Outside the canopy of her cockpit, the fog of the Oridol Cluster surged and pulsed like something alive. Six ships flew in formation around her: Rununja, Sata Neek, Wyl, and Skitcher in their A-wings, Glothe and Merish in B-wings.

"All fighters, ready for attack run," Rununja snapped.

*We know,* she wanted to say. *We all know the plan.*

Chass glanced at her instruments. Nothing red. Scanner showed the *Hellion's Dare* falling away behind the squadron. New signals blinked into existence as the enemy cruiser-carrier, far ahead and out of sight, loosed its TIE fighters. Nothing they hadn't seen a dozen times.

She set course, adjusted the audio filters on her comm, and slapped at a panel with her palm until noise—brutal noise, rhythmic and pumping—filled the shell of the ship. Synthtone and bass vye screeched chords over the rage of a gurgling Herglic singer. She felt the music in her bones and her horns, the pounding redoubling the ship's vibrations as she increased thrust. It was a song of agony and revolution, a track she'd played while reducing armored Imperial walkers to burning hulks.

*Not for this mission,* she decided, and fumbled with the panel until the music changed. The bass dropped out and a new voice, higher-pitched and rapid-patter, accompanied the sound of bells. This track was energetic and nimble, surreal and incomprehensible and obscene, and Chass knew every word. She had to resist the urge to jerk the B-wing from side to side.

*Now* she was ready for the attack run.

"Entering visual range," Sata Neek said. Chass barely heard him over her own singing.

She leaned forward in her harness, peering at the far-off glimmers that might have been ships and might have been cosmic dust. Much closer were the burning thrusters of an A-wing, perfectly positioned two kilometers ahead. Rununja was the front of the wedge, with the other A-wing pilots spread out in a V behind her and enclosing the three B-wing assault craft.

The plan was simple.

"We're developing a theory about how they're following us," Captain Kreskian had said at the briefing. "They're picking at the bones of the dead we leave behind, and we have no good way to stop them. Except—" He'd shown his teeth then, a pair of incisors that could have gnawed through a bulkhead. "—by *stopping* them."

*Finally,* Chass had thought.

She sang a high note and checked her range to the target.

"Incoming fighters," Rununja called. "A-wings, break formation and intercept but do not leave Hound—do not leave the B-wings exposed."

The jets of the leading A-wing flared, then dimmed as it pulled away. Chass spotted the first flashes of emerald lightning and glanced at her weapons panel. Her strike foils were still locked shut; with a few thousand kilometers left to travel, she wasn't ready to switch her power and heat dispersal settings into combat mode. "You guys got this?" she called, the music dropping in volume automatically.

"Maintain course and speed," Rununja answered. "We've got this."

"Have fun," she said.

As the B-wings raced forward, a battle took shape around them. First a handful of A-wings and TIEs swirled; then a dozen more fighters; then two dozen; then a thousand bolts of red and green glittered against the dust. The New Republic ships swooped and soared and forced the TIEs away from the B-wings, as if the assault ships flew through the eye of a hurricane. Chass jinked from side to side, evading stray shots from all parties.

Sata Neek cried, "Snapper attempting a variant Needle! Moving to disrupt!"

Wyl's voice came through the comm. "Char's heading for the *Dare*. Looks like he's got partners—do we pursue?"

"Negative, Riot Three," Rununja said. "The *Dare*'s expecting visitors. We stay on target until they signal."

The music faded. For a moment the cockpit was silent except for the roar of the engine and the rattling of metal. Chass's console blinked, alerting her to an enemy missile lock before the warning vanished almost instantly.

The cruiser-carrier came into view as another song started. This time, the beat was low and rapid and the words were long, slurred passages of pidgin Gamorrean. An outlaw song—flaunt music, rough and passionate and barely competent. Perfect, Chass thought, for what was coming.

The cruiser-carrier—*Quasar Fire*–class, outdated but functional— used the dagger design of a Star Destroyer rescaled to a fraction of a Destroyer's size. This particular carrier had turned ninety degrees away from the squadron, concealing the hangar bays built into its undercarriage and presenting a slimmer targeting profile. That was an irritation but not an obstacle.

Green sparks flashed off the cruiser-carrier's hull: turbolaser fire.

"Reduce speed. Lock S-foils in attack position," Chass called. "Get ready to move in."

She ignored the comm chatter from the A-wings and yanked the strike foil control cord. Servos hummed as automated locks released and metallic limbs extended, reshaping the B-wing into its familiar cross profile. Lethal weapons charged with an electric moan. She rotated the bulk of the B-wing around the cockpit, feeling a jolt as the gyrostabilizers kicked in.

The beat grew louder and a playful melodium joined as counterpoint to the low notes. Glothe and Merish signaled their readiness to Chass, and the three assault fighters made for their target.

This was the part she loved. She reveled in it without irony or embarrassment—racing toward the enemy, cannon fire baking her cockpit in emerald light. Swinging her fighter out of the path of a concussion missile, switching off her thrusters to confuse heat sensors, and relying on inertia to carry her forward. Refusing to flinch in the face of weapons that could reduce a city to slag and glass.

Running the gauntlet.

The ship jumped and swayed as particle bolts splashed against her shields and the protective electromagnetic bubble crackled and coruscated. The A-wings were too busy with the TIEs to draw fire from the cruiser-carrier. She was at the mercy of the enemy gunners. She considered her options: transfer power to her forward shields or transfer power to her weapons. She picked the same answer as always:

*Weapons. Definitely weapons.*

She checked her range again. Scale was deceptive with a Quasar Fire—it looked *too* much like a Star Destroyer, which made it tough to tell how far away the smaller vessel really was. *Just a few more seconds,* she told herself. *Soon as you can pick out the hull plates.*

A burst of laserfire lit her shields. *Close enough,* she decided.

The starfighter sizzled as she ignited her ion cannons. Three streams of electric-blue bolts streaked toward the carrier, sending out shock waves of lightning where they struck. Chass was barely aiming—she'd be lucky to short out a turbolaser emplacement or a sensor tower—but she only intended to cause confusion and panic. Glothe and Merish were firing as well, and together they descended on the vessel.

Her head slammed into her seat as a laser volley hit her dead-on. The ship rocked and the console glowed with alerts. She grinned and fumbled with the volume control until the music was deafening.

The cruiser-carrier was close enough to dominate her view. She cut short her barrage and turned, swinging the cross-body of the fighter to reposition her jets. Now she was passing over the carrier. Now she was a perfect target, and she could see her objective. She fired again and unleashed the B-wing's entire arsenal, proton torpedoes and laser-guided bombs tearing through space as her shields burst and particle bolts scorched metal. She smelled burning wires. She heard Glothe scream and saw his blip fade from her scanner.

Far below, lightning raged over the rear of the cruiser-carrier. She shot past the vessel and checked her readings.

"Direct hit! Direct hit!" Merish called.

"Quasar Fire's lost power to its engines," Chass said. "They're not following us anywhere."

"Interceptors, escort the B-wings home." Rununja's voice. For the first time since Chass had met her, she showed a hint of pride at her squadron's performance. It made her profoundly less insufferable. "Prepare to jump to lightspeed."

But they didn't jump to lightspeed.

They returned to the *Hellion's Dare* without difficulty, scattering to avoid TIE pursuit and taking the long route home. The TIEs that had broken away to target the *Dare* during the battle—the unit led by Char—fled as the Riot pilots approached, unwilling to face the combined firepower of the frigate and its escorts.

Chass immediately understood why: They'd already completed their objective. The *Hellion's Dare* was in flames.

Smoke billowed from three sections. Energy surged visibly across the hull, spilling out from torn conduits. The shield globe flickered in and out of visibility when it should never have been visible at all.

"Blistering hell," Sata Neek said.

A static blast of a message came in from the *Dare* a minute later: The damage was substantial but the ship was intact and its weaponry largely functional. The TIE fighters had concentrated their efforts on the frigate's reactor and hyperdrive.

Like the cruiser-carrier, it was going nowhere.

Chass stopped the music and listened to nothing.

## CHAPTER 5

# IDENTIFICATION FRIEND OR FOE

## I

The *Pursuer* limped toward the inner system. Colonel Shakara Nuress suspected it might be the Star Destroyer's last journey, and though the craft had been her home for years she was unsentimental about its fate. She'd had many homes, shipboard and planetside, over the decades. Even if this one survived, Shakara doubted she would walk its decks again.

"Approaching the minefield," Major Rassus called.

The *Pursuer*'s final mission had been bloody and unspectacular, and its skeleton crew was ready to disembark. The last regional threats to the 204th's privacy had been eliminated. No colony would witness the passing of Shadow Wing ships; no scout would reach sensor range of Shakara's new base of operations without triggering alarms. The only outstanding business was the *Aerie*'s quarry—the cruiser-carrier and its TIEs hadn't reported back yet, and that *was* genuinely concerning.

Shakara wasn't prone to panic or to underestimating her people.

Silence was not indicative of failure, and the best hunters were patient when tracking elusive prey. She wondered whether the enemy had fled as far as the Oridol Cluster, which would have explained a great deal—if the cruiser-carrier had plunged into that chaotic region, it could be some time yet before she received word.

*Quit speculating, you fool. Until you've docked, pay attention.*

"What's the minefield's status?" Shakara asked. She saw nothing but the distant orange sun through the viewport, and turned instead to the nearest screen.

"Still substantial gaps. At a glance, I'd call it sixty percent complete, but that's—"

"—better than when we left, yes. I'll check in with the minelayers later." She started to say more when the comscan officer rose abruptly and caught her gaze from the pit. "What is it?" she snapped.

"Incoming transmission," the man replied. "Badly distorted—it must be boosted and patched through ten different relays—but it's using the *Pursuer*'s transponder codes. They want *us*."

Shakara hurried into the pit, ignoring the ache in her knees as she climbed down. She took the headset from the officer without a word and slipped it over her ears. She strained to hear the voice through hissing and pops: "—on behalf of Colonel Madrighast, this is the *Unyielding*. We must sever communications in two minutes. Please respond."

*Colonel Madrighast.* The man was an idiot, but he was a loyal one.

"This is Colonel Shakara Nuress of the 204th Imperial Fighter Wing," she replied.

For several moments, there was no answer. Then Madrighast's colonial brogue came through: "Nuress. There were rumors you'd survived Cinder. I'm surprised you didn't reach out to me first."

"We've been isolated," she replied. "We're only just rebuilding the communications relays. You're the first to make contact, but—" She tried to eliminate every trace of scorn from her tone. Fool or not, he was still Imperial. "—I'm pleased you found us."

"You didn't leave much of a trail," he said.

"We didn't care to."

Madrighast snorted. "No, I imagine not. But it's past time—prepare to join my forces. We're moving to the Gordian Reach, where we'll regroup with the 108th." Shakara was unable to stifle her brief, surprised laugh. Madrighast's voice turned harsh. "Or you can transmit your location and we'll *discuss* it in person."

The threat was palpable. Shakara had heard of Imperials fighting Imperials for resources. But the threat wasn't *real*—not from Madrighast, not if she was right.

"I heard about your troubles during Cinder," she said, and though her words were conciliatory she lashed them like a whip. "I don't imagine you're in shape for battle. Neither am I, frankly—I'm building something here but I need time and I need space."

Madrighast paused awhile. He sighed noisily into the link. "I never took you for the sort to carve out your own little empire, Nuress. But I wish you luck with it."

Shakara laughed again, lower and without mockery. "You're right— I'm *not* the sort. Very soon I'll have a base of operations strong enough to supply a good portion of our surviving fleet, no matter who ends up in command. After that, I'll gladly follow whatever strategy Moff Pandion or Admiral Sloane or whoever takes charge has in mind." She scoured the last of the humor from her voice. "Instead of leaving for the Gordian Reach, pay us a visit in a short while. We'll have you repaired and restocked before you move on."

Madrighast sounded humbled as he asked, "What is it you've found there?"

"Somewhere to make a stand," Shakara said.

The transmission crackled out. The two minutes were over. She hoped Madrighast understood.

She put the headset aside and climbed out of the pit. The Star Destroyer was passing through the minefield now, transmitting clearance codes to avoid attracting the explosives and moving through gaps broad enough to admit the vessel. Shakara smiled tightly as she saw the first TIE patrols on the scanner.

*Very soon,* she'd told Madrighast, but the first phase was nearly done. The 204th had a new garrison. They'd blinded their enemies. Now the nature of her task would change, but she could adapt. So could her people.

The Star Destroyer adjusted course. A world shrouded in scarlet clouds came into view: Pandem Nai.

## II

Yrica Quell believed in the value of rules. Rules made a chaotic galaxy livable. Rules created pockets of sanity and predictability—sterile environments in which a person could live and breathe and think without fear. She'd believed these things as a child (often to the dismay of her older siblings) and she'd believed them while contemplating a future in the Rebellion.

The Empire had nurtured and refined her reverence for order. Obedience and deference, along with the knowledge of what was permissible and what was not, could take a person far at the flight academy. Where other cadets broke, Quell thrived.

But now she had defected to a nation founded by lawbreakers and anarchists. If she was to succeed in her mission, principles had to be bent.

Maybe someone would even respect her for it.

She stepped out of the turbolift into the darkened cargo bay of the *Buried Treasure,* her jumpsuit too loose and her oxygen mask too snug in the cold, nearly airless compartment. She swept her glow rod about the vast space, pausing where she'd hung her target with Tensent the night before. Aside from the scorched threads of fabric on the floor, there was no sign of their visit.

*Maybe they'll blame you for this one, Nath,* she thought. *You and your friend on the bridge.*

She shivered and strode briskly to the wall where the line of inert and depowered astromech droids waited. She thought of stories about the Clone Wars and the droid armies that had fought against the Old Republic, before the Empire; but these machines looked more absurd than harmful, squat cylindrical chassis giving them an affect of plump self-indulgence.

She knelt in front of a three-legged unit topped with a clear plastex dome—a window into a rat's nest of wires and circuit boards. She'd spent enough years studying basic engine mechanics to feel comfortable with the guts of a starfighter, but droids were another thing. The colored cabling meant nothing. The scratches on the chassis suggested the droid had been in service for some time but revealed nothing explicit. If she was looking for a sign—some indication she was making the right choice—she didn't find one.

Her gloved fingers touched the icy unit and quickly located a power toggle. The droid hummed softly as its energy cells revived. Function indicators glowed blue.

"You working?" she asked.

The droid responded with a lengthy high-pitched stutter. Quell understood none of it. She silently prayed that it was an initialization sequence—that the unit was, as its cargo status implied, freshly memory-wiped.

But hopefully not *entirely* memory-wiped.

"Basic functions check," Quell said. "Mobility? Technical interface? Astrogation?"

Three chimes. That boded well.

"Come on," Quell said. "I've got a job for you."

The droid rolled forward no more than two centimeters and rotated its dome, taking in the cargo bay with its photoreceptor. It made no evident objections and Quell rose, rubbing her torso to try to regain a semblance of warmth. She clutched the glow rod awkwardly in the crook of her injured arm.

She was rounding a stack of magnetically secured crates when she spotted a flicker within the cargo lift. She squinted, then flinched when she recognized the glow: the indicator lights of a visor.

"Kairos."

The woman moved inhumanly fast, apparently unimpeded by the cold and the near-airlessness of the hold; either her anatomy was truly foreign or her garb had a practical purpose. In her gloved hand was a metal rod—perhaps a multitool or a pry bar by design, but unmistakably a weapon in Kairos's possession. One swing hooked Quell behind the knees and slammed her onto the cargo bay floor. A second swing caught the straps of Quell's oxygen mask and tore it free, sending it skittering away.

Quell heard the droid squeal and roll forward. She turned her head in time to see it extend an arc welder, throw sparks into the darkness, but Kairos lifted her weapon and the droid halted. Kairos watched as Quell felt air escape her lungs.

"Listen—" Quell's voice sounded dull, muffled by the thin atmosphere. "You're right. You're right about what I'm doing. But I need—"

Kairos made no motion as Quell swallowed and gasped.

In horror, Quell thought: *She's going to stare at me until I faint. Maybe until I die.*

She'd been an idiot. She'd thought she could be a rebel, prove herself to her new masters. Fly for a good cause.

But she still hadn't earned it. Maybe she never would.

"I need a chance," she croaked. She couldn't hear herself over the sizzling of the droid's arc welder. "I want to make it right."

The visor flickered. Quell stared into it. She thought of lunging for her oxygen mask. She thought of lunging at Kairos, wresting away the weapon or tearing at the strange woman's wrappings until she saw flesh beneath. She doubted she had the strength, but she tensed her muscles anyway.

Then a hand pressed the mask back onto her face. She shuddered violently. The droid whistled. She thought she heard a voice say, "Make it right," before Kairos stalked away to the cargo lift.

She was trembling as she made her way to the moorings, half frozen and breathless from her encounter with Kairos. But there was no stopping now. She had bent the rules, broken her principles, and it was best to finish the mutilation rather than dwell on the pain.

She chose her ship the same way she'd chosen the droid. She didn't believe in intuition or luck and she certainly didn't put faith in the religion of the Rebellion's zealots—those heirs to the monastic Jedi and their cousins. No—the ship she chose, she chose at random. She would have to hope for the best.

Six starfighters were clamped to the underside of the *Buried Treasure,* accessible via hatches through a passage so small that, in places, it forced Quell onto her knees. Boarding the U-wing would have been simpler, but detaching it from the freighter would have set off too many alarms. The starfighters, like the droid, were cargo— comparatively insecure. Quell loaded the astromech into the connector tube and whispered her instructions. The droid chimed brightly and disappeared from sight.

She waited five minutes, looking from the indicator panels to the ladder leading back to the main deck. At last, a buzz indicated that her ship was locked into the loading ring. The pilot could now board.

She stepped into a hatch and dropped into the cockpit of a T-65 X-wing starfighter.

The vessel was still attached to the *Buried Treasure,* encased in a magnetic field, and the freighter's mass did little to conceal the cerulean storm of hyperspace. The yawning void of realspace was familiar to Quell, comforting for all its dangers, but a TIE fighter lacked a hyperdrive; she'd never been in a vessel with so little between her body and the weird, impossible flux that ripped apart all natural laws.

The zealots of the Rebellion revered a mystical, omnipresent, and undetectable energy they called the Force, claiming its ineffable power controlled destinies. The mysteries of hyperspace were fearful enough for Quell.

She tried to adjust her body to the seat as the canopy resealed. The cockpit felt too open, built to accommodate a hundred varied species rather than molded for humanoids alone. Controls crept over every panel like vines. But the basics were the same as in any vessel: sensors and scope, flight computer and comm, throttle and rudder pedals and repulsor controls. She squinted at an unfamiliar screen and realized, with a laugh, the purpose of the attached dials.

*Shield controls.* She'd always seen the rebel reliance on shields as contributing to sloppy flying. *Why learn to dodge when you can soak the damage?*

*Then again,* she reminded herself, *they won the war.*

She powered the ship for flight. Status indicators flashed. A message from the droid scrolled down the display, announcing the unit's readiness and designation: It was an R-series model with a twenty-character serial number it compressed to D6-L, and it claimed to be recompiling its code to optimize its performance for starfighter operations instead of capital ship maintenance.

That struck Quell as a poor omen. She hoped the droid's confidence in its own adaptability was warranted, but she had no way to judge; a TIE fighter pilot didn't need machine assistance.

She fumbled with the controls until she was confident the droid could hear her. "Prepare for unmooring and send this message upon detachment: Yrica Quell departing to investigate a lead for Intelligence working group. Intent is to rendezvous with the *Buried Treasure* within twenty-four hours."

The freighter would stop to refuel by then, and the X-wing's oxygen levels were already uncomfortably low. No ground crew had resupplied the ship for flight. If Quell wasn't ready in a day, she would have her choice between failure and suffocation.

"End communication. Detach now."

The X-wing rattled as the astromech droid disengaged the clamps. As the ship drifted clear, the *Buried Treasure* became a blur overhead, disappearing into the hyperspace tunnel even as the universe twisted and distorted around the starfighter. Streaks of color and flickering afterimages stained the cockpit for a paralyzing eternity. The console blared warnings. Quell wondered if, in her inexperience, she'd made an awful mistake by trying to drop directly into realspace.

Or maybe her mistake had been trusting the droid.

Then the spectral distortion vanished and night swaddled the ship. Strapped safely in her harness, Quell stared out at billions of distant stars.

She was flying again. Flying after too long.

She wanted to float for an age. To stroke the fighter's controls without going anywhere and let starlight soak into her bones.

But she had a mission.

"One last thing before we go," she murmured.

Gingerly, she removed the sling from her arm and rotated her shoulder. She was tender and stiff, but it was time. Even the torture droid had agreed it was almost time.

She was finally free.

Quell's task was to determine the 204th Fighter Wing's location and current activities. But Caern Adan had given her none of the tools she needed. She wasn't an analyst. She wasn't a detective. She knew Shadow Wing as well as anyone, but she'd been looking in the wrong place.

Intercepted communications wouldn't tell her anything. *Seeing* where the 204th had been might provide a clue.

When they'd met in Traitor's Remorse, Adan had told her that Shadow Wing had made nine attacks over the course of two weeks. Those were old sightings, too outdated to do her any good, but it was unlikely Grandmother hadn't acted since then. That meant, in turn, that Shadow Wing's recent attacks hadn't been identified as such—that the strikes had been either disguised (which seemed doubtful; the 204th was a decorated unit but not a covert one), swift and anonymous, or thorough enough to eliminate all witnesses.

So Quell had made a list from the databases Adan had provided. Missing ships, noncommunicative outposts, anything that suggested an Imperial fighter attack performed with brutal efficacy. She'd eliminated sites half a galaxy away and prioritized those remaining by date and location and target. What she had left was a set of star systems that *might* have been visited by her quarry.

She had approximately twenty-four hours to visit as many as she could.

Her first jump took her to the Paqualis system, where a New Republic supply transport had disappeared. She found the transport without difficulty at its last known coordinates, punctured by particle bolts and bereft of life and cargo.

An apparent pirate attack. Not useful to her mission.

She found no evidence of an attack at all in the intense crimson sunlight of the Shalam system—no debris, no wreckage. Nothing actionable. On the far outskirts of Telerath, where a captured Star Destroyer had gone abruptly silent, she gently navigated her X-wing through a sea of frozen corpses: the bodies of the Star Destroyer's New Republic crew, forced out of air locks and left to the merciless inevitability of hard vacuum.

She forced bile back down her throat. Shadow Wing could have retaken a Star Destroyer, but not like this.

She noted the Telerath system as a possibility and moved on.

Jendorn was haunted. She'd heard the stories from her father—that the great gray dust clouds of the star system collected *impressions* of anything passing through. The Empire called it a unique electromagnetic phenomenon. Quell's father had said the clouds were the work of a long-forgotten species. Whatever the truth, Quell's first sighting of a ghostly ship flickering like a malfunctioning hologram made her jump in her harness.

She followed a translucent New Republic corvette deep into the clouds and watched a swarm of flickering TIEs manifest around it. The impressions were incomplete—the phantoms came and went, leaving the ensuing battle a dreamlike fantasia—but she gazed with awe at the TIEs' maneuvers, the grace with which they spun around X-wings and drew black scars across the corvette's hull. She flinched when an Imperial fighter blossomed into fire after a missile struck its cockpit. She laughed in relief when the corvette began to list and burn and finally detonated into nothingness.

It was only after the company of ghosts finished its performance that she remembered which side she was supposed to cheer.

On her way out of the dust clouds she spotted an X-wing heading her direction. Its S-foils were closed; the vessel was in flight mode, weapons locked together and unpowered. In the cockpit sat a compact young woman in a New Republic jumpsuit, her expression somber and distracted. Quell waved to her ghost in passing and set course for the next site on her list.

She found a case of emergency supplies behind the pilot's seat and sipped a pouch of lukewarm water during her next hyperspace journey. She drank and dozed under cerulean lights, trying not to picture Telerath's sea of corpses superimposed over the battle at Jendorn.

In her waking moments, she began thinking not of her current mission but of an operation nine months prior. Every fighter in the 204th had descended upon Mek'tradi under the shadow of the *Pursuer.* That jewel of a planet, with its amber seas and pearl spires climbing into orbit, had housed a rebel cell. It had been the TIEs' responsibility to prevent any vessel from leaving the surface during the bombardment, and the pilots had performed their duty well: They'd chased X-wings in loops and burned ascending shuttles like children tearing wings from dragonflies. Quell remembered firing at landing pads, incinerating rebels racing to their ships.

She'd been horrified, yet she'd done her part.

In the aftermath, aboard the Star Destroyer, she'd debriefed with her commander and met with her ground crew and kept a stern face through it all before showering and panting into the water stream. She had felt suddenly *old*, like a woman whose heart was ready to give out.

Somehow, Major Keize had known.

He'd found Quell walking among the starfighter engineering teams, observing as they swapped out parts and attached cables and replaced paneling. With a silent gesture, he'd pulled her aside and walked her to his spartan office. She'd sat across from him as he asked banal questions about unit efficiency metrics and squadron power consumption.

She remembered studying his face. Brown hair dark enough to look black in the wrong light and thin, delicate lips out of place on a light, angular face. She remembered noticing the rumple of his collar and wondering if it was an affectation—a way of reassuring his subordinates that he was not, in fact, the perfect officer. That he was one of *them*.

"What's troubling you, Lieutenant?" he asked.

The question came unprompted. Quell flinched, though she wasn't surprised.

"I'm fine, sir. Mek'tradi shook me up, but I'm fine."

A smile appeared on Keize's face and vanished as swiftly as it came. "You can lie to me if you want. I can ignore it, and you can leave here no better off than you were. Or I can take offense and remove you from duty. Neither seems an ideal outcome for you. Or am I missing something?"

He asked it like he genuinely wanted her input. She thought it through. "No, sir," she finally said.

"Then what's troubling you, Lieutenant?"

She laughed. He didn't. She considered lying again. She trusted Keize, who had taken an interest in her since practically her start with the 204th. What she didn't trust was the systems that operated around them—the loyalty officers and the disclosure requirements and the recording devices that were monitoring them as they spoke.

Yet it was shame as much as mistrust that she warred against in order to say: "When I was an adolescent, I wanted to be a rebel."

"And now?"

"Of course not. Of course I don't now."

"Do you respect them?"

Again, she hesitated. The fear remained. The shame was gone. "No," she said. "But I think I pity them."

"If you respected them, that would be easier," he said. He waited for her to reply, then continued when she only stared. "When you believe people come to the fight with open eyes—when you believe they've judged their course of action rationally, however wrongly—killing them becomes simpler. You know they understood the risks and they deemed their cause worthwhile."

"And if I pity them? You think it's because I doubt their judgment?"

"Pity implies circumstances beyond your enemies' control. Circumstances that shaped them unfairly. Distorted their judgments. Pushed them into the line of fire.

"No one wants to be a butcher, Lieutenant. We all want to feel like we've bested someone fairly."

Quell considered the argument. Keize wasn't wrong, but nothing he said changed the situation. "The circumstances are our fault, though," she said. "The rebels' tactics are obscene but their grievances have merit and we're doing nothing to address the underlying causes—" She cut herself off, surprised at her own words.

Keize gestured with one hand. "Continue." As he spoke, he rose from his chair and began to pace. He stopped halfway across his office.

In front of the recording eye. "Continue," he repeated.

She did, though the words came slower this time. "The Emperor began by promising to reorder the decaying and corrupt Republic after the Clone Wars. And he did it. The corporate powers lost influence. Petty crime rates dropped. Local governments had to answer directly to him if they failed or abused their people." It was the history she'd been taught, though she'd heard other claims: that the Emperor had sought to militarize the Republic, and all else had been a side effect of the power grab. Stranger yet, she'd met Imperial patriots of her parents' generation who swore that a conspiracy of Jedi mystics had forced the Emperor's hand; but aside from wild stories, she'd never read anything suggesting the Jedi had been more than a marginal cult.

She went on: "Now, though, we've gotten inefficient again. There're probably more corrupt governors out there than there were ten years ago, and that can't *all* be blamed on the Rebellion. The famines in the Dryorkeen Cluster are real. Even petty crime is going up again in places.

"The rebels are making things worse. But we're not making things better."

Keize nodded thoughtfully and took his time before replying.

"Our Empire," he said, "is as corrupt as it is glorious. We've done so much wrong and so much right. But you're a soldier, Lieutenant, and that means you're faced with the burden of every soldier since the galaxy was formed.

"Soldiers can't choose their battles. A soldier fights for an imperfect nation, not a perfect ideal."

"We fight for the Emperor," she said.

Keize shook his head and stepped past her to the door. He gestured and they exited together.

They walked down the polished black corridors of the Star Destroyer, past ranks of stormtroopers and naval officers, technicians and pilots. Keize led the way to the hangar where dozens more men and women scrubbed scorch marks off TIE fighters or peeled off flight suits. He looked out and smiled with those thin, delicate lips.

"We fight for *them*, Lieutenant. We fight for our brothers and sisters beside us. Always remember that."

Yrica Quell had been a pilot once. She had been a great pilot, and proud. At last, she was starting to remember.

She emerged from her reverie when her X-wing jumped into the Jiruus system—prize jewel of the sector's Imperial moff and muster point for a missing New Republic reconnaissance expedition. The moff was dead now, and the New Republic frigate *Hellion's Dare* was days late to report in.

She checked her scanner as she approached Jiruus itself and saw no ships and few satellites. An automated signal from the planet indicated functioning landing pads. If nothing else, she thought, Operation Cinder hadn't come to the world.

But she was short on time. She would need to head back to the *Buried Treasure* soon in order to make her rendezvous. She saw no immediate evidence of a battle, no sign of TIE fighters or the *Hellion's Dare,* and she was preparing to jump out when a message came through from the D6-L astromech droid.

She frowned at her display as she read through what looked like a chemical analysis of—what? The composition of Jiruus's exosphere?

The droid had been largely silent on the journey so far, only responding to her explicit commands. She wasn't sure how typical independent action was for an astromech loaded into a starfighter, but this seemed well outside normal operations.

"What am I looking at?" she asked. "And why are you helping?"

Several lines in the compositional analysis blinked. *Tibanna. Iro-lunn. Clouzon-36.* Traces of hyperdrive fuel and particle weaponry.

Whatever had happened over Jiruus, it had happened in low orbit and it had been significant enough to leave scars.

She studied the display for several seconds. "All right," she muttered. "Good work."

The droid pinged a short, courteous acknowledgment.

She put the astromech unit out of her mind and adjusted her systems, diverting all power to her sensors. An X-wing wasn't a science craft, but maybe she could find enough traces to provide more information. If not, she could look planetside to resolve her two most urgent questions:

When had the fight happened?

And where was the wreckage?

Within an hour, she had her answers. The implications terrified her. They left her giddy and certain of her decisions. When she ordered the droid to set a course for the *Buried Treasure,* she was ready, she thought, for what was coming.

She had proved she was valuable to the New Republic. Now she had to convince the only man who mattered.

Caern Adan met her in the cramped mooring tube where she had stolen her X-wing a day before. With him were Nath Tensent and two *Buried Treasure* crew members, all of whom carried their pistols unholstered. Tensent would have been enough, Quell thought—there wasn't room to miss.

Adan stared with fury in his eyes, his antenna-stalks buried in his wiry hair. Quell was surprised he hadn't brought the torture droid; she almost said as much, but spitting in Adan's face wouldn't convince him of anything. It wouldn't help the mission. She'd found what she'd gone after, but she was still in the wrong.

"Lieutenant Yrica Quell," she said, "ready to report and submit to disciplinary action."

Tensent cracked a cold smile and aimed his blaster at the floor in lazy circles. He stood a half step behind and to one side of Adan.

"You stole a ship," Adan said. "The appropriate discipline is to throw you out an air lock."

"That's fair." *Not merciful, but fair.* She wondered if New Republic regulations allowed an Intelligence officer to execute a traitorous asset. She wondered if there *were* regulations constraining New Republic Intelligence. "Before anything else, though, download the ship's logs. Check them for tampering. And—"

She hesitated, then decided to take a risk. "—ask the droid what happened, too. I think it understood what I was doing and it can confirm our findings." For all she knew, the droid would incriminate her. But the thing *seemed* to like her.

Adan let out a grunt of a laugh. "We're not equipped for hostile information download. I'm not loading a malicious program into the ship's computers, or spending a day dissecting your droid in a clean room—"

"Then listen to *me*," Quell said. She heard the passion in her voice and tamped it down. "I came back. I'm worthless to you if I'm a traitor, but I can still be useful if I'm real."

"You can be real," Adan replied, "and still too much trouble to bother with."

Her eyes flickered to the crew. One of Adan's guards was fully focused on her, weapon clenched tight—*too* tight, in a nervous grip rather than a professional one. Another studied the status panels and the walls in something like shame. Tensent, however, showed no sign of stress. He looked as cold as when he'd tried to kill her in the Entropian Hive cantina, and as relaxed as when they'd shot targets in the cargo hold.

"Your play, but can I make a suggestion?" Tensent watched Quell, but his words were directed to Adan.

"Make it quick," Adan said.

"If she were in my crew? I'd give her five minutes. Then decide whether to toss her out the air lock." Tensent grinned, and Adan frowned dubiously.

Quell doubted Adan would execute her. She was less certain about Tensent. Nonetheless, when Adan turned away from the larger man Tensent's grin vanished and he caught Quell's eyes. He nodded very slowly, as if prompting her to act.

Tensent understood people better than Quell ever would. She tried to take the advice given.

"Two minutes," she said. "I don't need five. Just give me two."

Adan looked from Quell to Tensent and back. "Two minutes," he said.

Quell told him what she knew.

"Just over a week ago, a detachment from the 204th Imperial Fighter Wing ambushed the *Hellion's Dare* in the Jiruus system. The *Dare* was a New Republic frigate on a reconnaissance mission, with two fighter squadron escorts—enough firepower to defend itself.

"I know because I went to investigate sites of likely Shadow Wing activity. Jiruus showed traces of a battle in low planetary orbit but I couldn't find any wreckage."

Adan was paying attention. She was rushing, she knew, and she tried to slow down. She needed to seem confident, not desperate.

"I did a flyby of the planet surface and saw minimal damage from the fight. I made radio contact with the locals. They've got no galactic communications but they sent me scanner logs confirming that a conflict had taken place and that the *Hellion's Dare* had fled. The fact the cities are still standing indicates Shadow Wing didn't stick around long—they busted a few key facilities but didn't bother to purge a planet full of witnesses.

"I believe the *Hellion's Dare* fled the system into the Oridol Cluster. A Shadow Wing sub-unit pursued, and that the pursuit is ongoing."

She felt sweat under her arms. Her shoulder was sore from so many hours without the sling. She watched Adan's reaction, but his expression was flat. When he wanted to, the man could hide anything.

"You started strong," Adan said. "But you ended with speculation."

"I ran out of time," Quell replied.

Adan laughed—a genuine laugh this time, albeit a brief one. Quell let herself smile.

"Go on," Adan said. "Explain."

"We had a maneuver in the 204th we called trapping the bantha. Tricky to execute but very effective, and we got *good* at it." She heard her tone and cursed herself. *Sound humble. Sound penitent.* "When an enemy unit looked ready to flee to lightspeed, we'd pick a single fighter and separate it from the rest of the group. Surround it, harry it, but keep it intact right until the jump into hyperspace.

"As soon as the enemy started jumping out, we'd blast the trapped fighter. Everyone else would escape. We'd tractor the wreckage aboard our carrier and salvage the navigation system. Recover whatever jump coordinates the unit was using."

"That's some fancy timing," Tensent said. "Clever."

Adan's eyes half lidded and he nodded. "And you figure Shadow Wing chased after the *Dare* at Jiruus because, what—they didn't stay long enough to do much damage to the planet?"

"Yes. Shadow Wing went after a frigate on a reconnaissance mission. That suggests they wanted to prevent some discovery from reaching the New Republic, so why—"

"—why would they leave witnesses on Jiruus, yes. I'm not an idiot. What about the Oridol Cluster? Why there?"

"If Shadow Wing had destroyed the *Hellion's Dare*, they would've returned to Jiruus for mop-up. That means they're still in chase mode. Oridol's the obvious place for a rebel to flee and the—the abnormalities there would slow both the *Dare* and Shadow Wing to a crawl."

Again, Adan nodded. He shifted his weight from one leg to the other as if he wanted to pace but was frustrated by the cramped space.

"What makes you think," he said carefully, "that your Shadow Wing detachment wasn't destroyed by the *Dare*?"

He'd caught her. She thought of lying, but he'd just begun to trust her. *The truth, then.*

"The recon unit is a frigate and two fighter squadrons. Against the 204th, they don't have a chance."

# CHAPTER 6

# PAYLOAD

I

The goal was simple: Locate and extract the *Hellion's Dare* from the Oridol Cluster. But everything Yrica Quell knew about military strategy implied a thousand layers of complexity beneath that statement of intent. *Locate* meant scouting missions. It meant high-speed vessels and long-range scanning buoys; supply convoys and those convoys' fighter escorts; timetables and star charts and encrypted communications channels. *Extract* meant carriers and more starfighters and intelligence on the enemy force; detailed maps of the zone of action and meetings between wing commanders and squadron leaders; and in the end, for the briefest of periods, violence.

That was how the Empire had operated—with the slow, crushing inevitability of a tectonic shift. None of it was possible under the New Republic.

"If we want to find the *Dare,* we do it ourselves," Adan had told Quell, after he'd called off the guards and they'd returned to the main deck of the *Buried Treasure*. "I've sent a message to the commander of the Barma Battle Group but Shadow Wing isn't anyone's most urgent problem. It'll take us days to get reinforcements, at best."

Every passing hour increased the odds of the *Dare*'s destruction. Adan seemed to know that, and—testy though he was—he seized the *Treasure*'s conference room for his working group and didn't argue when Quell requested access to his files on the Oridol Cluster. They sat together with Nath Tensent and the silent Kairos, poring through intelligence reports and debriefings from past expeditions; reviewing technical specs for the *Hellion's Dare* and its escorts.

They debated ways to contact the *Hellion's Dare* and found none. They discussed whether to guess at the *Dare*'s course and follow along, but determined they would never find the ship in time. They considered what would happen if they *did* find the *Dare* and were forced to engage with Shadow Wing, and agreed engagement was to be avoided; they needed to help the *Dare* escape to friendly territory—learn what its crew had learned—not start a fight.

"We need a signal," Tensent said. "Send out a flare and bring them home."

*That's a metaphor, not a plan,* Quell thought. She said: "What kind of flare?"

Tensent shrugged. "Used to hear stories about purrgil. Living creatures that roam hyperspace. Old buddy of mine claimed he knew how they communicated. Said he could make them yell across a whole sector—warn his business partners without using Imperial beacons."

"We don't have purrgil," Quell said, "and the *Dare* wouldn't know what to listen for."

Tensent leveled his gaze at Quell and, one boot at a time, dropped both feet on the conference table. "It wasn't a suggestion. It was supposed to be *inspiration*."

She thought of snapping back, but Tensent didn't deserve it. She was irritable and they were short on time. She made a mental note to apologize later and hoped she somehow forgot.

Adan was silent through the exchange, drawing fingerprint-grease squiggles on the table. Tensent seemed as surprised as Quell when he announced that he'd found their solution.

Seventy minutes later, Quell was zipping up her flight suit when she heard a mechanical hum enter the berthing compartment. She turned to the doorway and saw the torture droid. "Adan agreed to let you fly," it said, as if the statement were a question.

"Yes."

"Into combat."

Quell felt a wave of heat and ire crest and forced it down like bile. "There won't be any combat if we're right. The outpost should be undefended. But Tensent and Kairos don't have the expertise to do the job alone."

She said it and almost believed it.

"Your shoulder is not fully healed. Your skull is not fully healed. Maneuvering at combat speeds will exert pressure that may cause additional fracturing—"

She edged around the torture droid as she stalked into the corridor. It kept talking. "—causing permanent loss of manual dexterity in one arm. You may suffer subarachnoid hemorrhaging. You may suffer brain injury—"

She spun around as the droid continued its litany of horrors. "Keep your little fantasies to yourself," she snapped. "Understood? Are we done?"

"When did you last sleep?" the droid asked in the same dull, relentless voice.

She had to think. She'd drowsed in hyperspace during her scouting mission, but it had been days since her last full night's rest—the night before Operation Cinder had replayed over and over in her ears.

The realization penetrated her body, weighing her eyes and limbs. "I'm rested enough to fly," she said.

"Medically speaking, you are entirely unqualified to fly."

*Probably true,* she thought.

"There's no one else," she said, "and Adan already cleared me. There won't be any combat if we're right."

"If you're wrong, are you prepared to fire on Imperial forces?"

That stopped her altogether.

She saw what the droid was doing. Torment her with images of suffering. Remind her of her exhaustion. Hit her with an emotional trigger to test her loyalty.

"Even if I'm wrong, any defenses will be automated. It's a *research* outpost." Her voice was soft, steady, and rational. "Are you going to stop me?"

"I've already passed on my recommendation to Adan," the droid said. "I'd hoped you would be more reasonable."

"You may think you do, but you don't know me terribly well." Quell started toward her ship. Her X-wing. Whether she succeeded or failed, she would fly for the New Republic today.

It might be her only chance.

Harrikos-Fifteen was classified as an Imperial research facility, and that was all the New Republic knew for certain. The rest—that it was studying the Oridol Cluster; that its defenses were minimal; that it held exactly what the New Republic Intelligence working group on the 204th Imperial Fighter Wing needed—was guesswork informed by old rebel reports and anecdotal evidence. There were a hundred ways the mission could go wrong and no time for study.

So Quell plunged into the azure fires of hyperspace (accompanied by Nath Tensent's Y-wing bomber and Kairos's U-wing support vessel) with a plan sketchier than any she'd encountered inside Shadow Wing. If it had come from the mind of Major Keize or Colonel Nuress, she might have taken more comfort in it; instead, the plan was her own.

The *Buried Treasure* was not a combat vessel, and its cargo was too valuable to risk. It would only follow the starfighters to Harrikos once the pilots signaled victory. Adan, too, had declined to come, despite Quell's suggestion that he ride with the U-wing's passengers. Before they'd parted ways, however, he had granted her provisional command of the mission. "You know their protocols. Kairos and Tensent will follow your lead," he'd said.

He'd taken Tensent aside immediately afterward and stared meaningfully at Kairos. Quell hadn't taken offense. She understood exactly how far her command extended.

Still, she was flying again.

She fell asleep to the tuneless whistling of the D6-L astromech and woke shortly before her X-wing erupted out of hyperspace. The stars fell into position and she blinked at the haze smeared across the black void—the scintillating cloud of the Oridol Cluster, its fractal patterns filling the vastness of space. She saw Kairos and Tensent wink into existence on her scanner. There were no other vessels. No communications signals. *One assumption proven correct.*

She activated her comm. "All ships report in."

"Tensent here." The voice came through, gruff and dour. "Don't get us killed."

Then a second voice—not Kairos, but one of the *Buried Treasure* crew members aboard the U-wing. "Corporal Shroi here. We're standing by."

"Stay close, but not *too* tight," Quell said. "The last thing we need is to stumble over each other."

She checked her scanner again and told her droid to make for the Harrikos-Fifteen Research Station—a speck of metal within the system's vast ring of frozen methane. The light of the burning blue sun glinted off the ice as the X-wing approached, and Quell's shields flickered as solar radiation beat against the electromagnetic bubble like rain. She kept her thrusters at low power to minimize the g forces; even so, she felt her shoulder throb and her forehead pound.

D6-L recommended she open the ship's S-foils and power her weapons. "Not yet," she said.

Before she'd stolen her starfighter, she'd barely seen an X-wing with strike foils closed. The ships were the backbone of the rebel starfighter corps, nearly as capable in a dogfight as a TIE though never *quite* as maneuverable, trading speed for shields and torpedoes and hyperdrives. Trading specialization for versatility. Her experience was as an adversary, not a pilot; if she did have to fight, she would be at a disadvantage.

She watched her estimated range to the station tick down and opened a new comm channel. The words felt natural as she spoke. "This is Lieutenant Yrica Quell, 204th Imperial Fighter Wing, to Harrikos-Fifteen Research Station. Authorization code—" She rattled off a string of eight numbers that had meant something before the Emperor's assassination and might be meaningless now. "Requesting emergency landing."

She didn't expect the station crew to believe her. She just needed to sow doubt.

The response came in the mechanical cadence of a droid. "Unrecognized vessel. You are not authorized to land. Do not approach."

She'd been hoping for a human. Now she had to persuade a machine.

She maintained her course and speed. "Do you know what's happening out there?" she asked. "The rebels destroyed DS-2. They say the Emperor is dead. My squadron escaped from a prison camp. We stole these ships, we're almost out of fuel, we need repairs . . ." She heard desperation in her voice. The role came to her entirely naturally.

"Do not approach. This is your last warning."

She couldn't see the station as more than a dark dot against the field of ice. But there was nothing on the scanner—no squadron of TIEs coming to greet them.

*Make the call, Yrica. Race for the outpost or circle and keep talking?*

Crimson lightning shot past her canopy, startling her out of her thoughts. The blasts had come from behind. She cursed and craned her neck as Tensent's voice came through the link. "They're not biting. Shoot the hostage and prepare for attack run."

*What?*

An indicator on the comm was flashing—a signal from D6-L. Tensent's message had been wide-beamed to the U-wing on an insecure channel. He was shouting so anyone could hear. He was *improvising.*

Her best reason yet not to like the blasted pirate.

Tensent fired again, the blasts a hundred meters off her port side.

She bit her lip and opened the throttle, felt the acceleration in her body like someone driving nails into her forehead and shoulder. She remembered the words *subarachnoid hemorrhaging*.

"Lieutenant Quell, this is Harrikos-Fifteen. Report immediately. What is occurring?"

She had to answer. Had to say *something* to keep the ruse going. But she didn't know how to lie when the lie didn't feel true. "Harrikos-Fifteen, please. I can't explain now—" She tried to inject panic into her strained breathing. "Just please let me land."

"Authorization denied."

She was outdistancing Tensent. The X-wing's thrusters handily outclassed the Y-wing's. The U-wing could've stayed closer, but Kairos had chosen to remain with Tensent instead of pursuing Quell at top speed. It made the ruse less convincing, but it gave Quell one less worry.

She could finally make out the shape of the outpost: two metallic spires, each wide at the base and tapering toward the tip, connected by a slender docking strip. The design was standard for a deep-space monitoring station housing no more than thirty permanent residents. If Quell was right, it had no fighter complement.

The outpost swelled in her view as kilometers flashed by. Sunlight reflected off ice blocks larger than cities, forcing her to squint into the glare. She decelerated to avoid racing past her target and felt as nauseated as a first-year cadet.

Emerald fires burned like halos around the spires' midsections. But the cannons weren't aiming for her—they were targeting *beyond* her, shooting at Tensent and Kairos. The lie had worked.

She was close enough to return fire, but she had to time it right. The outpost defenses were still treating her as nonhostile. She adjusted her heading and centered the docking strip in her viewport as if coming in to land. Particle bolts streamed by so quickly the beams became coherent. She saw Tensent and Kairos swerve rapidly on her scanner.

The docking strip grew larger. She saw guide lights and moorings and air locks. She strained forward in her harness and craned her neck, trying to identify the exact locations of the weapons emplacements.

*Time it right, or they'll blow you to pieces.*

She counted the seconds. She drew a breath. "Dee-six, lock S-foils in attack position."

The X-wing's strike foils separated and four cannons, capable of greater destruction than any TIE fighter, drew power from the ship's reactor. The targeting screen unfolded. Quell pulled up as hard as she could and cried out as she nearly collided with the outpost's hull; she skimmed meters above the plating, whipping past sensors and baffles and antennas. She fired and heard the rippling *crack* of the cannons, saw the crimson bolts impact gun towers protruding from the station. She flew through a cloud of sparks and twisted metal, blind until she reemerged into the soothing dark.

"Tensent here," the comm declared. "You handle the guns. I'll take the rest."

Quell saw the Y-wing closing on her scanner. The assault fighter would barrage the station with ion weapons and proton bombs—bursting enemy shields and shorting out defenses so long as it survived to make its pass. The U-wing, too, was closing in, weaving through cannon fire to approach the docking strip and unleashing swift, wild volleys of particle bolts in return.

Quell flew on, attuning herself to the X-wing's responses. The vessel seemed to flinch with every shot. It reacted more slowly than she was used to. But she reduced a second and third cannon to shattered steel and melted plastoid, spiraling her way up the spire of the station. A rotating turbolaser pumped dozens of particle blasts toward her from the spire's apogee, and she switched her weapons to proton torpedoes.

She saw, as the X-wing momentarily dipped, a viewport in the hull of the station—a command center, perhaps. She saw silhouettes inside, and faces: uniformed officers hammering at consoles, shouting orders, or staring into the battle.

Officers fighting for their dead Empire. The station defenses weren't fully automated after all.

*If you're wrong,* the torture droid had said, *are you prepared to fire on Imperial forces?*

She was a pilot for the New Republic. She had no cause for remorse. She let the proton torpedo fly and raced on past the destruction.

Two hours later—after the security team aboard Kairos's U-wing had taken control of the research outpost and rounded up the few survivors—the first pod streaked like a firework across the sky. It was a bright, burning thing, arcing toward infinity before vanishing into hyperspace. Another flew, then another. Ten, twenty, and more. Quell lost count as she observed from her cockpit.

Sealed inside each pod was a probe droid programmed to search for the *Hellion's Dare* in the labyrinth of the Oridol Cluster. Most of the droids' journeys would end in sudden and violent obliteration: The ever-changing hyperspace corridors of the cluster would toss the majority into stars or planets or other gravity wells. The few that survived would chart new paths. If one found the *Dare,* it could guide the New Republic frigate to Harrikos along the trail it had forged.

Probably.

Assuming the frigate was still intact. Assuming Quell was right about the *Dare* being in the Oridol Cluster at all. Assuming so many things.

*You did all you could,* Quell told herself. She'd planned. She'd fought. She'd flown. She'd killed.

The rest was up to the *Dare.*

**II**

Wyl Lark waited to learn whether he and his companions would live or die.

The *Hellion's Dare* drifted in the fog of the Oridol Cluster, orbited by the dull metal forms of its surviving escort fighters. The fires aboard the frigate had been doused. Electrical arcs no longer ravaged the hull. But the ship's engines remained offline. Wyl pictured the crew cannibalizing parts from weapons and life-support systems and droids, spraying coolant onto plasma coils and sawing through half-melted conduits with laser torches. While he sat in his harness, floating through the void of space, the *Dare's* engineers were fighting against time.

Thousands of kilometers and minutes away, the Imperial cruiser-carrier was fighting the same battle. Chass na Chadic had led the B-wing pilots in their struggle to incapacitate the enemy vessel. The B-wings—despite the loss of Glothe—had succeeded, and now the carrier's complement of TIE fighters enclosed it in a protective blockade. The Imperial crew was doubtless racing to repair the ship before the *Dare* could depart.

Wyl had wondered at first why the TIEs hadn't pressed the attack. He'd asked over the comm, and Rununja had explained, "If the TIEs abandon the carrier to attack our frigate, we'll send our ships to destroy the carrier. There's no hyperdrive on a TIE fighter. We'd be dead, but without their ship they'd be stranded."

That made sense to Wyl. He told himself that (unlike certain members of Riot Squadron) he didn't mind waiting. He just needed to understand the reason.

Yet for the first half hour, he stared at his scanner and sweated into his flight suit. At any moment, the enemy might attack. At any moment, the *Dare* might signal its readiness to jump to lightspeed. To maintain focus, to maintain alertness, was agonizing. If he quieted his mind, the lights of his instruments became hypnotic; if he let the roiling in his brain rise, the situation became unbearable.

The other surviving pilots—Rununja, Sata Neek, and Skitcher in their A-wings, Merish and Chass in their B-wings—checked in every five minutes. There was no news. No enemy sightings. Merish reported a power fluctuation in one of his cannons; then, five minutes later, reported he'd fixed it.

Thirty minutes and six report cycles in, the squadron's agitation was obvious. Skitcher flew in wider loops around the *Dare* until Rununja warned him not to waste fuel. Merish repeatedly asked Rununja to relay updates from the frigate, only to grow frustrated when no updates came. Wyl nervously checked his oxygen reserves. It was foolish, he knew; he had enough air for days. But each time his eyes drifted from the gauge, they snapped back. He thought of the patched crack in his canopy—still faintly visible—and the journey through hyperspace he'd taken while his oxygen had hissed away and his head had begun to pound.

*You could have gone Home,* he told himself. He laid his head on his console and whispered to his ship, "There comes an end to every war. Someday, we'll both be finished. You and me."

He inhaled the scents of metal and sweat and the floral perfume worn by one of the engineers. It wasn't the musk of the sur-avkas he'd grown up flying, but it was familiar, and it comforted.

Sata Neek's voice broke over the comm and said, "Riot Five to Riot Ten! Chass na Chadic!"

Wyl jerked upright and looked to the scanner. There was no change in the enemy position.

Chass didn't answer.

"Chass na Chadic!" Sata Neek cried again.

"Riot Ten?" Rununja's voice came through now, low and somber.

Wyl's breath came faster. Chass had saved him from suffocation. He didn't believe in life debts, but he believed in gratitude. If she'd been ambushed . . .

*"What?"* the lime-haired Theelin finally answered, abrupt and irritable. "What happened?"

Sata Neek clacked his beak—a sound nearly indistinguishable from static. "It was as I told you. The darkest secret of Riot Squadron revealed: Wyl Lark speaks to his ship!"

The others guffawed. Wyl fell back in his harness and looked at his comm—still open and broadcasting—with dismay.

"She betrayed you, Wyl! Your ship told us everything!" Skitcher cried, and absurd though it was, Wyl couldn't honestly say he didn't feel a twinge of betrayal. Sata Neek cackled the loudest. Chass protested, saying she'd missed it, asking what *exactly* Wyl had said and how embarrassing it was.

"Why didn't you answer before, Riot Ten?" This was Rununja again, and everyone fell silent.

"I don't think you want to know," Chass said. It sounded like a challenge. She'd never much liked Rununja.

"I might surprise you," Rununja said. "Or you might surprise me."

They waited. Then the answer came, soft at first, like metal vibrating so fast it hummed. The bass vye and the synthtone came through, and then the words, accompanied by Chass's husky, unselfconscious wails: *Red lights, dead state, we're gonna win too late . . .* The music was simplistic and overwrought and intimate all at once, and Wyl laughed. In that one instant, he loved Chass na Chadic more than anyone in the galaxy.

Sata Neek praised Chass's singing and Skitcher berated her ("Sheldra-Ko is barely music! It's a thousand years of art stapled onto insipid lyrics . . .") and Rununja, to Wyl's surprise, permitted it. When the pilots finished mocking Chass they returned to mocking Wyl; and when that was done, they began speaking of their lost colleagues again, of Nasi and Sonogari and Rep Boy and all the others. They spoke of cantinas and romances and pranks, and Chass sneered until Sata Neek reminded her that she, too, was now a part of Riot Squadron.

Wyl didn't forget to watch his scanner. But the time passed more easily, and he rarely looked at his oxygen gauge.

These are some of the stories they told.

Sata Neek spoke of his homeworld. "Coral reefs tall as the sky and sharp as knives! I would show you all, but I fear it is not what I remember. It's been too long since I returned, and I think I never will; I do not wonder what the Empire has done to Tibrin."

Rununja told of her early days as a rebel, when she had flown under the legendary General Dodonna. After she finished, she hesitated a long while before saying, "I wasn't a good woman before I joined the Rebel Alliance. I've tried to be a good leader, and I will stave off defeat so long as I have breath. But do not mourn me if I fall."

Merish wept and acknowledged that once, he'd prolonged a storm-trooper's death out of anger and rage. "He didn't deserve it," Merish whimpered. "Nobody deserves it."

Skitcher read from a book of found poetry he was assembling from fragments of comm chatter. Wyl recognized Sonogari's words and smiled.

Three hours in, with no news from the *Dare* and no movement from the Imperial cruiser-carrier, Wyl adjusted the frequency on his comm. Sata Neek was boasting about his romantic conquests again, but Wyl had heard it all before. He didn't tune Sata Neek out; he merely began a new unencrypted broadcast, transmitting to the nameless star system where they drifted: "Hello?"

He stared into the darkness and the fog. He couldn't see the Imperial cruiser-carrier, though every glimmer of dust resembled a distant TIE fighter.

"My name's Wyl. Tell me the waiting's not getting to you, too."

Sata Neek had stopped talking. All of Riot Squadron had stopped talking. They were listening to him, and they didn't interrupt or activate their jammers.

"We just spent the last hour telling stories," Wyl said, "but we know each other pretty well and we could use a fresh voice or two."

He squeezed his eyes shut; tried to imagine the TIE pilots in their flight suits, watching their own scanners and their oxygen gauges, listening to his voice.

"You missed the singing. I swear I don't have any plan here—we all know we're going to go back to fighting. But unless your ship's about to start moving, what would it hurt to talk?"

"You're an idiot, Wyl Lark." It was Chass's voice, followed by Skitcher's laughter—all of it on the open channel.

*Maybe,* he thought. *But I tried.*

Another hour passed before a smooth, low voice punctuated by static said, "Wyl Lark?"

Wyl tuned out Chass and Sata Neek's flirtations and startled upright in his harness. "I'm still here," he said.

"A-wing or B-wing?" the voice asked.

"A-wing."

"Identifying markings?"

"I clipped one of you a few days back—scraped up my canopy, almost broke it," Wyl said. He was trembling, but he couldn't help smiling. "Almost lost a cannon in the same fight."

"I saw," the voice said. "I've only got one cannon left myself."

*Blink,* Wyl thought. He was talking to Blink. He didn't quite restrain a laugh. "It's really good to meet you."

"Even under the circumstances?"

"Especially under the circumstances."

Wyl had never talked to a TIE pilot before. He'd barely talked to any Imperial troops—they hadn't prowled Polyneus like they had his friends' worlds, and Riot Squadron hadn't been given many chances to fraternize with its enemies.

So many of his friends were dead because of Blink and Blink's friends.

"So," Blink said. "You ever hear the myths around the Oridol Cluster?"

"I haven't," Wyl said. "Tell me everything." He checked his scanner and set Riot's channel to low volume.

Blink spoke slowly, shaping words with a craftsman's lazy confidence. "The Tangrada-Nii people—that's a culture, not a species—they said Oridol was the face of one of their gods, back in the days when gods were still something to be feared. Before we learned to kill planets on our own."

Wyl couldn't tell the pilot's species—human, he assumed—or gender. He couldn't picture a face beneath the Imperial flight mask.

"They were wrong, of course," Blink went on, "but their descendants—called the Tagra-Tel—sent hundreds of ships into the cluster over the course of centuries. They still revered the cluster in their way. During these long journeys, they experienced strange hallucinations—the light of Oridol suns, scattered and refracted by cosmic dust, crept into the ships and into the optic nerves of the travelers. Into the eyes and into the brain.

"Sometimes the Tagra-Tel imagined the Oridol god speaking to them. Sometimes they heard the voices of their dead, or saw the dust coming to swallow them. But most often, they dreamed of their own hearts pumping blood and of blossoms bursting from tree branches.

"That's how the Tagra-Tel came to conclude that the Oridol Cluster was alive. Not a god, but a vast, organic *thing* of dust and gas and energy, with a brain of starlight and crystal limbs. They would have said you and I are inside a life-form, and that all our battles are meaningless next to its vast antiquity."

Wyl heard no joy in Blink's voice. No wonder.

"It's a beautiful myth," Wyl said.

"You're going to rot here, Wyl Lark."

Wyl's breath caught. Blink kept speaking. "The Oridol god passes judgment on those who enter, and you and your comrades have been tested. You're going to be food in its guts, and if it bothers you to think your enemies don't want to *talk,* you can believe this is the voice of the cluster speaking—"

The comm filled with static. Wyl turned dials with fumbling hands until the sound abruptly dissipated.

"Ten-second jammer burst. Figured I'd cut off the signal for you," Rununja said. "No one worth talking to out there."

Wyl found that he agreed. "Thanks," he said.

"You all right?" Rununja asked.

"I'm fine. I really am."

Blink didn't speak again, but not long afterward, the enemy began broadcasting a series of Imperial marches and propaganda lectures. Wyl didn't tune to the open channel again.

In the end, it was the cruiser-carrier that moved first. There was no foreboding rumble or brilliant flare of thruster fire—just a shimmer on Riot Squadron's long-range scanners that meant the battle was about to resume.

"They're pulling away," Rununja called. "Cruiser-carrier withdrawing to safety and TIE squadrons incoming. They want the kill."

"Status of the *Dare*?" Sata Neek asked.

"Nearly ready." In Rununja's voice, Wyl heard: *Not ready enough.* "The *Dare* has already calculated the jump to lightspeed—we just need to buy her time to finish repairs."

"How much time?" Skitcher asked.

"I don't know," Rununja said.

There was silence on the comm. A dozen scanner blips brightened as the TIEs drew closer.

"There's another option," Rununja said—*Riot Leader* said. "We can run. We have functioning hyperdrives, even if the *Dare* does not. We could leave the frigate behind." She spoke dispassionately, as if posing a hypothetical.

"You're joking," Chass said. "You're joking."

"No," Wyl said, almost speaking over Chass. "We stay and fight."

"We stay and fight," Skitcher said.

"Stay and fight." Sata Neek, then Merish.

Rununja sounded approving as she echoed, "Stay and fight. We are united." Her voice regained its authoritative foundation. "B-wings stay close to the *Dare*—no point conserving ammunition, so use your proton torpedoes if you have a reason. A-wings, I want Riot Three and Riot Five off the *Dare*'s stern. Riot Four and I will take the bow.

"Beyond that, any plan is nonsense. You know how to fly. Stay alert, communicate, and may the Force be with you."

Wyl broke off with Sata Neek, curving toward the dark engines of the *Hellion's Dare*. The TIE fighters had already englobed the frigate and its escorts at a distance, and emerald fire lashed toward the Riot ships. The opening volley was only a provocation, not meant to do damage, and the particle bolts failed to strike metal; but the TIEs didn't stop firing as they drew near, and Wyl saw the *Dare*'s shields shimmer as the first bolts made contact.

Then the TIEs were upon them, and the fight began in earnest.

Wyl and Sata Neek called out to each other as they sped through the emerald storm and wove dizzying patterns. The enemy knew exactly how to space themselves to avoid friendly fire; how to target two rebel ships deep in their midst. Yet each moment that passed was a New Republic victory. Every shot aimed at Wyl was a shot not targeting the *Hellion's Dare*.

The other Riot pilots had engaged as well. Wyl listened to their chatter against the howl of his engines and the electric pumping of his cannons. Foolishly, he wondered: *What music is Chass playing now?*

He shouted a warning as he glimpsed carbon-scored Char head toward the *Dare's* sensor array. Together with Sata Neek, he spun his ship and chased a TIE through the chaos. His targeting computer pinged as he fired and Skitcher called: "Riot Leader is gone! Rununja's gone!" Wyl could do nothing for Rununja or Skitcher. His target erupted in flame and a swift exhalation was the closest thing to a cheer he could muster. He recognized the Twins sweep toward him in their perfectly mirrored TIEs and—knowing their patterns—slipped between them to escape.

"Riot Three!"

Sata Neek was calling him. Wyl swept his gaze across the field of fog and emerald fire, then down to his scanner.

"Wyl Lark, you fleshy peasant boy! Assist me!"

He located Sata Neek and fired a volley at the TIE fighter pursuing his partner. "You're clear!" he said.

Chass's voice came through. "They got Merish," she cried, as if it were a victory, "and now they're coming for me!"

Sata Neek responded instantly, breaking toward the *Hellion's Dare*. Wyl followed, and the TIEs followed him. He could see the crackling of the *Dare's* shields and eruptions along its hull where the shields had been pierced. His own ship leapt and jerked as particle bolts struck his aft deflector. He kissed the instrument panel. "For luck," he said.

He saw the spinning cross of Chass's B-wing against the background of the frigate. Her laser cannon and auto blasters burned, scattering TIEs intent on flanking the lone starfighter. Wyl saw Sata Neek's A-wing sweep in to intercept an enemy fighter that had survived the curtain of destruction; the TIE disappeared in a flurry of crimson particle bolts before Sata Neek's fighter, too, was reduced to a stream of ash and sparks and molten metal.

Wyl didn't see the fighter responsible. He blinked back stinging tears. "Riot Three to *Hellion's Dare*," he called. "We don't have long."

Chass was swearing, asking: "Where's Sata Neek? Where's Sata Neek?" Skitcher was calling for help. Wyl was no longer defending the *Dare* or distracting the TIEs—all he could do was try to escape death as it pursued him, surrounded him, pinned him down. His cannons pulsed, rhythmically tearing through fog, crimson painting the battlefield but failing to destroy anything. Below him, the hull of the *Dare* sped past, rippling with excess energy.

His navigation systems were blinking. Lowering his eyes to his screens was a risk; he did so anyway, and saw that the *Dare* had beamed him a set of jump coordinates along with an encrypted data package.

"Riot Three to *Hellion's Dare*—transmission received. Are we going?"

No one answered.

Was he supposed to wait? Was he supposed to run?

He saw a TIE fighter whip past him, ignore him, firing a single cannon like a blinking eye into the *Dare*.

Skitcher screamed over the comm.

"Riot—" Wyl couldn't remember Chass's designation. "Chass!" he yelled. "Chass!"

He rounded the bow of the *Dare* and turned, dipping under the bridge compartment. He was flying too close, but he'd be dead in moments if he left the frigate's cover. "We need to go," he cried. "We've got jump coordinates! They sent them for a reason. We need—"

She shouted back over the wailing brass of her music, "Are you kidding? We're not leaving them!"

He checked her position and spun his starfighter, flying between two TIEs as he tried to reach her. "Their engines are offline! We need—"

"They killed your buddy! They killed Sata Neek!"

They had. They'd killed everyone but Chass. He couldn't afford to think of that now, any more than he could think about Blink.

"Chass, please—"

His shield flickered bright enough that for an instant, he couldn't see where he was flying. He navigated by his instruments, and when the iridescent shimmering passed he spotted Chass ahead of him, spinning and firing and killing like a wheel of devastation.

He didn't know why he did what he did next. Anger or fear or love or gratitude overwhelmed him. In his mind's eye, he saw Chass dying and the *Dare* tearing apart in two massive broken sections before bursting in an explosion bright enough to shame a nova. He couldn't save the *Dare*, but he could save Chass.

He lined up the B-wing in his sights. He watched the cross-shaped ship spin. He timed his shot and squeezed his trigger.

Bolts flashed from the A-wing. The crossbar of the B-wing bled sparks as his blasts sheared off one of the assault fighter's cannons. Chass cursed again as Wyl took position near the slower vessel and said, "You can't fight back, and I won't let you try. We're going."

Chass said something in a language Wyl didn't recognize. Her voice was thick with loathing and sorrow.

Together, they ran the gauntlet of TIEs one final time. Together, they jumped to lightspeed and away from the *Hellion's Dare*. The freighter burned behind them like a star.

They didn't speak. Wyl didn't push because there was nothing to say. Instead they floated in clouds of shining white caressed by rays of jade and cornflower blue and violet. If the Oridol Cluster was a living creature, Wyl thought, they had surely found their way to its mind— birthplace of dreams and nightmares, an infinite expanse in which two lonely starfighters could be lost forever.

Maybe Blink was right. Maybe the Oridol god had judged them. Having been deemed unworthy, they were now beneath its notice.

"Screw all this," Chass occasionally muttered through the comm. That was the extent of their conversation.

Their onboard computers, linked together, attempted to plot a course toward the limits of the cluster. Toward freedom. The *Hellion's*

*Dare* had needed hours to calculate each jump; an A-wing and a B-wing, working together, might take days. Wyl didn't know whether the Empire's cruiser-carrier would come following, but if not, there were still limits to the rebel fighters' food, water, and oxygen supplies. Wyl and Chass might have fled a battle and turned their backs on their colleagues only to suffocate.

Wyl thought of Sata Neek and Rununja. He thought of the captain of the *Dare* and the droids aboard that no one ever seemed to care about. He thought of Home, and his brothers and sisters, and began to weep when he had difficulty recalling their faces.

"We have a mission," he told Chass. "We have a message from the *Dare* for the New Republic."

He told the same thing to his ship and received just as warm a reply. He laid his head upon his console and whispered, "Take me Home. Take me Home."

Then a miracle found them.

Wyl followed the message of light.

### III

Caern Adan drank in private. Not because he was ashamed, but because he wasn't. Because he saw enough horrors in the course of his work, feared enough of the outcomes he projected, confronted enough excruciating memories during an average day, that he had more than earned the privilege of a bottle before bedtime.

Besides, no one trusted a spy who drank. Not even if that *spy* was just an analyst. So it wasn't like he had the option of company.

He was enjoying a bottle of Corellian red in his cramped-but-private cabin when the alert came in. He fumbled his way into a shirt as he read the notification: Two single-occupant vessels had just jumped into the Harrikos system within sensor range of the *Buried Treasure*, apparently emerging from the Oridol Cluster.

It wasn't the *Hellion's Dare,* but it was a promising sign. If the frigate *had* met up with one of the probe droids launched from the Harrikos research outpost—received hyperspace coordinates leading out of the cluster's mire—the *Dare's* captain might well have sent scout ships ahead.

Caern was pleased. He had been right. (Quell had been right, but he had been right about Quell.) He was halfway to the bridge when an ensign intercepted him and steered him in the opposite direction. The captain had already spoken to one of the pilots, and the ships—an A-wing and a B-wing, both low on fuel and oxygen—would arrive in the hangar presently.

Quell and Tensent, along with a security detail, were already in the hangar when Caern arrived. *Who told them?* he wondered before lifting his eyes to the magnetic containment field. Gliding in on the *Treasure's* tractor beam came two distant white objects, swiftly resolving into the shapes of starfighters.

"They're scouts," Quell said. She was almost gaunt, as if she'd taken on a fever, but she was no longer wearing her sling. She didn't look at Caern, and instead stared fixedly at the fighters. "The *Dare's* captain won't follow our probes without knowing it's safe."

*Obviously.* Quell's ego was swelling daily, and she knew her reputation was at stake. *You shouldn't have let her steal a ship, Caern.*

Tensent grunted skeptically but didn't comment. Caern appreciated that about the man. He'd accomplished less than Quell but he knew his place in the working group and his loyalty was not in doubt.

Caern wondered where the last of his people had gone. He'd secured Tensent's loyalty, but Kairos was the one he *trusted* more than anyone in the galaxy. She had earned his faith long ago, and he had earned hers.

The first vessel into the hangar was a battered and scarred B-wing. Its strike foils were still spread for combat, apparently due to shearing and servo damage. Yet it couldn't land with the foils open, and the pilot must have realized it; the hangar filled with a metallic grinding and an acrid scent as the foils wheezed and stuttered and finally half folded enough to let the ship touch the deck.

The second ship approached the magnetic field as the security officers surrounded the B-wing and lifted the pilot from the cockpit. The woman was green-haired, compact and muscular, with thorny studs of flesh protruding from her temples. She stumbled down the cockpit ladder and was caught quickly by the security team.

"What's wrong with her?" Caern asked. He suddenly wished IT-O had come with him.

Quell's body and balance shifted beside Caern as if she wanted to run to the B-wing. She stopped herself, but she still looked like a hound on a leash. "Muscle fatigue," she said. "Dehydration."

"Probably been in there more than a day," Tensent added. "Not a lot of room to stretch in a B-wing cockpit.

The second ship—the A-wing—had touched down by now, and the B-wing's pilot struggled against the security officers, pulling away to hobble toward the other vessel. As the A-wing's canopy slid back, the man inside—the boy, really, dark-haired and olive-skinned—cried hoarsely, "There's a message!" He nearly collapsed as he clambered onto the wing of his ship. "Check the computer. There's a message."

"A message?" Caern called, as Quell silently mouthed the same words. "From who?"

But the boy ignored him, dropping clumsily off the ship's wing and wrapping his arms around the woman pilot. The security officers gave them room. Caern hurried over. The boy was mumbling something Caern couldn't hear—asking about the woman's health, maybe—and the woman was gripping his chin, lifting his head and looking into his eyes. "You're dehydrated and tired," one of the *Treasure*'s officers said, "but you're both safe now. You'll be fine."

Maybe it was the words *you'll be fine* that set them off. Caern couldn't tell, but in an instant the group was in chaos and everyone was shouting as one pilot wrestled the other to the ground. The woman straddled the boy, pounding her fists into his back and screaming, "You hear that? You're fine! You're fine and your whole *squadron* is dead—" Caern watched as two of the security officers tore the woman off her victim and Quell dashed to the boy's side. She was asking questions ("Who's dead?" "What happened?") almost lost under the woman's shouts.

Behind Caern, Tensent laughed. "This is who we rescued?"

Their names were Wyl Lark and Chass na Chadic. Two pilots without a unit. Two pilots who had survived the destruction of the *Hellion's Dare* by the 204th Imperial Fighter Wing and brought home a message—a data package containing everything the *Dare* had discovered during its reconnaissance mission.

The data package would take time to analyze. There was promising intelligence within, but Caern suspected even the crew of the *Dare* hadn't understood what it meant. They certainly hadn't organized it with clarity or ease of processing in mind. Yet even if the data proved useless, he felt confident that Shadow Wing was responsible for the attacks that had whittled away Lark and Chadic's squadrons—Quell's hypothesis about Jiruus fit too neatly, as did the pilots' descriptions of enemy tactics.

All in all, he decided, Lark and Chadic's recovery was a significant step forward for the working group.

(He wondered briefly whether anyone would hold him responsible for the *Dare*'s destruction—for not finding it sooner, really—but banished the thought just as quickly. Without him, the *Dare* and all its pilots would be dead in the Oridol Cluster, and no one would even know.)

"First priority," he told IT-O the afternoon after the pilots' arrival, "is to finish reviewing the data. I'm doing an initial sort before sending it home. If headquarters starts asking questions, I want to be able to answer them."

The droid observed him in the nearly empty conference room. "Will you be debriefing the pilots individually?" IT-O asked.

Both Chadic and Lark had spent the night in the medbay before summarizing their journey to Caern and the *Treasure*'s captain in the morning. Caern had sent IT-O in afterward; the droid's bedside manner was superior to his own. "I'd like to," Caern said, "but I want your impressions first."

"They've both suffered a great deal in recent days."

Caern let out a bark of a laugh. At another time he might have held it in, but he could express himself freely in front of IT-O. "They were *dehydrated*," he said. "Not exactly what I'd call suffering."

"They saw their comrades die. Neither currently has a social support system in place. Both feel responsible for what occurred—"

"You said they'd *suffered*," Caern snapped. "You know what suffering is. *I* know what suffering is."

"Their pain does not diminish yours," IT-O said.

Caern waved briskly, trying to move the conversation forward. "So you finished your interviews. I've pulled their personnel files. Spotty, obviously—" The Rebel Alliance hadn't been fond of record keeping. Its reasoning had been sound, but the New Republic was paying the price. "—but by all reports they're both capable pilots. And they survived, which is a point in their favor."

"Nothing otherwise remarkable?" the droid asked.

"No medals. The boy's homeworld has an interesting history, the woman is lucky to be alive twice over. No serious discipline problems recorded with either, but you know how reliable those assessments are. The most important question—" He frowned, drawn into the gravity of his own thoughts. "Are they right for the working group?"

"You intend to recruit them?"

"I intend—" He heard the impatience in his voice. IT-O didn't need to know the logic behind his decisions—but the droid had a way of helping him solidify his reasoning. "If the data we received is useful, there's a real chance the military will try to appropriate our operation. If the data *isn't* useful, we're certainly not receiving additional support. Either way, we've got a very narrow window before Lark and Chadic, along with their starfighters, are reassigned elsewhere in the fleet."

"So it isn't so much that you want *them*," IT-O said, "as that you see an opportunity to expand your working group and fear other opportunities won't come."

"I wouldn't have put it so cynically, but yes. Plus, I want their ships." He thought of justifying himself further—of reminding IT-O of the immediate threat they faced and the long-term ramifications of leaving New Republic security in the hands of the military—but the droid hadn't forgotten and Caern refused to be distracted. "So . . . ?"

The droid was silent, running assessments. Caern waited.

"I believe Chass na Chadic will join if you emphasize the threat that the 204th Fighter Wing poses. Be clear that she will participate in its elimination. Do not press her to decide rapidly. Do not emphasize the need to avenge her squadron. She will not respond well to overt manipulation."

"And once we have her?"

"That's beyond what I can predict from a single conversation. Her personnel record is a better guide than my profile."

*Evasive answer,* Caern thought, *but plausible.* "All right," he said. "What about the boy?"

"Wyl Lark will prove more difficult."

The droid stopped.

Caern waited. Finally, he prompted, "*Why* will he be difficult?"

"He spoke to me in confidence. I am reluctant to break that trust—"

"Please," Caern scoffed.

"—but I observe that he has already made one official request to be discharged from his duties and allowed to return to his homeworld. I believe a discharge remains the best means of preserving his physical and psychological well-being."

"Of course it is. War isn't *healthy,* but we keep doing it. What if I want to keep him?"

"He is devoted to his comrades. Argue that the working group represents the continuation of Riot Squadron's mission. Inform him that Chass na Chadic has already joined you. He will assent under pressure."

"Wonderful." Just what he needed: a fragile boy he'd need to coax into producing results. "Anything else I should know about him?"

"He is afraid."

*Even better.*

Caern considered the resources before him. Five operatives and five starfighters that hadn't yet been claimed, reclaimed, or requisitioned by the New Republic military. Those operatives ranged from absolutely reliable to—well, to Yrica Quell. Put together, they were barely enough to mount a raid.

But the work was necessary.

He'd spoken with Chief of Intelligence Cracken while Kairos, Quell, and IT-O had been at the Entropian Hive. The conversation had been brief, but the chief had made it clear that Shadow Wing was a secondary concern for the provisional government: that the unit responsible for massacres at Grumwall and Mek'tradi and Nacronis—*Nacronis*, where a whole planet had been slaughtered!—was, in the eyes of the New Republic, a drop in a sea of Imperial holdouts.

The Senate wanted the remnants of the Empire to surrender all as one. The military thought it could break the enemy's spine, forgetting the beast had already been beheaded. Only Intelligence understood the painstaking work of disassembling the Empire piece by piece.

Five operatives and five starships would have to suffice.

"One last thing," Caern said. "I'd like you to push harder with Quell."

The droid dilated its photoreceptor. "May I ask why?"

"You told me she was lying about something. She still is, and she's starting to get cocky." Caern cut the droid off before it could interject. "*Don't* say it. My threshold may be low but she's already disobeying orders, no matter how contrite she claims to be."

"I don't disagree," IT-O said. "I recommended against her recruitment."

"You did, and you were wrong. Let's make sure things stay that way." *Solve the problem now before she becomes a distraction.* "Push her. I'll see what I can find on my end. And if we don't discover anything soon . . ."

"Yes?"

"Watch out for a replacement. We can always toss Yrica Quell back to Traitor's Remorse."

# IV

The torture droid had made the arrangements, though Quell didn't know whether the droid or Adan was ultimately responsible. One way or another, the mess hall of the *Buried Treasure* had been cleared and—the IT-O unit had told her—a crate of produce defrosted and given to the galley droids. The temperature had been adjusted for optimum comfort. There were few other luxuries the crew could offer, but this was an occasion to celebrate.

Quell hesitated at the entryway, drew a breath, and reminded herself what was expected of her and why. She wasn't in a celebratory mood. She wasn't close to achieving her goal. But she was closer than she'd ever been, and the people inside needed her.

She needed them, too.

She tapped the door's control panel. The metal panel slid open, and she stepped past Kairos (who loomed inside, motionless, like a sentry). At the central table, seated around platters of apparently untouched finger food—cuts of fruit, miniature flatbread sandwiches, and a sweet- and musty-smelling bowl of crushed *something*—were three humanoid figures.

Nath Tensent was holding court, his boots on the tabletop as he spoke. "—never got to board one of those big Mon Cala–built star cruisers. Always wanted to. I hear they've got water tanks for—" He cocked his head and grinned in Quell's direction. "Lieutenant Yrica Quell, everyone. Say hello."

A young man stood. He looked healthier than the last time Quell had seen him, when he'd been carted to the medbay by the *Buried Treasure*'s crew; but now dressed in civvies instead of a flight suit, he seemed thinner than before. He extended a hand and Quell took it. "Wyl Lark," he said. He squeezed her hand without gripping. "It's good to meet you properly."

The third figure—the green-haired Theelin who'd piloted the B-wing—stood more slowly than Lark. "You're the one who found us?" she asked, shifting her weight as if ready for a fight.

Quell met the woman's gaze. "We all did," she said. "Tensent, Adan, Kairos, and me." She paused, then added: "I'm sorry we weren't in time to save the *Dare*."

She wondered how sincere she sounded—she'd never been any good at conveying empathy, no matter how real.

Chadic only shrugged. "Same here. Not your fault. Your boss from intelligence said you defected a while back, so—thanks."

Lark bowed his head. Chadic avoided looking toward him. Tensent, still seated, added, "Quell was there for Operation Cinder. Nearly got herself killed trying to save Nacronis. Woman's a hero all around."

The right thing to do would have been to deflect the praise or find something generous to share about Tensent. Quell only managed to nod awkwardly. It wasn't a subject she cared to dwell upon.

This was the working group now. Gathered together for the first time to celebrate one victory and begin planning the next. Staring in silence. At least Lark and Chadic weren't trying to kill each other.

Tensent snapped up a wedge of fruit, swallowed it, then rose to his feet. "If we're done with the party," he said, "maybe it's time we got to work."

Without speaking, they seemed to come to an agreement. Their postures changed. They transformed from patients into pilots, and even Kairos stepped away from the door to join the circle.

"Maybe we should start," Quell said, "by talking about Shadow Wing."

# CHAPTER 7

## GUIDANCE SYSTEM

I

The stranger arrived in Tinker-Town on foot, a duffel slung over each shoulder. Chestnut hair and a ragged, gray-specked beard gave him the unkempt appearance of a local, but the waterproof poncho gave his foreignness away—the people of Tinker-Town had made their peace with the rain.

He strolled down narrow streets, dim in the dreary midafternoon, past neon signs for junk dealers and droid repair shops and pawnbrokers. Metal scaffolding spread from building to building like creeping vines, and the gutter-water was the dull brown of rust flakes. If Tinker-Town had ever been a lively place, it had been during the heyday of Greater Xnapolis; and that city's glory had faded over twenty years earlier, when the Empire had cut resources to Mrinzebon and declared the colony a failure.

The spindly, amputated arm of an IG-series droid waved cheerfully above the entrance to Gannory's Cantina as the stranger marched inside. The cantina's interior was dark save for the light of the tabletops, and paint buckets caught water dripping from ceiling panels. But the surfaces were spotless and the smell of caf and stronger beverages was rich and appealing. The stranger lifted his chin as he approached the bar.

"Hello?" he called.

A topknotted Cerean, head tall as a human's torso, emerged from a doorway behind the bar. His hair was white and his face deeply lined, giving him the appearance of advanced age.

*You haven't met many of his kind,* the stranger reminded himself. *For all you know, they age in reverse.*

"Not so much business at this hour," the Cerean said, by way of apology. "Not so much business *most* hours. Here to drink?"

The stranger hadn't slid the duffels from his shoulders, and he didn't now. "I'm afraid not," he said. "I'm carrying salvage and looking to sell. Can you help me?"

The Cerean eyed the bags, then studied the stranger's face. "What've you got?"

"Power dampers. Stabilizing coil. Pressor control chip. Cold-weld arrestors. More besides, and tools."

The Cerean nodded, apparently deferring a decision rather than rendering one. "How fast are you looking to sell, and how much profit are you looking to make?"

"I'm in no hurry," the stranger said. "But I'd rather not spend the week haggling just to get a fair price." For the first time, thin lips ventured a smile. "You'd know what's fair around these parts better than I."

"You'll want Narlowe, then. Talk your ear off but she'll take it all off your hands. Third street on your right if you head straight out, end of the block."

The stranger nodded, slipped a hand into his pocket without adjusting the balance of the duffels, and withdrew a single Imperial credit chip. He slid it across the bartop toward the Cerean. "That's the last I've got," he said. "But I'll be back for a drink when I'm through selling."

The Cerean said nothing. The stranger left, maintaining the same steady pace with which he'd entered, moving out of the gloom of the cantina and into the gloom of the rain. He passed two intersections, then turned into an underpass running beneath a decrepit tram line.

The tunnel smelled of acrid mildew. Perhaps on Mrinzebon, the stranger thought, that was a natural scent. If so, it couldn't have helped attract colonists.

He was twelve steps into the dark when a rough voice demanded, "Turn around. Drop the bags."

The stranger turned around. He did not drop the bags. Wreathed in shadows were two bulky forms: One a jawless, toothy, and funnel-mouthed humanoid whose species the stranger failed to recognize; the other a Meftian in black leather, ivory hair matted by the rain. Neither carried a visible weapon.

"Drop the bags," the Meftian repeated.

"I have a right to my belongings," the stranger said. "I'm not looking for trouble."

The two figures approached. The Meftian grasped a duffel by its straps and yanked it from the stranger's shoulder, tossing it aside with a grunt. He repeated the motion with the second bag as the funnel-mouthed being circled behind the lone human.

"You have no rights," the Meftian said, and drove his fist into the stranger's stomach. The human bent over but did not fall. The Meftian struck him again.

Then again.

The stranger fell to his knees. The Meftian kicked his shoulder with a booted foot; slammed both fists atop the stranger's skull. Soon the funnel-mouthed humanoid joined the assault. The stranger absorbed each blow, protecting his vitals as well as he could and offering no resistance. When his attackers stepped away, his lip was bloody and his left eye was bruised and swollen. His poncho was torn and covered in mud.

The two assailants left the stranger behind, taking the duffels with them.

A short while later, the stranger rose. He gingerly touched his face, ribs, and legs, examining his injuries. He swayed when he took his first few steps, but steadied quickly before returning the way he had come.

Back past two intersections. Back to the waving droid arm and through the doorway to Gannory's Cantina.

"Hello?" he called, and again the topknotted Cerean emerged.

Upon seeing the stranger's injuries, the barkeep stepped back abruptly. "What happened?" he asked.

"You know what happened," the stranger said. His voice was uninflected yet rigid as iron. "You informed them I was coming."

"I did nothing!" the Cerean cried. He marched forward and slapped a trembling palm onto the bartop. Thick veins lined the back of his hand. "You should leave, sir. If you go into Xnapolis proper, you'll find a clinic and—"

The Cerean stopped speaking. From beneath his poncho, the stranger had drawn a hold-out pistol. He gripped it in a steady hand, aiming squarely at the barkeep's chest.

"You informed them I was coming," the stranger said.

Very slowly, the Cerean nodded.

The stranger canted his head toward the empty tables.

"We should talk," he said.

The Cerean introduced himself as Gannory. The stranger called himself Devon, and didn't show his pistol again after they sat down with two cups of caf. "No one deserves to weather what you weathered," Gannory said as they settled in, and this was the closest he came to an apology.

Devon didn't press for contrition. "Are you in league with them?" he asked, and when Gannory hesitated he clarified: "Are you part of an organization? Do you receive a cut of their take?" The Cerean assured him that, no, he was not *in league* with the beings who had stolen from Devon. He was neither victim nor perpetrator, but somewhere in between.

"They ask that I supply information," Gannory said, "that they may use to line their pockets. If I refuse, they'll burn my establishment to the ground; or burn me to the ground and take my establishment. If I hadn't turned you over, I'd have given them someone else this week—someone local. A friend, perhaps, or a friend of a friend."

"Better to protect your people and sacrifice a stranger," Devon said. There was no judgment in his voice.

"Better," Gannory agreed, "but not best."

Devon's attackers, Gannory said, belonged to a gang with no name—a gang of significance only to the people of Tinker-Town. "Once, the Empire kept their sort under control. There was still *crime,* of course, but criminals' ambitions were curtailed."

Gannory described, between sips of his beverage, the abandonment of Mrinzebon's garrison after the news of the Emperor's death; the riots and looting that followed in Greater Xnapolis; and the establishment of a new status quo. "Not quite anarchy, not quite order," Gannory said. "Strange, how swiftly it becomes normal."

"I can imagine," Devon replied. He'd commented little during the bulk of Gannory's story, simply listening and studying the Cerean. Now he tapped his empty tin caf cup like he was sending a coded message, producing unpredictable, staccato beats. "Would you go back, if you could?"

"Would I return the Empire to Mrinzebon?"

Devon nodded.

"If I had such power," Gannory said, "I'd use it to change a great many things. But I don't, so I don't think on it."

Devon grunted. The sound might have been a laugh. "No one fights the gang?" he asked.

"We've seen clones and battle droids march through these streets before," Gannory said. "No one here has an appetite for war."

"Self-defense, then," Devon said. "To protect your establishment."

"We've few weapons, and no training. Those who did joined the Rebellion—or joined the gangs."

Devon stopped tapping, then steepled his hands. His eyes fixed on his nails, three of which were encrusted with dried blood.

"I could train you," he said. Gannory began to object, but Devon continued, "You and anyone else who wants it. Not well—not as soldiers—but well enough to convince your gang to go elsewhere in Xnapolis. Some other neighborhood with easier prey."

He spoke with unflinching certitude despite the bruises on his face and the stains on his poncho. Gannory stared at the stranger who'd marched twice into his cantina and shook his head in refusal or disbelief.

"And your price?" Gannory asked.

"The credit chip I gave you," Devon said. "Return it, and we'll call the price paid."

The stranger Devon did as he promised.

Gannory found Devon his students—his recruits—as Gannory had once found Tinker-Town's gang its victims. In chatting with his customers and conversing with his family, he located neighborhood residents whose resentment contained the seed of determination. He sent these on to Devon, who spent his days in the Cerean's garden behind the cantina.

There, Devon taught. Devon fought.

He showed Gannory how to construct a single-shot stun weapon from the corroded blaster batteries that lined the garden's flower boxes, and how to judge whether an opponent could absorb the bolt and stay conscious. He showed Narlowe the junk dealer how to improvise a shock prod from an R2 unit's arc welder. He showed Shonessa and Brorn, who lived above the tram stop, where to strike to do maximum damage to human or Meftian anatomy.

He taught these people and others how to estimate their odds of winning a battle. He taught them when and how to run; when and how to join together and back one another up. Their goal, he explained, was not victory but deterrence; where deterrence failed, their goal would be survival. The lessons he taught were simple ones, but Devon had met the opponents the people of Tinker-Town would face. "Simple lessons," he told them, "will be enough."

He did not befriend his students. He told them nothing of how he'd learned his skills and didn't ask about their dreams or the tragedies in their pasts. Only with Gannory did he let his guard down, and then only twice—once as they returned the garden furniture to its proper place after a day's lessons, when they spoke of the incessant rain and their shared love of the weather-orchestras of Cousault; and once when Gannory saw Devon wince in pain from turning his bruised torso, and the human allowed the Cerean to bring him painkillers and ice.

Just as Devon did not befriend his students, neither did he protect them. When their first confrontation with the gang's thugs occurred, he was dining on baked tubers on the balcony of his flophouse. He heard a report of the scuffle the next morning and critiqued the performance of those involved—they had, he said, been overeager to protect their shop's earnings, but they'd done well all the same.

During the following week, his classes doubled in size. He began allowing his students to become instructors.

He was not surprised when, one night after he'd retired to his room, the Meftian pried his door open and said, "Come with me."

Devon touched his eye, recalling pain and swollen skin. He chose to cooperate.

They marched him through the streets to a teetering communications tower on the border between Tinker-Town and Little Neimoidia. There were three of them—the Meftian, the funnel-mouthed humanoid, and a short, stubby human woman who wore cheap cybernetics like a shirt. They pushed Devon and yanked him by the arm and generally abused but did not harm him during the walk. The few witnesses on the road swiftly hurried on.

They strode past guards and onto a cargo lift and emerged in a room part penthouse and part command center. Aging consoles and grease-stained machinery stood beside lounge chairs and coolers and holographic displays. Bull's-eye windows admitted pink and emerald light from billboards passing by on their Xnapolis circuit. Seated atop an intricately carved wooden desk at the room's center was a skinny human male barely older than Devon, wearing a fashionable Coruscanti jacket over a soiled engineering jumpsuit.

"Devon the troublemaker!" the man cried as he hopped to the floor. "So good to finally meet."

The Meftian held Devon while the cyborg woman waved a boxy scanner over his body. When she was done, she snatched Devon's pistol from where it was concealed at the small of his back. The Meftian released him, and Devon said to the man, "You lead them?"

"I do," the man said. "Call me Vryant."

Devon cocked his head and looked the man up and down. When his eyes reached Vryant's boots his thin lips twitched. "Who'd you kill for those, Vryant?" he asked.

Vryant furrowed his brow, then laughed as if he understood. "I'm ashamed to say I got them the slow way, by *earning* them. Six years on Herdessa, two in the trenches of Phorsa Gedd before I was shipped here."

"You're Imperial Army?" Devon asked. His words, normally crisp as winter, sounded breathy and inchoate.

"I was," Vryant said. "But the Imperial Army isn't on Mrinzebon anymore. It's just me."

Devon stared at Vryant awhile, as if turning over the claim in his mind. Finally he nodded.

"Why am I here, Vryant?"

The Meftian shoved him between the shoulder blades. Devon stumbled. Vryant cast the Meftian a look of disapproval. "Don't do that," he said. "I'm sorry, Devon. I—well. We've got a way to go but I don't want this conversation to be hostile."

"Tell me why I'm here," Devon said.

"My impression—correct me if I'm wrong—is that you're only a visitor in Tinker-Town. You came in, found trouble, and decided to make trouble back. That's almost admirable in its simplicity. Like the echo when you yell in a cave, or the recoil on a blaster."

Devon did not correct him. Vryant continued.

"You probably thought you'd earn a few credits making weapons for the locals and move on. We stole your salvage, after all. You've got no

love of us, and you have to make a living. But that's the thing of it—"
Vryant furrowed his brow again. "Do you have a plan, Devon? A place
to move on to after Tinker-Town?"

Devon said nothing.

"Because if you do," Vryant said, "I'll pay you back for your lost salvage right now and get you a shuttle schedule. I mean it—it's no loss
for me and if it ends this feud cleanly, why not?"

"Why not, indeed?" Devon asked.

"But if you *don't* have a place to go, I have another offer." He paused,
apparently waiting for Devon to prompt him. When Devon remained
silent, he kept going. "Work for me. Live here—not in Tinker-Town, of
course, but in the better parts of Xnapolis—and help me build something. Get rich if you like. Make a name for yourself if you like. Train
my people. Bring a little order back to Mrinzebon."

"Order," Devon repeated.

Vryant heard the skepticism. "I kept these people—" He waved a
hand at the gangsters. "—on a leash when the Empire was here. Mrinzebon has always been a cesspool, and our job was to keep the bacteria
under control. Gangs would rise up, we'd stamp them back down.

"I *still* keep these people on a leash; it's just a little longer."

"Is that why you stayed when the rest of the garrison left?"

"I saw an opportunity," Vryant said. "If I hadn't stepped in, my subordinates here would still be looting shops and marking their territory.
The difference would be a lot more bloodshed."

The enhanced human spoke for the first time. "All true," she said.
The Meftian seemed to laugh, emitting a series of growls and grunts.

Devon picked his way around the furniture and approached one of
the windows. He turned his back on Vryant and the others and stared
out onto Tinker-Town as billboard lights colored him in garish pastels.

"What about the Rebellion?" Devon asked. "The New Republic?"

"Am I afraid of them, you mean? No—"

"That's not what I mean." Devon kept his eyes on the window. "I
mean—why not look to them for assistance?"

He wanted to ask more: *Did they ignore Mrinzebon's calls for help
after the Empire left? Were the gangs here so vicious, so lawless, that they*

*had to be controlled immediately? Did you simply refuse to consort with the enemies of the Empire?* Yet he remained silent. He allowed Vryant to answer.

"Devon," Vryant said, in a tone of charmed bemusement. "The rebels are far away, and besides—do you really think they would've let me keep all this?"

Devon heard a sound very like a blaster sliding from its holster. He continued staring at the rusting structures and broken tramway and bright advertisements for businesses long since abandoned.

"Payment if I leave," he said, "or a job if I stay?"

"That's my offer, yes," Vryant said.

Devon nodded joylessly.

"I've made my decision."

The communications tower on the edge of Tinker-Town burned. Smoke billowed from the top, stinking and stinging. The lower floors of the tower hadn't all caught, but the structure was groaning loud enough to be heard over the flames. It would collapse soon.

The stranger Devon strode away from the tower and Gannory watched. Devon possessed a fresh limp and often brought his sleeve to his mouth to filter out the smoke. His expression revealed nothing.

"They brought you in there, didn't they?" Gannory asked. The rain was picking up, and the old Cerean wrapped his arms around his chest. "What happened?"

"The man had a second chance," Devon said. "I wasn't going to give him a third."

Gannory stared in bafflement, then looked past Devon to the tower. "Is anyone else coming out?"

"No," Devon said.

Devon stopped four paces from Gannory. The Cerean took a step back. Part of Devon thought of their conversations in the garden; part of him hoped to hear the Cerean say, *We'll get you to the cantina. Get you warm. You can be as cryptic as you like when you've got a mug of caf in you.*

Instead Gannory closed his eyes as if to listen to the moaning of the broken tower. He said, "There's a freighter that delivers to the space-port once a week. Should be arriving tomorrow morning. On the way out in the afternoon."

"I'll be there," Devon said, and stepped around Gannory to keep walking.

He didn't look back. He didn't ask the Cerean to check in on his students. He didn't lash out and speak of *ingratitude,* or demand he be compensated for all he'd done. He thought of these things, but that wasn't who he was.

And in Gannory's place, he'd have done the same.

There was no place for him in Tinker-Town. That was well enough; Tinker-Town could find its own way, and there was plenty of room in the galaxy.

# PART TWO

## MALADIES OF AN ENDLESS WAR

# CHAPTER 8

## DISUNITY OF PURPOSE

I

Hera Syndulla had always known victory wouldn't come easy. It was a lesson reinforced by every hard choice, every sacrifice she'd made and loss she'd endured over a decade of war. *This is the beginning,* she'd told an aide before the Battle of Endor, and weren't beginnings the hardest part?

Still, she'd let her guard down. She'd let herself hope when, in truth, there was so much work ahead. She'd—

She laughed aloud at her desk. Stornvein, who'd just delivered the latest intelligence brief and was halfway out the door, stopped to look back. "Something wrong, General?"

"Plenty," she said. "But if you ever find yourself frustrated? Think back to when smuggling fruit to starving villages was a triumph for the Rebel Alliance."

"I'll do that, ma'am," Stornvein said. "A bit of perspective never hurts."

The man exited with a bow of his head, and Hera resumed reading the brief. Yinchorr had devolved into a siege situation; Arkania was caught up in ground-level fighting; and Moff Pandion was continuing to sweep up Imperial strays to add to his fleet. The picture became clearer each day: While the Imperial Navy had scattered and dissolved at the galactic level, isolated fleets were entrenching under the control of admirals and regional governors. Any planet that hadn't freed itself already would be harder to liberate tomorrow.

The Barma sector had lacked an Imperial leader charismatic or tyrannical enough to consolidate sector defenses, which was part of why Hera had taken her task force to the border. Her official mission was to reclaim as much territory as possible, swooping into systems with her ragtag flotilla of battleships and starfighters and neutralizing naval opposition for the benefit of local resistance forces. But in truth, half her time was spent triaging distress calls instead of pushing forward; the other half was spent coordinating with New Republic operations in neighboring sectors, trying to maintain some semblance of a coherent galactic strategy.

These were good and necessary tasks. The New Republic was making progress, as was the Barma Battle Group. She'd seen the horrors of Operation Cinder, and she understood the consequences of prioritizing the wrong problems. She just wished the resources available were equal to the problems she faced.

"General Syndulla?" Stornvein was back already, leaning through the doorway with an apologetic expression. "Your appointment is here. He's early, but—"

*Speaking of problems,* she thought, and made a throw-it-here gesture. "Send him in, and call security if he isn't out in thirty minutes."

Caern Adan had been demanding a meeting ever since the *Buried Treasure* had rendezvoused with her task force. Now, almost two weeks and a minor planetary invasion later, she'd cleared enough room in her schedule to deal with the analyst face-to-face.

She recognized him from his holoreports when he strutted into the room. She arched her brow at the sight of his antenna-stalks, raised at attention as if he meant to monitor the entire ship. They looked somehow like slender imitations of her own jade head-tails, each thick as an arm and running down her back. She supposed she'd get used to them in time. She'd learned not to laugh at human hair, after all.

"Officer Adan," she said, gesturing to a metal stool. "I'm sorry we've had to delay this meeting so often—" He started to reply but she kept talking. "—and I wanted to thank you again for your work with the *Hellion's Dare*. That was a tough loss, but two survivors is better than none."

Everything in the man's communiqués had reeked of self-importance. The least she could do was *try* to start out on the right foot.

"Two survivors and vital information, General," he said, and she didn't find his tone—matter-of-fact and respectful—objectionable at all. "You saw the assessment of Pandem Nai?"

She nodded. Among her many problems, Pandem Nai wasn't the most urgent—but she recognized the potential for it to grow until, like a black hole, it swallowed everything else. "Gas mining world. Resource-rich, highly defensible, and behind enemy lines. Based on the *Dare*'s recon data, New Republic Intelligence thinks an especially nasty Imperial fighter wing has taken residence there. Does that sum it up?"

"It's a start," Adan said, and Hera heard the rising impatience. "If the 204th—they call it *Shadow Wing*—has locked down Pandem Nai, they can supply half a fleet with the planet's gas mines. Shadow Wing will turn the place into a fortress and launch who-knows-how-many attacks from it. Have you seen *their* file?"

She *had* seen the file on the 204th. She'd felt a numbing dismay when she'd read about their links to Orinda and Operation Cinder. The list of the Empire's atrocities was practically endless. "Yes, and they need to be addressed. So does Moff Pandion. So does the berserker fleet carving through Hutt space—"

"Then let me propose—"

"I know what you're proposing," she snapped. She let out a long breath and forced herself to calm. "Walk with me?"

She stood without waiting for him to answer and stepped into the corridor beyond her office. Ringing metal, shouts, and droid whistles echoed—the sounds of the latest round of repairs to the *Lodestar,* an aging *Acclamator*-class battleship that had carried thousands of clone troopers in the years before the Empire. Hera suspected there wasn't a hull plate left on the vessel that hadn't been replaced; its captain called it *sturdy,* a descriptor that Hera lacked the heart to dispute. If the *Lodestar* survived to the end of the war, she'd be pleasantly surprised.

Adan hurried to keep pace as she walked. "With every hour we wait," he was saying, "Pandem Nai becomes more heavily fortified. At the rate your task force is gaining ground, it'll be weeks before you get there."

"I'm aware, yes. We can't afford to ignore Pandem Nai for long—" She held up a hand as she made the concession. "—and we can't afford the resources to attack right now. Even if we could, we don't have the intelligence to know what we'd face. You don't need to convince me of the problem. You need to convince me of your solution."

Hera turned abruptly and hopped onto a ladder leading to the lower decks. She heard Adan swear softly as they descended. "I have a small working group," he called from above. "The same group that located the *Hellion's Dare.* My group is fully trained and equipped, dedicated to cracking the problem of Shadow Wing and Pandem Nai. All we need is an operating base."

She held back a laugh as she swung off the ladder and into the lower hangar. She swept her gaze over the vast enclosure and breathed in the smell of melted plastoid. Six columns of starfighters stretched before her, and half a dozen engineering teams hurried among the vessels (Meteor and Hail Squadron fighters, mostly, with others in for maintenance from Vanguard), rearming, refueling, and repairing them. A repulsor sled stacked with concussion missiles glided past her; a droid squawked orders from a catwalk up above.

"All you need is an operating base?" Hera asked, as Adan arrived at her side. "That's your way of saying, *I want to run a personal fighter squadron out of your fleet?*"

"*Specialized*," Adan said, "not *personal*. My group is tasked with analyzing the Shadow Wing threat and developing plans to counter their tactics; obtaining information from combat zones out of reach of New Republic Intelligence; and assisting or leading direct engagements against Shadow Wing itself." Adan was quoting from his own memoranda, but Hera didn't interrupt him. "You said you don't have resources? My people come with their own ships. You said you don't have the intelligence you need? That's our top priority."

"But what your people don't have is all *this*," Hera said, gesturing to the chaos of the hangar. "You're not just asking for space aboard a cramped ship. You're asking for supplies and expertise. You'd need my ground crews, my munitions, everything. And frankly—" She hesitated to say what she'd been thinking since she'd first read Adan's proposal, but she'd been in the Rebellion long enough to speak her mind about its future. "—what you're asking for looks a lot like an attempt to run a military operation without military oversight." She softened her tone and lowered her voice. "Officer Adan, the chancellor's made it clear she doesn't want a New Republic military at *all* once the peace comes. I don't like the precedent of this."

Adan met her gaze. The frustration left his face, but the harshness didn't. "I'm not asking you to like it," he said. "But my superiors have already authorized me to carry out the plan. I told you: All I need is an operating base."

Hera hid her surprise, squaring her shoulders and clenching her jaw. She could object, she knew—take her complaint directly to the chancellor, who owed her dinner and more than a few favors—but that wasn't how a situation like this needed to be handled.

"I have two conditions," she said.

"By all means," Adan said, almost graciously.

"First, if your squadron is operating out of the *Lodestar*, it answers at all times to the captain and wing commander on duty. We're not delaying a launch for you, and if we need extra fighters to defend the battle group you don't sit on your hands and watch. Understood?"

"Understood."

*That was the easy one,* Hera thought. *Now for the hard part.*

"Second, you don't get to command the squadron."

Adan's eyes turned hard. "Excuse me?"

"You never served in the Alliance military, did you?" Hera knew the answer—rushed as she'd been, she'd done her research.

"No, but—"

"What about before you joined the rebels? Any naval training? Local security work?" This time the question wasn't rhetorical.

"No."

She thought of asking: *What did you do, exactly?* But she wasn't trying to humiliate him. "Then I can understand," she said, "why you may not fully appreciate what running a starfighter squadron entails. But if you're going to operate out of my fleet, I need someone who can look at all *this*—" She jerked her chin in the direction of the ships. "—and know how to talk to the ground crews and account for support and logistics. Someone who knows how to plan an operation from start to finish, and who knows what a B-wing is capable of and what an A-wing isn't. I won't have time to review every flight plan your *working group* puts together, and for your own people's safety I want someone with flight experience signing off.

"You can oversee the squadron. Give it mission parameters, propose whatever you want. But when it comes to day-to-day operations, your squadron commander runs things."

His nostrils flared. His eyes were cold as diamonds. But he didn't object, and Hera was relieved that he seemed to accept the logic.

"I can live with that," he said. "I'll tell Wyl Lark to report to the *Lodestar*'s wing commander."

*Wyl Lark.* She tried to remember what she'd read from Adan's reports. "He's one of the *Dare* survivors? The one from Polyneus?"

"That's right."

"I'm sure he's quite a flier—" She'd seen two of the Polynean tributes in her career, and both had astonished her with their knack for piloting. "—but he's never come close to running a squadron. This isn't the time for him to learn."

Adan smiled sardonically. "I thought you didn't have time to micro-manage us?"

Hera mirrored his smile. "It took a while to set up this meeting. I may as well use the time we booked."

"So. Command experience. That leaves Tensent."

His resigned tone surprised her. "You don't like Tensent?" she asked. She had her own objections to the man, but he was qualified and capable. She'd met him in passing once, and found him smart and charismatic.

"I trust Tensent to do his job. But I don't trust Tensent to do his job unsupervised."

"You're afraid he'll steal your group away, aren't you?" She started to laugh, then swallowed the sound. "I'm sorry, that's not fair—"

But Adan was smiling again, almost chagrined. "It's a concern, yes. If you don't trust Intelligence running a side game, you certainly shouldn't trust Nath Tensent."

"In that case, you really only have one choice. Less command experience than Tensent, but enough, and plenty of time operating out of a carrier. Expertise in the enemy you're hunting."

Adan's reaction was swift and contemptuous. "She's a defector. She—"

"Some of the best pilots—the best *rebels*—I've known have been defectors. If you can't trust her she shouldn't be flying at all." Hera sighed and glanced at the nearest console. Her thirty minutes were almost up, and she had ten thousand other emergencies awaiting her input. "I'm not going to force this, Officer Adan. If you prefer Tensent, you can give him the position and hope we don't regret it. Quell would be my choice—I'll even overlook where her X-wing came from—but you know your people better than I do."

Adan held her gaze awhile, then looked out at the sea of starfighters. He seemed to be studying the workings of the *Lodestar* and its squadrons; as if he'd find an answer in the welding of metal or the uncoupling of fueling hoses. "It'll be Quell, then," he said, "until it isn't."

*Good enough,* Hera decided. She nodded briskly and strode toward the ladder. Adan was still looking away when she turned back.

"I said I don't have time to review your plans, and I meant it. But I will be keeping an eye on your squadron. Your pilots are operating out of my fleet. That makes them my responsibility.

"Keep them safe. Be smart. We've all seen enough funerals."

Adan faced her, arched his brow, and snapped a salute. "General."

She grunted an acknowledgment and ascended the ladder.

She was halfway to her office when the old longing hit her. *General Syndulla* never seemed to fit—like a perfectly tailored garment that nonetheless belonged to someone else. She had been a rebel before the Alliance to Restore the Republic had existed. Back before they'd had fleets and armies. Back when they hadn't been worried about setting bad precedents for a galactic government they were still figuring out how to run.

The Empire was crumbling every day. Trillions of people were free because of the Rebellion. Because she was a general running a battle group instead of a cell leader flying the *Ghost* on one mad assignment or another.

Still, she missed her old crew. Her family.

She wished they all could have been with her aboard the *Lodestar.*

**II**

*Fly, try, and die* was an adage of the Imperial Starfighter Corps: advice to undertrained TIE pilots fresh out of the Academy and desperate for practical instruction. It was bleak and demoralizing—enough so that saying it in public risked spawning stern memoranda from the security bureau—and not entirely unhelpful.

Survival in the brutal Imperial infantry was a matter of luck. Survival as a pilot meant pushing your fighter to its limits and coordinating with your squadron. Those who learned became aces. Those who didn't were dashed into nothingness in a thousand different ways.

*Fly, try, and die,* Yrica Quell reminded herself as her squadron—*her* squadron—maneuvered outside the perimeter of the Gobreton minefield. Four marks trailed her X-wing in a perfect wedge formation; in the dark between the ships, communications bursts linked droids and navicomputers, synchronized thrusters and maneuvering jets so that the five ships moved as one. She saw nothing ahead of her except the distant azure sphere of a gas giant and the endless starfield behind it.

"Ready for targeting pass," she said. "Lark, with me. Kairos, you're backup. Ready jammers. Weapons free but watch what you pull in."

"Lark acknowledging." Crisp and responsive. After only a handful of flights, Quell expected nothing less from Lark.

A low, computerized buzz was the only response from Kairos's U-wing. D6-L translated ACKNOWLEDGED on Quell's display, but it wasn't necessary. Building a vocabulary of sounds had been Quell's first task upon learning Kairos would be flying under her.

She still didn't understand the reasoning behind her promotion to squadron commander. She'd earned it—she'd proven her value, proven her skill, and the thought made her want to weep and cheer in triumph—and Adan had pledged his support and confidence in the most sober terms. But she didn't entirely *trust* it.

"Unlink navigation. Opening throttle," she said. D6-L indicated it would handle the first task. She felt the surge from the thrusters, felt her seat sculpt to her spine, as she handled the second.

She didn't trust her promotion. She didn't trust Adan's reasoning. She didn't trust—she didn't *know* her squadron, and though Lark and Chadic seemed professional Tensent and Kairos had each tried to kill her once already.

Those were interpersonal challenges, and ones she was steeled to face. But she also didn't entirely trust her own judgment. She'd earned her position as squadron second-in-command in the 204th. She'd been ready for elevation after almost a year building training schedules and filing maintenance and personnel requests; after taking command of more than one mission in times of emergency. Yet a squadron of disciplined Imperial pilots who had undergone the same training, who spoke the same shorthand, was different from what she faced now.

She'd told Adan she could have the group combat-ready in a matter of days. It hadn't seemed like a choice, when the 204th was supposedly fortifying Pandem Nai with every passing hour.

She spotted the reflective glimmer of a smart mine and chose her new trajectory. She turned and rolled, skirting the mine's targeting sphere as Lark and Kairos trailed far behind her. Her sensors flashed as the mine came alive and she continued her turn, accelerating and pulling away.

The mine was pursuing her now, locked and burning fuel in an effort to catch the X-wing. Quell's heart rate increased. She couldn't outrun it. She might be maneuverable enough to force it to expend all its fuel, but she didn't yet understand her ship's capabilities on that base, intuitive level.

She didn't trust her X-wing, either.

She felt exposed with the emptiness of space above her. A TIE fighter viewport faced straight ahead. In the X-wing, cold and dark enveloped her.

Lark's voice came through the comm. "Target acquired. Firing now."

Quell twisted in her harness, fighting against the pressure of acceleration, trying to peer back past the bulk of D6-L and the glow of her thrusters. She saw nothing. Heard nothing other than the rumble of her ship.

Her scanner flashed. Lark's voice came through again: "Target destroyed. You're clear."

"One down." Tensent this time, wryly amused. "Three hundred to go."

"It's target practice," Quell answered. She sounded confident, for which she was grateful. She hadn't been certain Wyl Lark would hit the mine in time. "I'm not asking you to clear the field. Just show me you can maneuver together and don't get hit."

"But if we leave any alive—" Chass na Chadic's voice. "—they'll come after us for revenge."

Tensent laughed. Quell wasn't sure who Chadic's sarcasm was directed at—maybe it meant something to Lark—but she chose to ignore it.

Together they ran through one drill after another. They dived toward the minefield in flights of two and three, drawing the mines away and detonating them safely. It was their fourth training mission together, and after three dissatisfying excursions spent on basic maneuvers, Quell was pleased to see that the element of danger focused her pilots' attention.

The problems she'd witnessed over the past week, however, remained problems. Assigning five different starfighters to five pilots who'd barely met was a dangerous way to build a squadron. Maybe a foolish one. Whenever the ships broke formation they risked colliding, thanks to wildly different speeds and turning radii. The pilots couldn't count on one another's capabilities because they didn't understand what their squadron mates were capable of. The 204th had been capable of astonishing feats because its pilots acted in union, but this . . . ?

Still, Adan had made it clear that there were no other starfighters available—that they would make do with what they had. Quell had agreed.

She didn't have other options. All she could do was apply her discipline to a new purpose, in service of a new master.

She made notes as the exercise continued. Chass na Chadic was a tremendous flier and a poor communicator. Wyl Lark's gunnery was decent enough but he maneuvered with a grace Quell had rarely seen. Nath Tensent, to her surprise, fell into an easy routine with the others, reflexively coordinating attack patterns and flight vectors. Kairos flew without excess motion or wasted shots.

Quell was nearly ready to end the exercise and return to the *Lodestar* when Tensent, moving to chase a mine pulled by Kairos, cursed over the comm and called, "Second mark on my six—must've flown too close."

Quell checked her scanner and saw it: another mine in motion behind Tensent's ship. His Y-wing didn't have the thruster power to escape. Kairos had a mine of her own in pursuit and Chadic was too far away to do any good. Lark and Tensent were both on the comm now, and Quell cut them off as she spun her fighter about. "Tensent, forget Kairos—I'll hit the first mine. Maintain course, double-aft shields!" She doubted shields would do much good against a smart mine, but there was no reason not to try. "Lark, grab the second ball!"

Lark replied—something confused—and Quell saw a distant flash of light. Not an explosion, but the glimmers of cannon fire. "The mine behind Tensent," she shouted into the comm. "Draw it away with your ship!"

Her body seemed to vibrate as the X-wing screamed toward Kairos. The ache in her shoulder, nearly forgotten that day, returned. She spotted the U-wing and the trailing metal sphere and counted heartbeats as her targeting computer obtained a lock.

Lark was calling, "Who's *shooting*?" as Quell squeezed her trigger. Her cannons crackled. The mine—the first mine—burst brilliantly, filling her viewport with white light. Chadic was saying something as well, and Quell spared her scanner a glance.

Six marks. Four allied starships. *Two* mines left, not one. Quell pieced it together, swinging toward Lark's A-wing: He had drawn off the mine from Tensent as Chadic had tried to detonate it. Instead of saving Tensent, she'd activated a third mine by sending stray shots into the minefield. Now Lark had two in pursuit.

An A-wing was fast. *Maybe* fast enough to escape, but doing so would leave two mines live.

"Lark!" Quell called. "Pull them into Chadic's field of fire! Chadic—"

"I'll try not to hit him."

Quell watched it play out on the scanner. She accelerated toward Lark, but she knew she'd never reach him in time. He lost speed as he maneuvered toward Chadic, the mines moving from his stern to his port side. By the time he entered the B-wing's firing range, the closest mine couldn't have been more than a dozen meters away.

The flash that followed seemed insignificant against the starfield. The atomizing destructive force could have devastated a city block.

"Lark! Chadic! Report, now!"

Chass na Chadic's voice was the first one through. "Scratch two. Wyl's in one piece, but only because half of him got vaporized."

Wyl Lark was alive. His ship could be repaired. That was the extent of the good news.

There was enough blame to go around such that Quell didn't waste time chastising her pilots upon their return to the *Lodestar*. After they'd finished cutting Lark's cockpit open with a laser torch—pulling him out intact and uninjured—she'd snapped something unproductive at Tensent and Chadic and sent them on their way.

She would review the flight recordings later. She knew what to expect: She'd hear her own voice shouting panicky and ambiguous orders before she'd gone silent to hunt the first mine. She'd find that Lark and Chadic's actions were reasonable on their own but poorly coordinated. All she wondered was whether Kairos had bothered acting at all.

So much for bringing the discipline of the 204th to a squadron of her own.

"You want to tell me what did this?"

The speaker stood beside Quell as they watched Lark's fighter rise off the hangar deck in the grip of a loadlifter. One of the ship's thruster nacelles was blackened and half shattered. Quell assessed the ship first, then the white-haired woman in a scorched and stained jumpsuit.

"Smart mine," Quell said. "Does it matter?"

"Tells me you got outwitted by a piece of machinery," the woman said, "which probably means I've got more repairs coming."

*In the 204th,* Quell thought, *you'd have been docked a week's pay for talking back to a squadron commander.* She wondered if the disrespect was typical for a rebel, or aimed at her specifically.

"How soon will the ship be up and running?"

The woman rubbed her face in both hands. Tattoos covered her flesh—elaborate, colorful whorls surrounding dancing figures and strange pictograms—and she seemed to try to wipe them away. "How many A-wings do you think we've got aboard the *Lodestar*?" the woman asked.

*You're not answering me,* Quell wanted to say.

"One," Quell said. "The *Lodestar's* shipboard squadrons are T-65B X-wings and BTL-A4 Y's."

"Good. You're paying attention. So how fast do you think I can get the parts? Not just for the A-wing, either, but for the whole High Galactic alphabet's worth of ships you brought—"

"I understand the challenge," Quell said. She heard the tension in her voice and deliberately eased it. "But this is the squadron we've got, and I need you and your crew to support us, same as any other. Sergeant . . ."

The woman folded her arms across her chest, waiting. Quell met her gaze. "Ragnell," the woman finally said.

"Sergeant Ragnell. I almost lost one of my people on a training exercise today and I'm meeting my commander in half an hour. I would really like a win right now."

Ragnell grunted and craned her neck to watch the loadlifter reposition the damaged ship.

"Four days," Ragnell said. "But I'm warning you: Try not to break more than one ship at a time, or you'll end up grounded longer than that."

Four days.

The words scarred Quell's brain, and she hadn't shaken her frustration by the time she was sitting with Adan in a two-person meeting room explaining her progress and setbacks with the squadron. Adan appeared distracted, barely speaking, his antenna-stalks raised. Quell wasn't sure what his inattention meant until he cut her off with a wave of his hand and said, "General Syndulla is striking at Berchest, maybe as soon as tomorrow. I'd like to capture one of the Imperial yachts there—see if there's useful data aboard."

Quell shook her head slowly, not understanding. Had he been ignoring her entirely? "We won't be ready," she said. "Lark's A-wing won't even be repaired. I don't know how long we'll be—maybe another week, but I can't take these people into a combat zone."

Adan's lips twitched, but he didn't seem surprised or even alarmed. "That's about what General Syndulla said, too. I was hoping you would give me a counterargument."

"She heard about the minefield?"

"She did. She says no more flight time until you've—I quote—*got your act together.* Simulators only. So I ask you again: Do you have a counterargument?"

"No," Quell said. It hurt her chest to say it, yet she was responsible for her squadron. She wouldn't bow to pressure. "They're good pilots, but they're not ready for combat."

Adan's antenna-stalks seemed to stiffen, then slowly retracted into his dark mass of hair. He nodded and stood. "Then *make* them ready. And in the meantime, double down on the tactical analysis—we may as well get some work done."

"How much time have you spent with your pilots off duty?" the torture droid asked. It floated above the table that filled most of the cramped meeting room, looking like some sort of dreadful centerpiece.

"Not much," Quell said. "Lark and Chadic summarized their service histories for me, but otherwise I've been focused on training, research, and operations."

She didn't mention the tasks she'd postponed: studying New Republic data on Pandem Nai; reviewing sector charts; evaluating her X-wing's specs and her droid's capabilities. The only reason she'd made time to speak to the IT-O unit was because it had promised to review her team's personnel records with her.

"*Lark* and *Chadic*," the droid said. "Not *Wyl* and *Chass.*"

"No."

"Did you fraternize with your squadron in the 204th?"

"Are we here to talk about them, or me?"

"I'd prefer to talk about the intersection *between* you and your people," the droid said. It dilated the red lens of its photoreceptor as Quell scowled. "But we can move on to that later."

"What do I need to know?" she asked.

The droid retreated half a meter and emitted a high-pitched whine as one device—a sonic pain inducer—retracted, only to be replaced by a miniature holoprojector. A burst of light signaled the creation of a rapidly changing hologram: a figure of Nath Tensent became a profile of Wyl Lark; the profile became a video of Chass na Chadic; Chadic's laughter vanished, replaced by the visor of Kairos.

"Four pilots, each with considerable combat experience. Each highly motivated to locate and neutralize the 204th Imperial Fighter Wing. They share virtually no training or pre-military history. They are effectively strangers to one another."

"What do I need to know," Quell repeated, *"that I don't know already."*

"You need to know," the droid said, "what they *do* share in common."

Quell waited. The droid froze the holodisplay on the image of Wyl Lark. "Nineteen years old. Homesick. A self-described warrior of exceedingly gentle temperament. Sole survivor of his squadron."

From Lark to Chadic, then. The droid continued: "Listed age is inconsistent, ranging from twenty to twenty-five. Homeworld unknown."

*Rim rat,* Quell thought, then felt a reflexive remorse. She'd learned the slur in the Empire, but she'd met plenty on Gavana Orbital growing up: humans and nonhumans born on the fringes of civilization, without the trail of personal data Imperial citizens relied upon to obtain employment, services, and transport.

"Considers herself Theelin, but family history is unknown. Sole survivor of her squadron for the second time," the droid finished.

Quell wondered what the *first time* was and made a note to check the records. "Keep going," she said.

From Chadic to Tensent. "Tensent you know. Thirty-seven years old. Attempted to retire rather than continue fighting without his comrades. Untrustworthy by his own admission. Sole survivor of his squadron."

The hologram rotated through the images again. "Four pilots," it said, "facing substantial psychological obstacles and personal tragedies that will affect their performance. I cannot breach confidentiality, but I can tell you—"

"What about Kairos?" Quell asked.

"Kairos," the droid said, "has her own challenges. They are classified."

Quell let out a long, hissing exhalation. *Of course they are.* "Can you at least tell me her species? It might matter, depending on the mission. If she's injured—"

"I can say nothing. She understands the risks."

Quell nodded slowly and let the topic drop.

"I'm not blind," she said. "I know they've got scars. But they'll learn to fly together."

"And what about your final pilot?" the torture droid asked. The hologram flashed, and Quell looked into a face she almost didn't recognize: her face, gaunt and battered and scraped. An image from when the New Republic had found her on Nacronis.

She snorted to cover her sudden discomfort. The droid didn't speak. She chose to play along. "Lieutenant Yrica Quell," she said. "Self-confessed traitor. Sole survivor of her squadron. Highly motivated to locate and neutralize the 204th Imperial Fighter Wing."

"Trustworthy?"

"As much as anyone."

"What made her into a traitor?"

"The death of the Galactic Emperor and the instigation of Operation Cinder."

"Why?"

"Because when innocents die in war, there should be a *point* to it." The words leapt from her lips like spittle. She hadn't paused between replies and she didn't pause now. "Because if you can't even begin to explain what good you're doing by fighting, you're fighting on the wrong side."

The humming of the droid's repulsors rose in pitch, softer and softer until they became the nearly inaudible whine of an insect.

"Have you given any further thought," the droid asked, "to *why* the Emperor ordered Operation Cinder?"

"We're done," she said, and rose from her seat on trembling legs. "We're done, unless—"

"Yrica." The hologram flashed away. Quell blinked the light from her eyes. "Please sit."

"Why?"

When the droid answered, its tone had changed, altering from bass and hollow to something gentler. "I'm not your friend. But I am concerned for your well-being and I have committed to helping if at all possible."

It paused, then finished:

"I understand what it means to change."

She peered into the red light of its photoreceptor. For a moment, she almost believed the machine.

She almost believed an Imperial *torture droid*.

"What happens if I walk out?" she asked.

"Caern Adan will promptly demand that you attend regular therapy sessions or be removed from the working group."

She sat back down.

"We'll talk about anything you like, then."

She meant it. She would talk about the Emperor and Operation Cinder. She would talk about her parents and her first girlfriend. Her last boyfriend. Her squadron. Anything else the IT-O unit needed to believe she was fit.

But she didn't trust her promotion to squadron commander. She didn't trust Caern Adan's reasoning. And she certainly didn't trust Adan's personal torture droid.

# III

Colonel Shakara Nuress sat in the copilot's seat of a *Zeta*-class cargo shuttle, watching the sprawling settlement of Induchron fall away beneath her. Induchron was an ugly little outpost, all squat warehouses and processing facilities; prefab housing units and rusting schools embedded in a dun-colored, gravelly plain. The locals doubtless viewed it as a grand metropolis, and Shakara didn't begrudge them their pride.

But she was ready to be gone. She was feeling like less of a warrior by the day, and she wanted to be among her people again.

"To Orbital One, Colonel?" the pilot asked.

"Yes. The long route today, I think."

"Colonel?" The pilot furrowed his brow.

Shakara withheld her impatience, plotting a course on the console instead. "Primary ascent at these coordinates. Take us into the exosphere and descend again—" She jutted her finger at the display. "—here, before proceeding to Orbital One. Understood?"

"Of course, Colonel."

She leaned into the torn leather of her chair and sighed. It was her own fault. She'd chosen Ensign Casas as her pilot not in spite of his unexceptional record but *because* of it—because he'd been stationed on Pandem Nai for two years now and, if someone had to fly her about for appearances' sake, she'd rather waste the time of a well-meaning errand boy than one of the veterans of the 204th.

At least he hadn't called her Grandmother. How she hated that nickname. Hated the reminder that she was old. Hated worse the reminder that somewhere along the line she'd gotten *soft*.

Someone from the 204th would teach him the name soon enough.

The shuttle pitched upward into the churning ocher clouds. It would be some time—Shakara hoped, at least—before she saw the sky from this angle again. She'd spent the last three days hopping from surface settlement to surface settlement, meeting with the planet's civilian leadership and inspecting the Empire's scant few ground-level installations. All told, she was satisfied with the results. The general populace showed no signs of rising up, and they lacked the weaponry to revolt at scale; the Imperial infantry forces were pledged to her command; and the discussions of gas processing quotas and transport safety protocols had gone well—if she could increase the orbital mines' Tibanna extraction rate, the surface processing facilities could adjust accordingly.

She should have felt victorious. Instead she couldn't help but think of how wrong it all had gone to bring her to this point. To transform her into an industrial administrator.

"Colonel?" The pilot's voice interrupted her thoughts. "Incoming message from Orbital One. Squadron Four has returned. They report no losses."

She gestured dismissively. "It can wait till I arrive."

Wisps of gas meters long and thin as thread unraveled about the cockpit as they ascended, and the clouds' coloration changed from ocher to tawny orange and finally to scarlet. With the change in tincture came thicker strands of the densest gas, lengthening from meters to kilometers. Under better circumstances, Shakara might have been moved by the beauty of the blood-lit sea; but not today.

She was lucky to have found Pandem Nai at all. After Operation Cinder, the 204th had been left without orders. Their Star Destroyer, the *Pursuer,* had sought out targets of opportunity while Shakara had desperately attempted to locate and contact a centralized authority within the vulnerable Empire. But she had been able to reach no one—no admiral competent enough to understand what the 204th could offer—and so she'd waited too long. The *Pursuer* had accrued too much damage, and she'd advised the Destroyer's captain to fall back, make repairs, and regroup.

They'd chosen Pandem Nai half expecting to find it overrun by local revolutionaries. Somehow, however, the governor had maintained control of a world rich in resources and uniquely positioned to defend itself. True, there had been desertions, but the orbital gas mining facilities had been largely automated anyway and processed Tibanna gas was vital for the proper functioning of heavy weaponry. An Empire without Tibanna mines—or without suitable substitutes—would be unable to wage war for more than a few months.

The shuttle emerged from the scarlet clouds. A cloak of darkness fell across the viewport, and the stars came into sight. The ship swept across the surface of the atmosphere, sending ripples like foam in its wake.

"Descending now, Colonel." The pilot hesitated, then asked, "Would you, ah, like to do it yourself?"

*Is he truly incompetent?* Shakara looked toward the man, bewildered, then realized he was attempting generosity. "No need," she said. "I'm content to enjoy the view."

They plunged back into the red and wove among the massive mining stations laden with gas pods; past gleaming colonies, their durasteel spirals buoyed by enormous antigravity repulsors and lit by a thousand habitation lights. (So much more civilized, Shakara thought, than the rude ground-level settlements.) They flew alongside tankers and cargo haulers and slipped into the current.

There were other worlds rich in Tibanna gas. But it was Pandem Nai's atmosphere that made it exceptionally useful to the 204th. The thick cloud cover was not only minable but explosive; there, any weapon larger than a cannon was prone to backfiring. A battleship bristling with turbolaser batteries was more apt to damage itself than its foes, and when the Separatists—or the Rebel Alliance, or the New Republic, or whatever the galaxy's anarchists called themselves nowadays—finally came, starfighter superiority would determine the victor.

The local governor and the *Pursuer*'s former captain had put up only cursory resistance when Shakara had assumed control and begun fortifying the planet. She'd scraped together three cruiser-carriers to transport select TIE squadrons wherever they were needed, and neutralized half a dozen attempts at enemy reconnaissance. She'd begun outreach to other Imperial survivors, using Colonel Madrighast as her first go-between to offer Pandem Nai's resources to whatever convoy could reach her. She'd inquired about enemy weapons powerful enough to ignite the atmosphere from orbit—Shakara put no faith in the foe's claims to value civilian life—and been assured the risk was minimal unless the enemy built their own Death Star.

She was ready for a siege. Ready to face the next stage of the war. She'd adapted herself and her people to the course of events, no matter the inconvenience.

Orbital One came into sight through the viewport. It was not a battle station, but embedded within the ring of the outer mining facility was a militarized stronghold established by Imperial forces long ago.

Two main hangars sufficed to house Shakara's TIE squadrons, along with a small fleet of shuttles and maintenance drones. Within a few short minutes the cargo shuttle had swept under the hangars and to the smaller executive docking bay, where Shakara disembarked onto a perfectly polished floor marred only by thruster scars and the boot scuffs of the officers awaiting her.

She left Ensign Casas to tend to the shuttle and strode toward the central access corridor. Three officers trailed her, each rapidly dispensing a series of updates she forced herself to care about: complaints about the orbital gas mining operations (the civilian workforce was stretched thin after doubling output, and tighter security was reducing productivity); shortages of equipment requested by the tankers; updates on the personnel reauthorization initiative she'd requested to weed out infiltrators. Mixed in were reports more relevant to her military experience: Squadron Four's summary of its mission to Vnex; fresh charts from the minelayer operating outside Pandem Nai's orbit; Squadron Five's repair and readiness update. But even these came with a reminder of the war's toll and the roles she and others had been forced to assume. Mere weeks ago it would have been Major Soran Keize who saw to the squadrons' readiness and morale. And it would have been Keize who met her in private afterward and allowed her to speak grimly, frankly, about how dire their circumstances were.

She missed that man. She was a good commander, where Soran had been a great *leader*. And she had trusted him.

She would endure.

She allowed the reports to continue, relying on her subordinates' ability to prioritize, until she reached the turbolift to her living quarters and cut the conversations off there. One last question reached her before the door slid shut: "People are asking, Colonel—any word yet from above?"

This from Lieutenant Preartes, who had been aboard the *Aerie* when it had pursued an enemy frigate through the Oridol Cluster. He'd taken the escape of two of the frigate's starfighters personally and was eager to redeem himself. So far as Shakara was concerned, the *Aerie* had done well under trying circumstances; she was content for Preartes to punish himself.

"I'm going to speak to my source presently," Shakara said. "You will know when I have an update."

Her source was waiting for her in her cabin when she emerged from the lift.

It stood silent by the door, floating noiselessly and cloaked in red leather and delicate fabric. It possessed the shape of a human but there was nothing human about it—it was a mockery of life, and the faceless black glass that stared in place of a face was without soul or spark. It was a wraith: the echo of a man who had died not long ago and haunted what remained of the Empire.

"Well?" Shakara asked, turning to stare into the faceless mask. "Do you have new orders?"

It said nothing. She'd have started if it had.

But she'd seen it speak once. A short while after Endor, when the chaos ran rampant instead of simmering and the *Pursuer* had fled purposelessly through space while the Separatist Rebel Republic took world after world. The wraith, the Messenger, had found her (not the *Pursuer*'s captain, but *her*) and demanded her blood to prove her identity.

She'd given it what it wanted. She still had the scar. Then its faceplate had shimmered with the static of a hologram and Emperor Palpatine had looked upon her for the first and last time.

*Operation Cinder is to begin at once,* it had told her in the Emperor's voice, and she'd obeyed.

She had found the operation distasteful, but she hadn't questioned it the way a handful of her pilots had. The Emperor had given the 204th purpose from beyond the grave—honored the fighter wing, along with other units across the galaxy—and set them on their course. Nacronis had not deserved destruction, but she trusted the Emperor's Messenger that such destruction was *necessary.*

Decades ago, during the Clone Wars, it had been the Republic losing its fight against Separatist aggressors and *Supreme Chancellor* Palpatine who had ordered distasteful but necessary deeds. He had identified the corruption at the Republic's heart—the religious zealots who called themselves peacekeepers—and expunged them. He had transformed the Republic into an Empire and maintained order for over twenty years.

She would fight on as long as she could. She would ready Pandem Nai for battle and offer aid to the scattered Imperial armadas. She would take the role of bureaucrat and charismatic leader and mass murderer if that was what victory demanded.

If that was what she had to do to survive long enough for the Emperor's next orders to come.

"No one else understands as he did," she said to the Messenger. No admiral had managed to unite the divided fleet with a plan to save the galaxy. No successor had emerged to take the Emperor's throne. "We will need more guidance, sooner or later."

It said nothing.

She wondered how much farther the Empire would fall before it began to win again.

# CHAPTER 9

## DELUSIONS OF GRANDEUR

**I**

The planet-killer filled the viewport: a world's worth of ashen metal and mad weapons that dissolved in streaks around the edges like a smudged painting of a battle station. Even unfinished, it was an obscenity—an utterance screamed by a murderous Emperor at a galaxy that dared defy him, and a rebuke of the rebel blood shed to destroy the first Death Star. Chass stared at the abomination and felt rage mingle with disgust.

"The objective is inside the superstructure. The shield is down. Kairos will deliver the payload." Quell's voice came through the comm, crisp and passionless. Chass was starting to get used to that tone from her new commanding officer—not Hound Leader's masked fear or Rununja's cult-leader egotism, but a machinelike determination to see the mission through.

"Shield's not supposed to be down," Chass said. "Ask Wyl."

"It's down *now*," Quell replied. "Go!"

Chass's B-wing rattled as she opened the throttle, though it rattled *wrong*—her seat heaved instead of trembling, and there was no ringing-glass trill from the panel behind her head. If she'd had her music, she could have ignored the flaws, but the simulator didn't permit music. (Quell probably didn't permit music, either, but Quell didn't have to know.)

"She's right," Wyl said. His voice was distant, lost in a memory he didn't deserve. "It wasn't like this."

"Count ourselves lucky, then," Nath returned. Chass had recognized the sort of man Nath was the first time he'd grinned at her; she hadn't had a reason to reconsider yet.

They flew in a wide formation into the heart of the conflict. Emerald and crimson particle bolts streamed across Chass's field of vision, punctuated by the flickers of distant explosions as rebels died and died again (or would have, if those deaths hadn't been cheap imitations of something meaningful). The planet-killer's superlaser erupted and the whole universe turned a pustulent green. Chass flew to the beat of her pulse, letting the rhythm tell her when to veer and when to rotate the gyroscopic body of her craft. TIE fighters flew in masses toward her and she fired restlessly into the swarm. *These* TIEs died more easily than the ones that had chased the *Hellion's Dare,* and she found only a dull satisfaction as they burst into component molecules.

"Tensent, where are you?" Quell called.

Chass didn't see Nath on the scanner. Wyl was weaving around her, his faster A-wing circling like a hound protecting its master. She tried to pull away. Kairos lagged behind, exposed to an attack from the rear, but—well. Quell could deal with that. What was the point of the exercise if it wasn't challenging?

"Tensent!" Quell yelled again.

"Trust me!" Nath said.

Chass could see the surface of the battle station now. The details weren't perfect—identical chunks of weapons towers and sensors and deflectors repeated over and over—but as fire raged around her she tried to imagine how it had *really* been, for pilots like (*don't think about*

*Wyl*) Sata Neek. She tried to place herself in the battle, fighting the same abomination that had risen once before; fighting the monster that heroes at Scarif had sacrificed everything to defeat.

She couldn't do it. The battle was a lie. The particle bolts flickered in and out, transparently false. TIE fighters ceased to exist. Her ship whined in ways a real B-wing never would. She screamed in frustration as Wyl made confused sounds and Quell shouted pointless orders.

Her ship was enveloped in fire. She'd been hit but she didn't care. The viewport went white, then black, and Chass was sitting in the sphere of a simulator pod.

"The hell was that?" she asked.

"Call it a win," Nath said over the link. "The Death Star's gone and only one of us died."

Nath had broken the simulation. Whether he'd *cheated* was open to debate. The program wasn't meant for anything as complex as the Battle of Endor, and Nath had increased the complexity by straying from the planned flight path. "More than one way into the reactor," he'd explained afterward, "so why go the route the enemy's prepared for?"

The computer, desperately trying to calculate the positions of hundreds of TIE fighters and thousands of particle bolts in proximity to all five living participants, had reduced the TIEs' already dim artificial intelligence, stuttered as it tried to maintain fidelity, and finally crashed outright.

But if breaking the program was Nath's fault, it was Wyl's fault they were stuck with simulators in the first place. Wyl was the one who'd gotten his ship busted at the minefield. His idiocy had persuaded General Syndulla that the squadron couldn't be trusted in the field; and Quell had gone along with it.

*We wouldn't be here if not for Wyl,* Chass thought. It was true in so many ways.

They stood together under the black spheres of the simulator pods in the *Lodestar*'s repurposed clone trooper barracks. Quell's face twisted with Imperial arrogance as she barked, "Are you clever? Yes, you've all proved it. But the point was to show we could complete this the *right* way."

Nath stood at ease, observing Quell with what might have been a sympathetic smile. "In that case, Battle of Endor might've been ambitious. The *right* way needs a different squadron makeup, and we can all tell those TIEs aren't real. Chass shot them down like decoys, and Wyl was playing to the pre-programmed blast patterns—"

"I wasn't," Wyl said, surprised.

"Sure you were," Nath said. "Maybe it was instinct, but you saw what was random and what was repeating. You could've kept that up for an hour."

Quell scowled at Nath, staring up at the taller man. "I take your point, but I still can't take these results to General Syndulla—and I don't need your suggestions. Not now."

Chass snickered. Quell didn't look at her.

"We're done," Quell said. "I've booked another run in the simulator tomorrow. Expect an operational summary tonight; preflight briefing starts at oh nine hundred."

"Ma'am, why—" Wyl's back was straight and his eyes were on Quell. Chass saw him struggle with how to treat his commander; he wasn't used to so much formality, but he was mirroring her demeanor as best he could. Calming her, intentionally or just by instinct. "We've been working hard on the 204th tactical analysis. Why aren't we simulating *them*?"

It wasn't a bad question. How many hours had Chass spent locked up with Wyl and Quell and Nath talking about the Shadow Wing capital-ship-spiral-of-doom and Char's habit of flying solo? She could replay Nath's fight at Trenchenovu in her dreams.

"I've been working on a program," Quell said. "It's not good enough yet."

"We have to learn to fight them," Wyl said.

Quell was a statue. A wind could have eroded her features. Then: "I'll send you the profiles I'm working up. Personnel files on everyone

I can remember. They're not finished—some are just names, some don't have anything on flying technique. I don't know who Blink is. But it's something to study."

Quell left without another word. Kairos followed a moment later. Chass hadn't spoken much to the strange woman in the cloak and visor, and Kairos hadn't given her more than a glance. Chass was leaving, too, when Nath reached her side and said, "You doing anything?" He wore the cocky grin of a boy half his age, and almost pulled it off.

"I'm getting out of here," Chass said.

"So grab a shower," Nath said, "or not, and then let's drink until we get our new reading material. Found the place to be after hours, and no one will say we didn't earn it."

"Quell wouldn't say we earned it."

"She won't know, will she?"

He said it with such affected bemusement that Chass laughed despite herself. She knew exactly the kind of man Nath was, and she knew she ought to loathe him as a liar and a snake. Instead she found his predictability amusing—as if Nath were a con artist *pretending* to be a con artist as part of his game, playing every note as broad as possible.

"All right," she said. "Twenty minutes?"

"Meet outside the B-deck turbolift," Nath said. Chass marched out without looking back.

The *White Book*—the Rebel Alliance's military field guide—officially prohibited possession of intoxicants under nearly all circumstances. But individual rebel cells and ships had always done as they pleased, and the *White Book* was seen as a joke by some and an insult—an attempt to impose Imperial order on the Rebellion's anarchic coalition— by others. The New Republic was trying to apply its own standards more rigorously, but *trying* didn't mean *doing* and Chass didn't know anyone who read the frequent handbook updates.

So she wasn't surprised Nath had found a place to drink aboard the *Lodestar.* Whether it was *permitted* only mattered if the captain or General Syndulla found out.

She'd changed out of her flight suit and into civvies when she found Nath waiting in the tight, low-ceilinged corridor on B-deck. Wyl Lark stood beside him, hair wet and gleaming.

"You didn't say he was coming." Chass jutted a finger toward Wyl but didn't look at him.

"Didn't say he wasn't," Nath answered.

"Besides," Wyl added, "Kairos said no, and it's better to have company."

*Are you that much of an idiot?* Chass thought.

"Are you that much of an idiot?" Chass said.

Wyl winced, but—to his credit—the expression passed almost before Chass spotted it. "We've got to try," he said. "What happened with the *Dare*—you're not going to like me, but we have to try."

"Tell it to Sata Neek." Chass pivoted and started to walk away. Even at her height, she had to duck under a power conduit to pass. Before she'd made it five meters she turned back and called, "For the record? I *am* trying. You know how you can tell?"

Wyl looked at her with the sad, confused, dumb expression of a hound kicked by its master. Like he couldn't comprehend why his provincial charm wasn't reaching her.

"Because you shot me," Chass finished, "and I never shot back."

*So stop clinging to me,* she thought, and went to find other drinking partners. Better drinking partners. Drinking partners lacking the self-involvement seemingly possessed by every human. On a ship full of soldiers, there had to be someone.

**‖**

"So what's the story between you two?" Nath asked.

Wyl sat beside the hulk of a man on a couch worn through to its metal frame, illuminated by the glow of a sign that said RANJIY'S KRAYT HUT. The sign's meaning wasn't clear to Wyl, but it wasn't the only mysterious object in the suite that had (Nath claimed) once been the ship-

board home of the Old Republic senator from Malastare. Over two
dozen pilots were packed into three rooms, most of them out of uniform. A line snaked across the suites to the makeshift bar in the restroom.

"Me and Chass?" Wyl asked.

"You and Chass. You put a bounty on her pet? Sleep with her boyfriend? She *hates* you, brother, and you've got to know why."

"She doesn't hate me. She barely knows me." He sipped at his drink—
mostly foam and water—and wondered how much to share with Nath
Tensent. Wyl was trusting by nature but he wasn't naïve, and Nath's
interest felt more manipulative than empathetic.

Yet Nath was part of his squadron now, and he deserved a fair shake.
Wyl managed a tight smile. "We served together on the *Dare*, but different squadrons. What happened at the end—she blames me for leaving the others behind."

"And for shooting her?" Nath asked.

"It was a bad day all around," Wyl said.

Nath laughed, as if that explained everything. Wyl was grateful the
man knew when not to press.

They both turned their heads as a cheer erupted on the far side of
the suite, where a cluster of pilots watched a newsscreen. Wyl made
out an image of a blue-gray planet and the word LIBERATION.

"Looks like we got Kerkoidia back. Another victory for the New
Republic," Nath said, raising his glass of wine. Wyl detected no sarcasm in his voice.

"That's great," Wyl said, and he meant it even as he frowned. The
pilots who had cheered wore the determined faces of men and women
who saw a shot at salvation. "So do you know why everyone acts like
we're losing?"

Nath didn't even pause to consider the question. "You were out of
touch awhile, right? The *Dare*?"

"Even before we ran into the 204th, yeah. Recon mission, checking
on systems that had been cut off."

"You hear about Cinder before you left?"

"It happened as we were heading out," Wyl said. He thought of Shadow Wing and the ruins of Nacronis; Caern Adan had shown him vivid images captured by New Republic scouts. "Reports trickled in, but—"

"But you didn't appreciate the damage till you got back. You were riding that *victory feeling* for a while." Nath shrugged. "Cinder hurt morale, but that's not all of it. Rebellion was always close to losing, and old habits are tough to shake, especially when they're what kept you alive."

"You think it's just pessimism?"

"Mostly. Sooner or later, though, the New Republic's going to have to remember it's on the offensive."

"*The offensive*," Wyl echoed. He glanced at the newsscreen again. He remembered the judgment of the Oridol Cluster; the fate of the *Dare*. "Winning or not, sometimes it seems like the Empire is doing more damage than we are."

Nath shrugged again. "Imperials are stuck living by old habits, too."

"You're a philosophical man, Nath Tensent." It was a joke, but not insincere. Wyl tried to decipher the crinkles around the older man's eyes; the faint curve in his lips. "Being on medical leave give you time to think about it all?"

Adan had told Wyl and Chass that Nath had been injured—and his ship and droid damaged—in the fight against Shadow Wing six months prior. Nath hadn't spoken of his recuperation, and Wyl had tried to respect the man's privacy; but Wyl needed to change the subject and Nath only waved it away.

"Suppose it did. I got pretty comfortable. But whatever mess the rest of the galaxy is in, seemed to me like—" He looked about the room, carefully lowered his voice without appearing deliberately discreet. "—well, I've got a grudge against Shadow Wing, same as you. I know what they can do, and it sounded like Adan and Quell were going after them with or without me."

"And you'd rather they do it *with*," Wyl said.

"Exactly. I'd like to see the job done right. I won't say I don't want a hand in shooting them down myself, but either way. It's why I don't mind all the tactical planning; why I put up with this simulation garbage." Nath downed half his drink in a single swallow. "This is swill. Come on—you want to see how your ship's faring?"

Wyl had, in fact, been wondering about his starfighter. They left the makeshift cantina for the hangar bay, and as they walked the conversation turned to trivial things: first jests about the A-wing and Nath's aging bomber, then stories about old comrades and past battles and rebel leaders. They stumbled into Nath's astromech droid—a C1-series unit creakier than his ship—whom Wyl embraced and chattered at like a long-lost brother while the droid muttered and warbled. "Don't patronize the old bastard," Nath said, giving the droid's chassis a solid kick; but T5 vented hot air and trailed Wyl as they continued on their way.

Soon they were strolling among crates and toolboxes and half the night had gone by. Wyl realized that he regretted none of it.

He hadn't spoken to much of anyone since escaping Oridol. Chass wouldn't talk to him. Caern Adan had briefed and debriefed him. Quell was focused on business. And there hadn't been opportunities to socialize with the crew of the *Buried Treasure* or the *Lodestar*.

No—that wasn't true. There had been opportunities. Wyl had avoided them, after losing Sata Neek and Rununja and Nasi and Sonogari. After failing his friends and squadron and ship. What could he say when someone asked, "Where was your last posting?" He hadn't had the courage for that conversation.

With Nath Tensent, he didn't need to. The man expected nothing.

After midnight shipboard time, they said their goodbyes. Wyl stepped back, ready to depart, when Nath said, "Does it bother you, what she did today?"

"Chass?" Wyl asked.

"Quell. The Endor simulation. You were there for the real thing— I know I'd be a mess if someone popped me back to Boz Pity, made me watch a few of my friends die."

Wyl nodded. The simulation *had* troubled him, but he'd set the notion aside, ignored the ghosts of Riot Squadron. "I'm sure she meant well."

"Probably. Seemed to mess with Chass's head, too. Don't know why." Nath snorted and clapped his hands together. "Maybe I'm overthinking it, but there's something off about Quell. It's not the Imperial style—I was an Imp pilot myself, once—but something else. Too focused on the mission, or not focused enough."

"She was part of Shadow Wing," Wyl said. "Maybe she feels she has something to prove."

"Maybe. Just keep an eye out, okay? Meanwhile, the rest of us can look out for each other. Got to get flying before the fleet hits Pandem Nai, or who knows what we'll miss."

Wyl considered the man before him, trying and failing to separate self-interest and truth. *Maybe with Nath,* he thought, *they're one and the same.*

"For you and for Chass, I'll absolutely keep an eye out," Wyl said. "If you can win over Kairos, let me know."

### III

Yrica Quell watched Caern Adan pace across the ready room, buried deep in his rumpled coat. They'd commandeered the place from Meteor Squadron while that squadron was deployed to Chazwa, and Quell struggled not to gaze at the mementos pinned to the walls or read the notices displayed on the seat consoles. She kept her eyes off the graffiti etched into her chair's armrest. The ready room told the story of two wars, and she wanted to escape into the tale—submerge herself in the history of the *Lodestar* and its pilots instead of wrestling with the unpleasant reality before her. Instead of keeping her eyes on her superior officer.

Had Major Keize ever felt so alone at a briefing aboard the *Pursuer?* She doubted it.

"New Republic Intelligence," Adan was saying, "has tasked additional stations with flagging intercepted communications concerning

Pandem Nai. We're still not picking up much, but we're hoping to learn more soon about the 204th's garrison. Our latest guess is that the Star Destroyer *Pursuer* is *not* operational in-system, but it's possible additional capital ships have been deployed."

She noticed him taking care to meet the eyes of his audience—to look directly at Tensent, Lark, and even Kairos. He lingered on the empty space where Chadic should have been; the Theelin girl hadn't shown for the status meeting and Quell had made an excuse rather than admit that Chadic was tardy.

"General Syndulla's fleet," Adan went on, "may be in position to strike in as few as three weeks, based on our previous estimates and our progress over the past several days. We have until then to gather additional intelligence on Shadow Wing and determine what vulnerabilities exist in Pandem Nai's defenses." He paused at the appropriate times. He did all he could to make scanty findings sound more momentous than they were.

"We can assume they know we're coming," Quell added. "The squadrons that destroyed the *Hellion's Dare* are almost certainly out of the Oridol Cluster by now, and they will have reported the escape of two rebel—New Republic—starfighters. But knowing Colonel Nuress, she'd be preparing for the worst anyway. So we need to determine not just what their defenses are now, but what they can construct while we're on the march."

Lark spoke up, cautious as he asked, "Are we assuming they're entrenching for a siege? Or could Shadow Wing plan to grab as much Tibanna gas as it can and then move on? Stay mobile?"

Adan's lips twitched in a suppressed wince. "Quell? You're the behavioral specialist. What are the odds they're gone before we get there?"

She didn't know. She didn't like answering questions she didn't know in front of her squadron; nor did she like admitting ignorance to the man who controlled her fate. "We think they've been stationed at Pandem Nai for almost a month," she said. "If they wanted to stay mobile I think they'd be gone by now. But I can't be sure."

"What about their other operations?" Tensent shifted his bulk in his seat, glancing to his console. "Any update on whether they're sending sorties out of the system?"

He asked this of Adan, but Adan again looked to Quell.

"I don't know," she said. "Adan, have you heard anything about additional operations?"

"I haven't," Adan said.

Quell reviewed her mental model for anything that might offer a clue. "What about transport capabilities?" she asked. "If we knew how many cruiser-carriers were at Pandem Nai before—"

"We *don't*," Adan snapped. "New Republic Intelligence accepts that Shadow Wing is a priority, but there's a whole galaxy on fire right now. You know what I know."

Quell bit back a retort and nodded.

Adan wasn't finished, though. "The *entire* Intelligence working group on Shadow Wing is in this room. My assumption was that by this time, you'd be conducting tailored reconnaissance and planting tracking devices on Imperial supply convoys. Instead I had to tutor Meteor Squadron on what to watch for at Chazwa, and why we should try to preserve local fuel samples to see if they came from Pandem Nai." He let his gaze slip from Quell, scanning the room before returning. "I didn't count on you needing the better part of a month to get your team operational."

Quell didn't flinch. She didn't say a word.

Adan was a bastard, but he was in command, and he was right. She'd earned herself a squadron, and now she was proving herself incapable of leading it.

Shortly afterward, Adan adjourned the status meeting. Quell excused herself and went hunting for Chadic. The search took her most of an hour; she went deck by deck, compartment by compartment, asking brusque questions of engineers and officers and droids. She didn't talk to the *Lodestar*'s other pilots—she'd heard enough sneering about the "alphabet's worth of ships" dropped aboard by New Republic Intelligence, and she didn't care to damage her working group's reputation further—but she walked through the hangar, eyes open and searching. Sergeant Ragnell, the tattooed engineer, greeted Quell with a polite wave before turning to scream obscenities at a droid dragging a repulsorsled loaded with heavy ordnance.

By the time Quell finally located Chass na Chadic, she'd pushed her failure in the ready room to the back of her brain and kindled her fury at her missing squadron member. In the medical bay, Chadic stood at the bedside of a man with leathery yellow skin and a bandage wrapped around his forehead. Three other figures stood with Chadic, laughing and arguing, all of them in New Republic special forces uniforms.

Quell stood in the doorway, waiting for Chadic to notice her. When she didn't turn, Quell approached.

"Friend of yours?" Quell asked.

Chadic pivoted toward Quell, snorted, then looked back to the man in the bed. "Bad friend to have," she said. "Man's a jinx."

"To you, the man's a hero." One of the upright soldiers—a human with a black beard that extended to his stomach—growled the words without looking at Chadic. "You got to earn the right to call him a jinx."

"Dirt-sucker," Chadic muttered.

"Spit-racer," the man returned.

Quell wrapped her fingers around Chadic's upper arm and tugged her away from the bed. The three specforce troopers, along with their wounded companion, observed but said nothing. Chadic hissed her own objection as they stumbled to the far side of the room, while Quell spoke over her: "You get one chance to tell me where you were. *One.*"

"Drop ship was short a copilot," Chadic said. "I was playing backup."

Quell didn't understand at first. Then realization dawned. "You were gone on a specforce mission? You volunteered for other duties?"

"Yeah," Chadic said. Her voice possessed the unbending surety of an Imperial flagstaff.

Quell stared at the compact young woman before her. *In the 204th,* she wanted to say, *you'd have been stripped of your rank and shipped to a military prison. A pilot fresh from the Academy would fill your seat and never hear your name.*

Chadic gazed back. Quell's rage seemed to break against her speck-led face and strong chin. "In the Empire," Quell said, not meaning to, "you'd be shot for treason."

"The Empire lost," Chadic said, unmoved. "Something happen in the status meeting I actually needed to know? Or are we still sucking our thumbs and waiting for Syndulla to say we can fly?"

Quell had never harmed a subordinate before—not like a dozen commanders she'd known in her career, who answered disobedience or failure with thrashings. She prided herself on her calm and reason. Yet she watched herself, as if from afar, as she grabbed Chadic and swung her into the wall and said, "You're only *alive* because of me. You're in this squadron because of me. If I tell you to suck your thumb, that's what you *do.*"

Four strong hands caught her arms and shirt. Firmly, but not roughly, they pulled her away from Chadic. Quell didn't struggle as a voice said, "She saved the jinx's life."

Chadic squeezed her hands into fists, then released. "So are you kicking me out?" she asked. "Are we done?"

The hands released Quell. She didn't look back at the specforce troopers. Chadic's words, smug and confident, echoed in her mind. They mixed with Adan's arrogance and her own certainty that she was failing her squadron.

"No more unauthorized flights. We've got a mission coming up," Quell lied. "If you're not ready, you never hear about the 204th again. If that doesn't matter to you . . ."

Chass na Chadic saluted. She *saluted,* swinging her hand to her horned temple and her shock of hair, showing teeth in a grin or a snarl. "Yes, sir. Whatever you say, sir."

Quell left the medbay and the infuriating Theelin behind. Her mind drifted to the yellow-skinned man in the bed and the words, "She saved the jinx's life."

She had to find a mission for her squadron. Something Syndulla would approve, even if it was outside a combat zone. Simulations and drills would destroy them by the time they proved themselves, and Chadic was only the first sign of trouble.

# IV

Nath recognized the fatigue in Quell as easily as he'd spotted Adan's opportunism and Wyl's sense of righteousness; as easily as he'd recognized that the Empire was just a shinier place for the same thugs and gangsters he'd grown up with. His new squadron commander was so desperate to prove herself that she was working herself to a hollow shell.

She hadn't been at her best at the last status meeting with Adan, and she'd grown worse daily. Her eyes were bloodshot and her voice was husky. She'd gained a ragged edge during drills, and Nath had followed her one night to find her slumped over a table listening to a headset. He wondered if she was taking stimulants, and if so, whether the torture droid was providing them.

He wasn't sympathetic. Quell loathed him, seeing him as a reminder of her own moral failings—where he'd been a rebel for years, she was still desperate to show she wasn't an Imperial spy. But Nath wasn't ready to see her fall apart, either. She was his best route to Shadow Wing.

He *needed* to find Shadow Wing. He'd made the bet and put everything at stake. He just chose not to show his desperation the way Quell did.

Nath's routine kept him busy seventeen hours a day even when the squadron ("Alphabet Squadron," the *Lodestar*'s pilots called it with a snicker) demanded fewer. Early mornings were for study: He'd never been much of a student, but he knew how to read the documents Adan sent over on Pandem Nai and Colonel Nuress. He reread the debriefing interviews Wyl and Chass had given on their run-ins with the TIE wing and Quell's profiles on squadron leaders like Broosh and Gablerone. While the other troops in his berthing compartment dressed and shouted and ran around like idiots, he sat in his bunk and jotted notes on the people he wanted to die.

He missed having his own quarters. He hadn't slept in a shared berth for years. He hadn't had a chance to meditate uninterrupted in weeks.

Daytime belonged to Quell and the squadron, or—when the morning drill didn't last long—to his ship and his droid, neither of which he trusted with the *Lodestar*'s engineers. The old Y-wing had enough custom parts and jury-rigging in its tonnage that even the best mechanic was likely to break something while puttering around. It worried Nath that T5 had taken a shine to the tattooed engineering chief, but there wasn't much he could do about that. T5 had listened to Reeka and obeyed Ferris out of fear of disassembly; Nath couldn't even wipe the thing's memory, thanks to carbon scoring around the circuits.

The drills themselves varied from tense to interminable. On the days when Quell re-created an old encounter between the 204th and rebels or pirates, breaking down tactical decisions moment by moment, the work seemed grueling but the effort well spent. Simulated dogfights, on the other hand, were both frustrating and tedious. The squadron could beat any computerized game, but it meant nothing in realspace. And racking up digital kills hadn't persuaded General Syndulla to let them fly again.

When evenings rolled around he engaged in less tangible work. Some days he put a few hours into the *Lodestar*'s crew, in either the mess or the Krayt Hut, eating and drinking and gambling with people who might eventually matter to his survival. He picked out the small-time crooks—a smuggler running contraband, a pilot running a rigged game of liar's dice—but didn't make more than cursory contact with them. He was staying clean for now.

Socializing with the troops came second to investing time in the squadron, however. Wyl Lark didn't trust Nath yet, but the boy *liked* Nath and he was too mild-mannered not to listen when Nath planted thoughts in his brain. Chass was more trouble, but she was warming to Nath, too—if he worked the two just right, he could keep them from killing each other and count them both as allies against Quell and Adan.

Because although he might have needed Quell, and Adan might have needed him, Nath wasn't a fool.

In her awkward, Imperial way, Quell had tried to convince him that he wanted vengeance for Reeka, the woman with a face full of scars and a heart even meaner he'd lusted after; Piter, whom he'd practically reared—never less than terrified, usually infuriating, but as trustworthy as any of his crew; even for Braigh, whom Nath had expected to put down himself. Back at the Hive, Quell had offered him the chance to learn the names of their killers and balance the scales. To see justice done.

He'd refused, of course.

Justice was the vice of bold, honorable men who died swift, stupid deaths, and vengeance was justice without the sheen of respectability. Nath had survived as long as he had by controlling his vices, not letting temptation lure him down suicidal alleys.

But he'd let himself take another offer, a better offer. One Quell didn't know about and he didn't plan on sharing. Now Nath was committed.

He hoped Quell didn't turn out to be more trouble than she was worth.

Nath slid into a chair in Meteor Squadron's ready room, two seats to Chass's side and one row behind Wyl, and slapped a meaty hand on the boy's shoulder. "Want to guess what we're up to today?" he asked.

Quell had called them to the briefing without notice. *Probably to see if we'd come running,* Nath thought, knowing he'd done the same thing with his own crew. Quell hadn't arrived yet, which also suggested . . . something. Nath wasn't sure what.

"We had an elder back home who said she could see the future," Wyl said, tilting back his head to look at Nath. "I don't have her talents."

"One day," Nath said, "we're going to talk about your crazy world." He turned toward the door as he heard the creak of leather and the rustle of cloth. Kairos had arrived, moving to take up a position at the back. "What about you?" he called. "You want to guess why we're here?"

Kairos lowered her head. Nath laughed. Chass snorted. It was a better answer than anyone had expected.

Quell arrived a moment later. She looked gaunt enough to cut in half with a paring knife, but she was rigid and proud as ever. Adan followed her in, giving the room only a cursory glance. After Adan came a woman Nath didn't recognize at first—a jade-skinned Twi'lek with white-patterned head-tails and a confidence that made Quell, in comparison, look like a trembling child.

General Hera Syndulla.

Legend of the Rebel Alliance. The woman who'd helped free Lothal, survived Scarif, and led the charge at Endor. Commander of the battle group and special guest aboard the *Lodestar*. If she was making time for a briefing, they were in for very good news or very bad.

"General?" Quell asked.

Syndulla shook her head. "It's your show, Lieutenant."

Quell showed no surprise as she stepped to the front. Syndulla and Adan lingered to one side. "The squadron has been authorized," Quell said, "for limited noncombat operations. Our first mission has been determined, and we fly in six hours."

Nath looked to Syndulla. *Limited noncombat operations* meant a trial run. Syndulla nodded at Quell and said, "The job is recon and asset extraction. I'd send my own people but as you know, we're short on resources. When this situation was brought to my attention, I agreed that it fell into your area of expertise."

Nath heard the tortured grammar and smirked. *When the situation was brought to my attention* suggested she didn't want to give credit or spread blame.

Quell touched one of the ready room displays, and a series of images flashed onscreen: An ancient city flooded by colorful mud, shattered airspeeders and human corpses floating past; a gleaming Imperial population center, modern chrome-and-crimson towers battered and streets silent and lifeless; a village in a field of black grass, residents running from a lightning storm that filled the horizon.

"Operation Cinder," Quell said. She spoke with the hoarseness of emotions smothered and stomped. "You've seen the reports. Most of the targets were saved. Some of them weren't. It'll be years before the full casualty count is known."

Wyl stiffened in his seat. Chass shifted uncomfortably. Neither had been around to help stop the genocides; Nath wondered if they felt guilty.

Quell kept talking. "For all the horrors of Cinder, however, it gave us useful intelligence. It exposed the enemy's most loyal and ruthless units—marked them by their participation in atrocities. We think that information can be useful."

She nodded to Adan, who paced as he picked up the briefing. His voice was crisp; he was a man used to persuading audiences of his brilliance. "The Empire is in disarray. That's obvious by the sheer number of splinter factions—we aren't fighting one enemy, but several dozen. Some are isolated by happenstance: Moff Royen's fleet is cut off from support near the Red Hand Cluster. Others, like Adelhard's faction in the Anoat sector, have decided they're better off securing their own territories and to hell with everyone else. We haven't seen a lot of interfactional warfare, though it's early days yet.

"So how does this relate to Cinder? You have to imagine that Imperials willing to commit atrocities on the orders of a dead Emperor—" Nath watched Adan's eyes, but the spy didn't so much as glance at Quell. "—probably feel a level of solidarity. They're *loyalists*. Even if they're scattered across the galaxy and attached to different factions, they'll look to one another as allies and make contact when possible."

Quell stepped in again. "The 204th Imperial Fighter Wing committed a war crime on Nacronis. Now they're sitting on a treasure trove at Pandem Nai. Who are they going to share those resources with? Who can they trust more than other Cinder veterans?"

Nath looked from Quell to Adan to General Syndulla, searching for a sign of doubt or hesitation. He could accept the logic of Cinder units sticking together, but it was *hunch*, not operational intelligence.

"The planet Abednedo," Quell said, "was a target of Operation Cinder. Thanks to local resistance and a New Republic special forces team, it barely escaped destruction. Following the battle, the specforce team relayed that all Imperial units had fled or been destroyed.

"Five days ago, a coded transmission was sent from Abednedo suggesting that the strike team was in error—that surviving Imperial forces are still hiding on the planet surface. It's not the first report to that effect—New Republic Intelligence has heard rumors of Imperial holdouts before—but it's the first to come through official channels."

"What's the source on this?" Nath asked. Everyone turned to him, and he cut Adan off before the spy could answer. "No, I know, I'm not cleared for that. Put it this way: How *reliable* is your source on this?"

"Not very," Adan said. "We don't have a full ID or background on the sender, but they used the right codes. No specific reason to think the intel isn't valid."

*No wonder Syndulla's not bothering to use her own people,* Nath thought, and graciously nodded to Adan. *She can't possibly believe this is worth pursuing.*

Quell grunted softly. "The purpose of the mission is, in part, to determine the source's credibility and authenticate their information. We will rendezvous with the source, transport them to the *Lodestar,* and if possible perform basic reconnaissance in an effort to locate the Cinder holdouts."

General Syndulla stepped forward again. "I've reviewed Lieutenant Quell's plan and I believe it has merit. Your squadron commander knows what she's doing, and so do all of you. This is what you're best at." She paused, let the words sink in, then dropped her voice an octave. "I want to be clear, however: You are not authorized for combat operations. You want to prove yourselves? This is your opportunity."

"Check your consoles for the flight plan," Quell said. "We resume in fifteen minutes."

Quell, Adan, and Syndulla exited the briefing room together. Nath saw the general place a hand on Quell's arm, but it could have been a warning as easily as a gesture of support. Wyl was already reviewing the flight documents, while Chass appeared to be punching them up on her screen with her feet. "This is what they've finally got for us?" she muttered.

"You figure it's busywork?" Nath asked. He knew the answer. He also knew his audience.

Wyl was the one to reply, which didn't surprise Nath. "I'm more worried we end up killing one another," he said.

That *did* surprise Nath, and he laughed. "That's dark, brother."

"I'm not entirely joking," Wyl said. "We haven't flown in atmosphere as a squadron. There're a lot of unknowns. And—" Chass was glowering in Wyl's direction. Wyl finished with a bitter smile. "—Chass wants me dead."

"Not true," Chass replied. "I just don't care if you live or die."

"Then start caring." Quell's voice, brittle and deadly as glass, broke through the chatter as she returned through the doorway.

Wyl looked chagrined, and his voice softened as he answered Quell. "My fault. But you're asking for a lot of faith."

"No," Quell said. "I'm not. I'm giving you orders, and I expect to be obeyed. This isn't a volunteer mission."

Chass and Wyl both looked to Nath, but Nath only shrugged. "Let's look at that flight plan," he said.

He needed Quell, he told himself. He needed her squadron. He had a job to complete.

*Double or nothing.*

## CHAPTER 10

# SPONTANEOUS ETHICAL RECONFIGURATION

I

From a distance of four hundred thousand kilometers, Abednedo resembled nothing so much as a clod of dirt wrapped in desultory clouds. It possessed no majesty; inspired no awe. For Quell, it was nonetheless her best hope for salvation.

She had been the one to dig up the obscure transmission from the New Republic Intelligence data banks. She had concocted the strangled reasoning connecting theoretical Abednedo holdouts to Shadow Wing. She'd done so knowing that her squadron was falling apart and required something more than simulations to stay together. She'd done so for her own sake, in response to the longing she'd felt when she'd seen Chadic return from her specforce sojourn.

It wasn't likely to work. She was ashamed at how quickly the others had figured it out.

"Chadic, Kairos, with me," she said as D6-L adjusted her X-wing's course toward the southern hemisphere. "Lark and Tensent, establish geostationary orbit above Neshorino and await further instructions."

"Shout if you need us," Tensent replied.

Quell watched two blips on her scanner peel away, while Chadic's assault ship and Kairos's transport followed Quell at a respectful distance. If all went well, Lark and Tensent would never need to make planetfall; the A-wing would make its scouting pass from orbit, if the opportunity arose. The Y-wing was there if everything went terribly wrong.

The X-wing trembled as the vessel penetrated the outermost layer of Abednedo's atmosphere. "We're in the soup," Quell announced as she thumbed through messages from the astromech—signals to and from computerized flight controllers in the city of Neshorino, transmitted far faster than she could read.

The droid's actions disconcerted her. A TIE pilot had no astromech unit to rely on—she was dependent on her carrier ship and flight controllers to plot her course and choose her dock. A TIE pilot needed to trust her team. Now Quell flew a ship that didn't even need her to function.

She thought about Tensent's ancient T5 droid, and how Tensent treated it like a member of the squadron—argued with it in the hangar, wandered with it through the corridors of the *Lodestar*. She'd barely crossed paths with her astromech off-duty. It hadn't seemed to mind.

She approved D6-L's proposed trajectory and let the droid take her down. The silence of space—broken only by the noise and rattle of the ship—gave way to the roar of wind as the X-wing cut through gray cloud cover. Temperature controls activated automatically, chilling Quell as the ship's exterior baked in the heat of reentry. She heard her repulsors thrum to life a moment later, adjusting for the planet's gravity.

Neshorino rose out of a mountain range of endless rust-brown rock. Jagged natural spires stood tipped by ornamental towers, and great cliff faces were carved with painted statuary. A thousand narrow streets and stairwells blurred beneath Quell as she made for one of a series of protruding buttes. There was a beauty to the city, but it was a foreign beauty—Neshorino had been built by a species native to caverns and stone, and no human could ever find comfort there.

Ten minutes later Quell was admiring the stonework up close, walking down a tessellated roadway studded with brightly glazed tiles. Chass na Chadic strolled toward her from a path leading to a neighboring docking platform as the wedge-faced, wide-eyed natives scurried on business around them.

"What are you wearing?" Quell asked.

Chadic scrunched her face and glanced down at her asymmetric leathers. Quell wasn't sure if they qualified as fashionable, cheap, or both—she hadn't owned much in the way of civvies for a while.

"Clothes?" Chadic tried. "I'm wearing clothes. I thought we weren't trying to draw attention."

Quell looked at the navy blue of her own flight suit. "The New Republic saved this planet. We're more likely to get what we need like this."

Chadic parted her lips as if ready to laugh, then shook her head. "Let's go, New Republic lieutenant."

Quell tried not to bristle. *She's egging you on. Respond and you'll just encourage her.* She felt like a child again, suffering her brothers' torments aboard Gavana Orbital. Only it wasn't, she realized as Chadic strode away, her brothers that the Theelin reminded her of—

*Shoot down that thought. Burn it. Focus on the mission.*

They swiftly moved from broad boulevards into narrow alleys so packed with pedestrians that Quell often lost sight of her companion. A faint odor of vanilla and dust and fresh paint pervaded the city—the natural musk of the Abednedo people, perhaps—and up close, Quell could see that Neshorino hadn't been unscathed by Operation Cinder after all. Scaffolds shored up cracked cliff faces and statues the height of skyscrapers stood battered and beheaded, cordoned off and surrounded by rubble. In a plaza walled on one side by a mound of boulders, thousands of gemstones painted like beetles had been placed delicately on the ground; Quell knew nothing about the culture of Abednedo, but she recognized a memorial when she saw one. She thought of the cargo bay aboard the *Pursuer,* converted to honor the victims of the terrorist attack on the Death Star.

They moved on into Neshorino's House of Strangers—the sector of the city reserved for the use of non-Abednedos, full of travelers' lodgings and cantinas enclosing micro-atmospheres. Quell paused long enough to contact D6-L through her comlink and confirm her destination, then led Chadic back into the maze of alleys until a staircase took them away from the crowds and into the rock of the mountainside. There, holographic flames set in crystal chandeliers lit the way to an intersection of eight narrow stairways like wheel spokes. Above the intersection hung an incongruous tarp, covering whatever ancient painting or mosaic had once looked down on pilgrims.

"Here?" Chadic asked.

"Here," Quell said.

They waited. Quell signaled the rest of the squadron and received short replies indicating that nothing of consequence had occurred.

They waited longer. Quell began to wonder if their contact wouldn't show when a figure emerged from one of the passageways and hobbled toward her. The newcomer's most prominent features were the bulbous, compound eyes set in its insectoid skull, and Quell tried to recall what she knew about the Verpine people—a clannish, intelligent species with a reputation for technical aptitude and an esoteric language.

The Verpine adjusted the layers of scarves around its face and made a chittering, squealing noise. It jerked up its left fist and uncurled two of three fingers to reveal a comlink, from which a voice declared, "You identify Republic not Abednedo. Commiserations and deals to be made?"

Quell grimaced. *A street trader with a broken protocol droid.* "We're waiting for someone. Move along."

The Verpine chittered again. "You identify Republic," the comlink repeated, and the insectoid jutted its right hand at Quell's flight suit. "Responding communication?"

Chadic was pacing the enclosed space and peering down the connecting passages. "What communication?" she called.

"Communication of Mission Ember. Confirmed?"

*Operation Cinder.*

"Confirmed," Quell said. It was suddenly cold beneath the mountain.

"Deals to be made," the Verpine said again. "Initial transaction to be confirmed. The Republic is understanding and the moneys?"

Quell amended her mental image of the Verpine: *a street trader with a broken protocol droid and a handful of New Republic security clearances.* Just because the Verpine had sent a coded signal didn't mean it had anything worth selling.

This was a situation she hadn't prepared for. She'd expected a member of a local rebel cell at best, a paranoid informant at worst. Once again, she was playing the role of a spy instead of a pilot and she felt paralyzed.

Chadic must have seen her hesitancy. The Theelin moved between Quell and the Verpine. "Plenty of noise but no one's hollering. You want a deal? You give us something to work with. Give us proof, we give you *moneys.*"

The Verpine clacked and shook in reply. Quell half expected to see it sneeze, or maybe to see another creature crawl out from between its chitinous plates. Instead it rapidly squealed and chittered into the comlink—it seemed to hold a whole conversation—before the machine said, "Merchandise samples provided. Goodwill indicative to Republic government."

*Merchandise?*

But she didn't have to ask. Shuffling footsteps echoed from one of the stairways, and the Verpine pointed a trembling finger at the two individuals who descended. The first was an Abednedo, burly and simply dressed as he escorted the second: a pale man in bone-white armor, his eyes wide, cheeks bruised, and hands cuffed together. He looked horrifyingly young under the dried blood that framed his mouth. On his shoulder was the white pauldron of an Imperial stormtrooper sergeant.

"Merchandise sample," the Verpine said. "Take? Take."

The stormtrooper's eyes locked onto Quell's flight suit and didn't stray. She looked at the grime and scars beneath the fuzz of his hair. He was bent forward and seemed unable to straighten.

Chadic swore and looked to Quell. Quell clenched her fists, trying to will herself not to tremble and to focus on her job. She moved until she was close enough to the stormtrooper that he could have torn her throat with his teeth.

"Operation Cinder," she said. Nothing more than that.

Quell had never been adept at reading body language; never known how to ask the probing questions an interrogator might. But she recognized the flash of uncertainty in the sergeant's face. The look that said: *It's classified, and anything I say could get me tossed into the brig.*

"More merchandise for moneys-purchase," the Verpine said. "This one take. Goodwill."

"The rest of the merchandise," Quell said. "You can show me?"

"Ready. Yes? Ready to show."

Quell stepped away from the stormtrooper and gestured Chadic to one side. "Kairos is waiting," she murmured. "Get this—" She shifted a shoulder in the stormtrooper's direction. "—this prisoner to the U-wing. I want to see what else is for sale."

"You don't want backup?" Chadic asked. She was more focused on Quell than on the stormtrooper. There was no concern in her voice, which might have hurt under other circumstances.

"I want to get out of here with a win. Even if that's just our—" *Our free sample,* she thought, but the words tasted bilious and she didn't complete the sentence.

Chadic patted the pistol strapped to her side as if reassuring herself. Like her clothing, the weapon was irregular—some sort of exotic slugthrower—and, Quell guessed, as illegal under the New Republic as under the Empire. "I'll handle it," Chadic said.

Quell nodded to the Verpine and left Chadic, the stormtrooper, and the Verpine's assistant as the Verpine led the way down a staircase and through another tunnel. "You want to tell me where you found the merchandise?" she asked.

The Verpine chattered into the comlink until the droid echoed back,

"Profession is traveler. Transporter. Merchandise requests secret non-standard transport offworld."

"The *merchandise* requested transport?"

"Nonstandard transport. Nonstandard is specialty."

They passed under an archway and onto a battered stone bridge spanning the chasm between two cliff faces. Airspeeders hummed above, and the stench of dust and rot rose from below. Quell looked down onto a massive rockslide being picked over by droids and Abednedos.

More signs of Operation Cinder, perhaps. She tried not to think about it.

"Nonstandard transport," she said. She wasn't sure if it was a euphemism or a poor translation, but either way she guessed it meant "smuggling." "You were contacted by the merchandise, and . . . ?"

They passed into another tunnel and up a staircase, arriving in a broad cavern open to the sky. In the cavern's center sat a Ghtroc 690 light freighter, filthy and dented as if it had flown through a sandstorm. Quell recognized the vessel from her youth, and tried to think about the agri-hauler who'd often dined with her family instead of the realization crawling up her spine.

"See? Look now. Look."

The ship's loading door slid open, rattling and hissing, and her eyes adjusted to the darkness inside as a reek of sweat and waste mingled with the sickening sweet scent of infected wounds. Scattered around the ship's hold like crates of unsorted salvage were a dozen or more figures in once-white armor encrusted with stains. Like the sergeant, each was cuffed, hands behind his or her back. Unlike the sergeant, these were gagged and tethered to support struts and cargo anchors. Many were motionless, asleep or unconscious on the metal deck. Others raised their grimy heads and squinted into the light of the cavern. A green-eyed woman shook hard enough that her cuffs rattled. A gray-haired man shifted protectively to block Quell from the prone figure beside him.

In the 204th, Quell's squadron had once disabled a slaver ship. The conditions there had been no worse.

These were the holdouts of Abednedo. The survivors of Operation Cinder, desperately seeking a way offworld. They'd turned to a smuggler for help, tried to flee, and instead the Verpine had chosen to sell them out to the New Republic—

Quell felt her heart rate accelerate. Her breathing turned shallow. She shuddered, every instinct telling her to draw her sidearm and bring the Verpine to justice for reducing brave stormtroopers to terror and humiliation.

But she *was* the New Republic now, and these troopers had attempted to commit atrocities.

This was necessary. This would lead to Shadow Wing.

"What's your price?" she asked.

## ||

Chass na Chadic didn't care for stormtroopers, but the sergeant didn't give her an excuse to exercise her aggression. He walked at the pace she set, never turned to face her or spoke in defiance. He was, if not broken, beaten.

Chass could settle for that.

She hadn't thought much about Operation Cinder. The *Hellion's Dare* had been too far from the worlds that suffered, receiving only snippets of news about slaughters carried out by the retreating Empire. She'd felt a reflexive anger, a surge of rage, that had quickly melted into the sea of affronts the Empire had committed. It hadn't been the Empire's first genocide, after all; just the most petty.

So it wasn't Cinder that made her loathe the man stumbling in front of her. It was the smaller indignities—the scandoc checks and extortion rackets and beatings she'd suffered back when. Maybe the sergeant was one of the *good* stormtroopers who never left a Rim rat with broken ribs because she looked at him wrong—but what did it matter? He'd chosen to support the Empire as it was, and every stormtrooper was complicit in something.

She was out of the House of Strangers and proceeding down a high-walled alley when she halted. She couldn't have said what triggered her wariness; maybe it was just being trapped between two stone barriers.

"Stop," she said. The sergeant stopped. "We're turning around."

The stormtrooper began to run. Chass cursed. Then she saw a flash of red light, smelled vaporized atmosphere, and felt chips of stone slash her cheek.

She didn't see the shooter. Shooters. Whoever it was wasn't at ground level, and there were enough windows and balconies built into the alley walls that there was nowhere she could be sure was *safe*. She sprinted forward, pumping her legs and feeling the stiffness in her thighs—she'd spent too much time flying and not enough on her feet over the past month—and rapidly overtook the sergeant.

She didn't assume the shooters *wouldn't* kill him, but she expected she could use him as a shield. He put up an anemic struggle as she wrapped her arms around him, yanked him backward, and put her spine against the wall. Particle bolts scorched trails through the air, and when the sergeant went slack Chass drew her weapon—a KD-30 pistol more expensive than anything else she'd ever owned—and scanned for a target.

She didn't find one. A blaster bolt struck the rock half a meter from her foot. She suddenly regretted drawing her weapon. With one arm around the sergeant, she had no way to reach her comlink and call for help.

This wasn't how she wanted to die. Not murdered by stormtroopers on a pointless mission on a nothing planet. She was shaking from the surge of adrenaline—the mix of thrill and frustration.

"We go," she snapped, and shoved the sergeant forward. She didn't look back, didn't focus on anything but pushing down the alleyway. She panted for breath, mouth hanging open and body cold with sweat. By the time she emerged into a broader boulevard packed with Abednedo pedestrians and merchant stalls, her vision was blurred from exertion and the rush of blood.

She was still alive, though.

The pedestrians shouted and scattered like startled birds. She didn't understand the language but she could guess the meaning of the cries. Half a dozen humans (almost always humans, with the Empire—that fact was enough to make Chass proud of her Theelin blood) rushed out onto high stairs and landings overlooking the plaza, each in civilian attire and carrying a blaster rifle. Even at a distance, Chass recognized the weapons as E-11s. Stormtrooper gear.

Chass took the first shot. She missed. Smoke curled up from the stonework beside her target: The KD-30 fired custom rounds instead of particle bolts, each loaded with a virulent acid that could dissolve almost anything. Not even a Hutt, layered with oil and fat, could survive a shot from the KD-30. But a Hutt was easier to hit than a stormtrooper, and Chass only had nine rounds left.

She took another shot. This time a stormtrooper howled in agony, but the Imperials were already maneuvering to pin her down. She couldn't run again—a dash across the boulevard would require moving through the kill zone—unless she abandoned the sergeant. Quell wouldn't be thrilled with that outcome, but Chass wondered if it was her only route to safety.

She heard a scream. She hadn't fired her next round. Then another scream, and she risked a glance toward the sounds.

Kairos stood on one of the overlooks, lifting an Imperial by the head with both hands. The man writhed in her grip, then sagged. Chass couldn't see what Kairos had done—snapped his neck, she hoped, though there were more nightmarish possibilities—but when Kairos dropped the body off the edge of the staircase it hit stone with the limp thud of a corpse. The man's pain hadn't lasted long.

The attackers turned their weapons on Kairos. Kairos moved through the red storm of bolts like an assassin, freezing and then dashing forward, hurling an enemy into a current of blasterfire or shooting a foe from across the boulevard with the weapon slung around her torso. Chass tried to recognize it between quick shots: a *bowcaster*, maybe?

There was something savage about Kairos's attacks. Chass realized what when she scanned the corpses around the boulevard and saw that nearly all of them had heads blackened and bloodied to unrecognizability.

Then Kairos was at her side and they were running, dragging the sergeant between them. Chass felt herself putting as much distance between herself and the strange woman as possible. She caught glimpses of dark stains on Kairos's battered cloak.

The U-wing was in sight atop its landing butte when Chass thought to holster her weapon and signal Quell. "We were followed," she panted, feeling the strain on her throat. "Kairos and I have the trooper, but if they found us—"

"Someone was watching our source," Quell replied. She sounded like her thoughts were elsewhere. Chass tried not to resent her for it and failed. "Get to your ship. Get the U-wing and the passenger safely into orbit."

"What are *you* doing?" Chass asked.

"There's more. The Verpine has a whole freighter full. He's agreed to fly his ship back to the *Lodestar,* but if there's trouble he'll need an escort and—"

"You want us to wait?"

"No," Quell said. She paused awhile. "Objective is unchanged. Get out of here with a win. Get the passenger into orbit, rendezvous with Lark and Tensent. I'll make sure the Verpine gets away safely."

It was a bad plan. It was *obviously* a bad plan, Chass thought, so much so that Quell had to see it. They'd been separated and now they needed to reunite.

But it was Quell's plan. Maybe she saw something Chass didn't.

"Good luck," Chass said. "And move quick. The guys chasing us play dirty." *And apparently so does Kairos,* she thought, but at least Kairos was on her side.

III

It wasn't more than a minute after Chass na Chadic signaled Quell that the cavern came under fire. The entrance was defensible—a tight enough bottleneck that even Quell, with only her rusty blaster skills and a light pistol, could keep the enemy at bay. But it was obvious the foe wasn't fully committed, either. The Imperials were waiting for reinforcements, which meant Quell and the Verpine had to leave.

"Now?" The question came through the comlink. The Verpine was already in the cockpit, anxious to launch.

"No," Quell said. "You'll know when."

She tried not to think of the *merchandise* aboard the Ghtroc 690. She was glad the Verpine hadn't started the ship's engines; she didn't want to inspire the enemy to barrel on through, desperate not to lose the cargo. Desperate not to lose friends and comrades.

Then a shadow crossed her body and her ragged hair shifted in the breeze. An engine roared louder than blasterfire. Her X-wing had arrived.

Another disconcerting advantage of flying with an astromech droid: Your ship came when you called.

The X-wing lowered itself into the cavern on its repulsors, barely edging around the freighter. Quell waited until it was ten meters away then made her dash. The enemy would pause for an instant to confirm she'd stopped firing, then pursue; if she wasn't under the canopy by the time the Imperials were in the hangar, she'd make an easy target.

"Now!" she called.

The X-wing hovered in place, canopy open and D6's dome spinning as the droid scanned its surroundings. Quell leapt and caught a strike foil—already locked into attack mode—as particle bolts lashed past her. She felt the exhaust of the freighter's thrusters against her cheek as she half swung, half fell into the cockpit seat. The transparent metal canopy was already lowering.

Then she was in position. Her body still felt uncomfortable in the rebel ship, but her feet located pedals and her hands, after a moment searching panels, found the controls she needed. She looked through the haze of crimson bolts and saw a squad of Imperials pouring through the cavern entrance.

The attackers were in civilian attire, yet they moved with the coordination of army veterans. They weren't the bruised and filthy captives

Quell had seen aboard the freighter. Neither were they polished fighters in pressed uniforms and grimly determined faces. They looked
desperate. They looked scared. They reminded Quell of the inmates at
Traitor's Remorse.

One carried a portable rocket launcher. As the woman hefted it
onto her shoulder, Quell made her decision and squeezed the trigger
on her control yoke. The cavern exploded in fire, and she watched the
faces of the soldiers as, one by one, they died to the X-wing's blasts.

She heard no emotion in her voice as she said: "Quell to squadron.
We're lifting off."

## IV

Wyl Lark's reservations about the mission changed nothing. When the
signal came from Chass he opened his throttle, checked his course,
and made to intercept Chass and Kairos as they emerged from Abednedo's atmosphere. He called for Nath to join him—the Y-wing wasn't
built for dogfighting but the assault craft would be vulnerable on its
own—and it was Nath who reminded him, "What about *not authorized for combat operations*?"

"The combat operation came to us," Wyl said. "If you know how to
avoid a fight, now's the time to say."

Nath laughed. Wyl saw the Y-wing match his course, and he reduced his acceleration to allow Nath to catch up.

There were three new marks approaching Chass and Kairos. Wyl
wasn't sure where they'd come from, but Chass called out an ID—
"Three dupes closing"—and snorted.

"You want to repeat that?" Nath asked. "They're really sending TIE
bombers?"

"Must be all they've got left," Chass said.

Wyl strained forward, staring into the starfield in search of the
bombers' double-sphere chassis (the *dupes*) and curved wings. He
tamped down his confidence. A bomber might lack speed and maneuverability, but its cannons could still tear a fighter apart.

He'd almost lost Chass in the Oridol Cluster. He'd failed there in many ways, but he didn't intend to lose her now. Nor Kairos.

The dogfight had already begun by the time Wyl spotted the foe. The TIEs swung in to fire a coordinated volley at the U-wing, then retreated before Chass's B-wing could snare a target. Wyl was preparing to pursue the TIEs on their next pass when another voice came through his comm.

"Tensent. Lark. I'm en route to your last coordinates but not seeing you. What's going on?"

Quell's voice. Wyl winced. "Kairos has three marks on her," he said. "We're about to intercept—you want us to turn around?"

There was a short pause, then: "Negative. I'm still in atmo. Got an allied light freighter ahead of me but no threats in sight. I'll get it to hyperspace, then join you."

"Acknowledged." Wyl glanced at the scanner and saw the exposed freighter at the edge of his range. He agreed with Quell's assessment of the threat: The U-wing was in imminent danger. The freighter was not.

He watched emerald fire blaze over the U-wing—even made out the shimmering of the transport's shields—and angled himself into position to pursue the last bomber as it came out of its dive. The other enemy pilots realized what was happening and tried to decelerate, to fall back and behind Wyl, but they weren't swift enough to save their comrade. Wyl latched onto his target, squeezed his trigger, and felt the pulse of his cannons ripple through his ship. He was forced to slow as the bomber detonated in a bright, powerful burst ahead of him, giving his pursuers an opportunity to draw closer. He would need the rest of his squadron to save him.

"Give them to me," Nath said, "if they're careless enough to follow."

"Roger that." Wyl angled the A-wing to bring it around, watching the two marks follow on his scanner. "We're doing good," he murmured to his ship.

And they were. For all their early troubles during training, the squadron seemed to be operating effectively. Wyl rolled and jinked, not trying to lose his pursuers but simply preventing them from getting a target lock. He veered into Nath's cone of fire and saw the closest

TIE careen away—damaged or attempting to escape, he wasn't sure. The second bomber remained in pursuit, and he pulled it into range of Chass; the mark disappeared from his scanner and the Theelin announced, "Scratch one."

"Where's the last TIE?" Wyl asked.

"Got away," Nath said. "Heading for the freighter."

Wyl grimaced and looked in the direction he and Nath had come from, but he saw only the bright curve of Abednedo above him. "Quell? You get that?"

"I got it. One bomber incoming. I can intercept. Lark, see if you can catch it before it arrives."

He adjusted his course and opened his throttle until he could feel the strain and rattle of the ship in his bones. He watched the scanner and allowed the computer to automatically adjust his vector—at his velocity, a one-degree error would send him kilometers from the TIE.

To his surprise, the bomber was still accelerating. The TIE wouldn't escape—the A-wing could keep up no matter how much power the enemy pilot diverted to engines—but what was it trying to *do*? At its current speed, it would only have a fraction of a second to fire on Quell or the freighter before whipping past. After that, it would need minutes to return and make another firing run, *if* the maneuver didn't tear the TIE apart.

"Quell?" he asked.

"I see it."

"What are you—"

"Go radio silent, Lark. I need to focus."

As his body protested against the g forces, he watched the blips on his scanner. The TIE approached the freighter. The X-wing moved to intercept. Like the TIE, Quell would have only one chance to destroy her target—one volley as the bomber came hurtling past.

Wyl realized what was going to happen. He saw what the TIE was trying to accomplish. But there was nothing to be done. He needed seconds more to enter firing range.

He watched the scanner as his ship roared. He saw the TIE pass

Quell's X-wing close enough for the dots to merge. He saw no explosion, no distant flash of light.

The flash came a moment later. The freighter and the TIE both disappeared from the scanner.

"They're gone," Quell said. "They're gone."

Wyl heard the despair in Quell's voice.

"What was on that freighter?" he asked.

## V

Caern Adan was waiting in the hangar of the *Lodestar* when they returned. With him stood a security team primed to take possession of the sole surviving prisoner. But Quell barely noticed either as she climbed out of her X-wing. She was cold—her flight suit was soaked through with sweat—and the afterimage of devastation was burned into her retinas. She still saw the freighter tearing in two as the bomber impacted; the specks of soldiers floating in the void before they were vaporized, their journey of misery and imprisonment ending in inglorious death.

Light-headed, she swept her gaze to the other ships—her squadron (*her* squadron) and the pilots climbing down onto the hangar deck. She summoned them with a wave of her hand as the security team boarded the U-wing.

Her people knew what had happened. They knew what to expect. Wyl Lark looked somber, head high, ready to take responsibility; Nath Tensent watched the U-wing; Chass na Chadic shifted uncomfortably, boredly; and Kairos was Kairos, motionless and unreadable.

"That was a disaster," Quell said.

No one replied.

"You—" She jutted a finger at Lark, then moved it to Tensent. "—should never have repositioned without authorization. I don't care what you did as a rebel, improvisation gets people killed."

Lark looked surprised. Tensent grunted. Again, no one spoke.

"You—" She turned her gaze on Chadic. "—could have signaled me for instructions. You could have reached me through my comlink if I wasn't in my fighter. You could have avoided engaging the bombers and just jumped to lightspeed. You could have—"

"I could've done a lot of things," Chadic said. "You'd have blamed me for them, too. *You* could've not split us up, paid more attention to the comms, actually *shot* the bomber heading directly for you—"

"You're not in command!" Quell heard her voice rise to a shout and forced herself to control her volume. She noticed Ragnell, the tattooed engineer, pretending not to watch while she unloaded D6 from the X-wing. "This is a debriefing, not a discussion. You want to talk tactics, we can do it later."

Chadic shook her head in evident disgust, but she held her tongue. It was the most Quell could hope for.

Chadic wasn't wrong, of course. Quell knew that, but she couldn't think about it now.

"We screwed up," Quell said. "People are dead. We'll have to live with it."

"We got one," Tensent said. "We screwed up, but we gained more than we lost."

"Only if the captive is useful," a new voice added. Quell turned to watch Adan approach the group. He wasn't looking at her, instead observing the security team half guiding, half carrying the stormtrooper sergeant from the U-wing. "That man doesn't strike me as the link to Shadow Wing we were hoping for, but I suppose you can't tell at a glance."

A shiver worked its way down Quell's spine. "No," she said. "You can't."

"And apparently," Adan continued, "you also can't tell when a mission will involve combat. At least the ships are all intact."

"We knew it was a risk," she said. "There's *always* a risk of engagement."

"Well, we'll just have to try *very* hard to get information from our one lowly sergeant—"

"*Stop*," Quell said. Her shuddering was constant now. She drew a long, ragged breath, but it wouldn't end.

Adan looked at her with sudden intensity. Something ignited in his eyes. "Excuse me?"

She stared at her superior officer. The man she'd fought to prove her loyalty and ability to over the course of weeks. The man who had given her a second chance after she'd abandoned the Empire. But she couldn't prevent the words from escaping her lips. "*Stop*," she repeated. "We were on this mission because we didn't have any other leads. Because you, the *intelligence* officer, didn't give us anything better to work with—"

"You should watch your tone," Adan said, and now his voice was loud, too, his eyes wide. Lark was saying something, stepping forward and trying to intervene, but Quell ignored him.

"You threw this group together from scraps," she said, "like we're supposed to know how to do this, but we *don't*. We don't have the training, we don't—"

"*None* of us had training!" Adan's voice was a roar. "None of us had the luxury of years in an academy, learning every damn protocol under the suns. We figured it out along the way, and when people got killed we knew it was the price of *rebelling* against your Empire! Maybe it's time you—"

The words began to blur together. Chadic was nodding slightly. Quell saw the dead prisoners floating in space. She felt the stiffness in her shoulder as she lunged forward and brought her fist into Adan's stomach.

He hadn't been prepared for it. He bent over, and Quell heard indecipherable shouting through the hangar. She didn't look at the others as she stormed out, making her way through the *Lodestar*'s cramped hallways until she found a restroom.

There she fell to her knees and vomited.

None of this was why Quell had joined the Rebellion.

She sat on her knees on the cold floor of the restroom, picturing the soldiers who'd died aboard the freighter. Picturing the infantry she'd slaughtered with her X-wing in the cavern. Thinking of the occupied research station she'd fired upon at Harrikos-Fifteen.

She was sick of bloodshed. She felt dirty from toes to hair. She'd joined the Rebellion—the New Republic—to get away from that feeling. To do something worthwhile.

She thought of her mentor, Major Soran Keize, and what he'd told her long before the incident at Mek'tradi—long before she'd confessed her youthful admiration for the Rebel Alliance. It had been after Mennar-Daye, when so many of their enemies had fallen and the bombers had made runs over the cave systems for *days*. She hadn't been able to sleep, knowing about those bombers, imagining rebels buried in grit and slowly suffocating. Keize had found her one night studying in the *Pursuer*'s mess hall, and gradually coaxed out her insecurities.

"War is always monstrous," he'd told her, "but that doesn't make us monsters."

It was the first time she'd heard him say that, but not the last. She'd eventually learned to repeat the words like a mantra, use them to calm herself after operations that seemed destructive beyond reason. She'd believed in the sentiment. It had helped her face herself and her comrades.

But Keize had participated in Operation Cinder, too.

The words weren't as soothing as they'd used to be.

# VI

"She *hit* me," Caern said. His stomach was still sore. He could feel the fist impacting flesh, the vertigo as he'd been thrown off balance.

"That is inexcusable," IT-O said. The droid floated amicably above the cot in the supply closet Caern had requisitioned for his private cabin. "But I must ask: Did you intentionally provoke her?"

"Of course not!" Caern scoffed, stood from his seat atop his cramped workdesk, and sat back down as the blood rushed to his head. He started to go on, then grudgingly replayed the confrontation in his mind. "No. I may have—I was irritable, and that may have affected me, but no. Would it matter if I had?"

"It would in no way justify her actions. It would provide additional insight into your motivations, and hers."

"This isn't about *my* motivations. This is about gross insubordination and—and she's testing her limits. She disobeyed orders. Now she's punching people? It's gone far enough."

"I agree completely," the droid said. "I suggest she be removed from duty immediately."

Caern let out a hoarse laugh. The droid knew what his response would be; did IT-O want to force him to say it? "We're stuck with her now. Even if I could find a new squadron commander—High Command might, *might* take me seriously enough to transfer someone from elsewhere on the battlefront, though it would be humiliating beyond belief—she's still the only one with inside experience. She's the one who's been training the squadron to work together. We don't have time to find someone else."

"Is it possible that the cost of keeping Yrica Quell is greater than the cost of delay? There are other squadrons beyond your working group."

Caern considered the question. His voice was softer when he said, "No. No, that's the sort of thinking that got Shadow Wing deprioritized in the first place. If we don't stop them here, there will be another Nacronis. Or another Blacktar Cyst. Or—something new and awful, the sort of thing only officers like Quell can dream up.

"I'm going to keep digging. Call in every contact I've got, in and out of the New Republic, to uncover her story. If we find the truth about Yrica Quell, maybe we can control her."

"I don't envy your position," the droid said.

"No," Caern said. "I suppose you don't."

He sat in silence awhile. The droid usually reduced its hovering altitude, dimmed its lights, and muffled its hum when it recognized that a conversation was over. It didn't do so now and Caern knew it was giving him space. A moment to reflect before moving on to the next awful dilemma.

The moment didn't last. "I understand the squadron brought home a captive. A stormtrooper sergeant who participated in Operation Cinder."

"What about him?" Caern asked.

"Do you intend to interrogate him yourself?"

He let the question linger. He savored the bitterness like a swallow of wine. "Yes."

"Would you prefer that I did so in your place?"

Caern met the gaze of the droid's red photoreceptor. "No. I would not."

The droid had asked that question before—more than once over the years. Caern had never said yes. He feared what would happen if he did.

"As you wish," the droid said, and drifted downward as if falling asleep.

The Empire had as many types of prisons as it had weapons, and Caern had seen most of them over his career. The labor camps were luxurious in their way—brutal, apt to work inmates to death, but the prisoners were more likely to be killed by one another than by a stormtrooper. They were the place for irritants and petty criminals whom the Empire preferred to ignore. Conversely, the mass education centers were exercises in brutality, where whole villages were packed into conditions rats would balk at and left to fester in their filth. There were the mobile prisons like Accresker, built to discourage rescue attempts. There were the biocontainment zones for species the Empire hadn't properly cataloged (and for any nonhuman who particularly irritated an Imperial officer).

Then there were the transitory facilities—transitory only in the sense that, officially, a prisoner was to be held at such a camp for a maximum of six months before being moved to a more appropriate location (or released, rare though that was). The transitory facilities were for prisoners who *might* be something special—rebel informants, or Crymorah syndicate lackeys, or accessories to some grand act of Imperial corruption—but whom the relevant authorities weren't ready to label yet.

Many prisoners in transitory facilities were never charged with a crime at all. They were locked away because a stormtrooper or a loyalty officer or a middling bureaucrat found them indistinctly *suspicious* and wanted someone else to investigate further.

That was how Caern Adan had come to be in prison. How he'd gone from writing articles about disputes within the InterGalactic Banking Clan and Corporate Sector solvency to being confined for twenty-seven months for reasons no one had ever fully articulated.

He hadn't been a rebel. He'd been a passable financial journalist, credentialed and censored by the Empire.

He drank before the facility, though not as much as he drank now. He'd always been a coward, but he'd never had *phobias* before his imprisonment. As was the way of things, his time there had radicalized him; persuaded him to join the Rebel Alliance. He'd made allies. Met Kairos. Met IT-O, though that relationship had begun as a rocky one.

He thought of all this as he made his way through the *Lodestar* to the brig where the stormtrooper was confined. He didn't know the man's name—the stormtrooper hadn't offered and Caern had ordered the man kept in isolation. He'd performed enough interrogations that he didn't *need* a name or a background check to predict how it all would go.

The stormtrooper would stonewall awhile. Caern would be polite, trying to coax out information with a smile and reassurances. When that didn't work, he would grow frustrated but try to hide it; a day later he would emphasize to the stormtrooper how little time they had, how swiftly the chance of a merciful outcome was passing. He would hint at a deep familiarity with Imperial interrogation techniques and ask whether the stormtrooper believed the New Republic would enforce its regulations regarding the treatment of prisoners.

Maybe Caern would play upon the stormtrooper's guilt, if he had any. Maybe he would lie about the man's comrades and say that they, too, were imprisoned and ready to turn. Maybe Caern would bond with the man over a sumptuous meal. In the end, Caern would get what he wanted.

He could've passed the job on to IT-O. That thought crossed his mind as he nodded politely to the guard on duty and passed into a cramped corridor where three little cell doors waited. But Caern had, as Yrica Quell had reminded him, been useless enough so far. He operated best from behind a desk, or with an enemy who didn't fight back.

Caern knocked on the door of the stormtrooper's cell.

"It's time for your interview," he said.

## CHAPTER 11

# PRIMITIVE CULTURAL REGRESSION

**I**

Yrica Quell flew through an endless night in the cockpit of an Imperial TIE fighter. No asteroids or planets moved through the vastness around her; not even stars marked the void to contextualize her journey.

The TIE wasn't real, though. It was a simulation, and while the scream of the engines was nearly perfect it didn't have the smell of old sweat and seat leather. There were no scratches around the edges of the viewport where panels had been imperfectly installed. It wasn't satisfactory, but it was better than an X-wing that had never fit her comfortably.

She changed course through the virtual blackness and grimaced when the thought came, unbidden, that her astromech unit would confirm her new vector. The X-wing might not have fit comfortably, but she was getting used to its luxuries.

She was surprised when a voice came through her comm. "Alphabet Leader, this is Spectre Leader. Bring it in for a landing, will you?"

She didn't recognize the call sign. A moment later she recognized the voice. *You can't hide anymore,* she told herself, and shut down the simulation. When she climbed out of the pod, General Syndulla was waiting.

"Alphabet Leader?" Quell asked.

The jade-skinned woman smiled crookedly. "It's what the other squadrons are calling you. I think you're stuck with it."

She didn't sound like a woman furious at being disobeyed, or at the deaths of prisoners, or at one of her subordinates manhandling a superior officer. Maybe she was just resigned—maybe Syndulla had known the mission would fail from the start, and she was ready to order Quell off her ship.

Or maybe she'd send Quell to a prisoner-of-war camp somewhere. She'd be within her rights.

"Walk with me," Syndulla said, "and let's talk."

The general led the way out of the simulation center, speaking as she went. "I've already gotten the story from the rest of your squadron," she said. "Interesting bunch. Rotten mission. Lots of people dead, and you should've known better."

"I know."

"Even your droid offered to resign. Sent me a report, said it mishandled the targeting calculations in that last run—that you were attempting an almost impossible shot, and it should've known as much."

"It wasn't the droid's fault."

"Agreed."

Quell was puzzled by the notion that D6-L had tried to take the fall, but she had other concerns for the moment.

"It was a tragedy," Syndulla went on. "You didn't want it. I realize that, and I'm not saying you did. Maybe you could've planned better, but you weren't anticipating an engagement and—" She stopped and turned to face Quell. "How many people died aboard that freighter?"

"Sixteen, I think. More, if the Verpine had a crew."

"Okay. You know the number. That means you take this seriously and I don't have to rub it in."

Quell nodded. She felt the ache in her shoulder and her skull return, as if her body revolted against the conversation.

"You should've anticipated how things could go wrong," Syndulla said. She was walking again, ducking under piping and conduits in the tight corridors of the *Lodestar*. Quell cleared the passages with ease. "But you're young. You're new to the job. You can learn from your mistakes. Your bigger problem—" She laughed to herself, and Quell wanted to bristle; yet there was no mockery in it. "Your bigger problem is that even if you *had* seen everything coming, your plan still would've fallen apart."

*Because I'm incompetent?* She let the general talk as they turned a corner and headed toward the hangar.

"You expected your people to fly like Imperials," Syndulla said. "You expected predictability and deference—and that's your right if that's how you want to run your squadron, but these people have spent years learning to trust their comrades and do what has to be done. I'm not saying it's the best way—the 204th obviously operated differently, and you outflew us plenty of times—but it's *their* way."

"I do understand that, General," Quell said. She wanted to quarrel with the particulars—with the notion that somehow rebel flying was more reliant on trust or more creative and improvisational, but there was truth to the idea that the Empire valued *squadrons* and the Rebellion valued *pilots*.

Syndulla nodded brusquely. The lights in the hangar had been dimmed in accordance with the ship's clock. A few droids hummed about the bay, disengaging fuel lines or polishing nose cones. Aside from Quell and the general, only one other person occupied the vast chamber, tinkering with the underside of an astromech unit.

"Ragnell," Syndulla called. "You working in the dark again?"

The tattooed mechanic slid out from beneath the droid and flicked her hand in what could have either been a cutting motion or the sloppiest salute Quell had ever witnessed. Quell felt a rush of discomfort, but the general seemed unperturbed. "My body's still stuck on Chandrilan time," Ragnell said. "Figured I'd get ahead before you broke more of my ships."

"Good attitude. You watch out for the ships, I'll watch out for my pilots," Syndulla replied.

Ragnell retreated back under the droid. Syndulla waved Quell along as they walked past rows of X-wings and Y-wings. Gold and blue stripes marked the Y-wings of Hail Squadron, while the starfighters of Meteor Squadron were decorated with brightly colored paintings of rock and ice. Like the sloppy salute, these personalizations discomforted Quell. The Empire permitted no customization.

Syndulla noticed Quell's gaze and murmured, "Ragnell's got more than a few hidden talents. Tattoos and paint jobs among them—but don't tell her I told you."

Quell cast another sidelong glance at the woman under the droid, but Syndulla was moving on and her voice was businesslike once more.

"How well do you know your people?" Syndulla asked.

*Well enough,* Quell wanted to answer, but she knew it wasn't the reply the general was looking for. "I've read their profiles. I've talked to IT-O—Adan's droid—and gotten its opinion. I've participated in—"

"All right, you're not the eats-with-the-pilots sort of commander. Let me put it this way: You know your squadron will fight, but will they fight for *you*?"

Quell said nothing.

"Do they know that *you'll* fight for *them*?"

Again, Quell said nothing. Syndulla waited as if she expected an answer, but Quell had nothing to give. "Come on," the general said, and marched at a brisker pace out of the hangar before climbing a ladder to the upper decks. Her tone became curt, and Quell wondered if she'd displeased her. "I'm giving your squadron an assignment—and don't you dare tell me I can't. So long as you're operating out of my ship, I'll go around Caern Adan whenever I want."

"Yes, General." Whatever Quell was about to be assigned, she doubted it would be to her liking; but any assignment at all suggested she wasn't about to be imprisoned.

"Alphabet's been chewing up resources I'd rather use on other projects. Not that Shadow Wing and Pandem Nai aren't strategically important—I've heard Adan's arguments and I believe them—but the *Lodestar* has its own battles to fight. You're using up fuel, power cells, food rations, and I'm short on *all* of it.

"The truth is, Lieutenant Quell, we weren't ready to win this war. Our supply lines are shot. I spend more time discussing logistics nowadays than I ever did when we were a patchwork fleet scampering around the galaxy."

"The Separatists had the same issue in the Wentrion Gaps." Quell saw a glimpse of surprise through the general's mask. "I've read a lot of military history."

"I imagine you have," Syndulla said. "In any event, since we don't have any new leads on Shadow Wing right this second, it's time for you to pay your dues. There's an old rebel supply cache not far from here. The base hasn't been used for years but we kept it stocked in case we needed a safe house." They reached a door with a roughly affixed plaque reading GENERAL HERA SYNDULLA. The general indicated for Quell to wait, entered the room, and returned a moment later with a datapad in hand. "I want your team to strip the base bare and lug everything back home. Nothing romantic about the job, nothing they'll sing songs about, but I can't spare other forces to do it."

Quell took the datapad and glanced down at a list of coordinates, topographic surveys, and inventory listings. "Noncombat, I assume?" she asked.

"You assume right. You show up, you land, you spend a day or two loading cargo. Best case, it turns out those inventories are accurate and we don't have to requisition more equipment for a bit. Worst case, at least pirates won't get whatever's there."

"Are looters a serious concern?"

"Only if someone's been stupid enough to talk about the base in public. But rebel secrets have been spilling out since Endor, so anything's possible." Syndulla tapped the door's keypad. The door locked with a metallic clunk. "I'm sure Officer Adan will have a laundry list of objectives he wants pursued when you get back. But how you handle *this* mission will help me decide if there's another."

Quell clenched the datapad until she feared the screen would break. "Understood," she said.

She was being punished, and deservedly so. She'd been given a menial task. But she was also being tested—if only to determine her willingness to *accept* a menial punishment.

She'd expected worse. She would see it through.

They started walking again. Quell felt reasonably certain she'd been dismissed, and cringed inwardly at the awkwardness of following the general all the way to the pilots' berths and crew quarters. But Syndulla made no comment, and they moved in silence.

Even at night, sounds of life echoed through the corridors: irritable shouts and calls for assistance; the whistling of droids and the replies of their masters; laughter drifting out of one of the ready rooms; and from somewhere—Quell couldn't guess where—the sound of music, real-time voices singing over recorded instruments.

"Can I ask you something?" she said to the general.

"Ask whatever you want while you've got me."

She hesitated. The question felt like a risk, but she wanted to know. "You've been doing this a long time," Quell said. "The Imperial Navy has massive dossiers about you."

"More a statement than a question." Syndulla flashed a good-humored smile, then answered: "More than a decade now."

"Is it worth it?"

Syndulla cocked her head.

"Not the Rebellion," Quell added quickly. "Not fighting against the Empire, but—being a soldier. Everything it costs."

Syndulla's face took on a look not—as Quell had feared—of disdain or suspicion, but of something approaching pity or maternal sympathy. "Look around you, Yrica. The answer's all over."

Quell didn't understand. When the general walked on, she didn't follow.

## II

The moon had no name. The planet only had a numeric designation. The star system was called Harkrova, after an ancient astronomer who—Nath could only assume—believed he'd found something worth discovering.

He had been wrong.

The squadron launched from the *Lodestar* at roughly sixteen hundred local time, as the *Acclamator*-class battleship moved on to the front lines of the sector conflict. Since returning from Abednedo, Nath had spent most of his free time buying drinks for the pilots of Meteor and Hail squadrons, gauging the status of General Syndulla's campaign and the likelihood that any of them would survive to reach Pandem Nai. He had his doubts. Meteor and Hail were joining Vanguard at Argai Minor to aid ground forces against what one pilot had described as "the citadel from Darth Vader's schoolyard sketchbook, with more weapons emplacements than personnel."

In his younger days, Nath had craved a decent fight. As he got older, his cravings waned. His appreciation for the thrills of combat was balanced by his desire to keep breathing. So he wasn't really sad to miss the Argai operation. He just had doubts about the salvage job he was stuck with.

He glanced at the console of his Y-wing and saw a message from T5 flash across the screen. He laughed at the obscenity and muttered, "You and me both, brother."

Harkrova I was the only planet in the system: a barren, sulfurous wasteland illuminated by a dim yellow sun that looked small and distant even from space. Its single moon was more hospitable, covered in mountains and lush forests, and Nath found himself peering below as he emerged from the moon's cloud cover. Needle-leafed cyan trees completely obscured the ground. Nath hadn't grown up with forests, and they still surprised him with their beauty.

"So where are we supposed to *land*?" he asked over the comm. "Tell me there's a clearing."

"Not exactly." Quell's voice came through clear and steady and dead as ever. "There's a mountaintop."

*Was that a joke?* he wondered.

It wasn't long before all five vessels landed on a stony peak overlooking the woodland, kilometers from the site of the supposed rebel cache. Nath shivered as he climbed out of his fighter and saw his breath wisp upward. He began checking his emergency gear. "Going to be a long hike," he called toward Wyl as the kid popped his canopy. "Pack well or don't whine on the way."

Wyl laughed. Nath gave the other ships a glance and saw Chass staring at him, arms wrapped around her chest. Were Theelins cold-blooded? He couldn't remember.

Quell was next to speak, confirming what Nath had suspected. "Topo maps indicate we're four, five hours from the cache. We may not make it by nightfall so be ready to camp. And keep in mind we've got a lot of supplies to cart back this way."

"Any chance there's transport at the cache?" Wyl asked.

"There's a chance," Quell said.

They unloaded. Nath was pleased to see that Kairos was strong enough to carry what must've been her own weight in camping gear, along with an ornate bowcaster the likes of which he hadn't seen in a decade. Wyl, once he'd cleared out the A-wing, spent the last few minutes on the mountaintop squatting in front of T5 and Quell's astromech droid, grinning and whispering like a toddler. Anyone else, Nath would've wanted to smack for that—yet he found himself reluctantly charmed by Wyl's boyish enthusiasm. It was unpretentious. Unperformative. And to give Wyl his due, the kid was a blasted competent flier.

The five pilots picked their way down the rocks. The descent wasn't steep, nor treacherous, and once the exercise took the edge off the chill Nath found the journey not entirely unpleasant. Quell led the way, while Kairos and Wyl took up the rear. Chass floated about, apparently focused on staying away from—well, either Wyl, Kairos, or both of them, Nath wasn't sure. The bright, metallic odor of the needles grew strong as they crossed the tree line.

Nath worked his way to the front until he hiked beside Quell. "Drink?" he asked.

"I've got a canteen," she said without looking at him.

He tapped the flask in his jacket, then shrugged. Maybe better if he didn't elaborate. "Didn't get to talk much after Abednedo. Wanted to say I was sorry how it went down. Glad Syndulla and Adan weren't too hard on you."

Quell grunted and leapt off a boulder, landing hard on both feet. Nath watched the way she rubbed her shoulder. She hadn't completely healed since he'd seen her in a sling.

When she didn't answer him, he followed and went on, "Don't think anyone blames you for taking a swing at Adan, either. Risky move, but no one doubts he's a scumball."

"Are you saying," Quell asked, "that you can forgive a swing at a superior officer? So long as he's difficult enough?"

He laughed. "Bet you wonder how *my* squadron worked, don't you?"

"I really don't."

Nath laughed again. Slowly, Quell was growing on him. It was a pity she didn't feel the same. "Anyway, I wanted to mention all that so you don't think any of this is personal. I wanted to chat about the problems we've been having—seems like we're not getting much closer to Shadow Wing, and Pandem Nai's pretty far off. Maybe if Syndulla let us off the leash more we'd be having more luck, but—well."

"We don't find something soon to jump-start this operation, part of me wonders whether the New Republic would rather live with Shadow Wing than take the next step. They'd lose a ship or a city now and then, but still easier than laying siege to Pandem Nai while the whole galaxy is a mess—"

"The New Republic," Quell interjected, quiet and curt, "fully understands the threat posed by the 204th."

"Just saying it's hard times. They'll be making sacrifices. Could be we'll see whole sectors turned over to Imperials when the peace comes. Trouble is—" He paused. "I'm only here because of Shadow Wing. You remember that, right?"

It was a lie, but it felt as honest as anything Nath had said.

"I remember," Quell said.

"So I'm telling you now, as a friendly warning: I'd like to do right by my old squadron. Take the whole 204th down. If I can't, though . . . ?

"Well, there's one Shadow Wing pilot in view right now." He let his lips twitch upward, but it wasn't really a smile. "I can always settle and cut my losses."

Quell kept her eyes on the path down the mountainside. Nath started to wonder whether she understood. Then she glanced back at him, colder than anything on the frigid moon.

"Thank you," she said, "for your frank assessment. I'll keep it in mind."

"My pleasure," Nath said, and trekked past his commander with a grin.

The chill of the moon was almost enough to make him forget about the real reason he was in the squadron. Vengeance was part of it, to be sure, but he'd known in the cantina on the Entropian Hive that there was no gain in it. He'd walked away from Yrica Quell, resisting the temptation to join her.

He would have stuck by his decision if Kairos hadn't come calling. If she hadn't stepped into his room while he'd been cleaning the mess Quell and the torture droid had left, presenting a recording from Adan that promised more than vengeance: a recording that had promised *money,* all the credits Adan could scrape together so long as Nath understood he was working as Adan's personal agent.

The reward was too big, the gain too great, to turn down the bet.

Now Nath was committed. And if he failed to find Shadow Wing, failed to shed blood after taking on the mission, he really would be letting his old crew down.

He could let down Adan, too, but the spy was just another customer. Nath had no qualms about backing out of a deal.

## III

They'd made it to level ground, but Chass was still miserable. It wasn't just the cold, or the fact she hadn't been on a world so wide open—so deathly silent, so full of wild smells—in ages. It was all those things, but mostly it was the company.

These weren't her people. Quell was an Imperial at heart, no matter what she did to try to show otherwise. Nath was entertaining, but Chass couldn't begin to trust him. As for Wyl—she risked a glance in the boy's direction and saw him angling her way.

"You all right?" he asked.

"Fine," she said.

It was—cockpit chatter aside—about the most they'd spoken since the *Hellion's Dare*. Wyl's face was stoic, but his posture was stiff. He was making an effort to show he accepted the brush-off and mostly failing.

Chass turned her gaze away.

He'd taken too much from her. He might not understand it, but he didn't have to understand any more than she had to forgive.

She slowed her pace. Wyl didn't pursue her and Chass fell behind. There was no path through the forest, but the undergrowth was thin and the trees were spaced wide—they must have been one of the few life-forms that could survive on the dim, dreary moon. Now and again she heard a birdlike trilling, but she saw nothing rustling through the branches or burrowing into the dirt.

She flinched when she heard footsteps behind her. She flinched a second time when she saw that it was Kairos.

*You need to do this,* she thought. *If not with Wyl, at least with her.*

She blew a funnel of breath and dropped back beside her colleague. Kairos tilted her head in acknowledgment but otherwise didn't react.

"You saved my life on Abednedo," Chass said.

Kairos seemed not to hear. Her pace was slow and steady, easy to match. Her cloak still bore dark stains from their last mission.

"I got kind of creeped out when I saw you fight. You're intense, and

I—okay. I'm grateful for the save." She forced out the words and felt satisfied with their sound.

Kairos turned toward her and Chass forced herself not to visibly tense. She met the gaze of the visor. She pictured the woman tearing through ragtag soldiers with cruel fury. Whatever Chass's visceral reaction, she could respect Kairos's ability.

Kairos inclined her head in a slow bow. Chass smirked in return.

"Still be easier if we knew you," she said. "You are kind of a freak."

# IV

The dim yellow sun hid behind the forest canopy long before its light disappeared altogether. Darkness brought life to the woods—or perhaps the absence of vision focused Wyl's other senses, alerting him to sounds and scents he'd discounted too easily. The ground chittered and murmured, as if chitinous insects called out to one another; the odor of wet fur and fungal matter drifted to his nose.

With the darkness came a sharper cold, and Quell swiftly called a halt, announcing that they were still several kilometers from the rebel base and that without even a trail to follow continuing through the night would be folly. The five pilots rapidly unslung their packs and established a makeshift camp around a cluster of heat lanterns. Only Nath and Kairos seemed unaffected by the temperature, and Wyl felt a moment of genial envy at Nath's layers of muscle and fat.

Soon they sat in their separate corners, eating gritty chunks of ration bars dipped into a citrus-chemical nutrient paste Chass's B-wing had been stocked with. They did all this in silence, and Wyl was struck—not for the first time—how different it all was from Riot Squadron. He remembered what Sata Neek had told him, the night he'd tried to leave forever: *We had the best times.*

If only to hear a voice, he struck up a conversation with Nath, and presently they were speaking with ease about their worst nights in the wilderness: evenings spent in the factory-deserts of Phorsa Gedd, which vented heat from sunset to sunrise; or in the fungal forests of

# STAR WARS
# TIE FiGHTER

## "SHADOW WING" PART 1 of 5

The Empire's glorious victory at the Battle of Hoth has all but smashed the pitiful Rebel Alliance whose dwindling forces now scatter and flee before the might of the Imperial war machine. Soon, peace will be restored to the galaxy and the feared TIE Fighter pilots of **SHADOW WING** will be the ones to secure victory for the Emperor!

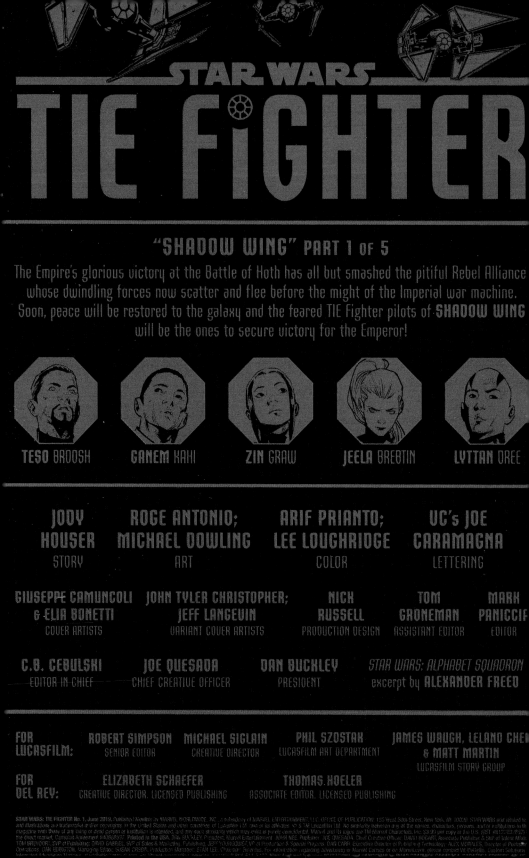

| TESO BROOSH | GANEM KAHI | ZIN GRAW | JEELA BREBTIN | LYTTAN DREE |

**JODY HOUSER**
STORY

**ROGE ANTONIO; MICHAEL DOWLING**
ART

**ARIF PRIANTO; LEE LOUGHRIDGE**
COLOR

**UC's JOE CARAMAGNA**
LETTERING

**GIUSEPPE CAMUNCOLI & ELIA BONETTI**
COVER ARTISTS

**JOHN TYLER CHRISTOPHER; JEFF LANGEVIN**
VARIANT COVER ARTISTS

**NICK RUSSELL**
PRODUCTION DESIGN

**TOM GRONEMAN**
ASSISTANT EDITOR

**MARK PANICCIA**
EDITOR

**C.B. CEBULSKI**
EDITOR IN CHIEF

**JOE QUESADA**
CHIEF CREATIVE OFFICER

**DAN BUCKLEY**
PRESIDENT

**STAR WARS: ALPHABET SQUADRON**
excerpt by **ALEXANDER FREED**

**FOR LUCASFILM:**

**ROBERT SIMPSON**
SENIOR EDITOR

**MICHAEL SIGLAIN**
CREATIVE DIRECTOR

**PHIL SZOSTAK**
LUCASFILM ART DEPARTMENT

**JAMES WAUGH, LELAND CHEE & MATT MARTIN**
LUCASFILM STORY GROUP

**FOR DEL REY:**

**ELIZABETH SCHAEFER**
CREATIVE DIRECTOR, LICENSED PUBLISHING

**THOMAS HOELER**
ASSOCIATE EDITOR, LICENSED PUBLISHING

## Commander Nuress, A.K.A. Grandmother.

I'M SURE YOU ALL HAVE HEARD THE *RUMORS* BY NOW.

MYSTERIOUS ORDERS. LARGE-SCALE MILITARY MOVEMENT.

WHATEVER *NEW STRATEGY* OUR EMPEROR IS PLANNING, THE MIGHT OF THE IMPERIAL NAVY IS A KEY ELEMENT.

AND THAT MEANS AS MANY HANDS ON DECK AS POSSIBLE.

WE'VE RECEIVED ORDERS TO SEND A SQUADRON TO ACCOMPANY A MAINTENANCE CREW ABOARD THE *SUMMIT* TO *THE KUDO SYSTEM.*

THE STAR DESTROYER *CELERITY* HAS REPORTED HYPERDRIVE ISSUES PREVENTING THEM FROM RENDEZVOUSING AS ORDERED.

I KNOW *SQUADRON FIVE* HASN'T BEEN FLYING TOGETHER LONG.

BUT YOUR PERFORMANCE UNDER COMMANDER BROOSH HAS BEEN COMMENDABLE.

ALTHOUGH...YOU LOOK LIKE YOU HAVE SOMETHING YOU'D LIKE TO SAY, COMMANDER BROOSH.

DO YOU DISAGREE WITH MY ASSESSMENT?

THE FOCUS OF *SHADOW WING* HAS BEEN PRIMARILY PUTTING DOWN THE REBEL INSURGENCY.

ESCORT DUTY SEEMS LIKE A RATHER SUDDEN SHIFT.

NOT AT ALL, COLONEL. I WAS JUST... SURPRISED.

Felucia. Since their first night together at Ranjiy's Krayt Hut, Wyl and Nath's rapport had only improved. It wasn't what Wyl had had with Sata Neek or Sonogari—it lacked the maturation of tested friendship, and tasted faintly of desperation—but it was relaxed and comforting. Wyl didn't know if he'd be able to call Nath his friend tomorrow or a year from now (though he hoped so), but he could do it tonight.

Wyl encouraged Nath to do most of the talking. Gently, without insisting, he asked for stories about the man's old squadron. It was when Nath spoke about Reeka and Piter and Rorian that the cunning glint in his eyes seemed to thaw and he laughed without artifice. Their voices grew louder as Wyl asked about Nath's night with T5 in the Red Isles of Thakwaa, and Nath described, in exquisite and implausible detail, how the astromech droid had convinced him to render plant stems into ointment for protection against the flies.

"By the third batch it's finally working," Nath said, "and I'm covered in rashes like a lab animal. That droid . . ."

"So what happened in the morning?" Wyl asked.

"Nothing interesting. We got offworld a few days later, and I swore off taking botanical advice from machines ever again."

Wyl heard a muffled snicker from Chass, who'd been pretending not to listen. But it wasn't Chass he spoke to when he raised his voice and said, "You've got to have some stories, Commander."

Quell, who'd been staring into the forest like a woman standing vigil for her dead, said, "Nothing to share."

"You've never ejected and had to camp?" Wyl tried. "Spent a night under a tarp in the rain?"

*Give us something to work with,* he wanted to say. *Something other than orders and drills. I'm trying to help you.*

"Nothing to share," Quell said again.

Wyl forced a smile and rubbed his face with his palms. They'd grown icy.

"Why don't you tell your own story instead of stealing ours, huh?" Nath grinned and slapped a meaty hand against Wyl's shoulder. "Or at least make up something good."

"What do you want to hear?"

"To start with? What sort of man acts like he's never seen a droid but flies like he was podracing in diapers?"

Wyl furrowed his brow. There was nothing hostile in the tone, but he didn't understand. "What—"

"He wants to know where you're from, you thick-skulled man!" Chass called in exasperation, falling backward where she sat.

"Pretty much," Nath agreed. "What sort of backward world are you from and how'd you end up *here*?"

Again, Wyl heard no hostility in Nath's voice—no judgment despite the phrasing. He paused, then nodded cautiously.

There was a door in his heart that he kept closed, separating the Wyl Lark of Home from the Wyl Lark of the Rebel Alliance and the New Republic. He opened the door in dreams and in flight, and he needed it to keep himself from breaking.

But if he *was* to call Nath—or any of the others—a friend, he needed to open the door for them. And though Wyl was not naïve, he was trusting by nature. He didn't want to be a man who hid what he was when asked to share.

"It's not a short story," he warned.

"You got somewhere to be?" Nath asked.

This is the story he told.

Polyneus was the name outsiders called the world. Wyl had grown up thinking of it as the *Empire's* name, a way of mocking his planet with a clumsy and meaningless designation, but that was both untrue and unkind—even before the Empire, no one had ever called it *Home* but his people. And Wyl's ancestors, along with all the progenitors of Polyneus, had been outsiders once, too.

"We were fortunate compared with many," he said, in a voice unlike the voice he used to speak at all other times. His audience watched him, rapt one moment and uncomfortable the next. Wyl didn't soften his candor.

The Clone Wars had damaged many worlds irrevocably. Wyl hadn't seen them, but he'd heard the tales passed on by elders and storytellers.

Polyneus had been unscathed. Ignored. The Republic had had no strategic reason to garrison there. The Separatists had seen it as a backwater, a primitive place full of primitive people.

The Polyneans were not primitive. They did not reject science or galactic technologies, but they were judicious in what they permitted on their world. Like the Abednedos, they built cities into mountainsides—but also into jungles and on mighty platforms above lakes. They milked beasts and grew crops, but where their needs would bring suffering to living creatures or exhaust the natural landscape they tasked their engineers with finding technological solutions.

"It wasn't like this," Wyl said, gesturing to the forest around them. "Not in the places where we lived. But it was closer to this than any city I ever saw in the Core Worlds."

The children of Polyneus grew up as children of all, playing together, studying under the Sun-Lamas, and moving among communal homes as their needs and desires demanded. It was at the age of seven that Wyl first mounted one of the sur-avkas, following a group of older children to the cliffsides where the half-tame, half-wild creatures flocked. There was no ritual significance to sur-avka riding, no cultural rite attached—but it was a source of mirth and challenge, and Wyl took to it like thousands of youths. He learned to grip the beast, to breathe as it breathed so that it saw him as an extension of itself, and in time he joined races and displays of skill.

The Empire didn't interfere with Polyneus when Wyl was young. (At least not the way he remembered—maybe the elders and the Sun-Lamas had sheltered young children from the truths of the galaxy.) But when he turned twelve, the Empire's presence became unmissable. "They chose to build a weapons platform in low atmosphere. I don't know why—if it was to intimidate us, or if they worried about rebels or some other invader. Everyone said it would be the first of many.

"You could see it in the sky. This black, spiny thing that passed over us once a day. The clouds around it turned the color of rust. Soon you could smell it on the wind, like the acid from your stomach. The sur-avkas didn't fly quite as fast anymore. The birds—"

The elders of the settlements petitioned the Empire when they saw the damage being done. The Empire promised inspections and studies, assured the Polyneans they'd compile reports and long-term impact projections. Those were only promises, though, and they were never kept. A brave and wise messenger was sent to Coruscant to seek the advice and aid of the Galactic Emperor, but that messenger never returned.

Slowly, Polyneus's biosphere began to die. The Empire didn't care.

"That's when the elders knew they couldn't solve the problem alone."

"That's when they reached out to the Rebel Alliance."

Wyl didn't know how contact had been established. Maybe, he admitted, the Sun-Lamas of the Peak, learned masters and keepers of the Polynean ways, had been in touch with Senator Mothma or other rebel leaders for years beforehand—but he doubted it. He imagined the search for a rebel contact had been perilous, and that the rebels had been skeptical of Polynean aid until they'd heard the offer.

"The Hik'e-Matriarch—translate it as 'queen,' maybe, though it's more complicated—she knew the rebels needed pilots. So she offered, on behalf of us all, to send one of the finest sur-avka fliers from each community to serve with the Rebellion until Polyneus was free of the Emperor's shadow."

The proclamation was passed among the Polyneans but never written: *Let every village send a warrior-tribute, for the battle against the Empire has become our battle; and no people in the galaxy fly as the people of Home fly.*

Some villages held competitions. Others allowed volunteers to step forth and let the elders choose among them. Neither method was needed in Ridge, where Wyl had been raised. Only one other sought to deny him his place, and that was an act of kindness. But no one doubted that Wyl Lark was the finest flier they had.

He wanted it. He wanted to do right by his people, and to make a difference in the galaxy.

He left Home. He made an oath to return when the Empire was defeated.

"They called us the Hundred and Twenty—the volunteers from Polyneus who found their way into the Alliance. We didn't know one another. We left separately, made our way to different rebel hideouts, but I hear the others fared well. Some lived, some died, but they *fought*. They made us all proud.

"As for me, you know the rest. I ended up in Riot Squadron. I left behind my siblings, my family on Polyneus, and I gained a new family."

Wyl told them the truth, but there were truths he didn't tell. He didn't mention how much he missed Polyneus. How joining the Alliance, traveling the galaxy, had forced him to take up the wider galaxy's ways and lock the teachings of his people away in his heart.

He didn't tell them how he had longed to return Home after the Battle of Endor, and that he still longed to go back now.

He was tired of war. Tired of the galaxy.

Yet Polyneus was not free of the Emperor's shadow, and he was the last survivor of Riot Squadron. He owed it to both families not to run again; not to flee as he had in Oridol, when he had failed the cluster's test.

Dawn came slow and early. For a long while, as the night-noises faded, the world seemed filtered through a blue haze like campfire smoke—the effect of the forest canopy or unseen particles in the air. Wyl tasted grit on his lips when he rose. It tasted of capsaicin and mint.

They ate breakfast and broke camp before resuming their trek. None of them spoke as they walked, though the silence seemed less tense than it had the previous day. Maybe they were simply exhausted. It wasn't yet midmorning when the ground sloped upward and Quell called, "Shouldn't be far now."

Wyl had seen enough rebel safe houses to know what to expect: a rude bunker planted in the soil or a hatch leading to a natural cavern. Something well camouflaged. He swept his gaze over the forest, searching for a sign, and saw the others doing the same. But the search wasn't necessary.

It seemed to form out of the woods as they approached. The structure was wide at the base, with spokes like roots leading into a central tower like a cathedral spire. Wyl assumed it was made of painted duracrete at first, until they drew nearer and he saw that it was both tree and stone—the structure appeared to be an unbroken, gargantuan piece of petrified wood.

It was an impossible creation, unlike anything built on Polyneus. Wyl felt both awed and somehow ashamed in its presence. Why, he wondered, had the teachings of the Sun-Lamas never manifested so beautifully?

He spotted openings—windows, he thought—in the upper reaches of the spire but none toward the base. He heard Chass laughing and glimpsed her running, disappearing from view around one of the spokes. Quell snapped, "Everyone, careful," but even she didn't seem to mean it.

"What *is* it?" Nath asked.

"It's a rebel base," Wyl said.

It took them fifteen minutes to find the entrance: a set of disguised double doors carved into a joint between the spokes. The doors opened at the slightest touch. The interior was more conventional, but only marginally—the central enclosure was airy and vacant, with the fossilized walls of the spire stretching as high as the forest canopy and glittering with reflected sunlight. The spokes were rough, round hallways off the main chamber, each narrowing as it went so that a human would be forced to crawl to reach its end.

"This isn't a rebel base," Nath said, as the five walked and gazed in wonder. "It's a Jedi temple."

"You sure?" Quell asked.

"Not sure," Nath said. "But it would explain a few things."

Wyl knew little of the Jedi—he'd barely heard the word on Polyneus, but during his time in Riot he'd heard stories from officers who'd served in the Clone Wars. The Jedi were warrior-mystics, attuned to the "universal Force," who believed themselves guardians of justice. Wyl had encountered whispers that the rebel General Skywalker was the last of the Jedi Order—heir to an ancient tradition, whose preternatural wisdom had helped lead him to victory time and again. But troops told a lot of strange stories. Wyl didn't know the truth of it.

"It's some sort of temple, anyway," Wyl agreed. "It can't be anything else."

"Look for the supplies," Quell said. "Maybe there's a storage area somewhere."

But only Quell, so far as Wyl could ascertain, was really trying to look. Kairos stood in the center of the main chamber, peering directly upward into a shaft of sunlight. Nath rubbed his hands against the walls. Chass, Wyl saw, was deep in one of the root-spokes, her back against one wall and knees bent, feet pressed against the wall opposite. Her head was turned to face the dark terminus of the spoke.

She was shaking.

*Leave her be,* Wyl told himself. She'd made her needs clear.

Nonetheless, he bowed his head and took three steps down the passage toward Chass. Etched into the walls were thousands of pictograms, whorls and lines and figures depicting nothing he could identify.

"Are you all right?" he asked softly.

He promised himself he would withdraw if she said nothing. Instead she looked at him and he saw a gentleness he'd never seen from Chass.

"It's beautiful," she said. "I'm not used to thinking of cults as beautiful."

There was meaning in what she'd said, hints of something old and painful. But he heard no invitation to pry, so he only nodded.

## V

They discovered a removable panel in the floor of the main chamber. Underneath was a storage cellar that appeared to have been built separately from the rest of the temple—the walls and ceiling were reinforced with metal beams, and artificial lighting was strung haphazardly throughout. This, clearly, was Syndulla's cache—there were stacks of crated ration bars, disorganized piles of power packs and engine parts and loops of cabling, and who-knew-what else. Raising it all out of the basement and getting it back to the ships would be slow work, but that, Nath supposed, was why they were there. It wasn't supposed to be a *fun* job.

They jury-rigged a system of rope and low-power repulsorsleds and began hauling up the goods by early afternoon. Nath stripped down to short sleeves—the exertion and the shelter more than warded off the chill—and stayed in the main chamber with Quell while the others loaded sleds down below. Quell wasn't much of a lifter, but she put in her share of effort and she supervised well enough.

They spoke only about the work. Nath figured that was fair, given the last real conversation they'd had he'd threatened to kill her. But eventually, Quell surprised him with a question:

"How'd you know? About this being a Jedi temple?"

"I don't *know*."

"But you were confident. Like it's something you've seen before?"

Nath studied Quell's face awhile. "You're younger than me. Older than the others—except Kairos, maybe, who knows?—but young enough to have gotten the *second* revised history of the Clone Wars."

Quell bristled and tried to hide it. "What does that mean?"

"The Empire's been erasing the Jedi from history, step by step. First they said the Jedi tried to murder the last chancellor—Palpatine, before he was Emperor—in some sort of coup at the war's end. It's what I grew up hearing."

"I heard that version from the older officers. It never made any sense because—"

"Because you were taught there weren't many Jedi to begin with, right? That they were relics, mostly forgotten?" Nath grinned. "That's the trouble when they keep changing the story. Nah, there were thousands of them, and real influential in the Republic. Believe me, you hear a lot about the legend of the Jedi and the Force when you join the Rebel Alliance."

Nath saw Quell trying to reason through it all. He'd seen that look from more than one rebel recruit. "How do you know it's not all propaganda on your—on the rebel side?" she asked.

"I don't. That's the nasty thing about the Emperor changing history. Leaves you *doubting,* doesn't it?"

They tabled the conversation long enough to haul up a hunk of metal, piping, and glowing lights that Nath guessed somehow related to battleship hydraulics. When that was done, Quell asked, "What about now? The Rebellion had its share of fanatics. Is the New Republic going to bring back the Jedi? Are we going to live in a theocracy?"

"Don't know, but I don't expect so," Nath said. "For all that the Rebellion liked to win converts, I never saw many practitioners of the Jedi religion. You're not uncovering any great conspiracy here, sister— you're just a little behind the times."

Quell hesitated, then nodded and began hollering instructions down to Chass and Wyl.

Nath decided to leave out the rest: that the Jedi might not be worth worrying over, but that the fall of the Empire would bring a thousand lesser cults crawling up from the sewers, piggybacking off the Jedi legend and the fame of General Skywalker. He'd seen the dark side of pilgrim worlds, and he didn't care to see *that* make its way into the wider galaxy.

But that was a problem for another day. For the moment, better to keep Quell focused on Shadow Wing. *Poor girl has enough worries.*

He'd still kill her if he had to.


By nightfall, they hadn't completed the extraction nor made a run back to the ships. Rather than risk an accident, Quell called for them to make camp. Without anyone saying a word, they agreed to do so outside; somehow, it seemed wrong to set up bedrolls inside the temple.

As they sat around the heat lanterns, Nath and Wyl chattered about the joys and perils of atmospheric flight. Even Chass, to Nath's pleasant surprise, threw in the occasional opinion. Quell remained characteristically detached.

Nath wasn't sure how long Kairos had been standing before he noticed her. When he did, the others' gazes followed.

She was a silhouette in the shadows, standing between the trees. In her cloak and wrappings and half lit from below, Kairos looked more monstrous than usual. She was staring toward the group, both fists clenched at her sides.

Wyl asked, "Is something wrong?"

She strode forward until the camp light splashed across her body. She knelt, slowly opening her right hand. A trickle of dust—of loose soil or gravel—slowly poured onto the ground, as if out of an hourglass.

"Kairos?" Quell was tense, ready to rise. "What's going on?"

As the dust grew to a small pile, Kairos moved her fist in an arc, drawing a line from the first pile to a new, second mound. She reached out with her other hand and a second stream began to fall; soon she was moving arms and wrists in deft gestures, creating intricate patterns before the lanterns. When her first hand was empty, she caressed the piles of dust and gathered up a fresh fistful.

She stroked pictures into existence. Images formed, were cast away and remade. Nath couldn't comprehend it at first, but at some point during the process the pictures resolved in his mind into something greater. One led to another. He saw meaning.

"This is her life," Wyl murmured.

This is the story she told.


Great spirals and a hundred motes portraying the galaxy, all swept into a mound of dust in the Outer Rim. From the mound comes the next image—a fire, a bowl, an endless horizon. A simple life on a world far from the Core.

A Star Destroyer in the sky. A cloaked figure walking below. A dozen quick slashes through dust create a storm of blaster bolts, disrupting the simple life.

A series of images more difficult to decipher: More stars, perhaps. A circle with a chord cutting between points of the circumference. A dozen little squares, little boxes. A humanoid figure constantly shaped and reshaped, artistically adjusted, until it becomes clear that the changes are not the refinements of the artist—of Kairos—but an aspect of the art itself. A humanoid *changing*.

The boxes aflame. The changing figure aflame. The circle with the chord on one side and the starbird symbol of the Rebel Alliance on the other.

The changing figure, no longer changing, standing amid ashes and bones.

There the story ended. Kairos swept away the dust and stepped back, seating herself far from the group.

It was beautiful and disturbing. Quell was trembling. Wyl was watching Kairos. Chass was staring into the dust. Nath suspected they'd all read what they wanted into the tale.

He wondered how much of it was truth.


# VI


It was well after midnight when Quell woke to a sonic boom above the forest. She immediately recognized the sound of *speed* but not its form. The trailing engine whine suggested a Kuat Drive Yards craft. She scrambled out of her bedroll and after a moment of indecision activated her comlink to her astromech droid.

"What's on the X-wing's scanners?"

The others were half dressed and pulling their equipment together when Quell got her answer: an image transmitted to her handheld holoprojector showing a single ship flying over the moon.

*Probably a scout,* she thought. General Syndulla had warned her about pirates and looters. The newcomer was moving fast and low, reconnoitering the forest.

She looked between her pilots and the temple. She glanced at the dust Kairos had scattered across the ground. "Stand down," she called. "I'll handle this for now."

Chass na Chadic was rubbing the sleep from her eyes as she turned toward Quell. "What's that mean?"

"It means," Quell said, "that we're well hidden. Whoever is out there is searching for the temple but won't find it quickly. Maybe not at all. Stay focused on the salvage job while I head back to the ships—they're easier to see than anything down here, and if a hostile spots us I'll be in position to launch."

"Maybe we should *all* launch," Tensent said. "Chase down whoever's out there while surprise is on our side."

Lark frowned. "We don't know they're hostile. But I agree it doesn't make sense to—"

"I'm not asking for input," Quell said. "If more ships show, I'll call you. If it's just one—even hostile—I can deal with it. Get some sleep, keep your comlinks close, and resume work in the morning."

She began to pack her own gear. She heard Chadic mutter, "Because splitting up worked great last time," and felt her body flush with cold ire.

*Last time,* she wanted to say, *I trusted you to act like Imperials. This time, I'm letting you be what you are.*

But she didn't say it aloud.

No one troubled her as she slung her pack over her shoulders (ignoring the ache from her right side) and started back the way they'd come the previous morning. She kept her glow rod low to keep herself from tripping over roots or deadwood, and to avoid any risk of detection. She heard the chittering sounds of the burrowing night insects—or whatever it was that caused the ground to murmur.

She'd been watching her team over the past day. She'd seen Lark and Tensent and Chadic begin talking to one another like comrades. Now even Kairos was opening up. Quell didn't know *why* it was happening—she didn't think it was Tensent's manipulations or Lark's natural ability to harmonize—but she knew it was valuable.

She also knew that a group bonded best as equals. That as their commander, she was only holding this process back. And she remembered General Syndulla's words: *Do they know that you'll fight for them?*

This was her chance.

If there was a threat out there—an enemy she could face alone, for the benefit of the mission and the squadron—so much the better.

But the night was cold and the sounds were strange, and after an hour of walking Quell began to see things flickering in the distance between the trees. Figments and faces, like the ones she saw when she closed her eyes tight and the blackness churned and took form.

She saw the soldiers from Abednedo dying to blasts from her X-wing or suffering in the cargo hold of the Verpine smuggler. She saw the battered dead of Nacronis floating in silt, flesh torn from the storms and bodies bloated from the flood.

And whenever she turned her head, seeking the source of a soft padding sound upon the frigid ground—what seemed to be footsteps close behind—she caught a glimpse of black robes and a withered face like running wax. It was a face she recognized from the rarest of video clips and public proclamations: the face of Palpatine, Galactic Emperor, to whom she had sworn an oath. Palpatine, who had brought nearly all known worlds under his command. Palpatine, who had ordered the cleansing and destruction of many of those worlds, even before Operation Cinder.

She wondered what she would say to him, if he had really been there—if his ghost were haunting the Jedi temple, awaiting a group of New Republic pilots to torment. If he had another order to give, would she listen? If he could explain, justify Operation Cinder, would she accept it?

She shut it all away, sealed it up in her mind, and set her eyes on the path to the mountain.

## CHAPTER 12

# SPIRITUAL REAWAKENINGS

I

There were no further signs of raiders that night. They posted a watch, and Quell checked in every sixty minutes, reporting no sightings or sensor readings. Chass was surprised to find she wasn't disappointed. She wasn't *enjoying* the work at the temple, but she wasn't spoiling for a fight.

In the morning Nath scrambled ration bars and nutrient paste in a skillet over a heat lantern. "Won't do a *lot* to improve the taste, but it'll perk it up," he said as he handed out helpings. When they got to work, Nath played den mother as he had the day before, watching from above while the rest of them loaded equipment in the basement. They didn't speak often, but when they did it was in good spirits.

Quell didn't return by nightfall. "Better to stay on guard," she told them. They'd brought almost everything up but still needed to load and secure the repulsorsleds and move them to the U-wing—another half day's work, at least.

"By this time," Nath was saying at their camp, "Vanguard Squadron and the rest of Syndulla's fleet are probably wrapping up on Argai Minor. Unless they *really* got their butts kicked, in which case we're hauling a lot of equipment for no good reason."

"Nice." Wyl shook his head. "Let's assume they win. Then it's Pandem Nai not long after—"

"—we hope," Nath said.

"We hope," Wyl agreed. "Following that . . . how much longer, do you think? Until it's all over?"

He was asking Nath, which was why Chass felt obliged to answer. "Not very," she said. "Mop-up will take years, but it's going to be *stomp a dirtbag here, stomp a dirtbag there, don't let them gather in one place.* Without the Emperor, the Empire's done."

"You in a hurry?" Nath asked, watching Wyl with a grin.

"I was supposed to be back home by now. Of course I'm in a hurry. But . . . one more mission, right?"

"I hear you, brother." Nath raised his canteen in a toast. Chass had seen him pour something into it earlier; she lunged suddenly, her shadow leaping under the light of the heat lanterns, and snatched the canteen for herself.

Nath laughed and clapped as she took a swallow. Whatever was in the canteen, it was awful—bitter and herbal, like drinking someone's garden. She thrust the container back into his hands before she returned to her seat. "I don't want to know," she said. "I don't want to think about that ever again."

"Be glad," Wyl said, his voice soft, "you never went drinking with Sata Neek. Man had interesting tastes."

A picture of the bird-frog flashed into her mind and she felt more sorrow than rage. She'd liked Sata Neek—he'd been strange and funny and kind, and he'd fought at Endor, and he'd liked her. He was dead because of—

She looked at Wyl and smirked back. She was tired of loathing him.

"You know it's your turn," Nath said.

She looked back at the older man, who took a deliberate, luxuriating sip from his canteen. She asked, "My turn for what?"

"Storytelling. Wyl did it. Kairos did it. You going to hold out?"

Chass snorted. "*You* didn't tell a story."

"I'm an open book. Anything you don't know about me, you probably don't *want* to know." Nath grinned broad enough to flash teeth, and even Wyl looked away in distaste. "If you've got questions—"

"No," Chass said. "No one has any questions."

The night was cold but she felt hot, flushed as Nath and Wyl and even Kairos watched her. She turned away from the lot of them, toward the temple, and studied the great spire extending into the starry sky.

"You don't have to." Wyl's voice, disgustingly smooth and calm. "No one expects—"

"Shut up," she snapped, and didn't look toward him.

Wyl's decision to share his tale two nights earlier hadn't surprised her. His mix of sincerity and unwarranted confidence had made it almost inevitable—Chass had cringed even as a part of her admired his honesty.

But Kairos had been a surprise. Kairos, the nightmare girl, had chosen *here* and *now* to reveal herself to all of them. Just the same as Wyl.

"You don't have to," Wyl said again.

He might as well have said: *I know you're afraid to do what I did.* Worst of all, he was right.

She looked from Wyl, to Nath, to Kairos, searching for a thread of condescension or mockery. She found nothing. The air outside the temple seemed too still for anger or judgment.

"No dirt drawings or legends about the Hundred and Twenty, but I'll talk," she said. "Just don't—you get what you get. Remember you asked for it."

Her audience waited, politely attentive. She thought of her secrets—not all of them, because she couldn't *remember* all of them, but she riffled through the ones she could bring to mind like playing cards. Secrets about her childhood; about the Unignited Stars; about figuring out what it meant to be Theelin without guidance in an Empire made for humans.

Finally, she decided on a tale they would want to hear.

This is the story she told.

"You know Jyn Erso?" she began, because if they didn't the rest of the story would be meaningless. "The woman who started it all and destroyed the Death Star? The first one, the real one, I mean."

"General Skywalker and Red Squadron destroyed the Death Star," Nath said.

"Skywalker fired the last shot, was all. Jyn did everything that mattered. I met her once."

It had been in the Five Points system, on an awful little world called Uchinao. "I was out of work—" Chass said, which wasn't true; "—and out of credits," which was. "There was someone looking for me back then, and he had connections. I had scandocs that would pass a mobile inspection but would trip alarms at a real checkpoint. All of which is to say it wasn't a great time in my life."

Uchinao was a decaying orb specked with massive metal rigs plugged into bergs floating on a liquid surface. The liquid wasn't water, and neither were the bergs—their ice was dark and veined with yellow, like a bruise on pale skin. There were rumors that creatures lived deep inside, but on top it wasn't so different from any other city-world, with a thousand cramped streets filled with garbage and inhabitants treated worse than the waste.

Chass had stolen a coat—heavy and bulky and warm, the best thing she'd ever stolen and a garment she still missed—and had come barreling down a side street only to run into a Chevin four times her size. The Chevin's leathery gray skin stank of cheap perfume and its snout alone was nearly as tall as Chass. She'd backed up rapidly and found the Chevin wasn't alone.

"There were maybe five or six of them. The Chevin and his buddies, making a deal in this alley with a human woman not much bigger than me. Selling or buying, I don't know. But the Chevin decided not to let me go."

*You have offended me,* the Chevin had said, and one of his buddies had pulled out a shock collar.

Chass had worn a shock collar before. She knew what would happen if she didn't escape. But she didn't have a weapon, didn't know anywhere to run to. She'd eyed the Chevin's blaster, readied herself to snatch it.

She hadn't needed to.

"The woman kept talking to the Chevin, trying to get his, her, whatever, attention off me and back onto whatever deal they were making. But the Chevin kept *looking* at me, making these sleazy comments, saying I shouldn't have been wandering around at night . . ."

She hadn't been watching the woman. The shooting took her by surprise—the sudden flare of light, the Chevin stumbling in shock. Chass had backed into a corner, covered her ears, and waited for it all to end.

"I looked up and she was the only one left. I don't know why she did it. She certainly didn't tell me. But you looked at her, and—you know how some people have this *thing,* where you know they're the most amazing people you'll ever meet even if they're just drooling in their sleep?

"She had that."

They'd spoken briefly—very briefly—but Chass didn't tell Wyl and Nath and Kairos what the woman had said to her. She didn't say the woman had given her name as Liana Hallik.

That was it, though. They'd gone their separate ways before local security could make a fuss. Chass had returned to her life and it wasn't until a year later, on Koiogra, that she'd realized who the woman had been.

"I found this little black-market shop. Specialized in holovids. Guy owed me, didn't have the credits, so he gave me an armful of banned recordings."

She'd robbed him.

"I went through them at home. Some of it was pervert stuff, but some of it was music and—that's the stuff I liked. There was weirder stuff, too, and I started watching a rebel propaganda vid and recognized this girl. It was a grainy shot, with most of the room filtered, but she was making a speech. It was Jyn Erso—it was *my* girl, the girl who'd saved my life, talking about attacking the Death Star. I didn't really understand back then. I wasn't political. But she was—if you've seen it, you know."

Chass had memorized the words long ago.

*You give way to an enemy this evil with this much power and you condemn the galaxy to an eternity of submission.*

*The Empire doesn't care if you surrender. The Empire doesn't care if you're hopeless. I've given up before, and it doesn't help. It doesn't stop.*

*Rebellions are built on hope.*

"It was after that speech that she went off to Scarif. Led a strike team, led a whole armada, to steal the plans of the Death Star battle station the Emperor had built to kill billions."

Jyn Erso had died on that mission. Legend had it that she'd sent the last transmission to the rebel fleet—the Death Star plans themselves— moments before the battle station's weaponry had boiled the planet's seas and burned away its surface. Jyn had been a martyr. She had been a hero.

"That's when I knew. That's when I knew if—I thought, *I met her. I could be like that, too. Crawl out of the gutter to do something great.*"

She'd seen Jedha, after that: the ruined pilgrim world where Jyn's rebels had come from, to which Chass had made her own sort of pilgrimage. She'd flown with the Cavern Angels and eventually joined the Rebel Alliance. But she didn't say those things aloud.

Nor did she say anything about how desperately afraid she'd been all her life before finding Jyn Erso.

"That's it. That's the whole story."

It wasn't even close, but it was something.

Chass woke before dawn to a ringing sound like a struck gong. She burrowed deeper into her bedroll but the sound didn't stop, and as she listened it steadied to a soothing tone that seemed to warm her chilled digits. Nath and Wyl were climbing upright, and as Chass gradually emerged from her cocoon she saw that Kairos had started toward the temple.

"Where's it coming from?" Chass asked.

"Sounds like the forest canopy," Nath said, "but if Kairos thinks it's in there I'm not going to argue."

Kairos showed no sign of alarm. She waited for the others as they pulled on their boots, then padded inside. Chass followed with Wyl and Nath and caught her breath as they entered.

The temple was dark, but drifting about were motes of light: thousands, maybe millions of sparks in the night like stars. They covered the walls and the spire of the main chamber, and Chass felt her eyes drawn upward as if gravity pulled her body toward the chiming. Unselfconscious, she raised her arms like a dancer and turned as she marched into the chamber's center. They stood at the center of a universe that existed only within the temple.

The stars rotated around her. The others were present but, like her, they were looking up and were only shadows in her peripheral vision. Chass had never been interested in astronomy, but somehow she recognized what she saw: familiar stars and around them, flecks that were the worlds she had visited, worlds she'd loathed and run from along with worlds she'd secretly treasured. Uchinao and Lyran, Nar Shaddaa and Jedha. They whirled and blurred together one moment, then crystallized as if viewed through a corrective lens. The universe blazed and burned, furious and beautiful.

"The galaxy as it was," Wyl said.

She knew that he was correct, but she couldn't have said *how.* She was looking into the distant past.

Then the whirling increased in speed, and the dark between the stars grew deeper. The emptiness became a *hungry* emptiness, and the stars became food for the ravenous void. Against the dark the light stood out clearer in contrast, almost too painful to watch. Chass's body trembled. She wanted to dance. She wanted to fight.

"The galaxy as it became," Wyl said.

This, too, was correct. In the stars, Chass saw war.

Then dawn came.

The dim light of the yellow sun encroached through the windows of the spire. The deepest blackness turned pale and imperfect and unthreatening. The brightest stars dimmed, and they were only stars like any Chass could see—like the stars she took in at a glance from her cockpit, mundane and unstoried. There was no longer a shadow over the galaxy.

Then the stars disappeared. Daylight filled the temple.

All that was left was the four of them.

"The galaxy as it is," Wyl said.

Chass lowered her arms. It should have been a letdown—the loss of it all, the change from a cosmic struggle to something less extraordinary. She felt lighter nonetheless; the loss had made her buoyant.

"Jedi knew how to build," Nath said, and Wyl laughed, and then Chass laughed, and even Kairos bowed her head in something resembling amusement.

They left the temple, maneuvering three repulsorsleds through the forest and bearing packs stuffed to overflowing, murmuring to one another and smiling like old friends.

*It's time,* Chass thought. As they trekked through the chill morning, she passed her sled to Nath and strolled over to Wyl.

"Hey," she said.

"Hey," he said.

"You understand now?" she asked. She didn't explain. He would figure it out or he wouldn't.

But he nodded slowly, and she thought, perhaps, she'd underestimated his perceptiveness.

"I do," he said, "a little bit, I think. I'm glad you told us."

"Then you won't do it again?"

Wyl pursed his lips and blew a trail of pale breath. He didn't look at Chass for a while, but she gave him time. Eventually, he glanced back and still didn't speak.

She didn't want to do what she knew came next. It would've been easier when she hadn't liked him. (When had she started liking him? she wondered.)

"Wyl," she said. "What happened at the *Dare*. You—" *You took away my chance.* "You ran, and you took me with you by taking away my choice. I don't know if it's because you were afraid to go alone, or afraid to fight, or because you're *interested* in me—"

Wyl flinched. Chass saw him doubting himself and hurried on. The pain was necessary, but she wasn't a sadist. "—or because you really believed you were doing the smart thing, tactically. It doesn't matter.

"But you can't do it again."

"I know," he said. "You wouldn't allow it." He grimaced and shook his head, and he looked more serious and concerned than even Quell ever had.

Chass tried not to pity him. Wyl tried, she knew. Even with all his idyllic past and his I'm-your-humble-savior ego, she knew he tried.

Then he said, "I—are we a squadron, now?"

"Meaning?"

"Meaning, do we have each other's backs? Are we together in this?"

Now it was Chass who looked away. The toe of her boot found a clod of dirt and sent it arcing into the air.

It was a good question. She *had* underestimated him, at least a little. "Yes," she said. "I guess we are."

"Then I owe it to you not to make your decisions for you," Wyl said, and shrugged. "Even if they're the wrong ones."

She processed it slowly. She laughed softly after a while, and Wyl smiled, and she wrapped an arm around him and squeezed his shoulder as they walked until he finally laughed, too.

He said he understood, but she was sure he didn't. Sure that he wouldn't have agreed if he had—but she could live with what she'd been given. She could find joy in the morning chill of a strange moon.

**II**

Quell hadn't slept more than a few hours at a time each night, alternating watches with D6-L. (Nath's droid, the ancient C-series unit, didn't volunteer for a shift and Quell didn't ask.) Her astromech ran nearly silent, only pinging or chirruping in response to orders and questions, but each time Quell woke she found a thorough report awaiting her on her X-wing's onboard computer: detailed scans and analysis with a top line summary of "no unusual activity."

The droid was thorough. The droid was professional. It wasn't until their third morning on the moon that Quell remembered what it had done after Abednedo.

The droid had offered to resign. It had taken responsibility to protect her. That was an act more than thorough or professional, and it needed acknowledgment. But she had no idea what to say.

Exhausted and filthy, she approached it after she'd finished her breakfast and crouched by it near her starfighter. "Dee-six?" she said.

The astromech rotated its dome and offered a questioning ping.

"You weren't built for combat, were you? For starfighter operations?" She remembered its mention of *capital ship maintenance* when she'd first loaded it aboard the X-wing.

The droid let out a lower humming sound, its chassis momentarily wobbling.

"You've done well," Quell said. "Very well. And I'm grateful for your assistance."

For a few moments, D6-L did not audibly respond, though its indicator lights flashed as if it were processing an influx of information. Then the unit emitted a stern, dignified buzz, rotated, and rolled away in the direction of the ridge. As it gained distance, it began to whistle softly.

Of all the lessons Quell had learned about leadership from Major Keize, managing droid personalities hadn't been among them.

An hour later, D6-L let out a loud ping and Quell joined it looking down onto the forest. Below, she could see her team creeping up the mountain. She fought back her weariness and saw the ease in their body language, heard the lightness in their voices, and pride rose inside her as the four arrived at the peak.

Not only pride, though. Something less pleasant, too—a tinge of frustration, of bitterness, that leapt further into her consciousness when she saw Chadic with her arm slung around Lark.

She would get over it. Her team was coming together at last.

### III

It took another two hours to load the gear aboard the U-wing and prep for launch. Wyl focused on the task throughout—strapping down machinery and power packs wasn't difficult, but the cargo was too volatile to trust to the usual netting. "We've had a pretty easy mission so far," he told Nath when the older man urged him to wrap up. "You want to be the one to explain to the general why the U-wing exploded in hyperspace?"

"Sounds like you're volunteering," Nath said with a grin, and went to plug his droid into the Y-wing.

Wyl didn't think much about his conversation with Chass. He'd dwell on it later, he suspected, after returning to the *Lodestar;* but for the moment he was grateful for the armistice between them.

In time, the job was finished. Quell called them together, the five ships already powered up and humming. "Should be an easy flight back," she said. "That pirate scout jumped out of the system a day ago, and I got a signal from the battle group with rendezvous coordinates. No alarm, no warning to come in hot, so I'm assuming operations are going well." She paused and added, "Good work," before sketching a rough flight path for departure.

Wyl's A-wing was ready for takeoff when he decided to check the U-wing one last time. He hurried through the loading door and into the main cabin, dimly lit and packed full of cargo. He shook a stack of crates, confirmed the settings on the repulsors they'd used to lock everything in place, and finally stepped back, satisfied they'd done the best they could. "You're set," he called to Kairos, eyes still on the load. "Give it a final look if you want."

Kairos didn't reply, of course. But neither did Wyl hear her emerge from the cockpit. He frowned, stepped to the cockpit door, and saw that no one was inside.

Where *was* she?

He left the U-wing and scanned the mountaintop. The other pilots were in their ships. He saw no sign of Kairos. He could've called her on his comlink, but he was more curious than worried. He started back toward the slope where they'd made their ascent.

There, a dozen meters down the trail, stood Kairos. She was still, staring across the forest in the direction of the temple.

Wyl sauntered toward her, careful to make enough noise to announce his approach. When he reached her side he followed her gaze, trying to see what she saw. The noise of the engines fell away; the calm of the forest swept over him. The moment was tranquil, but if there was any glimmer from the top of the temple spire, any sign of the ancient structure at all, he couldn't find it.

He thought back to the images he'd seen inside. The burning stars, the darkness—it felt like a faded dream now, half remembered and impossible, exposed as fakery in the light of day. Only the last moments remained with him in full: *The galaxy as it is.*

He found peace in that.

"Wyl Lark."

The voice was low and wet and guttural, and at first he didn't understand where it came from. When he saw Kairos facing him he flinched.

"The Emperor's shadow is long," she said.

Then she looked away and began to hike back toward the ships.

Wyl felt his muscles quiver. He felt a chill more profound than anything the forest moon had inflicted.

# CHAPTER 13

# THE DETERMINATION OF SOLDIERS

I

The *Lodestar,* along with the rest of Syndulla's battle group, was waiting on the outskirts of the Borleias system. Quell saw fresh damage on the *Lodestar*'s port side as she flew to dock, but the fleet as a whole appeared intact—she noticed a corvette with one of its sections exposed to the vacuum of space and a freighter trailing sparks, yet she noticed no vessels missing altogether.

Syndulla was waiting in the hangar when the squadron landed. That surprised Quell—the general presumably had more important things to do—but Quell climbed out of her X-wing, offered a cursory nod to Ragnell as the engineer waved teams into position, and marched crisply in Syndulla's direction.

"General," she said. "Mission accomplished."

"Glad to hear it," Syndulla replied. She was looking past Quell, to Lark and Chadic and Tensent as they called to one another and hopped out of their vessels. Quell saw the general smile, but the expression only lasted an instant. "No problems on the ground?"

"None," Quell said. "We found the rebel base without issue. One scout ship—we're assuming pirates—flew by but didn't see anything. The team reported some odd visual phenomena on our last day, but nothing that interfered with the job."

"Visual phenomena?" Syndulla cocked her head. "In the temple, you mean?"

"Yes, ma'am," Quell said.

"But you didn't see it yourself?"

"I was off-site at the time."

Syndulla peered at her in a way that Quell found vexing. "Too bad," the general finally said. "I think you would've liked it."

Behind her, Quell heard Ragnell yelling about the repulsorsleds. "We're highly trained engineers," the woman called, "not your blasted labor force." Quell resisted the urge to turn and see what, exactly, was happening. Instead she kept her chin up as she waited for the general.

"Regardless," Syndulla said, "it looks like you've come out of it in healthy shape. Which is good—because I've got another mission for you, if your squadron is ready."

Quell nodded cautiously. Before she'd gone to the cold Jedi moon, the general had told her: *How you handle* this *mission will help me decide if there's another.* And though she didn't understand *how* she'd passed Syndulla's test, she knew better than to question the result.

"We're always ready, ma'am," Quell said.

It was another salvage operation. The fighting on Argai Minor had been brutal, and New Republic Intelligence suspected Imperial forces planetside had been receiving logistical support from elsewhere. "We want to know if their supply lines reached all the way to Pandem Nai," General Syndulla had told Quell. "Since Shadow Wing is your specialty, you get first crack."

The plan was to patrol the battlefields surrounding the ruined Treinhaus Citadel, holding off any remaining Imperials and buying time for a New Republic salvage team to collect data from the wreckage. The enemy had already been decimated by orbital bombardment and precision strikes from Syndulla's fleet, so resistance was expected to be scattered and desperate. "Three-legged walkers and stormtroopers with surface-to-air missiles ought to be our biggest problem," Quell told the others at the briefing.

They'd proven they could avoid bungling a mission altogether. Now Syndulla was giving them a chance to show they could operate in a combat zone. She'd done so without embellishment or warnings about the risks, but they all understood the significance.

For a hundred reasons, this couldn't go like Abednedo.

Yet it didn't take long for things to go downhill. The salvage team, upon arrival at the citadel, immediately increased its time estimate from two hours of work to sixteen. The fortress itself was missing most of its eastern wall—the kilometers-tall sheet of durasteel had been crumpled and melted by Imperial sappers using deep core mining drills. And the surrounding battlefield—rather than offering excellent visibility, as the pilots of Vanguard Squadron had predicted—was littered with the wreckage of speeders, troop carriers, walkers, and other vehicles, many of which had been ignited by Imperial guerrillas and now spewed toxic smoke into the air.

Quell scrambled to adjust her planned patrol patterns and to organize shifts for the sixteen-hour wait. Four ships would stay in the air at any given time, in two two-ship elements. One pilot would be permitted to rest and stand watch over the citadel itself.

She assigned the slower vessels—the Y-wing and B-wing, both poorly designed for atmospheric flight—to patrols closer to the citadel, while the A- and X-wings patrolled farther out. The U-wing could substitute for any single vessel. The resulting schedule appalled Quell's sensibilities: She didn't trust Chadic to fly with Tensent. She didn't want to leave Lark and Kairos without support. She didn't believe any of them would coordinate, following their assigned patrol routes and covering all necessary ground.

But she said none of this. When she took off with Wyl Lark for the first patrol, she told her squadron, "Keep to your assigned sectors. Stay with your partner. Follow your instincts. And alert everyone the moment something happens."

They were rebels. She couldn't remake them into Imperial pilots in the time she had. As she'd done on the nameless moon, she had to treat them as what they were.

For the first three hours, they encountered no resistance. They took potshots at infantry squads maneuvering below, simply to force the Imperials into cover; they caught glimpses of a TIE scout at the limits of their sensor range; but for the most part, they watched and waited.

During the next three hours, as evening fell and the smoke grew thicker, they found themselves repeatedly targeted by Imperial ground forces. One moment, Quell would peer through the poisonous smog and adjust her course across the battlefield; the next, her console would flash, alerting her to a missile lock, and she'd frantically bank and ascend, bank and ascend, trying to reach an altitude where the missile couldn't follow. She never ordered a counterattack after these frantic, furious encounters. She knew the starfighters would become vulnerable if they dropped low enough to strike at the infantry.

For the next five hours, through the Argai night, they fended off waves of TIE bombers. The bombers came infrequently, in flights of two and three, unescorted by fighters and taking weaving paths through the smoke and darkness to reach the citadel.

Wyl Lark destroyed three. Kairos and Chadic neutralized two each. Quell never even saw one.

She should have been pleased. She *was* pleased—the squadron was performing admirably and the mission was going well. But she'd hoped for a chance to prove herself. General Syndulla's question remained unanswered—*Do they know that you'll fight for them?*—and she'd failed to demonstrate the risks she would take to keep her people alive.

When morning came, the attacks stopped. The final patrols were uneventful, and in the misty light of dawn the pilots joked and traded stories. Quell didn't discourage them.

They returned home with the data. The mission was a success.

Quell thought her "Alphabet Squadron" might have a chance after all.

After Argai Minor—after two days of downtime, during which Quell spotted Tensent and Lark frequently mingling with the pilots of Meteor Squadron—the next mission took them to Rentaxius VIII, where they were to intercept and capture an Imperial cargo vessel believed to have resupplied at Pandem Nai.

The operation had begun well. The New Republic ships had surrounded the enemy vessel. Quell demanded that the freighter surrender, and the captain agreed. Then she had to sit listening as the captain was murdered, a new commander took over, and the freighter opened fire. What happened next was neither a success nor a disaster: Tensent and Chadic disabled the ship, but a stray shot from Lark aimed at a laser turret hit an oxygen generator instead. They'd had to evacuate the survivors and tow the escape pods to safety.

Lark didn't mingle with the *Lodestar* pilots that night. Quell went looking for him after her debriefing with General Syndulla and Caern Adan. When she found him in the hangar drinking with Tensent—D6-L and T5 flanking Lark like loyal hounds—she backed away quietly before she could be noticed.

Her pilots were supporting one another. Again, she was pleased. Again, she felt the flash of bitterness. Major Keize, she thought, would have been ashamed—by Quell's neediness and doubt, as well as her inability to forge a bond of blood and trust with her people.

The next mission was a support operation, backing up Hail Squadron after the Y-wings had been decimated by a run-in with an unidentified Imperial cruiser-carrier—possibly a Shadow Wing vessel, but more likely an escapee from Argai Minor. Hail's new target was a half-wrecked Star Destroyer that had been limping through the Haldeen sector for weeks. Quell very nearly had the opportunity to draw the destroyer's fire—another chance to prove her devotion to her squadron—but the moment passed and superior tactical options became available. Quell had no death wish, and together, her squadron and Hail delivered the killing blow to the enemy craft. Quell ached as she watched the ship fall—she couldn't help but imagine the crew aboard scrambling through the flames. She imagined what battles the Star Destroyer had fought in its past; the squadrons it had hosted.

When they returned to the *Lodestar*, she smiled grimly and said nothing of the dead as she reviewed the operation with her troops.

"I understand," the torture droid said, "that your relationship with Adan is improving."

"Did he tell you that?" Quell asked.

She still met regularly with IT-O, though their sessions were shorter now. She had more work on her hands; she had missions to plan, reports to file, meetings with the ground crew to attend. These were all excuses, but they had the benefit of being real.

"There have been no further physical altercations," the droid said. "That alone qualifies as improvement."

"We don't—" She paused. She wasn't sure what was safe to share with the droid—what it was fishing for and what would make its way back to Adan. "My sense is that he's content to let General Syndulla assign the missions. He's focused on analyzing the data we're bringing in. When he wants my opinion on Shadow Wing or Pandem Nai, I'll be available."

"I'm glad to hear it," the droid said. "You understand that while he may have stepped back from direct supervision, Adan is ultimately in control of—"

"My fate, yes. He can always send me back to Traitor's Remorse."

"I wouldn't have focused on the negative possibility. However, you will need to come to an understanding with him, sooner or later."

"We *have* an understanding."

"You have a cease-fire agreement. If I may make an assertion, Yrica Quell, you have a tendency to view half measures as finished journeys—" The droid's photoreceptor dilated menacingly as she straightened in her seat. "—when it comes to issues relating to psychology and interpersonal relations. You complete an important first step and, feeling justifiably triumphant, see no purpose in a second."

*Don't argue with the droid,* she told herself. *Just nod and get it over with.*

"Where do you get the gall to say something like that?" she asked.

The droid's voice was steady. "You felt recruiting your pilots was sufficient to command them. You agreed to sessions with me but have shown little interest in taking our lessons beyond these walls. Even your adjustment to the New Republic has involved remarkably little—"

"Stop," she said. The voice still told her not to argue, but it was drowned out by the roar of blood in her ears. "You don't know what I've done to try to adjust. You have no idea. Just because I don't talk about something doesn't mean I'm not thinking about it. It doesn't mean I'm taking *shortcuts.*"

The droid contracted its photoreceptor and reduced its altitude by several centimeters. "Of course," it said. "I may have overstepped."

It almost sounded *hurt.* But it was still a torture droid, and *almost* wasn't convincing.

The droid was wrong about Quell. If it had been right—if she really had been the sort of person to call a first step a victory—she wouldn't have spent so much time dwelling on her squadron. The question of how to cement her bond with her pilots lingered in the back of her brain as she reviewed munitions supplies with Ragnell in the hangar, arguing over concussion missile requests and Lark's "damage-prone" flying techniques. "You're shutting us out," Quell snapped. "We're not *guests* aboard the *Lodestar*—we're part of your complement, so treat us like it."

"I *am* treating you like you're mine," the mechanic sneered. "You think Meteor and Hail are thrilled when I prioritize Vanguard? Hail still has four ships too broke to fly, and I've got their commander nagging me every day like I'm all that's holding them back."

"You think you're not?" Quell asked.

Ragnell didn't answer, instead glowering at Quell from where she squatted amid a pile of datapads and toolboxes.

Aboard the *Pursuer,* Quell thought, a mechanic was *always* responsible for the state of her squadron. She'd never heard excuses about workforces and supplies in the Empire.

"We're stretched thin," Ragnell said at last.

"We're *winning*," Quell said.

"And we're not built for it. I've worked with some of these ships for years—I've kept them functional all this time. But that was when we were hiding. Keeping these squadrons ready for missions *daily*? That's a whole separate set of problems." She locked eyes with Quell. "Meteor and Hail get that. General Syndulla gets that. Even Vanguard gets that. You need to adjust, too."

Quell grunted. "I don't have much choice."

The mechanic looked triumphant. They went down the list of Quell's needs and Ragnell's time estimates, and Quell assisted with the triage as best she could.

She found her eyes tracing the woman's tattoos—the dancing figures and whorls like waves or fire, intricate and connected on every centimeter of flesh. The two finished up and Ragnell walked with Quell between the rows of starfighters—Meteor and Hail's vessels, scarred and blasted but still painted bright. Quell thought of Ragnell and the *Pursuer* and the words of the droid and the words of General Syndulla.

"Before we go," Quell said, "I need a favor."

"Of course you do." Ragnell sighed.

**II**

Nath hadn't slept more than five hours. The latest mission—a raid on an Imperial outpost caught relaying messages to Pandem Nai—had gone too well not to celebrate, and he'd spent until the wee hours in the Krayt Hut comparing notes on Y-wing repair with Hail Squadron. He didn't much like the Hail Squadron pilots—to a person, they seemed much too proud of landing a spot aboard Syndulla's flagship—but Nath might need them down the line. Humbly accepting a few accolades and acting friendly seemed worth the time.

But he hadn't been expecting a wake-up call from Quell and orders to head down to the hangar at an unnatural hour, and he clearly wasn't the only one: Chass's eyes were bloodshot as she marched down the corridor, and even Wyl didn't look fresh. Only Kairos seemed unperturbed.

*Thing probably doesn't even sleep,* Nath thought with a mix of annoyance and admiration.

"They can win," Chass muttered. "The Empire can win. Shadow Wing can win. Don't make me fly this early."

"Reasonable compromise," Nath said as they strolled into the bay.

Quell was waiting in her flight suit. She offered a curt nod toward the group and jutted a thumb behind her at the rows of fighters. "Got word there's an admiral coming today. He'll be doing a full inspection of the *Lodestar* and its complement. Give your ships a walkaround, check your cockpits, don't embarrass me. Understood?"

*In other words,* Nath thought, *hide anything you can hide and clean up your mess.*

Wyl mumbled a "yes, ma'am," though Nath felt the boy must have been sarcastic. Chass paused, seemed on the verge of marching out, then lurched forward like something was dragging her by puppet strings. Nath eyed Quell, who shrugged at him as the others moved on.

Before Nath could follow, he heard Wyl's laugh—a swift bark—followed by Chass swearing. Puzzled, he sauntered past the Meteor Squadron X-wings and came into view of the rear of his ship. His Y-wing sat there, scratched as always but scrubbed and polished like it was fresh from the factory.

He walked slowly around the vessel. His eyes widened. He must have looked absurd, he knew, but it was his ship—*his* ship. Someone had touched *his ship* and painted a crest on the gleaming metal depicting five vessels—an A-wing, B-wing, X-wing, Y-wing, and U-wing. Above the crest, a banner read: ALPHABET SQUADRON.

He looked to his comrades. Each stared at his or her own vessel; each ship had been similarly branded. Chass went from swearing to laughing loudly, while Wyl turned around to look over at Quell. Kairos gazed at the U-wing's markings as if transfixed—she extended a hand and touched the paint gingerly, like it was something ancient prone to crumble in the light.

"You do this to my ship?" Nath called toward Quell.

"Do I look like I can paint?" Quell asked, voice humorless.

"Don't do it again," Nath said, but he was smirking despite himself.

"It's fantastic," Wyl said. "Thank you."

"There's something else," Quell said, and she strolled down the central aisle between fighters. Kairos stepped away from the U-wing reluctantly. "Thought I'd show you, while we're at it."

When her audience was gathered together, Quell tugged up the sleeve of her flight suit and rotated her arm. Stenciled into the irritated flesh of her biceps was a tattoo: the same squadron crest that now adorned the ships.

"In case I get stranded planetside," Quell said. "They'll know where to send me."

"That they will," Nath said.

"You're a freak," Chass added.

"I'm also your commanding officer," Quell said.

Chass shrugged. "Still a freak."

They were all smiling. Chass and Wyl continued ribbing Quell, and Nath complained about the early hour. But he could see what she'd done and he respected the effort. Maybe she couldn't bond with her team like Nath had with his squadron, but Quell had managed to bring the team to her.

It wasn't a bad outcome. Whatever Nath's issues with Quell, he hoped she would keep them all alive.

"Time for breakfast," Wyl said. "You coming with us, Lieutenant?"

"Not this time," Quell said. "But thank you."

Nath laughed and waved Wyl and Chass to follow him. *Yrica Quell. You're still Imperial at heart,* he thought, but he didn't spoil the moment.

## III

Caern Adan was being outmaneuvered. He'd seen it coming—could have planned it himself, for all the details he'd predicted—yet it was still happening. Worst of all, it was his own fault.

"I let General Syndulla have them," he told IT-O as he toweled off in his quarters. He'd been saving his water rations, hoping a long shower would bring him some semblance of peace. (It hadn't.) "I could've held them in reserve but I didn't, and now she's handing *my* working group their assignments."

"If you were handing out assignments, you wouldn't have time for analysis. General Syndulla is sending them after leads *you* obtained from our captive."

*Our captive* was IT-O's way of saying "that war criminal stormtrooper you spent a week interviewing." It was true that Adan had extracted useful intelligence from the man—scraps about Shadow Wing's garrison and Pandem Nai's developing status as a key refueling post for Imperials on the run. And Adan had obtained that intelligence without spilling blood, albeit not without compromises. He'd shipped the man off when they'd finished; Adan expected he would languish in a cell for months before anyone figured out what to do with him.

Now he was neck-deep in data from Argai Minor and elsewhere. Data that, piece by piece, revealed an image of Pandem Nai's defenses and Shadow Wing's operational status. A map of the Pandem Nai star system was burned into his brain.

"It doesn't matter that *I* know my contributions," he said, "or that *you* know my contributions. We're all thrilled that the general and my superiors are finally taking Shadow Wing seriously, but if this ends with 'General Syndulla's Alphabet Squadron' achieving a major strategic victory, it—"

"Leaves your heroism unsung?"

"—leaves the New Republic Senate more convinced than ever that firepower is the solution to every problem. What will they do when the next Shadow Wing comes along? The goal ought to be to predict and prevent another Nacronis, not to send a fleet in after the fact."

"We agree that New Republic Intelligence must play a more prominent role in galactic security. But your working group was never going to neutralize the 204th on its own. Military assistance was always inevitable."

"*Assistance.* But now I'm assisting them. They're not assisting me. The whole point of this operation was to show what's possible when intelligence takes control."

"The point," the droid said, "was to bring a dangerous enemy to justice and prevent future massacres. Besides, Caern—your involvement isn't over yet."

That was true. It wasn't satisfying, but it was true.

Caern dropped onto the cot that passed for his bed and found his fingers stroking a bottle of Corellian red. The bottle was half full—a fact he made sure to file away in case IT-O complained about his drinking. *If I were really drinking too much, would I have so much left in the bottle?*

But the droid didn't say anything as Caern took a sickly sweet swallow. The silence was almost worse than the rebuke.

"I *may*," Caern stressed, "have another option. A last resort, in case Syndulla tries to shut me out altogether."

"Do tell."

"Yrica Quell," he said. "You weren't able to dig up much. But I got an interesting note yesterday from one of my contacts in Hutt space. Check my files—you have the decryption codes."

The droid contracted its photoreceptor and hummed as Caern took another swig from the bottle. A few moments later, IT-O's servo whine rose in pitch.

*Got your attention, did I?*

"Assuming the information is accurate," IT-O said, "that would represent a significant discrepancy in Lieutenant Quell's story."

"It would," Caern said, and waved a hand airily. "And no, I'm not confident it's true—my contact is competent but not picky about his sourcing. *If* it's true, though—*if* I can confirm it—it could help me rein in the team. Remind them they answer to me and not Syndulla."

"If Yrica Quell is not what she claims, it could also do considerable damage to your reputation. Assuming her intent to neutralize the 204th Fighter Wing is genuine at all."

"Details," Caern muttered. "I'm making progress, Ito. Be happy for me."

The droid didn't reply. It wasn't happy for him, Caern knew. Not that it wasn't capable of the emotion—he'd seen the droid express pleasure and empathy in the past, when one or another of its patients performed some feat of psychiatric recuperation. But that wasn't—had never been—Caern and IT-O's relationship.

Caern realized that the bottle was now empty and thought about procuring another. Then the intercom chimed.

When he saw who his caller was, he decided to remain sober.

General Syndulla's battle group had secured six systems over eight days. Aside from being formidable in its own right, that accomplishment positioned the fleet to take control of the Skangravi-Mestun Regional Hyperlane without exposing the newly freed systems to an Imperial counterattack. The Skangravi-Mestun, in turn, led nine-tenths of the way to Pandem Nai—close enough to open dozens of potential paths for the final leg of the journey. Shadow Wing presumably had early warning mechanisms set along the longer, easier, more obvious routes to the system (like the Celanon Spur, which Caern had spent hours studying since learning of their enemy's location; or the winding path through H'Grathi, where the scouts of the *Hellion's Dare* had originally been spotted), but access to the Skangravi-Mestun multiplied the New Republic's options tenfold. Shadow Wing couldn't possibly watch *every* path to Pandem Nai.

Nor was Pandem Nai itself the mystery it had been. Between intercepted communications and everything the battle group had procured, Caern's dossier on the enemy garrison had grown to considerable length. The next natural step was to go beyond a general overview to obtain detailed schematics, personnel information, and security codes.

"Do we have time for that?" Quell asked, after he finished his assessment.

He was pleased that she asked him instead of assuming. He was pleased she'd come to him at all instead of sequestering herself with the general to plan an assault on Pandem Nai. They sat in the dimly lit tactical operations center, surrounded by transparent screens displaying hyperspace charts and system layouts, with no one but the *Lodestar*'s droids for company.

"No," he said. "We don't."

"What happens if we don't find a weakness?" she asked.

"A formal decision hasn't been made, but the New Republic recognizes that leaving an enemy unit responsible for who-knows-how-many atrocities sitting on a major strategic resource isn't an option. If it were just Shadow Wing, frankly, it might be different—the military would ignore the problem until your people shot down a dozen command ships and blew up a small moon—but Pandem Nai is already supplying several smaller Imperial factions. That's only going to get worse.

"So *what happens,* most likely, is that Syndulla's battle group joins a protracted siege of the system. Pandem Nai gets blockaded. The damage is contained until the enemy breaks the siege or finally succumbs."

"Which could take months," Quell said, soft and tentative. "The Empire makes gains across the galaxy while our fleet is besieging Pandem Nai."

Caern leaned back in his seat and clapped his hands. "Exactly. All of which you already knew, didn't you? It's why you're here."

He expected an argument and didn't get one. Quell nodded, staring at a display. "Yes." She tapped the console, changing the screen to show the Pandem Nai system's orbital paths.

"It's on us to make a plan. To find a weakness," Caern said.

"Yes." Quell scrolled through additional screens of data: defensive estimates, minefield positions, historical data on Pandem Nai's gas extraction operations.

"You understand what that means?" he asked. "This was never going to be the Death Star. We weren't ever going to find a secret vulnerability in Shadow Wing that could shut the whole unit down, or a path through the system the enemy somehow missed."

She looked from the display to him and said nothing. He heard the condescension in his voice and tried to moderate it. IT-O had told him many times that smugness wasn't *helpful;* in this case it might have even been unwarranted. "Lieutenant Quell—*you* are the vulnerability. Your insight into Shadow Wing is the only reason you're here. It's our only substantive advantage.

"So if you want to neutralize your old unit swiftly and as bloodlessly as possible, you need to take into consideration all of this—everything we know about Shadow Wing and Pandem Nai—and tell me:

"What are they going to do when we attack? And how do we counter it?"

He couldn't tell if she heard the words. She kept staring at the display, absently rubbing at her biceps beneath her shirt sleeve.

"Three days, maybe, till we're in position?" she asked.

"Give or take."

"Then we have time to go through scenarios one by one. Until we find a plan that works."

# IV

It was a terrible plan, Hera Syndulla thought. It would get Alphabet Squadron killed and leave the fleet in a precarious position, forced to retreat or begin a siege that was very likely to fail.

"It's a solid plan," she told Quell as the young woman skimmed a datapad at the front of the ready room. Hera had learned to read Quell, at least a little—she knew the lieutenant turned serious and quiet when she was most nervous. "Present to your squadron what you presented to me. I promise they won't revolt."

"It's reckless," Quell said. She cast a glance toward Adan, who was speaking quietly into his comlink at the opposite end of the room. "You and I both know it."

Hera smiled wryly. "It's a *rebel* plan. You've been watching how we operate. You kept your people's abilities in mind, and the capabilities of the battle group. All rebel plans look reckless on the surface."

*And they all look terrible,* she thought, but Quell looked anxious enough without that particular truth.

Hera had spent the last thirty hours alternating between cloistered sessions with Quell and Adan and larger meetings with her captains and New Republic High Command. Lindon Javes had studied and agreed with Quell's prediction. Hera had argued to Admiral Ackbar himself that Quell's approach was their best chance, and the man who had won the Battle of Endor had given his approval. Yet there was still something that felt foreign about the plan—some nuance that eluded Hera but was embedded into its structure.

Maybe, Hera thought, it was just that it was *Quell's* plan and not her own. It had the fingerprints of a stranger on it.

She hoped there wasn't anything more.

Quell's pilots filed into the room. Hera hid a smile when she saw them sit together. She'd been watching them since they'd come back from the Jedi temple. *You haven't lost your touch, Hera.*

She waited until they'd settled and began, "In fifty-three hours we will be in position to reach Pandem Nai, where—according to the best of our intelligence—the 204th Imperial Fighter Wing is currently garrisoned.

"You've all seen the reports. Shadow Wing has fortified the Pandem Nai system with minefields. It patrols the inner system with fighter squadrons and cruisers. Pandem Nai itself is sheathed in a volatile atmosphere that causes heavy weaponry to backfire—effectively rendering capital ships ineffectual in any assault."

*That* had been a point of contention during the battle group's planning meetings. *What if we reduced the power output to the turbolasers? What about coherent beam weapons? What about—?* Hera had been surprised by her captains' desire to find a scientific solution—some engineering trick—to the problem presented by Pandem Nai's atmosphere.

But she'd spoken with Tibanna gas extraction experts who'd once worked in Cloud City and a defecting Imperial scientist from the Tarkin Initiative. They'd tried to explain the chemistry, but what it came down to, they said, was mathematics: Add enough energy to Pandem Nai's atmosphere and its gas would combust. The more energy, the bigger the explosion—similar to starting a fire in an oxygen-rich environment. Capital ships would be forced to keep thruster temperatures low and use their weakest weapons or else risk immolation. If they got too close to the planet, they'd only get in the way.

"That means," Hera continued, "that starfighter supremacy will determine victory or defeat. You're all intimately familiar with the capabilities of Shadow Wing, so I won't dwell on what it means to face dozens of TIEs under the command of Colonel Nuress."

She looked among Nath, Wyl, Chass, and Kairos, and saw nothing less than resolve. It was what she'd expected, but she'd been ready to change course if she'd seen fear or doubt. "Finally, we have reason to believe that Shadow Wing's base of operations is not on the planet surface but on one of the orbital stations designed to extract and process Tibanna gas from the planet's atmosphere. That gives us a clear target, but the station is as heavily armored as any battle station. It may not be capable of annihilating a planet—or even a ship like the *Lodestar*—but it *will* be designed for anti-starfighter operations.

"Under the protection of a lesser unit, Pandem Nai would be a tough fight. Under Shadow Wing, it's almost perfectly defensible against direct attack. But Lieutenant Quell and Officer Adan have given us an alternative strategy.

"It depends on you. Your skill. Your bravery. Your willingness to neutralize Shadow Wing while the fleet acts as backup. It's a solid plan—" She resisted the urge to glance at Quell. "—but it is exceedingly dangerous. Which is why I'm telling you all, no matter what you think, you have a choice here.

"I can find other pilots. You don't *have* to do this."

Chass snorted. Wyl smiled kindly. Kairos stared ahead. Nath leaned back in his seat and said, "You're joking, right?"

"I knew what to expect," Hera said. "But I never send my people on a mission like this without asking. If you change your minds, just say the word."

She stepped back and gestured to Quell. "That's all prologue. Start the briefing, Lieutenant."

They spent four hours in the ready room. The initial overview was short, but Quell's detailed flight plan was a work of art in minuscule type—page after page of likely Shadow Wing response scenarios, reaction time estimates, footnotes citing squadron psych profiles and Wyl and Chass's own encounters in the Oridol Cluster. Every assumption cited intelligence or precedent. They reviewed all of it together, and then, of course, came the questions. Hera was glad to see the pilots engaged—glad that Nath and Chass, in particular, seemed to take the dangers seriously and had expertise to offer—but she was exhausted by the time the briefing was over.

*And you're not even putting your life on the line,* she thought.

Quell drew Adan aside as soon as they broke, confirming one of the latest intelligence drops. Wyl looked preoccupied, not so much as glancing at the others. Chass had a nervous, excited energy that didn't surprise Hera. She couldn't get a read on Nath or Kairos, which *also* didn't surprise her.

"So," Hera said, before anyone could disappear out the door. "Drinks on me?"

"You're kidding," Chass said.

"Why not? You're not absorbing anything tonight you haven't learned already. And don't tell me you have anything better going on."

Kairos bowed her head and stepped past Hera into the corridor. Quell and Adan were intent on their discussion. *Most of you,* Hera amended to herself.

"I'll go," Wyl said. "And while Chass and Nath might hesitate, they're not going to make me drink with the general alone."

Chass muttered under her breath. Nath laughed and said, "Kid puts a lot of faith in us."

"You're his squadron," Hera said.

She slipped away long enough to get her messages from Stornvein— to swiftly review the alerts from High Command she'd missed during the briefing and confirm that the pile of memoranda and requests from her battle group could wait until after dinner. When she finally reunited with Wyl, Chass, and Nath, they were already sharing a plate of military-grade "imitation braised bantha" and working their way through bottles of cheap swill at the Krayt Hut.

She settled in while Nath told a story from his Imperial Academy days. She'd come with stories of her own prepared, in case they were needed—stories of her old crew, her *family,* to inspire the pilots or frighten them or ease the tension, as required. She'd told her stories so many times for so many reasons—taught lessons to so many squadrons—that it almost felt artificial now. Like the stories had never happened to her, and only existed to help others.

But they'd all happened. They were real. It's why they were still precious.

Nath finished his tale, and the pilots snickered and Hera asked questions. She encouraged Wyl to talk about Riot Squadron and the *Hellion's Dare,* and she mentioned the time she'd met the *Dare's* captain, the strange little Chadra-Fan called Kreskian. She asked Chass about the Theelin's B-wing. "I was there," Hera told her, "when we brought home the first prototype. They're not like any other starfighter—anyone who can climb out of a B-wing and not fall over dizzy is a hero in my book." Chass was slow to reply, but Hera kept putting out bait and eventually even Chass engaged energetically. *Tough girl,* Hera thought, *but she's got as much heart as anyone.*

She didn't force the conversation. She let it flow and race along and double back. She didn't *need* to force it—Alphabet Squadron really had come together.

At the same time, though, she saw the faults. Nath would ask a question of Wyl and glance sidelong at Chass, checking her reaction. Wyl's expression brightened into something beautiful the moment he mentioned his homeworld; everything else, in comparison, was mere professional courtesy. Chass was often distracted, looking across the room to a crew of special forces operatives or staring into the distance.

There was a bond between them. There was. But it was new and tender, like young love or fresh skin over a deep cut.

Hera's crew had taken an eternity to bond. Rough, angry arguments had aged into comfortable disagreements through years and shared suffering. Shared hope. She wanted to give the same to Alphabet Squadron, but she worried there wasn't time.

And what of Kairos? Hera only knew what she'd read in the New Republic Intelligence files, and that was enough to trouble her dreams. And Quell? Quell, who was trying with every fiber of her being to make this operation work . . .

Quell was a good soldier. But Hera wondered if she could handle what was coming. If she could fly against her people without hesitating or letting the memories overwhelm her.

"You look worried," Wyl said.

Hera snapped out of her reverie and smiled at the boy. She shrugged and gave him the most honest answer she could. "I'm a worrier. Don't let it bother you."

"It won't," Chass said. "Wyl's worse than a worrier. He's an *idealist*. He figures it'll all come out right in the end."

"It's good to have one," Nath offered. "Gives the rest of us something to calibrate against."

They were back at it in a moment. Hera let them talk.

Fragile bonds. An untested commander. Back in the old days—back with her family—she would have judged a mission like this, with well-intentioned but unstable pilots, too risky. *You're not ready,* she might have said.

But now she was a general. She didn't have the luxury to think like that anymore.

*May the Force be with them,* she thought. *And please—let me not be wrong.*

# CHAPTER 14

# THE EXPLOITATION OF FANATICS

I

The Harch, whom everyone called "the Harch" as if her species were a royal title, flexed two of her claws high above her head, focused six eyes on the supplicants before her, and clacked her chelicerae as she cried, "Receipts, soft-things! You wish reimbursement? You bring receipts!"

Rikton protested in an unpersuasive stutter. Devon placed his hand on the younger man's arm and cut Rikton off in a crisp, authoritative voice. "Eightmarket doesn't give receipts, but the transaction was recorded. If you need proof, we can get a copy."

"Receipts," the Harch said. She rotated her body back toward the landspeeder suspended from the garage ceiling, her upper arms prying back the hood of the engine compartment. "I prefer receipts."

"But the recording will do?" Devon asked.

"Yes," the Harch hissed.

Rikton let out a relieved noise like a deflating pressure hose. Devon nodded to the man and, as one, they exited through the back of the shop. "You knew she wanted receipts when you bought the parts," Devon murmured. "You got the repairs done. The customer was happy. But you won't handle things that way again."

It was a statement, not a question, and Rikton seemed to know it. "No, sir," he said.

Devon laughed. Rikton looked confused. "Go home," Devon said. "Work orders are piling up, and it'll be a long day tomorrow." Rikton hesitated, then headed for the lockers.

Devon liked Rikton. He wasn't much more than a boy—nineteen, twenty years old at most—but Rikton was hardworking and naïve and arrogant all at once, in the way only young people could be. Devon even liked the Harch, who ran a disciplined crew without brutality and with a forgiving heart. She claimed to have eaten human flesh once, and Devon both believed it and suspected the victim had deserved the fate.

He liked Rikton and the Harch and the whole crew. Every time he thought it, he found himself surprised.

After Tinker-Town, he had traveled awhile, from planet to planet and spaceport to spaceport. On Mon Gazza he'd been caught up in a war between rival spice traders and moved on when the bloodshed had escalated. On the Ring of Kafrene, he'd made an enemy of a one-eyed weapons smuggler and slipped away in the night. He'd been present when the Bazaar of Esoteric Obscenities had burned to the ground. At each stop, he'd done his best to keep his past from following and to begin anew.

He hadn't planned to stay more than two days aboard the *Whitedrift Exchange*. The aging *Lormar*-class space station crawled through hyperspace, serving as a mobile trading post and as a home—temporary or otherwise—for its ten thousand passengers. Devon had intended to disembark upon reaching the next inhabited system; but the Harch had offered him work and a place to stay in the corroded, cavernous reaches of the station, and he'd agreed for reasons he couldn't entirely justify. He didn't regret his decision.

Maybe this time, no one would pull a weapon on him. Maybe this time, the war really was over.

Despite the many work orders, the next day's first job was also the last. A century-old cargo hauler had lost its plasma transvertor, and the owner—twice as old as her vessel, by her looks—had promised the Harch a cut of her freight if Devon and Rikton could get her ship online. The Harch had barely glanced at the particulars before sending the two on their way, and what should have been a one-hour task stretched to eight. Devon and Rikton spent the morning removing a dozen layers of hull plating and radiation shielding, and spent most of the afternoon swapping out components by feel.

They talked as they worked. Rikton was cagey about his life before the Harch, but that wasn't uncommon with workers aboard the *White-drift Exchange*. Prior to the Battle of Endor, the trading post had been subjected to frequent Imperial raids in search of fugitives, bounty hunters, and traffickers. Since the Empire's fall, the *Exchange*'s workforce had been vetted no more thoroughly.

Still, Rikton didn't strike Devon as a bottom-feeder hoping for a score. They'd talked about Rikton's upbringing on Corulag and his grandfather's declining health. "Never really got on with my parents, but my grandfather understood life, I figure. Always talked about serving alongside the clone troopers, how it taught you what matters is heart. Doesn't matter if you all look alike—inside we're all different."

Trite as it was, Devon appreciated the sober sincerity of Rikton's statement. "Your grandfather's a wise man," he said.

"Was a wise man," Rikton said. "Passed away. When I left Corulag to—to seek my fortune, yeah?—my parents disowned me. Haven't been back since."

Devon heard the evasion. He smiled sympathetically, stuck his arm deep in the guts of the cargo hauler, and didn't ask what *seek my fortune* meant. He nodded toward the glow rod in Rikton's hand and the boy raised it over Devon's head, illuminating the narrow access compartment.

"You got here not long before me, yeah?" Rikton asked.

Devon grunted, found a melted mass of wiring with his fingers, and tore out the entire clump. "Maybe two weeks," he said. "But I've been fixing machines much longer."

"You're good at it," Rikton said. "Real good. You going to stay on?"

"For a while, I think."

"The Harch likes you. Bet you could earn enough to start your own shop, if you wanted."

"Is that what you're looking to do?" Devon asked.

Rikton looked surprised by the question. He stuttered over the start of an answer, began again, then said, "Not for me, I don't think. Got a long trip in mind. Just trying to make enough credits to book passage."

"Where to?"

Rikton looked to their toolbox, pulling out a fresh spool of wire. "Don't know yet. I'll figure it out when I've got the money."

Another evasion, Devon decided. But everyone had their secrets.

The work continued. With a surgeon's precision, Devon excised a dying power pack and spliced two meters of fresh wiring into a panel ten centimeters wide. The public address system declared (in six languages) that the *Whitedrift Exchange* was arriving in orbit around Karazak. *That*, Devon thought, would have triggered Imperial scrutiny in the old days. Karazak was a slaver world, and for all that the Empire had tolerated slavery it had at least regulated the trade. By contrast, the Old Republic had ignored slavery outside the Core Worlds despite officially forbidding it; Devon doubted the New Republic would treat the matter any more seriously.

Devon and Rikton kept at it, and as afternoon became evening and they focused on reaffixing the ship's plating, they spoke about cleaning solutions and the droids they'd loved as children and whether the Harch would scold them for finishing so late. At last, as they packed their equipment and Devon scrubbed grease and oil and acid stains from the hangar floor ("We're not janitors, Rikton, but it's our mess"), he asked, "That old power pack we took out—can you grab it? It's a class-T hazard; need to handle it properly."

Rikton was latching the lid of the toolbox. "Already done," he said. "While you were finishing with the shielding."

Devon grunted and nodded.

The boy had a right to his privacy. Devon wasn't troubled by most of his lies. But *that* one surprised him.

He watched Rikton more closely after that. He didn't follow the boy or ask prying questions; but he did take more care to inventory equipment brought to the job, the parts they junked along the way, and the items they returned to the Harch's shop.

He spotted irregularities four more times in the following weeks. Rikton wasn't a thief by the conventional definition—he never took anything directly from the Harch's supplies. Mostly, he collected items destined for the scrap heap. Once, he purchased a naikon matrix using the Harch's bulk discount, then "forgot" to ask for reimbursement.

It wasn't any of Devon's business, but now he'd seen too much to let it go.

He began asking questions—not *prying* questions, but simple questions, natural ones, spread out over time. "How many more jobs before your trip off station?" he asked, and learned he had a month before Rikton planned to leave. A month to get the answers he needed. "Any other family besides your parents out there?" he asked, and wasn't surprised when Rikton told him no. He asked technical questions, too, about whether the boy could handle an XJ9 hypercharger or if he could show Devon how to disassemble a servo-pulsor. Nothing there surprised him, either.

"Not a lot of strangers worth trusting," Devon told the boy one night at the lockers. "But you find the right crew, you look out for them. You understand? You help them, they help you, no matter the trouble."

"True, that," Rikton said.

But he didn't seem to understand, and Devon couldn't force him to see.

Later that same night, after the rest of the crew had gone home, Devon found the Harch in the garage. "I need your help," he said.

The Harch chittered and scoffed as she closed blast shields over the windows. "I have given you work. I have given you purpose and pay. Now you ask more?"

"Are you still providing Rikton with his shipboard comm?" he asked. The *Whitedrift Exchange* offered passengers and crew limited access to the galactic communications network, but the price was high. The Harch leased a portion of her bandwidth to her workers.

"I am," she said.

"I'd like to review the logs. I know you have that ability. I don't want Rikton to hear about it."

The Harch swiveled toward Devon, focusing all six eyes on the human. "He has found trouble?"

"Maybe."

Her chelicerae folded and unfolded. She was thinking. She was smarter, Devon suspected, than anyone gave her credit for.

"Is it related," she asked, "to his service with the Empire?"

"I don't know," Devon said. "I'm hoping not. But what are the odds a boy that young has *two* secrets?"

Rikton lived in a habitat capsule on D-deck. The capsules were private and soundproofed, and those were the kindest things anyone could say about them—each was smaller than an escape pod, built to accommodate the most budget-conscious traveler. Devon waited until the shipboard lights illumined to their early-morning radiance, then tapped Rikton's door chime.

He'd read the logs. What happened next would prove difficult and potentially dangerous. The boy deserved a full night's sleep.

"It's Devon," he said into the comm. "We need to talk."

Rikton's voice mumbled a reply. Several minutes later the capsule door slid open and Devon caught a glimpse of the vertical bed against the wall, the empty shelves, and the duffel on the floor behind the blinking boy. "I'm not late," Rikton said. "Promise I'm not, I saw the schedule."

"We need to talk," Devon repeated. "Come on. I'll buy you breakfast." His tone was matter-of-fact. Almost friendly. Rikton nodded briskly and fell in behind Devon like a man condemned.

They purchased tin cups full of poached eggs and curdled green milk and carried them to the catwalks above subsystem engineering. They saw no one but repair droids making their rounds. Devon ate hungrily—he'd learned long ago not to ignore the value of a meal—while Rikton prodded at runny yolks. "What's going on?" Rikton asked. "You're acting odd. You know that, right?"

"I know," Devon said. "I wanted to talk to you about your plans."

"What plans?"

Devon smiled—just the slightest curve of thin lips. "Exactly. Last you said, you hadn't picked where to go with all your traveling money. I thought I'd make a recommendation."

"Yeah?" Rikton smiled in return, but his eyes were cast low, peering at Devon's throat.

"Heard of a place you could use your skills better. They're hiring mechanics by the cargo-load out in the junker systems. Not just scrappers, but folk with real expertise. They're desperate. The pay's good."

"Not sure I want to be a mechanic forever," Rikton said. "No offense."

"None taken. But you don't have to do it forever—do it for a month. Word is the guild got their hands on not just one Star Destroyer but *two*." He held up a hand to silence the boy. "You know that technology. I've seen you, and I haven't asked why. Truth is, I'm not interested in judging your past, or why your parents disapproved—I just want to help you find a good place. And for a little while, so long as there's demand, salvaging battleships is as good a place as an Imperial greasetrooper is apt to find."

The tin cup trembled in Rikton's hands. He put it down on the catwalk where they sat and looked into the abyss of piping and conduits. "I don't appreciate you making assumptions—"

"Rikton. You don't have to be afraid." His voice was smooth and honed as a knife. "You don't have to be ashamed. You're *good* at what you do."

Rikton's eyes flicked upward to meet Devon's at last. "I am."

"Good. Should I reach out to the junkers, then? Find you a contact?"

"I don't—" Rikton started to turn away. Devon placed a hand on his shoulder. "I've got plans," Rikton said. "I've got other plans already."

"You care to tell me?"

Rikton looked to Devon's hand. Devon drew away and took another stab at his eggs, finishing the last moist morsels as the boy considered his answer.

This was the moment, Devon thought. Rikton would open himself or he wouldn't, and that would determine his fate.

"I wasn't a *grease-trooper*," Rikton said. "I was navy, not army. Shipboard engineering. Served on a Gozanti cruiser eighteen months. Was studying to become an officer."

"Not a bad start. Then Endor happened, and, what—half the crew left?"

"Half the crew *died*. Got caught by the rebels; captain decided to fight. I found an escape pod, ended up alone. Wasn't a plan or anything, but I didn't have anyone to report to after. Didn't have anywhere to go."

Devon nodded and gestured for Rikton to continue.

The boy shrugged. "Wandered a little, ended up here," he said. "Never expected it to fall apart so fast, you know?"

"No one did," Devon agreed. "You try to contact them at all?"

"Tried. Didn't get much back."

"But you got something."

Rikton flinched. Devon saw it and decided to press.

"Is that why you're building a bomb?" Devon asked.

To his credit, the boy didn't seem surprised. His shoulders fell. He seemed to shrink inside himself. But he wasn't *surprised*. "You noticed the pieces?" Rikton asked.

"Not until the power pack. After that, I caught on. They give you a target?"

"I can't—" Rikton's voice was shocked and pleading—appalled that Devon would ask more than afraid of the consequences of answering.

Devon kept his own voice steady, if not soothing. "I have to know, Rikton. If it's here on the station, it—"

"It's not."

"Then where?"

"It's not!" Rikton repeated.

"Then *where*?" Devon asked again, and the last of his compassion was gone. There was only the *demand* now, the confidence and authority.

Rikton trembled, as if the words tore through him. But his voice was soft. "Traitor's Remorse."

*Traitor's Remorse.*

The last riddle was answered. Devon understood, now—understood exactly what had happened to Rikton the Imperial and driven him to become Rikton the mechanic and soon, once he had paid his transport fees and lied to the New Republic, Rikton the martyr. The boy whose parents had hated the Empire. The boy with nothing, who still wanted to serve. The boy who had somehow found an Imperial loyalist urging the lowest and most vulnerable to throw themselves back into the fires of war.

Devon understood, and he believed that Rikton *knew* he understood. With both hands he reached out and clasped the boy's shoulders, pulling him into an embrace.

"We need to talk," Devon said.

So they did.

They sat on the catwalk for hours, long after Devon had sent a message to the Harch indicating that neither of them would be working that day. They spoke about loyalty and honor and treason; about Traitor's Remorse and about pride and sacrifice. Rikton confessed his secrets and Devon confessed his—secrets a thousand times more valuable than the boy's, but all he had to offer in trade. They spoke until the station lights dimmed and the next morning they returned to work and spoke throughout the shift.

"There's no shame in defection," Devon told Rikton as they toiled over an airspeeder for an oblivious customer. "No shame in making a new life."

"I swore an oath to the Empire," Rikton said.

"The Empire's gone. Every soldier has to find his own way."

For days, they talked. Then one morning Rikton failed to arrive at the Harch's shop. Inside his own locker, Devon found a note attached to a duffel stuffed with mechanical components—including a power pack—he'd never expected to see again.

"Rikton's gone," Devon told the Harch after her other employees had left. "Says he's going to Corulag."

"A good worker, gone." The Harch folded and unfolded her chelicerae. "Your fault?"

"Not mine," Devon said. "Blame me for the destination, but not the departure."

The Harch considered this, then took long, silent strides to her console and began shuffling through datapads with all six arms. "Fine. You will not be docked pay. Not be peeled like fruit to feed the others when our income is reduced."

Devon smiled his thin-lipped smile. There was no apology in his tone when he said, "I'm leaving, too. Haven't decided where, but it's best if I keep some distance from the shop."

The Harch let out a sound he'd never heard before—a sort of low rumbling. "You disturbed something," she said. "You summoned a problem?"

"Odds are against it, but it's possible. Rikton was involved with certain people. He isn't anymore. If they care enough to blame anyone— and I don't imagine they will—they'll blame me."

"But you leave, despite what you *imagine*."

"You've been nothing but fair to me," Devon said. "I don't want trouble for you or your crew."

"Nor I for them," the Harch said.

It was the first time he'd ever heard her say it directly: that she felt a degree of responsibility, if not care, for her workers. He nodded deeply, respectfully, and hoped she understood the gesture.

"You will seek work elsewhere?" she asked.

"I've got to eat somehow, and I don't have your peeling claws."

The Harch chittered with laughter and tapped at one of the data-pads long enough that Devon began to wonder if he'd been dismissed. Then she turned his way and declared, "Vernid. Synonymous with squalor and barbarism. Outer Rim system."

Devon had never heard of Vernid. But there were a thousand Outer Rim worlds that could be described as squalid and barbaric. "What about it?"

"I know someone there who would welcome you."

Six eyes stared at Devon. He stared back before bowing his head once again. "I'll consider it," he said.

A short while later, he left the shop of the Harch—and the *White-drift Exchange*—for the last time.

# PART THREE

STAGES OF A RAPIDLY DECAYING PLAN

## CHAPTER 15

## PREFLIGHT PREPARATIONS

**I**

**N**ath spent his last hours with his ship and his droid. He wasn't a sentimental man, or a superstitious one—he didn't have any preflight rituals or gods to square himself with. But if he was going on a mission that might well result in his death, he wanted to make sure that he'd stacked the odds beforehand.

So he squatted underneath his Y-wing, unbolting panels and bolting them back on. He checked cable connections and power levels in isolated components. He had to resist the urge to disassemble a proton torpedo to confirm its warhead was operational. *You're getting self-destructive in your old age,* he thought. T5 rolled back and forth nearby, uncharacteristically silent.

Now and then, one of the engineers would pass by and call to him by name. He'd peek out far enough to wave and grin, ask Mayus about his family or Jems about the centuries-old protocol droid he'd been assembling as a hobby. Only Ragnell, the chief, seemed to notice Nath's heart wasn't in it. "Looking a little nervous," she said, as she eyed him from her seat on a riding sled. It was the first time she'd ever spoken to him. "Big mission up ahead?"

"Don't pretend you haven't heard," Nath answered. "It's not attractive."

Ragnell smirked. "If I were worried about *that*, I'd have lived my life very differently. You're Nath Tensent, right? The guy who complains whenever we touch his ship?"

"I am."

"You want my advice?"

"I don't."

She gave it anyway. "You want to live through Pandem Nai, let a professional do the final check. You think you know what you're doing, but my people do this all day, every day. You're an amateur."

Nath grunted, though he recognized there was an inkling of truth in it. "Your people know Y-wings. This is *my* Y-wing," he said, "and no one knows it like I do."

"Suit yourself," Ragnell said, and rode on, leaving Nath behind.

It was his Y-wing. T5 was his astromech droid. Both had been there the last time he'd fought Shadow Wing, when the bastards had executed, one by one, his entire crew. Reeka, Piter, Pesalt, Braigh, Ferris, Canthropali, all of them. But Nath had survived, not because he was a brilliant combat pilot (he could admit that to himself—he wasn't bad, but he'd flown with better), but because he was lucky and because his ship had taken hits and not burst into shrapnel. That's what it took to survive, at the crux of it all: not dying.

He held a hydrospanner in one hand. His fingers closed tight around the metal, his knuckles going white. He slammed the tool against the hangar floor and listened to it ring.

The memories came back, dulled by time but still intense. He hadn't meant to raise them up. Reeka, Piter, Pesalt, Braigh, Ferris, Canthropali. His crew. His responsibility. He hadn't kept them from dying, and wiping out Shadow Wing wouldn't do anything to help them.

But it would balance the scales.

And his mother had raised him with a rule that still lived in his heart: When someone attacks your family, you punch back.

He wasn't in the mood to continue working on his ship. He blamed Ragnell for that, though the thoughts had been brewing beneath the surface before she'd come along.

He double-checked to make sure the panels he'd removed were secured in place, then shuffled out from under the Y-wing and gave T5 a thump on its upper chassis. "Come on, you little trash heap. Let's you and me—"

The droid let out a series of squeaks and squawks. Nath arched his brow, then laughed in surprise. *Should've expected that,* he thought, though he really hadn't.

"All right," he said. "Let's go have a chat with our friend Adan."

## II

Chass deliberated over her choices with the sober dignity of a woman going to an execution. She sorted through the little plastic box full of datachips, taking out one chip at a time as she sat on her bunk and considered the implications.

*Herglic rage-metal?* Too heavy, and it hurt her ears. She put the chip in her left hand.

*Warbat trance?* She considered the flight plan, smiled tightly, and put the chip in her right hand.

*Glimmik?* Too saccharine, she decided, and tossed the chip back in the box.

She'd forgotten she even had the glimmik files. If she remembered right, that chip had been a trade from a girl who collected lost art: music and imagery from people murdered by the Empire, whose identities were forgotten and whose work would disappear if not preserved. Chass had gone looking for a Theelin singer and received the glimmik instead.

In a moment of inexplicable panic, she wondered who would get the box full of music if she didn't make it back from Pandem Nai. Would it be tossed in the garbage compactor? Left for the crew of the *Lodestar* to pick through, divvying up their favorites and destroying the rest?

She'd found a pen and was halfway through scrawling GENERAL SYNDULLA on the box when she felt—filling the void of her panic as it began to recede—a deep and pervasive shame. Was this what Jyn Erso had done before Scarif? In her last hours at the Rebellion's Base One, had Jyn picked out strangers to donate her belongings to?

She tossed the box back on her bed, scooped up her two handfuls of datachips, and marched out of her berthing compartment toward the hangar. Instinctively, she took the route that led to a ladder, and swore as she realized she would have to climb with her fists full.

"You all right?" a voice asked.

She flinched and whirled to find Wyl walking up behind her.

"Fine," she said. "Yeah, I'm fine." She held up both hands, indicating the source of her frustration.

Wyl smiled sympathetically, but there was less warmth to it than she would have expected. She thought of Wyl as endlessly, irritatingly compassionate, yet there was something suppressed in his demeanor. "Are *you* okay?" she asked.

"I am," Wyl said. "Just—taking stock of it all. I came from the aft observation area. Watching the blue."

"Hyperspace still look like hyperspace?"

"It does. No matter where you are in the universe, it always looks the same." He wrinkled his nose. "Maybe that should be comforting, but it isn't, really."

"Brings up memories."

"Yeah."

She recalled the hyperspace journeys through the Oridol Cluster aboard the *Hellion's Dare*. The tension. The worry that the Empire would follow the moment they entered realspace.

"You sure you're ready?" she asked.

Wyl held out cupped hands. She poured some of the datachips in and flexed her fingers as he leaned back gingerly against the corridor's piping and conduits. "I am," he repeated. "I don't want to be here. I don't want to be doing this at all, but—we're the only ones left."

Chass nodded. Wyl wasn't finished, though the words came out slowly. "Riot Squadron had a mission. Hound Squadron had a mission. Someone has to finish it, and I think—we have a certain responsibility. Being part of a squadron means working together. Watching out for one another, and picking up the burden when someone else falls."

"You could go home," Chass said. "If you wanted. No one would stop you."

"I would stop me," Wyl said. "I stopped me once before, on Jiruus. And in Oridol maybe I failed the test, maybe I was a coward like you said—"

*I never said that,* Chass thought, but she let him finish.

"—but maybe the test isn't finished. Maybe I only fail if I run now." He sounded sad and quiet, but he smiled anyway and pushed himself off the wall. "I'm ready for this."

"Me, too," Chass said.

They climbed down the ladder to the hangar. They strolled to Chass's B-wing and Wyl returned the datachips to her as she climbed into the cockpit. As Wyl turned away, she called him back and said, "Remember: We watch out for one another, right? We don't make each other's decisions." *Your words, not mine,* she thought. *Which means you can't argue.*

Wyl nodded cautiously. "No," he agreed, "we can't."

He still didn't understand, of course, any more than he had on the moon.

But Chass was confident he didn't need to.

### III

The *Lodestar* erupted out of hyperspace on schedule, arriving in an empty star system off one end of the Skangravi-Mestun Regional Hyperlane. Wyl was already in his flight suit by then, and the announcement of "Alphabet Squadron to Ready Room One" seemed redundant. They all knew what was expected of them. Even the briefing felt perfunctory—Quell stood alone at the front of the chamber, reiterating points they'd all been thinking about for two days.

Then it was time to go.

Wyl climbed into his A-wing and stroked the console, whispered gently to his vessel as the reactor powered up and his comrades swept out of the hangar one by one—great roars and wind filling the space as Quell, then Chass, then Nath launched from the battleship. Kairos would follow Wyl.

He tried to think of the sur-avkas of his homeworld. He tried to remember the warmth of the beasts' flesh, the unpleasant odor of their hide, the sensation of mighty muscles moving beneath him. But the memories were gray and dull and distant, and he found himself thinking instead of that last day in the Oridol Cluster: of floating in space, of telling stories with Riot Squadron one last time, and of reaching out to the pilots of Shadow Wing. He thought of Blink and Char, and of Chass and Sata Neek.

He could do better this time. He had to, for Chass, Nath, Quell, and Kairos along with all those he'd left behind and all those the Empire threatened.

*One last mission,* he told himself. *Home can wait.*

# IV

Yrica Quell felt the lurch of the X-wing as it tore out of the pocket atmosphere of the *Lodestar* and into space. Her body bounced against her seat and she winced—not out of pain, but out of the *memory* of pain, the instinctive certainty that agony would rip through her shoulder and radiate from her temple.

Those injuries were healed. There was no pain. She stared into the void and listened to the rumble of her engines.

"Dee-six El?" she said. "Run an in-flight systems check. Weapons, power, hyperdrive, everything."

Quell watched the results scroll down her display. The droid, thorough as always, provided more than she could possibly make sense of and summarized it neatly at the bottom. She saw nothing to be concerned about, but it was always better to be certain. "You ready?" she asked, and D6-L replied with a straightforward chime of acknowledgment.

She'd never expected to find herself conversing unnecessarily with an astromech droid. But times had changed.

She tapped her comm controls. "Quell to squadron. All ships, report in."

The calls came back, sharp and swift:

"Lark standing by."

"Chadic standing by."

"Tensent standing by."

The computerized tone of Kairos's acknowledgment followed.

Quell could have assigned them numbers. They were, after all, no longer an unnamed intelligence working group. They were Alphabet Squadron, and they could follow military protocols. But with only five pilots, and with so much effort spent bringing them together—getting them to *know* one another—it seemed counterproductive to reduce them to designations.

The method she'd chosen, like so many of the methods she'd adopted lately, was the way of rebels. The Empire had done its best to treat its pilots as disposable so that when one died—and someone always died—a replacement could be inserted without a loss of efficiency. The Rebellion—and the New Republic, now—was messy. Mixed pilots flew mixed starfighters.

Quell wondered if the detachment the Empire had inculcated in her would make it easier for her to shoot her comrades in the 204th. If learning to treat pilots as disposable made it easier to defect. If she could fire her cannons and not think of the names and faces she'd learned over the course of years.

She suspected so.

And when it was over, and Shadow Wing was neutralized, she would be free. She would be a soldier in the New Republic. She would finally have done what she'd set out to do when she'd run off to train in the Imperial Starfighter Corps.

She'd wanted to be a hero, once. This was her chance.

"All pilots," she said, "form up. Set course for Pandem Nai and prepare to jump to hyperspace."

## V

Colonel Shakara Nuress stood in the command center of Orbital One and listened to the murmur of her subordinates as she paced the perimeter. She took satisfaction in the overlapping voices; the calm professionalism of com-scan officers as they guided freighters and light cruisers in and out of the system, and the succinct acknowledgments of her lieutenants receiving reports from fighter patrols.

Not even the fact that the voices were too few—that a command center designed for two dozen officers had barely half that number on duty—nullified her satisfaction altogether.

"Colonel?" a voice said.

Shakara turned to the speaker. Narston, an engineer half Shakara's age who had taken on the burden of liaising with the orbital gas mining crews, clutched a datapad in both hands as if she were a schoolgirl completing a craft project.

"What do you have?" Shakara asked—not unkindly, she thought.

"Latest set of progress reports, ma'am. Automated production is up by twenty-three percent and the gas storage pods are at eighty-five percent capacity. That puts us on track to—"

"It's all in there?" Shakara asked, nodding toward the datapad.

Narston paused, then seemed to comprehend. "It is," she said, and passed over the device.

Shakara waved Narston to one side and resumed pacing as she skimmed the report. She continued to loathe this part of her routine, but she'd gotten distressingly capable at it. Gas production *was* increasing, even without the staff and expertise she would have preferred—

the computerized procedures and droid workers had managed to boost Pandem Nai's Tibanna gas extraction rates nearly to a point of strategic relevance in the galactic war. More Imperial vessels were coming to restock and refuel at Pandem Nai daily.

The price, of course, was that the Separatists (the rebels, the New Republic—she heard the correcting voice of an aide even in her own mind) were taking an active interest in Pandem Nai's status. She'd noticed the enemy battle group stalking Imperial cruisers that had passed through her docks; seen the pattern of worlds falling to give the foe access to the Skangravi-Mestun Regional Hyperlane. There was an attack coming, and coming soon.

She wasn't worried. But she was alert.

"Narston," she called, and the woman was immediately at her side. "The civilian extractor crews—how's morale holding up? Any indications of disloyalty?"

"None that I'm aware of."

Shakara finished her scan of the report, then set the datapad on the nearest chair. "Let's shift a third of military personnel off supervisory duty and back to combat readiness, then. Just a temporary measure— don't let anyone get excited—but the civilians can manage themselves for a few days."

*At least,* she finished to herself, *until we see what the Separatists are up to.*

She wondered if she was engaging in wishful thinking—if her desire to be a soldier instead of an administrator was causing her to overestimate the odds of an attack and overprepare for a siege. If that was the case, the only harm would be in quotas unmet and ships left unsupplied.

If she was *right,* however—if the threat was real and she failed to meet it? Well, the Empire might be collapsing. But she was still a colonel. The Emperor had chosen her for a purpose.

She would defend her people until the end.

## CHAPTER 16

# TACTICAL ENGAGEMENT

## I

Alphabet Squadron dropped out of hyperspace at the edge of the Pandem Nai system in a tight wedge formation. Quell's vision still swam with glimmers of cosmic ribbons as she confirmed her comrades' arrival and slapped urgently at the comm. "Kairos," she snapped. "Now! Do it now!"

The channel filled with static. Her scanner registered the rest of the squadron for barely a second before the U-wing's jammers flooded empty space with electromagnetic signals on ten thousand frequencies. As her sight returned, Quell craned her neck and peered out her canopy, catching a glimpse of Wyl Lark's A-wing off her port side—the only indication that she wasn't alone.

She tried not to feel unnerved by the closeness of Lark's fighter, or the knowledge that Chadic, Tensent, and Kairos were equally near, less than fifty meters above, below, and beside her—close enough that a sudden turn or unexpected deceleration could easily result in collision. Their navicomputers and astromech droids were incapable of synchronizing the ships' flight: The jammers that hid their presence from the foe would also block all communications.

But this was the mission they had planned, and they were prepared.

"Give me visual confirmation, Dee-six. They're all in position?"

A readout of ships, their relative distances, and their current speeds scrolled across her display. They were, indeed, in proper position.

The enemy would notice the jamming signal in moments, if an alarm hadn't been triggered already. Quell was confident in that much—she knew the protocols the 204th would have in place. But so long as the squadron stayed clustered around the U-wing their numbers would be concealed. Their location, too, would be untraceable. Unless Shadow Wing sent a scout close enough to *see* the five ships invading Pandem Nai, Alphabet Squadron could slip through whatever web of perimeter sensors the Empire had erected.

They just had to do it blind.

*Adan, I hope your information is right.*

The inside of Quell's cockpit glowed with the ember light of the star system's distant sun. Pandem Nai was the second planet from its star, and between that world and the system's outer reaches were a dozen lifeless satellites—crumbling, uninhabitable lumps of rock—along with a great belt of frozen methane, ammonia, and water. Quell could make the belt out already, a glittering stroke of cold against the warm radiance.

She adjusted her vector ever so slightly, letting her maneuvering guide the others behind her as she dipped below the densest section of the belt. Ahead, the first real challenge of the mission waited.

"How much longer?" she asked the droid.

An estimate appeared on her console: twenty seconds.

She leaned forward in her harness. The great frozen field filled the sky above her, but that wasn't what she needed to see. Instead she tried to pick out silhouettes against the black—perfectly symmetrical objects hidden away in the dark.

D6-L let out a shriek of alarm, and visual overlays filled her display.

Quell saw it: the first smart mine, far ahead and a hundred meters beneath her. She resisted the urge to pull up hard so as not to alarm the ships behind her. Instead she veered gently, clearing the mine's trigger radius and passing by unharmed.

*One down,* she thought as they entered the minefield. *Three hundred to go.*

The mines would be inhibited by the jamming, but only to a point— they wouldn't pursue, but they were calibrated to detect the smallest gravitational fluctuations and detonate if a vessel got too close. The margin of error was thin. Quell and her people knew it and all of them were at risk—with their ships clustered so close, one mine might destroy them all.

Quell could see a dozen of the smart mines now, tiny spots that seemed to exist only in her peripheral vision. She looked for gaps, steering by degrees but never slowing. Every moment gave Shadow Wing more time to notice the jamming signal. More time to ready a defense and locate the intruders. Hesitation would kill them as surely as speed.

D6-L trilled again, but this time the droid's alarm was almost musical. Quell saw the mine, aimed for a gap between three others, and flew on. Her squadron followed, swinging out behind her like the tail of a kite.

She was sweating, but soon she forgot the danger. Conscious thought dimmed until all that remained was the sensation of flight— the glorious sense of a vessel at her command, weaving through the vastness of space. She banked and climbed and *felt* the nonexistent drag of her trailing allies. She saw a mine pass so close above that she could make out the seams between its metal panels. She swept beneath it and up again with a joyful laugh.

Had she forgotten what flying could be like? This was why she had become a pilot like her father, like her mother. This was *flight,* pure and undiluted, without the electric sizzle of a laser cannon to break the spell.

She flew on. Ten kilometers, a hundred, through the minefield. The planet Pandem Nai came into view: an orb shrouded in scarlet mist, shadowed by a single black moon. She could imagine the orbital stations floating in the upper atmosphere, the gas extractors and colonies—along with the TIE patrols and Imperial cruisers. She could *imagine* these things, but they were too far away to see.

Five hundred kilometers through the minefield.

How long had it been? How many minutes since they'd activated their jammers and warned Shadow Wing that they'd arrived?

Quell saw the final gap in the minefield—a ring of devices no more than two hundred meters wide—and, for the first time since arriving in the system, accelerated. She went no faster than what the slowest ship in her squadron could match, but they had delayed too long. The orb of Pandem Nai grew larger. The ring of mines drew closer.

If she was off by half a degree, she might plunge directly into a mine herself.

Then she was through. She glanced behind her and saw no bright explosion, no chain of mines detonating, but only Kairos's U-wing at her back. She resisted the urge to open her throttle further and instead rolled gently toward the planet. Now she *could* spot the shapes of other vessels: Gozanti cruisers and gas tankers, the specks of cargo shuttles and a TIE Reaper drop ship. She didn't see the cruiser-carrier Lark and Chadic had encountered, nor whatever remained of the Star Destroyer *Pursuer;* if she was lucky, both were disabled or away on missions. More likely, they were docked somewhere close.

She plotted a route in her head and swung out to avoid the busiest traffic. Someone would spot the squadron anyway, but she needed as much breathing room as she could muster. The visiting ships—the ones not affiliated with the 204th—were one element she'd been unable to predict in detail.

They raced forward, and the scarlet mist of the planet's outer atmosphere filled Quell's view. The orbital stations were murky shapes beneath the uppermost layers. She tried to determine whether any of the Imperial ships were moving to intercept her (she saw none) and warned D6-L, "Brace for impact."

She hit atmosphere with a metallic shriek and a jolt that felt like it would snap her neck. The gas wasn't dense at higher altitudes—if it had been, the X-wing would have burst apart on impact—but it was thick as steel in comparison with the emptiness of space. Automated stabilizers and cooling devices hummed and rattled as the ship shook and red enveloped her. In a haze of terror, Quell pitched hard to one side, trying to create maneuvering room for her squadron. She saw Lark's A-wing tear past her—sleek and aerodynamic enough to cut through the mist—while Chadic's B-wing tumbled behind.

But there were no collisions.

Her scanner blinked online. A dozen, two dozen marks appeared alongside her allies. Kairos had deactivated her jammers.

"Go!" Quell shouted. "Fighters incoming! Start your passes now!"

Her teeth cut her tongue as she bounced and slowed. She watched Lark decelerate and reposition himself alongside Tensent. Together the two broke off, maintaining their altitude as the first TIE squadrons approached. Chadic drew up behind Quell and they veered away on a separate course. The sensor blip that represented the U-wing plummeted and disappeared.

Over the comm came a cacophonous noise: an electric buzz like a thousand wasps combined with a rhythmic, warbling voice in a foreign tongue. The noise vanished almost as soon as it began, replaced by Chass na Chadic: "Forgot to filter the music. Systems online and ready to go."

Quell didn't reprimand her. There would be time for that if they survived.

Alphabet Squadron had arrived on Pandem Nai. The battle was joined.

**II**

Colonel Shakara Nuress wasn't easily impressed and she wasn't impressed now. The enemy had passed through the minefield with jammers active, and that had cost Shakara a handful of seconds—a brief period of confusion during which her com-scan officers had frantically checked for glitches and the minefield monitoring station had checked its own systems for fault.

There were no glitches. The fault was not in the monitors. Now the enemy had dropped the mask and begun its assault.

The enemy was clever, studied, even daring. But Shakara saw no need to be *impressed.*

"We have visual confirmation of two fighter elements," Major Rassus called from the tactical station. "An interceptor and assault ship in each. They're heading straight for Orbital One."

"Only four ships?" Shakara asked.

"Still assessing. If there's another squadron, it's hiding somewhere. Could be in the dark of the moon—"

"But no capital ships? Nothing outside the minefield?"

"Not that we detect, Colonel."

A precision raid, then—barring surprises, easily neutralized. Shakara doubted it was a suicide mission, which meant it was likely a prelude to a larger-scale attack.

"Have the patrol squadrons intercept and destroy the enemy craft," she said. "Meanwhile, scramble the fighters in Orbital One—I want everything we have in the air and ready to act."

Rassus snapped an acknowledgment, which Shakara didn't hear. She considered the timing. It would take five minutes, perhaps, to launch the rest of the 204th. That was enough for a Separatist fleet to arrive in-system but not enough for such a fleet to penetrate the minefield. She considered recalling the squadrons outside Pandem Nai, but *that,* she decided, was premature.

She had all she needed to solve the problem at hand.

She was interested to see what the enemy had in store.

### III

The cockpit rolled and bounced despite its gyrostabilizers, but it was the music that Chass felt in her body: the swift synthesized beats and the knife-smooth notes from the singer's throat, telling Chass's heart when to pump and her hand when to squeeze the trigger. She rode the rhythm as she rode the scarlet winds of Pandem Nai.

She laughed. She sounded like a maniac and she laughed anyway.

She skimmed the port side of Shadow Wing's orbital command center—an enormous wheel of black metal scaffolding and compartments, festooned with mining equipment and Tibanna gas containment pods. It wasn't built to be a battle station but laser cannons sprouted from hull plating every few dozen meters, targeting Chass with rapid bursts. The weapons weren't powerful enough to backfire in the volatile atmosphere, but they could punch a hole through a B-wing starfighter.

"Target in sight!" Quell's voice, urgent through the comm. "You see it?"

"I see it," Chass said. "Watch what I do next."

She spotted, at the edges of her vision, the marks on her scanner—eight TIE fighters closing from all angles. She rotated the bulk of her ship around the cockpit, let the thrust send her spiraling to keep her trajectory unpredictable, but she didn't worry over the opposition. Quell's job was to pull away the TIEs. Chass's was to be destruction personified.

Emerald splashed against her shields, and the electromagnetic bubble protecting her vessel shimmered through the color spectrum. Chass ignored that, too. She leaned forward and peered at a crease in the orbital station's skin—the closed maw of the port hangar bay doors.

She fired every weapon she had—ion cannons and lasers and torpedoes, spewing streams of electric energy and crimson bolts and warheads toward her target. Fire and lightning erupted at the point of impact, obscured the hangar doors from sight, but Chass kept firing and let her ship drop into the smoke and chaos. When her console began screaming alarms, warning of power drains and overheating, she switched to firing one set of weapons at a time—but she didn't stop.

Her whole body snapped forward as a volley from a TIE fighter nearly punctured her aft shields. She braced for another burst, then grinned as the pursuer disappeared in a thunderclap and a blossom of flame.

"You love me," she laughed. "You'd do anything for me."

Quell didn't reply for several seconds. When she did, her voice sounded strained. "I can't keep them all off you. Did you hit the target?"

"Of course. It's not small." She wasn't sure how much *damage* she'd done, but the fireworks had been spectacular. "If you're worried, we can do it again . . ." She heard the lilt in her voice and realized how giddy she sounded.

"Agreed," Quell said. "We make another pass. We'll make a third if we have to."

Three TIE fighters emerged from the scarlet mist ahead of Chass, silhouettes against the red. The music stopped, then started again with a slower, ethereal voice in command.

The mission, Chass thought, was impossible.

It was perfect.

# IV

Wyl Lark twisted above the Y-wing, clinging to it like a jealous lover as he warded off TIE flights and laser volleys. He felt every burst of particle bolts against his shields, saw the warnings glare at him from his console, but he didn't slow. His purpose—his only purpose on this mission—was to protect Nath Tensent.

He intended to do so.

They raced together along the starboard side of the orbital station. Nath skimmed only meters above the superstructure—wisely, Wyl thought, as it forced the TIEs to be selective about their shots—while picking off turrets and closing on the primary target. Wyl hadn't downed an enemy yet, but he'd discouraged the hostile forces by alternating swift, precise shots with rapid-fire sprays.

He wasn't sure he *could* kill any of his enemies. The last time he'd met Shadow Wing, the Imperial pilots had calmly slaughtered his squadron mates while evading nearly every attack he'd made. He'd studied all the files Quell had provided since then, but personnel evaluations weren't the same as lived experience. His eyes followed the fighters through the fog of Pandem Nai, seeking identifying marks and scratches—looking for Blink and Snapper and Char, who had haunted the *Hellion's Dare* for so long.

"Yes, I'm scared," he murmured to his ship. "I'm not ashamed to admit it."

He jumped in his harness when Nath's voice came in response. "All right, brother—coming up on the objective, but we're getting swarmed, here."

"Have you taken a hit yet?" Wyl asked.

"Not yet."

"Then trust me," Wyl said. "You'll make it there just fine."

He pushed the images of Blink and Snapper and Char out of his mind. He opened his throttle until the orbital station became a dark blur and Nath's Y-wing was far behind him, then looped up and over until he'd reversed course toward his TIE pursuers. He let momentum hold him in place—they were deep enough within the planet's gravity well that *upside down* had meaning, and his stomach lurched as his harness straps dug into his shoulders—and he screamed as he flew straight toward the surprised TIEs, whipping through a storm of particle bolts and dodging blasts with swift, almost imperceptible motions. He squeezed his trigger and scattered the enemy fighters.

No kills. He heard Nath laughing.

"Target acquired," Nath said. "Weapons locked. Be careful if you're close—might be some splash."

Wyl was curving back around to rejoin Nath when he saw explosions and felt the shock wave. The Y-wing had unleashed a flurry of cannon fire and torpedoes at the orbital station's starboard hangar bay, and the detonation sent ripples through the atmosphere that buffeted the A-wing like storm winds.

"Tell me you did damage," Wyl called. "Tell me you've got good news . . ."

"Good enough," Nath said. "We bought a couple of minutes, at least."

That was all they'd been sent to do. Buy time. Cripple the hangars and keep them shut long enough to prevent the TIEs from swarming. Face a dozen Shadow Wing pilots instead of seventy. The real mission would happen elsewhere.

Just like in the Oridol Cluster. Just like when Wyl had waited to be saved or doomed by the *Hellion's Dare*.

"Another pass?" Wyl asked.

"Another pass," Nath said.

## V

Outside the cockpit of the U-wing, as Kairos descended through the layers of Pandem Nai's atmosphere, the gas changed and the dense clouds thinned. Scarlet bled its darker hues and became tawny. Tawny wisps became pale ocher. It was as if she were passing through the layers of a painting; as if there were beauty surrounding her instead of violence and disaster. She longed to press her face through the viewport; to extend her tongue and flare her nostrils and taste the colors, as she might have when she was young.

But in truth, there was nothing beautiful at Pandem Nai.

She eased out of the descent, passing a hand over the console as if reading its instruments by touch. She had dived far enough to elude Shadow Wing's notice. Now it was time to return. She checked her course and leaned back as the ship pulled up and the pale-ocher wisps became tawny once more. She heard a series of thuds and groans from the cabin and a deep-throated shout:

"Warn us next time, huh?"

The thought hadn't occurred to her.

The ship vibrated until her skin seemed to burn. She made out the murky wheel of the orbital station above and aimed for a section of spoke near the center. This was the plan of the traitor—the woman soaked in blood and ash who had promised to *make it right,* and Kairos had accepted the plan because it aligned with her purpose. Through these acts, she would achieve vengeance. Through these acts, she would derive restitution from all the murderers of worlds—from the killers of Alderaan and Nacronis and Hetnagaro.

The Emperor, she thought, would be pleased at the violence she committed. But there was nothing she could do about that.

The U-wing soared. Its wings—its strike foils—stretched forward for flight instead of combat. Flickers of light around the orbital station suggested a storm, though Kairos knew they meant battle. The part of her that craved death grew excited at the scent, but she did not relinquish control.

There was another reason why she followed the plan of the traitor. This thought came to her unbidden and caused her pain: She thought of the face of Caern Adan, delicate and stubborn and scarred so deeply that the scars had become flesh.

She knew the debts she carried.

She leveled out her ship as she reached the underside of the orbital station, weaving through scaffolding and evading the gas storage pods that hung like fruit. She saw a TIE fighter flash past, but it twirled, spun as if regaining control of its flight, and returned the way it had come, apparently oblivious to Kairos. She reduced her speed to nearly nothing as she leaned over the control panel and peered above her at the station's hull.

"There! Right there."

The same voice as before, closer this time. She retreated into her seat and delicately positioned the U-wing to rise into the orbital station's executive docking bay. The magnetic containment field flickered but offered no pressure or resistance. This surprised Kairos. It suggested that Shadow Wing had neglected to secure the bay.

Or that someone had prepared a trap.

Kairos's organs seemed to twist and compress at the thought. She didn't like the notion of a trap. She never wished to be trapped again.

The docking bay was compact, designed to house no more than three vessels. Only one other was present at the moment—a *Zeta*-class cargo shuttle hooked up to power and fuel. Kairos saw no guards, no white-clad stormtroopers, and glided to a stop without landing. Her thrusters quieted while her repulsors whined.

She stood and turned to the main cabin. Pressed against one another in the confined space were fourteen humanoid figures wrapped in bulky jackets and armor plating, bearing packs and satchels and weapons gleaming with polish. Kairos had seen them on the *Lodestar* before they'd come aboard for this mission—they were New Republic special forces, full of bluster and efficiency.

A man with leathery yellow skin looked to Kairos questioningly. She inclined her head and gestured at the loading door. Someone tapped the control panel, the door opened, and the soldiers poured into the bay, sweeping the vicinity without firing a shot.

"All right," one of them called—a squat woman with skin weathered by burns. "We're ready to head in. You're holding our exit?" This last was directed to Kairos.

Kairos inclined her head again and began to heft and assemble the equipment left aboard the ship. The troops accepted this answer and noiselessly hurried away as Kairos swiftly attached barrel to battery to base. Soon she had a weapon—a turret able to rotate and fire and obliterate anything that entered the bay. She stood behind it and waited.

She was not patient. She wished to pull the trigger. To have a *reason* to pull the trigger.

She wished she were a better creature. That her metamorphosis would soon be complete, and that she could emerge as something bright and wondrous, shedding the atrocities of her life.

For now, however, she was what she was.

She readied herself for slaughter.

# VI

Caern Adan didn't particularly want to be aboard the *Lodestar*. He had no desire, as some of his colleagues did, to be "close to the action." He'd *been* close, and lacked the egomania required to want to repeat the experience.

Nonetheless, he knew that if he left prior to the assault he had masterminded—the operation he had planned from the very beginning, when he alone had had the foresight to see the danger of Shadow Wing—it would raise questions among his superiors. It would erode confidence. And there was, he supposed, some chance he might be useful.

So he sat in a corner of the tactical operations center (staffed with two dozen officers and aides to General Syndulla, all jostling for elbow room and attention) and watched a hologram of the *Lodestar*'s captain proclaim that the fleet would emerge from hyperspace in two minutes. He watched the general pace and murmur platitudes to her people. He gripped his seat as the whole ship lurched, arriving in the Pandem Nai system.

Numerous indicators flashed onto the transparent display screens as the *Lodestar* was followed by the rest of Syndulla's battle group: corvettes and cruisers with weapons primed and starfighter squadrons in protective formation. Additional indicators began to light a moment later, showing Imperial ships in orbit around Pandem Nai.

"Jump coordinates were correct, General," someone said. "We're just outside the minefield."

"Good." Syndulla's voice was unhurried. Unafraid. *All soldiers are suicidal,* Caern thought. She went on: "Send the signal to spread out and form a blockade. Remind our ships not to drift too close to the mines—we're not planning to push through until we absolutely have to."

A dozen voices echoed Syndulla's orders, passing them down from general to unit commanders to communications officers to individual ship captains and squadron leaders. A hundred fingers tapped at consoles and droids chattered as they turned vague intentions into numbers and angles and coordinates. Caern couldn't decide whether the chain of activity was something to be admired or a stunning example of military inefficiency.

"What's it look like in orbit?" Syndulla asked a com-scan officer. "Has Shadow Wing launched its fighters?"

"Not yet, General. Looks like two TIE squadrons active. Alphabet must be doing its job."

"Signs of movement from the Imperial capital ships?"

"None."

"What about reinforcements?" Caern asked, though he knew it wasn't his place. "Any Imperial presence in the outer system?"

The com-scan officer looked to Syndulla, who gave a curt nod. He replied, "Nothing we've spotted so far. We're scanning for hypermatter particle traces—if anyone's coming out of lightspeed, we might get a few seconds' warning."

"All right," Syndulla said. "Then we hold position until something changes."

Caern tried to force the tension from his body and failed to do so.

This was the plan—*his* plan, in part. The fleet could go crashing through the minefield, but it would take considerable damage in the process and engaging over Pandem Nai would be pointless. Heavy weapons were, after all, effectively neutralized by the atmosphere. Meteor, Hail, and Vanguard squadrons might be able to join Quell and the others by picking their way through the minefield more slowly, but that would give the enemy capital ships time to leave orbit and intercept the fighters. In the gap between the minefield's edge and Pandem Nai's exosphere, the squadrons would be easy prey.

The best thing Syndulla's fleet could do was ensure that nothing interfered with Caern's working group. With his *squadron*. If Shadow Wing acted unpredictably, the fleet would respond. Otherwise, well—

They would discover whether they'd won or lost in just a few minutes.

Caern Adan sat back and thought of how long he'd been pursuing

Shadow Wing. How certain he'd been that this mission was *necessary* for the safety of the New Republic and the reputation of New Republic Intelligence. It was all still true to him, still real, yet somewhere it had transformed from a theory into an operation risking the lives of hundreds or thousands of New Republic troops.

He didn't much like that part. They'd all volunteered, but he still didn't like it.

A voice deep inside him offered some small comfort: *It's not your responsibility anymore.*

He hoped Quell was up to the task.

# CHAPTER 17

# UNEXPECTED COMPLICATION

**I**

Colonel Shakara Nuress remained unimpressed. She remained unalarmed. She was, however, growing irritated.

The arrival of the enemy fleet was not a surprise, but it confirmed her theory of the attack—that the initial starfighter raid had been a prelude, and that the foe intended to throw its full weight against Pandem Nai to crack its defenses without a prolonged siege. The fleet's composition was in line with what she'd predicted, as well—an *Acclamator*-class battleship and a dozen smaller capital ships along with fighter escorts. It was too large for her to engage directly, but it didn't necessarily pose a problem.

"How many vessels," she asked Major Rassus, "do we have between the minefield and the planet?"

"Our own ships? Or all Imperial craft?"

*If they're in this star system, they're mine,* she thought. "All of them, Major."

"Eight," he replied. "Supply ships, mostly. Two cruisers, a corvette, and a troop carrier."

Nothing that could turn the tide of battle, she decided. "Recall them into low orbit. They're exposed out there and I don't want the enemy taking shots at them."

She'd barely given the command before another voice broke in. Ensign Nagry was looking over from her station with an alarmed expression. "The captain of the *Lancer* requests clearance to depart. He thinks he can slip past the enemy blockade, and worries his ship would be vulnerable to New Republic fighters if he stays—"

*For pity's sake.* "The enemy isn't after *him*. Recall him into low orbit! Make it clear that's an order, and that disobedience still carries consequences."

She didn't have time to worry about self-important corvette captains. She'd felt the bridge shudder twice from the enemy fighters' attacks—seen the deflector generators strain and heard the damage reports from the hangar bays. The foe was outnumbered but they were inside her perimeter and doing their damndest to prevent her from launching reinforcements.

There was a reason for that (one beyond the obvious), and she hadn't yet figured it out.

She waved off another complaint from Nagry and looked to her chief of operations. "What's our time estimate on the hangars? When can we launch?"

The old man's voice shook, though Shakara knew him well enough not to interpret it as fear. "Fifteen minutes. Maybe twenty. The fighters are intact but the doors are a wreck and the magnetic containment field on the port side is offline. If we somehow *did* open the doors we'd lose pressure through the whole compartment—"

She didn't need the details. "All right. Anyone you have to spare, put them on the task. I need those fighters in the sky."

"Respectfully—" She'd already started to move away. She turned to face him again, waiting. "—we don't *have* any spare resources. You know we've been stretched thin."

She was tempted to snap. To rage. She'd seen lesser commanders do so when challenged. The deck plating beneath her trembled as another enemy volley struck Orbital One.

"*Find* resources," she said. "Take stormtroopers off sentry duty. Halt gas extraction if you have to—pull every last man and droid from the Tibanna mines. You have my authorization to do whatever you need—just get my hangar bays operational."

There was no further argument. She stretched arthritic fingers and balled them into a fist. During the glory days of the Empire, a Star Destroyer had carried tens of thousands of trained crew. Never in her career had she been told that there weren't grunts to spare for a repair job, and now—well, now she was faced with fresh problems to solve.

She forced herself to consider contingencies. If she couldn't get the hangars open, what defenses were available? The orbital stations—Orbital One, in particular—had basic anti-fighter armaments. Some of the midsized ships did as well, though she didn't necessarily trust their captains not to use their more powerful turbolasers. The *Pursuer* was in no condition for combat, though perhaps she could employ it in some capacity.

She wondered if she'd been wrong not to call for reinforcements. *Too late now.* The enemy fleet would annihilate any new vessels arriving out of hyperspace.

The situation was exactly as it appeared to be, then. She was Colonel Shakara Nuress, commander of the 204th Imperial Fighter Wing, and she could win any battle with her squadrons deployed and time to prepare.

Without her pilots, she was helpless.

"Colonel?"

She felt the change even before she heard Rassus—the quieting of voices, anxious chatter turned to whispers. She saw where the major's gaze was directed and turned to the main entrance to the command center.

There, gliding silently forward, was a figure cloaked in red leather and fabric with a pane of black glass in place of a face. She knew it intimately. *The Emperor's Messenger.*

The droid had spoken only once, demanding the destruction of Nacronis in Operation Cinder. Since then it had watched. On rare occasions, it had strayed from her quarters. She had never seen it in the command center of Orbital One.

She approached the wraith and murmured so that her crew could not hear, "Are there instructions?"

The droid did not speak. It halted before her and did not move further.

Did it know? she wondered. Had it been monitoring transmissions and somehow determined the danger that Pandem Nai was in? Or had it predicted something else about the battle? Something about the enemy forces or Shakara's own decisions?

Her heart seemed to seize. Had it anticipated her doubt? Had it come to the command center knowing that she despaired at the condition of the Empire she'd once served well?

It seemed unlikely. It seemed like paranoia to even wonder as much. Nonetheless, the Emperor's Messenger was bearing witness to her decisions now.

"We will emerge victorious," she said softly. "In your master's name, we will."

## II

Nath Tensent had a plan. It wasn't, one could argue, the *official* plan—but even that was debatable, given the source. If he felt guilt over keeping secrets from the rest of his squadron, it was a guilt indistinguishable from sympathy; he felt no hesitation or regret, but it was *a pity,* he thought, that he was about to make Wyl Lark's life much harder.

"Give me a little space, will you?" he said. "I've got a thought for this next pass."

Wyl responded in a voice full of unconvincing cheer. "If I give you space, you're going to pick up tails. Sure you can handle it?"

Nath grinned. *Brave kid. Means well.* "You've got talent, but I've got experience. Keep yourself alive and watch for me coming out."

He wondered if he would feel *actual* guilt if he got Wyl killed. *Maybe,* he decided, but only if there was no mistaking his culpability. In a fight like this, where one stray shot could end everything, it was always hard to pinpoint blame.

He swung in a wide arc back toward the orbital station. He'd made three bombing runs already, coming away each time with new scratches. He counted seven TIEs on his scanner; same number they'd been facing awhile now. He'd delivered a glancing blow to one, and Wyl had sent another spiraling toward the planet, but Nath didn't hesitate in his analysis: If they kept going like this, they would lose.

All part of Quell's plan, of course, but it wasn't part of his.

The Y-wing shook in the atmospheric winds, and Nath drove his foot onto the left rudder pedal to coax his ship away from a volley of particle bolts. He transferred shield power from fore to aft as he passed under a flight of enemy fighters and into the shadow of the orbital station, hopeful he could run the gauntlet of turrets without getting incinerated. He felt every seam of metal ready to burst; he smelled wires overheating as he squeezed his control yoke. His teeth ached from the vibrations.

He knew his ship and he knew how far he could push it. He still had room to stretch.

The metal lattice of the station raced overhead—a dark sky contrasting with the endless sea of scarlet mist. Nath watched Wyl fall away on the scanner, taking most of the TIEs with him, but one of Nath's foes still pursued. That wouldn't do—he couldn't have witnesses for this run.

Particle bolts slammed into the ship's aft end and sent him lurching forward in his harness. He spat a curse. The Y-wing lacked the maneuverability and the speed of the TIE, which meant he'd have to get clever. *Figure it out, Tensent. Be the bastard they all say you are.*

He spotted his opportunity: a gap in the station framework leading to a maintenance shaft hung with gas pods, running partway along the station's outer arc. It was built for a droid, not a Y-wing, but he could squeeze in. T5 let out a vitriolic screech as Nath adjusted his ship's repulsors, mocking Pandem Nai's gravity as he penetrated the structure.

Almost immediately he heard a metallic wail as one of his nacelles caught scaffolding and tore a piece of the station loose. His damage indicators flashed red. He didn't have time to examine them as he rolled his ship, trying to avoid another collision with the shaft's protruding machinery. "Slow her down!" he called. "Cut the thrusters and give me repulsor drag!" He trusted the droid to do so without tearing the ship apart, though he felt a crushing weight against his chest.

His velocity dropped by half, then by half again. Maneuvering through the shaft became easier, but that wasn't the reason he'd done it. As he reached the shaft's far end and emerged back below the station's mass and into the scarlet sea, he grinned. The TIE that had pursued him was now directly ahead, having failed to curtail its own speed after losing Nath.

*Right in the line of fire.*

Nath squeezed his trigger. The TIE flashed, erupting in a piercing wave of light that whipped into the Y-wing, sent it nearly flipping. *Careful when you blow those things,* he thought as he regained control. *Atmosphere really does burn bright.*

"All right," he said. "We've got privacy and a few seconds to spare. How do we look?"

A primitive schematic appeared on his display: a diagram of the orbital station constructed during the bombing passes they'd made. A section two hundred meters ahead blinked, and Nath nodded.

"Good enough for me. Keep piping all transmissions my way. Don't do anything stupid."

One hundred meters. Fifty meters. Nath checked his helmet and activated the seal, binding it to the collar of his flight suit and lowering the visor. T5 replied sardonically on the console, and Nath smirked back.

"And hey—keep Wyl alive if you can, okay?"

There was no time for a response. The cockpit depressurized with a roar as the canopy flipped open, leaving Nath exposed to the frigid, blasting Pandem Nai atmosphere. The ejector equipment came to life, and magnetic fields launched him and his suddenly detached harness up and out of the Y-wing. He slammed hard into the orbital station's underside barely five meters above.

His harness's power supply wouldn't last more than a few seconds, but it generated a magnetic seal that allowed him to cling to the metal and scurry to the emergency hatch he'd seen in the diagram. Blood rushed to his head as he silently prayed that the control panel wasn't secured—he had some confidence that T5 could swing back around to catch him before he fell to his death, but it wasn't a risk he wanted to take. He slammed his palm against the panel once, then a second time, before the hatch slid open and he crawled inside.

His flesh was burning with cold as he collapsed on the floor of the station air lock. The hatch slid closed. Air blasted from the vents. He unsealed his helmet and sucked in a breath. He saw nothing to indicate he'd tripped an alarm.

"You all right?" Wyl's voice came through his comlink. "Lost track of you for a second."

"I'm fine," Nath said. "Get ready for another pass—didn't manage to do much damage this time around."

He rose to his feet, felt for the blaster on his hip, and studied his surroundings.

He had a plan. He had a mission, assigned to him by Caern Adan.

It was going to be a pleasure.

### III

Yrica Quell watched another TIE burn. It streaked through the scarlet atmosphere and sparked like a firecracker before disappearing under the shadow of the orbital station. There was a chance, she thought, that the pilot might survive—if he could slow his ship's descent, he might eject before hitting ground—but it wasn't likely.

That was the third of her comrades she'd killed today.

She recognized the squadron pursuing her and Chass na Chadic above the station. Captain Gablerone's unit had always favored maneuvering in groups of three, eliminating targets with brief, intense bursts of firepower; those signatures were unmistakable in her current opponents. Quell hadn't known Gablerone's pilots well, and she was grateful for that, yet she could still picture them in the mess hall of the *Pursuer*. She saw their faces as she aimed and fired, and she felt no grief.

She observed the memories of her life in the 204th through a distorted lens. She remembered it all, yet as she flew and fought she was without pity or care. Each shot she fired seemed to warp her view further, distancing her from the scenes. Particle bolts seared away all attachment.

She forced herself to assess her situation in the present. Her shields were oscillating rapidly, strained to their limit and flickering in and out of visibility. One of her thrusters was cutting out intermittently. Chadic's B-wing trailed smoke.

*If you keep fighting like this,* she told herself, *you will die.* It didn't matter if they kept the rest of Shadow Wing contained inside the hangars. She couldn't outfly her old comrades. She couldn't outfight them. The moral questions, the psychological toll, none of it mattered when she was in an unwinnable situation.

She had to buy more time for Kairos and her team.

*Be clever as a rebel.*

Emerald bolts tore through the mist around her ship, and she wove through the pattern, angling her starfighter between paired blasts and spinning away as soon as she could. She was high above the orbital station now, and she saw the speck of Chadic's B-wing drift lower. Quell's opponents stopped shooting. That meant they were going after Chadic.

*Be clever as a rebel. Be ruthless as an Imperial.*

She dived at an angle, gravity increasing her momentum as she plunged in pursuit of her foes and toward her partner. She scanned the battlefield with the same dispassion as before, searching for solutions. Searching for a way to delay or to kill.

She recognized it without a jolt of joy. She simply saw it there, plain and unguarded.

"Quell to Chadic. Listen carefully: I have a new plan."

## IV

Chass laughed, her ship twirling and rising and plummeting as if it were carried by a thrashing sea. The cramped pod of her cockpit felt like it was ready to tear free of the B-wing and fall into the endless scarlet. She'd almost lost the cannon on one of her S-foils, thanks to a blast that had nearly sheared off half her ship. But her music still played and her hair was wonderfully sticky with sweat and she was terrified and ecstatic at Quell's words.

"You sure about this?" she asked. "Is it even going to work?"

"Yes," Quell responded. "Just get close enough to blow the pod and stay far enough not to die. The explosion will consume the bulk of the gas instantaneously. No different from dropping a bomb."

"What about you?" Chass asked.

"I'm going to pull the fighters into position. Go!"

The playlist reached a Zeltron power anthem. A single, powerful voice cried out as synthesized notes urged the singer on and a single instrument became an orchestra. *Almost too obvious,* Chass thought, *but it'll do.*

She powered her thrusters in short bursts—bad for the equipment, bad for her neck and back, but great for confusing her pursuers—as she dropped through the atmosphere and beneath the artificial horizon line of the orbital station. She swung the cross of her vessel upright, bringing three of her four weapons above the cockpit as she raced below the station's structure, turning toward her target.

The enormous gas containment pod reminded her of a Star Destroyer's deflector generator: a faceted metallic sphere attached by stubby moorings to the orbital station proper. She wondered if she actually had the firepower to puncture it—she'd exhausted her supply of bombs and torpedoes, and she wasn't certain she'd do more than scorch the pod with her cannons. It must have been built to withstand collisions and industrial accidents. It must have been built to prevent *exactly* what she was about to attempt.

Chass felt her terror crest over her ecstasy as she redirected all available power—shields, repulsors, thrusters, and the rest—into her weapons systems. Her fighter bounced as momentum alone kept her moving. TIEs crawled across her scanner like a swarm of insects, and she saw Quell swinging toward them, trying to draw their fire.

*Not my problem anymore,* Chass thought. She saw the flashes of particle bolts in her peripheral vision and ignored them as the pod grew large in her viewport. She checked her targeting computer, calculated optimal firing range, and squeezed her trigger.

She felt a flash of heat, heard the sizzle of the cannons and a series of pops that brought the music to an abrupt end. She smelled components melting as destructive energy poured from the four points of the starfighter's cross, filling the viewpoint with sun-bright particles capable of vaporizing a small mountain. She kept squeezing as, one by one, instruments turned red on her console. But she heard no terrible thunder—she couldn't *see* through the firepower she'd unleashed, but she'd have known if the gas pod had detonated.

Wouldn't she?

She had to turn away. If she didn't, she would fly directly into the pod.

Would *that* be enough to detonate it, though? Would that be the answer?

She heard a shriek—a whistling and crackling from outside her cockpit. The sound of a proton torpedo.

*Not yet, Chass. Not your time yet.*

She tried to pitch downward, to escape the coming blast, but her maneuvering thrusters were sluggish and she remembered that she'd redistributed their power. As the thunder arrived and white filled her viewport she slapped wildly at the console, trying to retract her S-foils and turn the cross of the ship into a dagger that would plunge straight down. A wave of heat cascaded over her vessel, singeing her skin through the cockpit canopy, but then the B-wing dropped away and she looked up to see an explosion like a battle station detonating. Like Scarif burning under the Death Star's superlaser. Dark specks dashed themselves against the fiery wave and she realized that they were TIE fighters, perfectly positioned to take the blow.

She wanted to sit back. To rest and let the B-wing fall. But Quell's voice came through the comm and said, "Chadic! Where are you?"

She rerouted power away from the weapons. Her thrusters came back online, arresting her fall. "About a kilometer below you," she said, "but I'm okay. And just 'Chass,' all right?"

"Station's scorched—whole port side looks like it's burning—but it's not coming apart. We took out three TIEs, which gives us breathing room. Maybe the time we need."

"Maybe?" Chass asked.

"Still no word from Kairos," Quell said. "Get back up. We're not through fighting."

Chass could live with that.

She angled her ship back toward the battlefield and smiled as the music started up again. It was garbled and staticky, but it was exactly what she had hoped for.

# V

Wyl recognized Char, the TIE covered in ash. He recognized Blink, who had mocked him when Wyl had reached out—who had said *You're going to be food in the guts of the Oridol god* on the day that Wyl had been tested and found wanting.

He didn't know how he recognized them. Char was no longer black with carbon scoring and debris. Blink no longer fired a single laser cannon. If he'd told Nath, the man would have mocked Wyl's certainty and insisted he was imagining things.

Maybe he was. But the ghosts of Riot Squadron had flown with Wyl for weeks now. Was it any surprise that the ghosts of Shadow Wing had arrived at last?

He spun his A-wing away from Blink's latest volley, opened his throttle, and tried to lure his enemy into pursuit. Nath raced ahead below, maneuvering between the orbital station's turrets and taking potshots at sensor arrays and gravity generators. "I could use a hand!" Wyl called. "Pulling one into your targeting zone, assuming he'll take the bait."

"I'm a little busy," Nath said. His voice was almost inaudible through the static, as if he were whispering. "Any chance you can handle this one?"

"I'm handling all of them," Wyl said, doing his best to suppress his irritation. *You've never flown a Y-wing,* he reminded himself. *You can't know what he's dealing with.* But Wyl's shields had nearly burst and another solid hit would tear his fighter apart. "Please—I need a few seconds to recharge my deflectors and I can't get it by myself."

Nath hesitated before answering, "Do what you have to."

Blink remained the closest TIE behind Wyl. There were others ahead and farther back, but they were problems he could deal with fifteen seconds into the future. Blink, however, was loosing shot after shot, close enough to illuminate Wyl's cockpit with emerald light.

Wyl was about to let him get closer.

He kept his thrusters at maximum output—he couldn't afford to hint at what he was doing—while dipping and soaring to shear off speed and draw Blink in. Wyl cast a glance behind him and saw the dark eye of the TIE cockpit silhouetted against the scarlet mist, then plunged toward the orbital station at a forty-degree angle. His breathing was shallow and his bones felt ready to crack as he leveled out a few dozen meters in front of Nath's Y-wing.

Blink followed. They were a perfect line: Wyl, in Blink's sights. Blink, in Nath's.

*Come on. Shoot him. Shoot him!*

Wyl saw the ripple of the Y-wing's cannon blasts outside his cockpit. The shots had gone wide—maddeningly wide, not even close to Blink—and Wyl knew it meant his own death. He didn't have time to spin away. Didn't have time to shunt all power to aft deflectors and hope for the best.

He tried to think of Home and saw Sata Neek instead.

Yet he didn't die.

A rumble like thunder passed through his ship and through his body. His A-wing leapt as if slapped aside by a god's cosmic hand, off to starboard and away from the orbital station. Emerald flashed where Blink had aimed his weapons, but the green was pale and dim compared with the bright glow in the distance, on the opposite side of the facility.

When Wyl regained control of his fighter he saw flames racing across metal.

"Lark to Quell! Lark to Chass!" he called. "What happened?"

"Blew a gas pod," Chass answered. "You should try it."

Wyl didn't smile. He glanced at the TIEs on his scanner—scattered by the shock wave but quickly regrouping—and permitted himself another look at the fire. From a distance, he saw no gaping hole, nothing sheared off by the destructive power, but the station was *burning*.

Suddenly all his thoughts of Riot Squadron and Shadow Wing and Blink and Char seemed limp and selfish—they weighed on him still, but it was the crushing weight of a corpse.

Kairos was still on the station, along with her strike team. The station was burning. What were his problems compared with hers?

*Be safe*, he thought, and returned to the fight.

# VI

Orbital One was on fire, but that wasn't Shakara Nuress's biggest concern.

The blown Tibanna gas pod wasn't a catastrophe. It was a knife in the guts of her production schedule and the resulting damage would be considerable, but she could still recover. The warning indicators shining from every console in the command center were a badge of shame, not defeat—she'd read the specifications of Orbital One and it was built to survive a massive industrial disaster. The fires would spread only until they met the reinforced bulkheads between station sections and then slowly die as they exhausted all oxygen in their compartments. Even if she lacked the staff to see to the fire suppression systems, the safety shutdowns, all the protocols that were meant to be followed, Orbital One would remain intact.

No, her biggest problem was the same as it had been from the start. Her pilots were still trapped in the hangars. She had no defenses—no path to victory—without them.

"Rassus!" she cried. Only three other officers remained in the command center—she'd begun short-staffed and sent the others to check on her pilots after internal comms had shorted out—but she had to shout to be heard over the wailing alarms. "How much longer?"

"Till—?"

"Until we can release the fighters!"

She saw the answer in his eyes. *Too long.* The fires had disrupted repair of the hangar doors.

"Fifteen minutes," he said. "Another fifteen minutes."

Shakara had the dignity—and the presence of mind—not to swear. The wailing alarms dropped abruptly in volume; for that, at least, she was grateful.

Her eyes found the black glass stare of the Emperor's Messenger. The wraith had said nothing since its arrival, and it remained at its post near the doorway. Shakara wanted to approach it, to shake it, to demand answers—not just to her current predicament, but about why it was there at all. What the Emperor intended it to *do.*

*We wiped out a planet for you,* she thought. *The least you can do is tell us why.*

*Tell us how to survive.*

*Tell us how to preserve your Empire.*

She said nothing. She knew she would receive no answer, and the Empire she had fought for—the Empire she knew—had rewarded determination over groveling. She was among the Empire's best. She had seen the Empire grow and evolve and surpass the legacy of the Old Republic.

If she couldn't win today, perhaps Pandem Nai deserved to fall.

"Blast them open," she said.

Rassus didn't seem to hear. Then he turned abruptly from his console. "What?"

"The hangar doors," she answered. "Seal off the sections—as best we can, given the damage—and give the fighters permission to blow a hole through anything in the way. Yes, it won't be a simple fix. Yes, we'll do serious harm to subsystems and we'll need to evacuate additional compartments. But we've no other recourse."

Rassus didn't question her further. He brought his link to his mouth and started snapping orders.

Shakara looked again to the Emperor's Messenger. It didn't react, of course. Had she been expecting approval? A pat on the cheek from the Emperor's ghost?

Rassus nodded to her. Shakara stepped to the railing behind one of the tactical consoles and clasped it with both hands. A moment later a shudder ran through the deck. A new set of warnings lit up. The shudder became a jolt and a low, hollow boom like the beat of a metal drum resounded through the station.

She imagined the first TIE fighters hovering inside the wreckage of the hangar, directing their fire at rubble and carving through a bulkhead. She imagined a whirlwind sucking air and debris through the newly created gap, and the TIE pilots struggling not to collide in the face of such chaotic force. In a matter of moments, each squadron would creep through the gap and arrive in Pandem Nai's atmosphere. Above the burning Orbital One, they would swarm the handful of enemy ships and regain control of the battlefield.

The enemy fleet outside the minefield could press toward the planet if it wanted. Against the full force of the 204th Fighter Wing, Shakara was confident it would lose.

Victory had a price. But it was coming.

# VII

The turret was warm beneath Kairos's gloved hands. Like a living thing, it would grow hot with fury, its heartbeat pulsing, and then creak softly when it was quiescent. Kairos stroked the metal of the barrel, turning it away from the burning corpses of the three stormtroopers who had entered the docking bay.

She wondered why so few had come. She could only assume that the enemy was not aware of the U-wing's presence, or of the presence of the strike team. She had noticed the orbital station shudder and been certain that her mission was complete, but the special forces troops had signaled her with a single, oblique transmission confirming that the task was not done.

So she waited. When there was the opportunity to kill—to puncture and incinerate the creatures who crawled through the station in the name of their fallen lord and Emperor—she killed. When she was forced to wait, she waited. She was not patient, but neither was she an animal.

A deep booming sound, resonant and metallic, shook the station a second time. The U-wing, still aloft on its repulsors, barely shook. Kairos shifted her weight all the same.

What was happening? She was needed to guard her vessel, yet was she needed elsewhere, too?

The cockpit comm spoke. "Strike team to Kairos. Detonators in place. Returning to the transport now."

She stepped away from the turret and entered the cockpit long enough to trail her fingers across the controls and send a signal of her own.

She might not know what had transpired. But that was not her purpose.

The signal was sent. The defector would determine all their fates.

# VIII

Quell watched jagged metal tear through mist as a section of hull along the station's side erupted. At first she didn't understand what had happened—maybe, she thought, the fires from the gas pod's destruction had detonated some volatile piece of machinery—but then she saw shadows within the cloud of smoke and wreckage.

A trail of TIE fighters emerged from the station's wound like insects roused from their nest. First one, then a pair, then a steady stream. Whole squadrons, no longer captive.

They were blasting their way out of the broken hangars. Shadow Wing was free.

Quell's eyes were fixed on the dark trail. She barely had the presence of mind to touch her comm. "Lark! Your side of the station. Are you seeing—"

"I see it!" he replied. "They're coming out!"

*Then we've lost,* she thought. They'd barely been able to survive against two patrols. Against every squadron in the 204th, they were doomed.

But though her mind was nearly paralyzed, her body was not. The enemy still pursued her, and she pulled up and away from the station, her vision swimming as she looked toward a gas tanker drifting far above. Streaks of emerald flared past her and she twisted to and fro, trying to shake the enemy. Her fingers ached as she clutched her control yoke. She plotted a course in her head that would take her back to Chadic. It wasn't a *plan*—she had no plan—but it was the least she could do for her squadron.

She was diving when a miracle occurred. Her comm chimed. A message from D6-L appeared on her console.

Kairos's mission was complete.

She cried out her response in a voice of clarity and desperation: "Blow the reactor! Do it!"

She risked another glance toward the station. The great spoked wheel was a monstrous thing, flames licking one side and smaller fires, dimmer and ornamented with electrical arcs, crackling where the two starfighter hangars should have been. The trails of TIEs hadn't stopped, and the clouds of enemy ships could have been mistaken for ash and dust.

Quell waited for what she knew would come next.

# IX

Caern Adan didn't understand the look of horror on General Syndulla's face. He had watched the battle progress from the same vantage, seen the same esoteric tactical displays and heard the same shouted reports as her. He had felt his underarms dampen with sweat and his stomach churn and he'd yearned desperately to stride to his quarters and find a bottle of—well, just about anything.

But even with Shadow Wing released from its prison, they were on the verge of triumph. He saw energy readings spike on the long-range sensors. Someone called, "Visual confirmation! The reactor has been detonated!"

This wasn't the plan. The plan had been to disable the 204th's orbital headquarters with the fighters still inside, crippling Pandem Nai's defenses so that the fleet could move in. But the attack could still prevail. A Shadow Wing without leadership, without a base of operations and support crews and fuel and equipment, would last days against a siege, not months.

So why did General Syndulla stare at the strategy grid and the scanner readings like she was watching the end of the New Republic?

"Critical temperature," she called across the room to a tactical droid. "What's the critical temperature?"

The droid began rattling off numbers. Caern didn't understand. By the looks of it, neither did the general. "Just tell me this," she said. "What happens if they don't get those fires under control?"

Then Caern understood.

He sat back in his chair and tried to determine whether he'd won or lost.

# CHAPTER 18

# CATASTROPHIC FAILURE

I

**Q**uell watched the orbital station lurch, its burning port side listing downward. The center of the spoked wheel flashed and glimmered with fire and electricity and radiation bursts triggered by the detonation of the main reactor. Yet even inside her X-wing's airtight cockpit, she heard the blasts more than she saw them; from above the station, she lacked a direct view of the reactor casing.

The detonation wouldn't destroy the station. A dozen secondary reactors would power the repulsors and keep it aloft, with minimal power throughout. But it would no longer be a threat. As the last of the TIE fighters trailed out of the broken hangars, Quell hoped that the loss of their headquarters would force the pilots to pull back to the planet surface. They might yet cede the upper atmosphere to Syndulla's fleet.

Her pursuers fell off her trail—confused or responding to new orders—and Quell dived toward Chadic's last position. She was glancing at her scanner when she heard another peal of thunder and felt another shock wave below her fighter. The jolt passed, but she was searching for the source when a third shock wave hit her and slammed her helmet against the back of her seat.

Light burned beneath the orbital station as if it sat on a field of fire. The flames along the port side now enveloped half the structure. When the next roll of thunder came, Quell realized what was happening.

The fire spawned by the gas pod was growing in intensity. Whether due to the initial attack, the hangar explosions, or the detonation of the reactor, it was now strong enough to heat the other Tibanna containment pods to bursting. One by one, the pods were igniting, and with each pod ravaged the fire grew brighter and more terrible. The atmosphere began to churn, as if the orbital station had become the center of a storm.

Another pod ignited, then another. Tendrils of scarlet mist lit up and wove away from the station, like burning serpents or arteries pumping blood.

The sky of Pandem Nai caught alight.

All Quell could think of was Operation Cinder. The storm that the Empire had stoked to destroy Nacronis.

*It's happening again,* she thought. *It's happening again.*

## II

There was nothing but fire—fire and the dark specks of TIE fighters against the light, riding thunder and destruction. Chass rode the waves as well, but no matter how unsuited for atmospheric flight the TIEs were, the B-wing was worse. Only the gyrostabilizers in the cockpit prevented her from being dashed against the canopy a dozen times over as the firestorm threw her higher. The slow, rhythmic beat of cymbals and soft words from the comm was nearly lost in the howl of the wind.

She didn't know what was happening. Something had ignited the gas clouds of Pandem Nai, clearly. But *how*? She supposed it didn't matter.

Was this a success? A failure? She wasn't sure.

The TIEs were still firing. She opened her throttle, trying to escape the storm as her enemies—shooting wildly in her direction—did the same. She grinned and rolled her ship and prepared to counterattack. Success or failure, nothing *really* changed.

She would fight until the end.

She adjusted the comm system until the music became deafening, overpowering the rush of flames and the sizzle of particle bolts. She thought briefly of Jyn Erso on Scarif, standing defiant before the battle station that would destroy a planet to stop her, before even that thought faded away, replaced by the beat of a furious song.

## III

Wyl Lark felt the heat through his canopy and through the metal shell of his fighter. His shields flickered in and out of visibility. He rode the shock waves of the detonations, but the A-wing, for all its speed, was a fragile vessel. It wouldn't last long in a firestorm.

Had Quell planned this? Was this all the result of destroying the reactor?

The TIE fighters wouldn't last, either. Like him, they sped away from the detonations—yet still they pursued him. Char and Blink looped and wove together, coordinating their shots and forcing Wyl to choose between particle bolts and burning clouds. The orbital station fell away beneath him as he tried desperately to elude his enemies without incinerating his craft.

Did they recognize him, as he recognized them? Did Char and Blink long to kill the last survivor of Riot Squadron, completing the mission they'd left unfinished?

Why else would they still be following him, even amid catastrophe?

Other thoughts nagged at him, and he prized aside layers of fear to reach them. Kairos was still inside the orbital station. He couldn't help her. Nath had been flying close to the initial blasts when Wyl had been tossed away. Even now, he was failing to protect his partner.

He activated his comm, adjusting frequency to try to breach the firestorm's interference. "Nath! I lost track of you—can you get clear of the blasts?"

Only static came in return.

"Nath!"

With a fraction of a second to spare, he dived out of the path of a particle bolt volley.

He tried to make out the orbital station through a wall of flames. This *couldn't* have been some secret plan, he decided. The fire was spreading too far, too quickly, and he couldn't imagine what could occur if it—

*One problem at a time,* he told himself.

He glanced back at Char and Blink. He squinted at the burning clouds, readying himself to plunge through. He didn't know whether the Y-wing was still out there, didn't know where it might be, but he couldn't leave Nath unprotected.

Then the comm crackled, and a garbled voice said: "I'm all right. Forget about me right now and take care of yourself."

"Nath?"

But the voice disappeared, buried in distortion.

Wyl fled the fire and Shadow Wing, unsure what to do next.

# IV

The orbital station trembled steadily, the deck jittering and rattling beneath Nath's feet. Lights flickered but the artificial gravity remained stable. Officers and stormtroopers rushed past him in the corridors, ignoring the burly man in a New Republic flight suit in favor of reaching their posts—or the escape pods.

Nath wasn't sure what was happening. He assumed the New Repub-

lic strike team had eliminated the main reactor, but automated an-
nouncements had mentioned *containment pods* until the alert system
had gone offline. Wyl's message was even more concerning, and the
last transmission he'd received from T5 had mentioned seeking shelter
"out of the blast zone."

He suspected he'd made a mistake in coming aboard. But he was
here now.

*Might as well finish the job.*

He strode through the chaos as if he belonged there. No one halted
him as he worked his way against the tide of fleeing bodies; he wondered if he *had* tripped an alarm in the air lock and the crew had simply ignored it. He kept his hand near the blaster on his hip but never
touched the weapon—better not to draw attention—and increased his
pace to a jog when he saw others doing the same. Twice, he was forced
to alter his route when he reached a sealed blast door. Both doors radi-
ated intense heat, as if they held back miniature suns.

At last he arrived at the command center. Peering around the door-
frame, he saw that the broad chamber was nearly deserted—only a
middle-aged major, an ensign hammering at her console one-handed
while gripping a comlink, a red-cloaked figure that might have been a
droid, and a crisply dressed colonel remained.

Nath's gaze held on the colonel. She was keen-eyed, with a face of
dark and crumpled parchment and thin hair leached of all color. *Shakara Nuress,* he thought. *Grandmother.*

"We lost another gas pod," the major said. He visibly struggled not
to stammer. "The firestorm's diameter is expanding—"

"Give me a tactical map," Nuress snapped. The only sign Nath saw
of nervousness was her hands, as she stiffly wove and unwove her fingers. "Show me all ships and orbital stations—gas extractors and
colonies—within five thousand kilometers."

The major glanced toward the ensign—still consumed by her own
task—then dashed to another console. One of the displays blinked and
showed a sea of bewildering symbols Nath couldn't decipher from
afar. Nuress grimaced as she studied it.

"Should we have the colonies evacuate?" the major asked.

Nuress paced in front of the display, apparently deaf to the major's question. "You see them?" she asked. "Seven supply ships and three gas tankers in addition to the extractors."

"Major?"

"Tell them to withdraw. Top speed. If the firestorm reaches them—" She cut herself off and tapped quickly at her own console. "The storm is burning fast and bright, and there's a chance it will exhaust itself. If it finds a damn tanker, though—or three—it could have enough fuel to spread over this entire planet."

Nath saw her glance toward the red-cloaked figure—a tall, utterly still presence with a plate of black glass in place of a face.

"I don't need that on my conscience," she said.

*There's a story there,* Nath thought. But it wasn't what he'd come for.

The major bent over another control panel, checked something, and looked back to the colonel. "We're having trouble broadcasting. I can—"

Nuress waved him off. "Go. Do it manually."

The major left the command center at a run, streaking past Nath without a glance. Nath assessed his options—looked from the sweat-soaked ensign to the droid to Nuress—and decided he wouldn't get a better opportunity.

He stepped through the doorway and raised his blaster.

"Grandmother? Nath Tensent." He grinned his broadest, meanest grin and waited for her to turn. "You're a little busy, but you killed my friends. I thought we should chat."

He was pleased to see that for all her poise, Colonel Nuress was still capable of looking surprised.

## V

Buffeted by the storm, Quell's X-wing spun and burned. Wind and flame swirled around the orbital station, streaking outward in ribbons of annihilation. Quell's legs still worked her rudder pedals and her gloved hands played along the control panels, but her mind was trans-fixed by the hell that surrounded her. The holocaust of her own making.

Images of Nacronis—of the colorful siltstorm, wet and flaying and catastrophic, battering structures and flooding city streets with mud—mixed freely with nightmares of the present. She envisioned firestorms consuming the stations housing thousands upon thousands of civilian colonists. She pictured citizens on the planet surface looking up and knowing that they were doomed.

Her mind flashed to planetary bombardments—operations she'd dutifully joined at Mek'tradi and Mennar-Daye—where she'd watched ordnance fall and atomize settlements. She recalled those missions' preflight briefings and the professionalism with which she'd carried out the slaughter. She remembered cheering with a crowd on the ob-servation deck of the *Pursuer* as she beheld the mighty Star Destroyer annihilating its targets. She recalled the face of Major Soran Keize and every mistake she'd ever made.

One of the spokes of the orbital station's wheel began to buckle as the fires melted scaffolding and support struts. Metal plating tore loose and fell in hundred-meter sheets. From a vague, analytical distance, Quell remembered that there was a city somewhere below—a settle-ment on Pandem Nai eking out its existence in the station's shadow.

Quell had an extremely good memory, yet she couldn't recall the city's name.

She pictured molten slag and jagged wreckage falling from the pyre and impacting houses and factories. Crushing. Burning. Whatever the *Pursuer*'s bombardments had done, this would be worse—just as de-structive, but more callous and imprecise.

She was flying over a graveyard.

Her X-wing was diving. She wondered momentarily if D6-L was responsible, but the movements were her own—she hadn't heard from the droid since her ship had first been engulfed by the flames, and though she should have been concerned for the astromech she didn't have the space left in her consciousness. She sucked a thin, hot breath between her teeth and saw spots as she dipped below the horizon line of the station. She ignored the dots of TIE fighters on her scanner and angled under the station's center while maintaining her near-vertical descent.

Gravity pulled her down. Thrusters pushed her. She felt a wad of saliva catch in her throat and nearly choked. The atmosphere around her changed from deep scarlet to tawny orange. Finally, she spotted her target: an enormous girder as wide as her starship, shed from the orbital station and speeding toward the planet's surface.

She squeezed her firing trigger and loosed a flurry of particle bolts that sheared and shattered the metal. She kept firing, kept plummeting, reducing shards to shrapnel and shrapnel to ash.

"Lark to—Lark to anyone." The comm buzzed and popped. If Lark hadn't identified himself, Quell wouldn't have recognized his voice. "What happened?" he asked.

She tried to pull out of her dive. Her engines groaned and rebelled. Repulsors were useless, more apt to tear the X-wing to pieces than steady it. She leveled the ship and continued to fall. For three seconds she was certain she would crash; then she angled herself upward again and flew.

The comm crackled a second time. Lark's voice came more clearly now: "What have we done?" he asked.

The question tore her out of her dream and back to reality. It demanded an answer.

"*I* did it," she said.

The responsibility was hers. The mistakes were hers.

She wasn't sure whether anyone but Wyl Lark could hear her, but as she shot skyward and saw another black mass above—another scarred chunk of debris from the decomposing orbital station—she knew that her responsibility demanded action.

Alphabet Squadron was hers. She gave her final orders.

"We failed to take Pandem Nai," she said. "This is now a rescue mission."

The debris hurtled toward her, and she fired.

## CHAPTER 19

# EMERGENCY READJUSTMENT

### I

*This is now a rescue mission.*

"What does that mean?" Wyl called. "What are we supposed to do?"

Quell didn't reply. The comm buzzed and hissed. Wyl called Nath's name, and Chass's, and heard nothing. When he called to Kairos, he heard a squeal—an electronic tone that might have been acknowledgment or might have been a burst of static.

He was, for all practical purposes, alone. Barring his Shadow Wing pursuers and the ghosts of Riot Squadron.

He heard the clacking of Sata Neek and the steady drone of Rununja giving orders, warning him to elude the weapons fire aimed in his direction. Yet over the voices of his old squadron mates came Quell, again and again: *This is now a rescue mission.*

In the Oridol Cluster he had been left without comrades, forced to choose the fate of himself and his mission. He had been tested by the

Oridol god and haunted by Riot Squadron ever since. Now he was again forced to choose, pursued by the same enemy, and he felt suddenly calm as he spun his A-wing about and ascended away from the station.

*This is now a rescue mission.*

Not a mission of revenge against Shadow Wing. Not a mission of conquest to take worlds for the New Republic. For the first time since leaving the *Lodestar,* he felt sure of himself and his purpose.

He didn't know if the dead of Riot Squadron would approve. But his ancestors on Home would.

There was nothing he could do to prevent the station's collapse. There could have been thousands of Imperial crew aboard, and though he felt a pang he couldn't usher them to the escape pods. (He suspected that the Imperials weren't who Quell wanted them to rescue, but the decisions were his now.) Nor could he arrest the spread of the firestorm directly—and it *was* spreading, but shooting particle bolts into the burning clouds would do no good.

He glanced at his scanner—flickering and distorted by the storm—then looked through his canopy. This was a rescue mission, he thought, so who could he *help*?

He adjusted course and spotted the distant silhouettes of Imperial vessels racing away from the storm front. Supply carriers; a corvette; and among them a massive slab of a ship lined with spherical containment units: a gas tanker.

It crawled through the sky. Wyl dipped his port side and peered at the churning flames beneath him. At the rate the storm was expanding, it would surely catch the tanker. It would ignite the pods and—

Another cascade of emerald particle bolts tore past his ship. One struck home, tearing the targeting sensor off his starboard cannon and causing the ship to rock and howl. "Leave me alone!" he snapped, and accelerated toward the tanker.

He could outrace the firestorm with ease. The tanker could not. He glanced at the containment pods sprouting from the tanker's hull like the legs of a crawling insect. There were at least two dozen.

He tapped his comm and opened a channel. "Imperial tanker ship!" he called. "How can I assist?"

There was no reply.

He'd lost sight of his pursuers, and his scanner was useless. Another glance showed him that the tendrils of flame were rapidly closing. He crossed the distance to the enormous vessel and chose his first target.

His cannons blazed and sung. He turned and rolled as he flew closer to the tanker, bolts flying and sparking as they struck the moorings of the first containment pod. Metal blackened, crumpled, and finally buckled, sending the pod plummeting toward the planet surface.

It didn't feel like a victory. Wyl hoped the pod would strike somewhere in the wilderness beyond the ground settlements, crumpling without detonating. If not, however—he had no other options. Better to burn on the ground than to fuel the conflagration in the skies, obliterating the tanker and engulfing the planet in an endless inferno.

Flame caressed the tanker now, rushing to fill the gaps between the pods. Wyl tried to match the vessel's course and speed, steadying the A-wing as he aimed at the next set of moorings, but the storm winds bounced him ten meters into the air and his blast went wide. He lined up another shot and loosed a second volley; the pod creaked and swung from the moorings but didn't detach as fire flowed around it.

Wyl grimaced and swallowed a curse. With the pod hanging precariously he no longer had a clean shot. He didn't know how long the containment unit had before the gas inside ignited. This close, any blast would rip through his A-wing along with the tanker.

He angled for the battered moorings anyway. *One last try,* he decided, and laughed as he saw emerald bolts rip through the air around him. His pursuers had caught up, and there was nothing he could do but hope he survived long enough to complete his pass.

He was fifty meters from the pod when crimson streaked across his view. The half-broken moorings flared white and the containment pod dropped away.

Wyl traced the afterimage burnt into his vision and looked to the shooter: a New Republic U-wing racing toward him from the direction of the orbital station.

He couldn't make out any details, but he was certain that the crest of Alphabet Squadron was painted on its nose.

"Good to see you, Kairos," he said, "and glad you made it. Take the port-side pods. I'll handle the starboard."

The TIEs behind him poured streams of emerald destruction through the space Wyl's A-wing had occupied seconds earlier. Blink and Char wanted him dead, rescue mission or not.

But he thought of his last encounter with Shadow Wing. He knew what he had to try.

## II

The swarm had found her. A mournful song of bandfill tones and gasped vocals accompanied Chass as she rotated her ship, accelerated and dived, charged into squadrons and sprayed cannon fire across burning clouds. Shadow Wing's TIEs englobed her, and her shields were long gone. Second by second her systems were failing as particle bolts seared her primary airfoil.

She was doomed, but she wasn't defeated yet. One TIE strayed into her field of fire and she annihilated it with a cannon burst. Another mistimed its shots, and she dropped twenty meters and watched the charged beams strike another of her foes, sending it spinning away.

She sang along with the music, though she didn't know the words.

She'd heard a staticky voice—Quell's voice—declare something through her comm minutes earlier, but she hadn't understood it and the voice hadn't returned. She didn't know where the rest of her squadron was, or what their mission had become. The whole planet seemed to be burning. She was pretty sure that hadn't been the plan.

She no longer cared. She was frightened and satisfied as her mission came to its end. She intended to kill as many Imperials as she could.

The instruments under her right arm snapped and sparked and her cockpit lit up with electricity. The fabric of her sleeve blackened and she pulled her arm to her chest as the suppressors kicked in and the side panel fizzled and died. Another enemy shot pierced one of her S-foils, disabling its cannon and shaking her ship. She spun the B-wing around, saw the globe of TIEs closing, and decided on a final plan: She would let her starfighter fall, cockpit and weapons aimed to the sky, and spin and shoot and spin and shoot until her enemies were gone or she was destroyed at last.

She was ready. It wasn't the martyrdom of Jyn Erso, but it was good enough.

Yet as she lay in her seat and pitched her B-wing back, the rain of enemy fire ceased.

Above her, the TIE fighters rose into the air, turned, and retreated into the obscuring firestorm. She wanted to shout at them, to demand they return. She laughed in outrage and confusion.

Then she heard the voice through her comm, garbled and tinny. "I repeat, this is Wyl Lark of New Republic squadron 'Alphabet' to all ships on all frequencies. Please cease hostilities and provide immediate assistance.

"If we don't—" The voice hesitated. "If we don't, everything burns. If we don't, we could lose the planet. Nothing else matters. Nothing else, if we can stop this. This is Wyl Lark—"

*Wyl Lark,* she thought. *You're doing it again. You're taking it all away from me.*

She reignited her thrusters and slammed her burnt arm against the console to reset the scanner. Somewhere in this storm of death she could find a fight worthy of her.

III

"Now? You're choosing now to do this?" Colonel Nuress's voice wasn't so much outraged as astonished. Nath heard the subtext: *How stupid can you be?*

"Best chance I've got," Nath said, and swept the blaster pistol from Nuress to the ensign. The former remained standing. The latter sat motionless at her console. Nath stepped to the side, well out of reach of the red-cloaked droid. "Anyone moves, I shoot."

"This station is falling apart," Nuress went on, as if lecturing. "The whole planet is in danger."

"Then let's hurry it up. Answer my questions and we'll be done."

He walked slowly around the perimeter of the room, making sure he hadn't missed any obvious threats and giving himself a clear view of the entrance. He'd taken hostages before. He preferred doing it with a crew, but Colonel Nuress had taken his crew away from him.

As he passed the ensign—the woman's back to Nath, and Nath's back to the wall—he saw her hand slide toward her hip. It might not have been an attempt to pull a weapon, but he thought it better not to take the risk. Pistol still aimed at Nuress, he brought his fist down on the ensign's head, slamming her face into the console. She slumped in her chair.

*Could be unconscious, could be faking,* Nath thought. He was ready to shoot when the ensign slid from the chair and hit the floor. *Not faking,* he decided.

That left the Grandmother of Shadow Wing and the droid.

"What do you want?" Nuress asked. She didn't protest, didn't cry out to protect her officer. Nath appreciated that.

"About seven months back," he said, "you sent fighters to the Trenchenovu shipyards to repel a rebel attack. You remember?"

Her eyes held on Nath. He saw no flicker of hesitation, no moment in which she searched her memory. "I remember the operation," she said, "but none of the details. One squadron, I think. A minor altercation."

"You got it logged?"

This time she did hesitate, if only for an instant. "Yes."

"Pull it up." He gestured to the nearest console with his blaster. "Slowly."

She bent gingerly over the console—he wondered if she had spinal problems—and tapped at the controls. Reluctantly, he put his back to the red-cloaked droid in order to supervise. He didn't see her trigger any alarms or attempt to signal for help. She was sensible, he thought— she knew the station was a mess anyway, so her odds of getting rein-forcements were slim.

Or maybe she genuinely wanted to keep her people at their current tasks. Her alarm about the planet had sounded sincere.

"I have it," she said. "Trenchenovu shipyards. The 204th loaned out a squadron to the Star Destroyer *Sanction* to defend against an antici-pated terrorist raid. As I recall, the *Pursuer* had been meant to partici-pate as well; but a crisis arose elsewhere, forcing our squadron to remain at Trenchenovu while awaiting the *Pursuer*'s return."

"Two Star Destroyers against one rebel bomber squadron?"

Nuress shrugged. "Our intelligence about the attack might have been wrong. Better to be overprepared."

She could have been lying. Nath had no way to be sure. It didn't matter in the slightest, yet an unexpected rage welled up inside him. He'd come here for certainty. He'd come for an ending. If he walked away without knowing the truth—

*It doesn't matter,* he told himself. *Ask what does.*

"Who was on the flight roster? Give me the TIE pilots."

Nuress tapped another key, and a list of names appeared on the dis-play. She read the names as he did. "Captain Alyord Smythe. First Lieutenant Denn Maskar. Second Lieutenant Samnell Peers. Second Lieutenant—"

He heard the hitch in her voice and ignored the rest of the names. "What?" he asked. "What is it?"

She looked at him blankly. Irritated, he waved the blaster. "You paused for a second," he said. "What did you see?"

Nuress straightened gradually and turned to face Nath. "They're all dead," she said. "I'd forgotten, is all."

Nath stalked to the console—too close to Nuress, he knew, despite her age—and held the barrel of his blaster centimeters from her throat as he tapped the controls, opening the pilot records.

She hadn't had time to alter the data. The records supported her claim. His guts clenched as he opened each file in turn. Captain Alyord Smythe: Deceased. First Lieutenant Denn Maskar: Deceased. Twelve pilots, and every one of them gone.

This wasn't what he'd come for. He heard his breathing coming fast, hot and tasting of bile. "How can they all be dead?" he snapped.

"Seven months is a long time for a TIE pilot."

Nath remembered. Most fliers didn't make it a year.

"But your guys were *good*," he said.

He caught a flash of a smile and resisted the urge to club her face. "They were. These weren't our best. But it's been a difficult period, and once you start replacing pilots the whole squadron's survivability goes down." She eyed the records on display. "Maskar went almost a month after Trenchenovu, victim to an explosion on the flight deck. Sabotaged fuel piping purchased from Separatist sympathizers."

"Separatist?" Nath asked. Was she senile?

"Separatist, rebel. It's all the same."

He grunted, and she went on. "After Maskar, we lost three more across five months. It was only after the Emperor's assassination that the massacres began. We lost good people at Nacronis, at Indu San, in the Oridol Cluster—" She suddenly laughed, a crisp barking sound that suggested as much disdain as mirth. "Look around: Why do you think there's nobody *here*? Why do you think you *won*?"

Nath forced himself to slow his breathing and quash the trembling in his blaster hand. The pilots who had slaughtered his crew were dead. He had no proof of this beyond Shadow Wing's own records and the word of their commander, but it was as much evidence as he could ever hope to obtain.

They were dead. They were dead already.

He'd come for vengeance and they were dead.

"Who authorized the mission?" he asked.

"It's the Empire," she said. "Who *didn't* sign off, at one level or another?"

He growled. "Who approved the plan? Who said yes to the ambush?"

"I did," Colonel Nuress said.

That was the answer he'd been looking for. He tightened his grip on the blaster and let the rage boil inside his mind. Time to balance the scales as best he could.

Then he remembered his other mission, and he almost laughed.

"I have another question," he said. "You know a pilot called Yrica Quell?"

Her brow tightened. "I know the name."

"You got any opinion on her? Anything you want to share?"

"She was capable. As I recall, her record was undistinguished but not without merit. One of my majors quite liked her. I don't recall ever speaking to her directly."

"Let's see her file," Nath said.

Colonel Nuress shrugged and turned back to the console. "No use protecting the dead," she said, and the screen flickered and displayed a new record. Nath watched Nuress out of the corner of his eye as he read the contents, skimming over mission details and performance evaluations until he reached the end.

*Well*, he thought. *That's interesting.*

"Transfer it to datachip," he said. Nuress eyed him with a sort of revolted pride and he laughed, entering the commands himself. When the transfer was complete, he stepped across the room to the transfer unit and pocketed the chip.

"Are we done, then?" Colonel Nuress asked.

He looked at her. She stood straight as any junior cadet on the receiving end of an inspection, full of Imperial pomposity. She knew what was coming—Nath was sure of that—and she was ready to meet it without fear.

"Yeah," he said.

He wanted to see if she would reach for her sidearm. He'd noticed the pistol on her belt the moment he'd entered the command center, but he'd allowed her to keep it in order to narrow her options—it gave Nath one thing to worry about instead of many. Ultimately, though, she was too slow. Age or indecision kept her from taking up the weapon in the half a second Nath permitted himself to wait.

He pulled the trigger and felt his pistol tug at his hand, flare with heat. The bolt struck Colonel Nuress square in the chest and filled the room with the odor of ozone, melted fabric, and burnt flesh.

There was no chorus of spirits. No approving nods from the ghosts of Nath's crew at the death of their destroyer. Just a dull, numbed satisfaction in his rib cage.

He'd done what he had set out to do.

As the deck shuddered beneath him, he ran out of the command center and hoped his droid was still waiting.

# IV

Colonel Shakara Nuress lay on the cool metal floor of the command center and knew that she was dying. Every tremor through the deck plating sent quivers through her chest. There was little pain—the blaster bolt had cauterized the wound instantly, leaving only a radiant halo of heat around the burnt hole—but the numbness was disquieting in its own right.

She considered her options and obligations in a flash and found little to do of any use. There were no final orders to be issued. Nothing she could do to stop the Separatists or save Pandem Nai or wake Ensign Nagry or even avenge herself on the grandstanding bastard who'd shot her.

She twisted her body and felt a hot spike jab at her abdomen. She looked across the command center, and her eyes found the red-cloaked wraith.

The Emperor's Messenger.

It observed her with its eyeless glass faceplate and did not move.

She dragged herself forward, clutching at the seams in the deck plating. The tremors—her own along with the station's—nearly dislodged her fingertips from the cracks, but she tightened her grip and pulled. The journey took her one meter, two, three across the command center before her strength was gone.

"Tell me," she said in a desiccated voice.

The Emperor's Messenger bowed its head, tracking to her new position. It did not speak.

"Tell me why," she said. "Why observe us? Why say nothing? Why Operation Cinder?"

The Emperor's Messenger only stared.

"I can't tell anyone now. *Look* at me!" She tried to roll over to reveal her wound to the machine, but she lacked the vigor. "I served him for decades. I just want to know what he intended."

She had trusted that the destruction of Nacronis was necessary. Cinder had failed on other worlds—on Naboo and Abednedo—but not on Nacronis. Her unit had done its duty.

"Tell me it was worth it. Tell me *why*."

Her vision began to leave her, obscured by a fog that crept inside her eyes. She shook her head to clear it, not knowing how much time had passed yet aware that her death was imminent. She parted her lips to make demands of the Messenger one final time but the words failed to come.

Her gaze fell to the floor. She saw red leather whirling and retreating as the Messenger turned to leave.

There, in the command center of Orbital One, Shakara Nuress—loyal servant of the Emperor and grand strategist of the 204th Imperial Fighter Wing—died in despair, wondering if she had made a mistake long before and far away.

# V

*Induchron.*

Quell remembered now. The city's name was Induchron.

She caught glimpses of it as she accelerated toward the surface and penetrated the lowest layer of ocher clouds: an expansive, flat settlement of squat factories, prefab housing, and metal silos, sweeping across the rocky plains of Pandem Nai like moss. It was an ugly thing compared with the glittering skyscrapers of Coruscant or the citadels of Nacronis or even the carved mountain metropolises of Abednedo.

It was barely worth saving. Barely worth dying for.

But she would if she had to.

She dived in her X-wing, chasing burning clusters of debris plum-meting from the orbital station. Over and over, she targeted blackened metal sheeting and tumbling pylons with quick bursts of cannon fire, then reversed course—ascending skyward to intercept the next shower of industrial flotsam. The stress on her body was terrible—her muscles ached as if she'd been running for hours, and every motion released pain and lactic acid—but the stress on her ship was worse. She'd pushed her thrusters to their maximum for minutes on end in a planetary environment, subjected every bolt and computer system to immense pressures. Her astromech droid no longer seemed to be repairing her systems as they broke down one by one.

As she tore through the ocher clouds on another ascent, a horrify-ing *bang* exploded on her port side. She recognized the sound: Some falling shard of metal had struck one of her S-foils. It wasn't the first time. She hoped she hadn't lost the cannon, but if so? She had three left.

She tried to pull up a damage report but the display had gone black. Heat was becoming a problem, too—the hull of her ship was practi-cally glowing from her maneuvers, and she would melt her own can-nons if she didn't adjust.

She licked her parched lips and strained to see the next target. Things were only going to get worse. It was only *pieces* of the station falling now, but there were enormous modules that hadn't yet lost their repulsors. All of it would come down.

If she couldn't save Pandem Nai, maybe she could save Induchron. She wouldn't make the same mistake a second time.

# VI

The transmission came in seventeen fragments that the *Lodestar*'s computer strained to patch together. The firestorm above Pandem Nai was to blame—it had disrupted communications, degrading signal strength and necessitating the use of data recovery programs to process the simplest messages.

That was fine with Caern Adan. He smiled grimly to himself as software tried to make sense of the communiqué sent to his station. *No point hurrying when you've already lost the race.*

Outside his isolated corner, the rest of the tactical operations center was in a panic. General Syndulla was shouting orders, demanding that the New Republic fleet breach the minefield and approach Pandem Nai. "We have to get in there," she called. "We have to help them. Tell our ships to divert all power to forward shields and ram straight through if they have to!"

"General—" A white-bearded old human was protesting. "—if we do that, our entire fleet will be vulnerable as it emerges from the minefield. The Imperial warships are ready to battle. They'll cut us to pieces."

"They won't," Syndulla said. "Look at the tactical display—they're not maneuvering for an attack."

Caern looked to the transparent plate overlaid with ship markers and course vectors. The general was right—the Imperial vessels were scattering, too busy trying to escape the firestorm to pay attention to the New Republic fleet.

He stood from his chair, suddenly alarmed. He couldn't be the only one to see it, could he?

"They'll try to flee," he said. "If we break formation, we'll lose the blockade. The Imperial ships will jump to lightspeed. *All* of them will get away—"

"I'm aware of that, Officer Adan," Syndulla said. "My biggest concern right now isn't a dozen Imperial supply ships and cruisers escaping the system."

"What about the 204th?" he asked. It was, despite the sharpness of his tone, a genuine question; he could barely read the displays, he was no military strategist, and as much as he disliked looking foolish he needed to *know.*

But Syndulla retorted without patience: "Pandem Nai is burning. What happens to the 204th? I don't really care."

Caern started to snap back, but she had already turned away. He tuned out his inner ranting and forced himself to examine what he knew. Most—maybe all—of Shadow Wing's squadrons were present in the firestorm. The TIEs lacked hyperdrives, which meant they were stuck in system unless they docked with a carrier. That would take time, but given the catastrophe they might have the time they needed; clearly Syndulla wasn't about to intervene.

If Shadow Wing wanted to escape, it had a chance. That was the stark truth of it.

But Pandem Nai would no longer be a threat. Whatever became of it, its days as an Imperial stronghold were over.

Somewhere in his head, he heard IT-O's voice ask in a low, unthreatening tone: "Does that bring you comfort? Given the fact you can't change the situation or quench the fires?" Caern almost snarled as he shook the thought away. The last thing he needed was the droid playing conscience in his imagination.

He felt the *Lodestar* rumble softly as its thrusters pushed the battleship forward. Then a jolt shook the vessel with a metallic ring like a bulkhead buckling, nearly tossing Caern off his feet. *That must be the first mine.* He hoped Syndulla and the captain knew what the ship could endure.

His hands were trembling. He wanted a drink. The console in front of him chimed and gave him something better.

The transmission, reassembled, had come from Nath Tensent. It contained Yrica Quell's personnel record from the 204th Imperial Fighter Wing.

# CHAPTER 20

# REDEFINITION OF VICTORY CONDITIONS

I

The TIEs were no longer trying to kill him. Not most of them, anyway. Instead Wyl flew alongside the pilots of the 204th, through the battering storm and toward the last of the gas tankers. He'd seen a second TIE squadron head for one of the surviving extraction stations, and a third set course for a supply ship. With his newfound comrades, he'd cut dozens of volatile containment units loose from their moorings.

He prayed that it would be enough to stop the firestorm—that all their efforts wouldn't result in a charred ember of a planet and a blaze too hot to burn out even without the fuel they denied it.

Kairos led the way to the tanker in her U-wing. Her vessel had endured the inferno's wrath well—its shields and hull were sturdy, built for punishment that would obliterate an A-wing or a TIE fighter. Its additional weight meant the winds were less likely to hurl it into the tanker's side or cause a midair collision with an ally. Meanwhile Wyl's ship had lost one cannon entirely and he'd burned his hand through the glove of his flight suit trying to touch the canopy.

He tried not to pity himself. Char and Blink, flying behind him and capable of destroying his ship with the squeeze of a trigger, were probably worse off. A TIE fighter didn't even have shields; the pilots must have been roasting alive.

He adjusted his comm with tender fingers. "Approaching target. Counting forty gas pods. Divide them up, same as before."

Static roared in reply. He couldn't make out a word, and his systems diagnostics were down—he wasn't even sure if the problem was on his end or the TIEs'.

"All right," he murmured. He wanted to stroke the console but feared being burned again. "One more tanker, one more mission, and we'll get you home. Nothing wrong that can't be repaired."

The TIEs, the U-wing, and Wyl broke formation as they neared the tanker, dipping below its mass to access the pods. Streams of emerald and crimson poured from the fighters, carving away at metal. But fire washed over them like a tide, and each swell forced them to scatter— the pods might last against the full force of the storm for a few moments, but the TIE fighters and the A-wing couldn't.

The first pods fell toward Pandem Nai even as TIEs were blown away by the gale and failed to return. Wyl saw one fighter—he thought it might have been Char—swept into the flame and burst like a nova, providing more fuel and heat to the blaze. Wyl wanted to mourn but he didn't have the time. He tried desperately to cut away at a pod's moorings, but even his single functioning laser cannon sputtered and crackled and caused his ship to vibrate with every shot. The target barely looked scorched.

The pods closest to the storm front began to glow with heat. The surviving TIEs and Kairos didn't stop firing, didn't stop flying.

Wyl Lark believed in his mission. It felt *right*. It was a shame, he thought, that they might fail anyway.

## II

There was no one left to fight.

Chass drifted through the storm, thrusters at low power and energy diverted to stabilizers and repulsors. The wind carried her ship and fire licked her hull. She had nowhere to go—she saw nothing through the flames, had no functioning scanner. Only gravity suggested a difference between up and down.

Her music had stopped, the beat replaced by the throbbing of her burnt right arm. Without a battle, she saw no point in trying to fix whatever had gone wrong. She felt anxiety like withdrawal in her veins—a desperate craving for the fear and tranquility and *certainty* she had felt only moments before.

*Is this all I deserve?* she wondered.

Would they find her corpse charred to the bone, broken to ashen fragments in a B-wing crashed on a cinder of a world? Would anyone even discover that much, or would she just be counted among the thousands—the tens of thousands—who'd died in a disaster that had wiped out two warring fleets?

She didn't want to boil to death in her own sweat. She didn't want *this*.

*Maybe I do deserve it.*

Something burst far below, lifting her ship on a shock wave. She bounced in her harness and the B-wing leapt forward, tumbling through the heat and light. Chass leaned over the controls, trying to level the ship out and searching for some scrap of information on the console to guide her.

When she looked up, her dry lips parted and she stared. Far beyond the B-wing, silhouetted against the burning sky, was the wedge of a *Quasar Fire*–class cruiser-carrier orbited by at least twenty TIE fighters. At one time in her life, from so far away, she might have mistaken the cruiser-carrier for a far larger Star Destroyer—but after the chase through the Oridol Cluster, recognition came instantly.

Was it Shadow Wing? Were they trying to escape?

How could it be anything else?

She fumbled to redistribute power to her thrusters as she resettled herself in her seat. The starfighter lurched, her engine emitting a sweet, chemical odor. The cruiser-carrier was moving away but it, too, appeared hampered by the storm winds. She could catch it.

Panting for breath, ignoring the pain in her arm, she reached under the console and pulled a manual toggle to reset her subsystems. Nothing happened, and she tried again; finally, beneath a tinny ring and the roar of the storm, her music started up again: a deva pop track with an easygoing beat and saccharine lyrics recalling some local holiday banned by the Empire.

Chass couldn't remember why she'd even brought it with her, but she liked the rhythm and the irony in the verses. *Leave it on,* she decided. *You're lucky it's playing at all.*

Weapons came next. If the cruiser-carrier hadn't spotted her yet, a test would give away her position. Still, she gave her trigger a squeeze and was satisfied to see the auto blaster below her cockpit and her laser cannon spit particle bolts. The ion weapons were less responsive, but two stuttered out white pulses of energy.

Against a cruiser-carrier and twenty TIEs, she'd have to move fast. Get in close to the carrier, she decided—fry its deflector generators on the first pass, go for the hangar on the second. Maybe she could get inside—rip through the thing like a bullet from a slugthrower.

She could stop Shadow Wing. Where everyone else had lost sight of the mission, she could finish it.

*No shields, broken weapons, and the target we all came for. The people who killed Fadime. It's your sort of fight, Chass.*

She eyeballed her distance from the cruiser-carrier. Twenty seconds till she was in range, maybe. The TIEs had noticed her but they weren't leaving the larger ship—just forming a defensive barrier at its rear. Chass picked her first target, ready to scatter the swarm.

"Chass?" A voice broke through the music. "Chass! Is that you?"

*Wyl Lark.*

The man who'd stolen her targets. Who'd stolen her choices twice now. Not the man she wanted to deal with. Not the voice she wanted to hear in her final moments.

"Chass, we need you up here—trace the transmission vector if your scanner's down. We need to cut away the fuel pods on this tanker, or the whole thing goes up—"

"I'm *working!*" she shouted. "I've got a carrier full of TIEs *right here,* and they're making a break for it."

"You can hear me?" he replied. *You're an idiot,* she thought, but he sounded so relieved she couldn't muster much spite. "Listen to me, we need you. Quell's orders were that this is a rescue mission, so—"

"Screw Quell. Our mission was to stop Shadow Wing. *I'm here. I'm stopping them.*" She forced herself to draw a deep breath. She was coming into firing range of the TIEs. "You don't need me, Wyl. You keep the fire contained. Let me finish the job."

She squeezed her trigger, aiming at one of the TIEs. Particle blasts and crackling energy streaked through the burning clouds; her foe neatly evaded the volley with a quick horizontal cut. The TIEs didn't scatter. Their defensive formation remained intact.

"Please," Wyl said.

The TIEs returned a volley of their own. Chass's viewport flashed emerald and she spun and dodged, her breathing accelerating. She felt the music reverberating in her skull, calming her and guiding her motions.

If she couldn't scatter the TIEs, she could blaze through the center of the formation. She could overcharge her weapons, build enough momentum to crash past the fighters and ram the carrier. It *had* to be in bad shape already from the firestorm. She could deliver the finishing blow.

She redistributed her power again, keeping an eye on the steady streams of particle bolts outside. "Goodbye, Wyl," she said. "Do what you got to. Tell people about me, huh?"

But it wasn't Wyl's voice that replied.

"I know what you're thinking. But look around you—we all blew it. There aren't going to be any damn heroes today, sister."

Wyl's voice cried, "Nath!" and the older man snickered.

A cannon blast passed close enough that she heard the hissing interaction of charged particles and gas. She kept her course steady, eyes locked on the cruiser-carrier, but her shoulders were quivering.

Nath's words repeated in her brain. She tried to brush them away but they grew into an image of the *Lodestar,* of General Syndulla and the aftermath of the battle. She heard angry shouts and accusations about the fate of the planet Pandem Nai.

No one would care about a cruiser-carrier.

"Chass," Wyl said, "we need you *right now.*"

She slammed her fists against the console. It was a childish, petulant act. She let herself indulge, then pulled up and away from the Quasar Fire.

Because Wyl was right. Nath was right. Of course they were right.

Her ship rattled and bounced as she cut through the burning sky, the blaze cascading across her canopy as she penetrated a gas pocket. When she emerged, she saw the tanker—a massive vessel somehow more intimidating than any Star Destroyer—and a handful of TIE fighters along with Wyl, Nath, and Kairos firing haplessly at the containment pods. One of the pods was aflame, some layer of insulation between the metal shell and the Tibanna inside already ignited. She rolled her fighter in the pod's direction and squeezed her control yoke. The auto blaster pumped bolts out of sync with her music.

The pod detached and plummeted like a meteor. Nath and Wyl were laughing and cheering and shouting in desperation, strafing moorings as a team, while Kairos matched the tanker's speed and cut away metal with precise, powerful blasts. The TIEs danced around all of them, thrown from one end of the tanker to the other by the storm winds. Chass flew beneath the tanker's enormous bulk and hoped the storm wouldn't smash her into the underside.

As they worked, Chass heard faint, distorted messages from other TIE squadrons reporting success defending gas extractors and supply ships. "It's up to us," Wyl urged as one by one the tanker's containment pods fell away. But Chass's burnt arm throbbed and sent pain up to her skull and the music became harder to hear. She increased the volume until it felt like her ears would bleed.

Her fighter's strike foils scraped against the tanker more than once, leaving sparking trails. Her cockpit's gyrostabilizers failed, forcing her to keep her ship upright to prevent her body from being brutalized. But she held the vessel together. She found new targets. She tore another pod free, and another. She set her comm to broadcast to anyone listening, inflicting the saccharine deva pop on all the ships above Pandem Nai.

Together with her squadron, she stood against the storm to save a world.

### III

She couldn't see anymore. The canopy of her X-wing was plastered with ash and dust and oil, and a thick crack ran halfway down the center pane. Only one small patch remained blessedly clear, and Yrica Quell twisted her aching body so that she could glimpse the sky and the falling debris outside. She was down to a single functioning laser cannon, but that would suffice.

She soared and dived and soared and dived, blasting at the crumbling remnants of the orbital station above Induchron. The wreckage she couldn't destroy she broke into parts, hoping they would burn up in descent or land beyond the city borders. She thought she'd glimpsed the flare of a turbolaser from far below—a turret defending the city from ground level—but it might just have been a flicker in her sore eyes.

In truth, she didn't want to look below. She didn't want to know the state of Induchron.

She'd never heard sounds quite like the whines and moans her thrusters made. If she'd been in her TIE, she could have diagnosed the problem, made a guess at how long the starfighter could stay aloft, but the X-wing was too unfamiliar. A flashing indicator—one of the few lights on her console that still operated—warned her to eject. She didn't even know how an X-wing's ejection mechanisms worked; in all her studies, it hadn't occurred to her to check. If she'd had the breath, she would have laughed at the thought that that, of all things, would kill her. *Choked to death in your ejector harness. Your teachers would be proud, Yrica.*

She wasn't going to eject, though. Not until her last cannon stopped working.

She soared and dived, and she was less effective with every pass but she didn't stop firing. The metal rain hammered her ship and her body shook every time debris struck her canopy and lengthened the crack.

She chased a charred metal wheel like a gear toward the surface, firing staccato blasts as she attempted to see through the gap in the viewport ash. She had trouble contorting herself to observe, stay on target, and fire all at once, and she'd long since given up hope of assistance from D6-L. But the wheel was large enough to blast ten city blocks into a crater, and she had no choice but to snap shot after shot and try to do more than simply dent the metal.

She blindly slid a hand across the console, trying to divert more power to her weapon. Instead the whole fighter rumbled and she saw a white-hot streak race from beneath her cockpit toward the wheel.

She should have been out of proton torpedoes. The display had *told* her she was out, and she hadn't even done anything to trigger the weapon.

The torpedo struck. The wheel fragmented as the explosion bloomed, and Quell flew down through the white fire.

"Thank you," she whispered, though she doubted her astromech droid could hear her.

She was in the midst of pulling out of the dive when another metallic shriek rang through the X-wing. The fighter rolled and tumbled, ignoring Quell's attempts to right it and lurching haphazardly in response to the throttle. She peered outside and realized with alarm that her port-side foils were missing altogether, sheared entirely off at the base.

She couldn't fly. She couldn't stop. With her last functioning cannon now separated from her starfighter, she couldn't even fire at one final plummeting pylon before she fell onto the rocks of Pandem Nai.

# CHAPTER 21

## AFTER-ACTION REVIEW

**I**

**S**he woke in the cold and the dark. Her lips tasted of dust and ash. The gentle wind against her cheeks smelled like smoke and sent her consciousness whirling. She wanted to vomit at the overwhelming vertigo, but then the breeze died and she pried open her eyes.

Yrica Quell sat in the broken cockpit of her X-wing, drifting in and out of consciousness. There was no canopy between her and the night sky, and the starfighter was half buried in dirt and gravel, but she had somehow leveled out the ship while crashing. Between moments of numbing oblivion she determined that her body was intact—she'd surely broken bones again, but she had her limbs. She could *feel,* even if what she felt was pain in every extremity.

Eventually, aware that she was likely concussed and therefore likely to die if she continued slipping into blackness, she forced herself to unbuckle her harness and straighten in her seat. She fought through the sting in her neck to survey her surroundings and saw scrub plains extending in all directions, broken up only by low hills and distant mesas. Behind her, she saw faraway lights blinking and fading.

*Induchron?* she wondered. Had the city survived?

Her mission—her mistakes—swelled up in her at the thought. Dragging a breath into her raw lungs, she looked skyward and saw a pulsing glow beyond the thick clouds—a great swirling mass like a hurricane of flame. It churned high above the city lights, but as she watched it—and she watched it for a time she couldn't estimate, minutes or hours—it seemed to ebb instead of swell, slowly collapsing upon itself.

She wanted to take comfort in that. Maybe she hadn't ruined the planet after all.

But her mistakes were still too great to forgive.

A sound drew her attention: a chortling and screeching like a bird or a child's toy. She lowered her chin, turned toward the noise, and saw the source scurrying her way—a four-legged animal, wiry and mangy and sharp-beaked, colored the same dun as the surrounding landscape. It flinched and scampered half a meter back when it saw her move, then leisurely resumed its approach.

Other screeches rose up. There were five of the things, encircling the wreckage of the X-wing and watching Quell with glittering eyes.

*Scavengers.*

She peeled herself away from the chair and felt her body throb with pain as she searched for her pistol beneath the seat. She felt skin scrape off her digits as she dug ineffectually under levers and springs. At last, she found what she was looking for and gripped the weapon in both hands as she stood.

She almost lost her balance, but she wedged her feet in place and rested her elbow against the top of the ship. She could see now, just a meter away, the dome of her astromech unit. The droid was covered in black dust and char, and its indicator lights were off. For an instant Quell thought: *I'm sorry, D6-L. You never wanted to fly a starfighter,* and though she was struck by the absurdity of mourning an astromech she couldn't bring herself to laugh.

The scavengers screeched. Together they crept forward. Quell lowered her blaster and aimed at the dust.

Whatever she'd done today—no matter how many people she'd killed or nearly killed—she didn't want to die torn apart by beaked monsters.

She wasn't sure she had the heart to live, but that was a problem for later.

The screeching became an angry trill. Quell pulled the trigger. Nothing happened.

She wanted to shake the blaster or toss it furiously aside, but she didn't have the strength for either. She squeezed the trigger a second time; she heard an electrical pop and smelled burning plastoid. One of the scavengers was loping ahead with beak parted, now, and she pulled the trigger again and again, until finally the weapon leapt in her hand and a crimson bolt slammed into the dust, raising smoke and sparks.

The scavengers scuttled back over the rocks, but they didn't go far.

Quell felt another spell of vertigo. She rested more heavily on her elbow and waited for the creatures to return.

She stood there as the fire waned in the night sky, forcing herself to stay awake and shivering in the easy breeze. She observed the scavengers as they circled and sniffed and crept forward, and every time one charged she jolted to alertness, frantically trying to bring her blaster to life before Pandem Nai's monsters could tear her guts out. Each time, she was convinced she was going to die. Each time, the blaster sent the scavengers retreating at the last possible moment.

In the back of her mind, she knew she should have searched the X-wing's cargo compartment for emergency supplies. Found a flare, or better yet a signaling device to alert someone that she was still alive. She lacked the strength. She doubted the compartment remained intact. It was all she could do to hold off the scavengers.

Would they leave in the morning? Would daylight scare them away? she wondered.

She wasn't sure she wanted to see Pandem Nai in the daytime, exposed and scarred.

When the scavengers began squawking and clacking their beaks, she was slow to perceive that something had changed. The creatures were no longer looking at her, and the wind had suddenly strengthened and turned warm. There was a humming sound beyond the awful drone inside her head—the low, distant rumble of a ship.

By the time the scavengers fled back across the plains, she finally spotted it: a U-wing performing a vertical descent, positioned to land within a stone's throw of the X-wing. Quell felt a lurch of hope, then realized the crest of Alphabet Squadron was missing from the hull. The ship *might* have come from the New Republic fleet, but it wasn't Kairos.

It settled delicately onto the dust plain, its running lights painfully bright. The loading door slid open and she saw two figures inside: one, a humanoid silhouette, and the other a sphere hovering a meter above the deck, distinguished by a glowing red dot like an eye.

*Hello, IT-O,* she thought. *Hello, Adan.*

Her knees bent, and she rested them against the interior of the cockpit to stop herself from sinking.

Adan emerged from the ship, antenna-stalks raised. After stepping out onto the dust, he looked to either side as if expecting to be ambushed; then he clasped his own wrists and marched toward the X-wing. The torture droid didn't move, observing from inside.

Quell heard the blaster slipping from her hand and striking the floor of the cockpit.

"Why you?" she slurred. She should have been more grateful, but she lacked the strength for courtesy. She was as barren and open as the plains of Pandem Nai.

Even so, she'd expected Adan to smile.

"I know about your last mission," he said.

She tried to comprehend. "What last mission?"

"I know about your last mission with Shadow Wing. I know the truth about Operation Cinder." His voice was edged with steel.

"I don't know what you mean." That was true—the lies and the guilt and the confusion of her concussion blended together.

The intelligence officer's antenna-stalks curled inward. His shoulders stiffened. Quell had heard him rage before, but she'd never learned to tell what was real and what was performance. "You want to lie about it *here*? After what happened today?" He did smile now, but it didn't reach his voice. "If you have so little shame, maybe we should leave you on Pandem Nai."

It wasn't the threat that stung.

*If you have so little shame . . .*

She'd been drowning in shame for a month. She could barely breathe.

"What do you want?" she asked.

"Start with a confession," Adan said, "and we'll go from there."

It wasn't too much to ask.

This is the story she told.

Yrica Quell had never believed in the Empire. Not the way some of her comrades had—not with the patriotic fervor of a true disciple or the resigned sense of necessity she saw in Clone Wars veterans. She'd left home and joined the Academy with the fantasy of learning to fly and defecting to the Rebel Alliance; nothing she'd seen since had convinced her that her Empire was just, or that her Emperor was a righteous man.

What she believed in was her unit. Major Soran Keize had told her once, in a moment when she'd doubted her mission, "We fight for our brothers and sisters beside us." She'd clutched those words since then.

She'd believed in the 204th. She'd believed in Major Keize. And when rebel terrorists had assassinated the Galactic Emperor, she'd seen it as an attack not just on the Empire but on every Imperial.

"Those last six months before Endor—you don't know what they were like on our side." She didn't hear the words as she said them. She didn't see Adan's face. Instead she pictured Major Keize's angular cheeks and thin lips. "Every day there was a new rebel attack, and we kept trying to hit back but—no matter how hard we hit, no matter what we did, you kept coming.

"We shed so much blood just trying to stop you, and it didn't work. No one wanted to do the things we did. We were tired of killing, but we didn't have a choice."

It wasn't completely true. There were those who'd joined the bombardment of Mek'tradi eagerly instead of with somber determination, but Quell hadn't been among them.

In those last months, she'd forgotten her fantasies of joining the Rebellion. She'd fought with the 204th because she had nothing else to fight for, and closed herself to enemy propaganda and sightings of prisoners and anything that gave a face to her foe. In the days after the Emperor's death, she'd walked the decks of the *Pursuer* in shock and slept in the same bed as Sergeant Meriva Greef just for the warmth and comfort. She hadn't been alone in her distress. If anything, she'd kept her senses better than most.

For two weeks the *Pursuer* had jumped from system to system, trying to find a battle worth fighting. When orders had finally come in, everyone knew—the senior officers vanished like exorcised ghosts.

The briefing had come six hours later, after two squadrons had already departed on secret tasks. Quell had sat in her rigid seat as Major Keize declared, "Operation Cinder is under way."

"This is the first galactic counterattack since the Battle of Endor," he said, "based on contingency plans prepared some time ago. The 204th has a small but critical role to play, and I expect the very best from all of you."

Major Keize had displayed holograms of the Nacronis system, describing in detail the planet's defense systems and its unique meteorology. He'd discussed each stage of a complex assault leading to the deployment of specialized explosives in atmosphere to stoke Nacronis's siltstorms. Quell had listened, yet the pieces hadn't coalesced in her mind until she'd stood and asked:

"Sir? What is the strategic objective of the mission?"

"The strategic objective," Major Keize said, "is the elimination of all enemy presence on Nacronis, up to and including all resources that could be subverted by the enemy."

She understood then what Operation Cinder was: the destruction of worlds.

She didn't ask any more questions.

In the fourteen hours between the briefing and the mission launch, she did the same thing she'd learned to do over the course of many months. She pushed away memories of broken bodies and burnt vehicles. She buried her youthful fantasies in the dark of her mind. And she told herself she fought for her unit.

She could have spoken with Major Keize. He was busy—meeting with the squadron commanders in strange, private conferences in cargo bays and machine shops—but she knew him well. He would have made time for her. Yet she'd asked enough of him, and he had other tasks, and she knew her duty.

Just after twenty-three hundred hours shipboard time, Quell checked in with the ground crews and her comrades and confirmed that her squadron (commanded by Captain Nosteen, who had appointed Quell his second-in-command upon her transfer fourteen weeks prior) was ready for combat. She climbed into her TIE fighter and, moments after the *Pursuer* jumped into the Nacronis system, launched from the Star Destroyer's hangar with her fellow pilots and raced toward Nacronis.

Nosteen was a competent commander, and after Major Keize transmitted final instructions to the wing and ordered his own squadron to intercept the first rebel defenders, Nosteen directed Quell and the others—Tonas and Barath, Xion and Hastun, and six more—to escort the TIE bombers into the atmosphere.

Tonas was the first to die. He went in the line of duty, positioning his ship between an enemy X-wing and the bomber it targeted. With quick, efficient movements through the sky, Quell maneuvered to the X-wing's rear and shot it from behind. Barath was the next loss, struck by a surface-to-air missile no one detected until it was too late.

The bombers began delivering their payloads. The vortex detonators—customized explosives programmed for one purpose— increased the fury of the siltstorm forming in Nacronis's atmosphere. The TIE fighters were buffeted by the gale as they continued their defense of the bombers. Captain Nosteen died then, incinerated by a bolt of lightning, and Quell took command of the remaining pilots in her squadron.

Theirs was one of many storms stoked across Nacronis. They nursed their charge to the size of a sea, then a continent. The enemy stopped attacking by the time all the planet's storms merged together.

Quell observed from above even after the bombers returned to the *Pursuer*. She watched as the siltstorms ravaged the surface and the planet's life was snuffed out. Without Captain Nosteen, no one tried to order her home.

She didn't understand why she stayed. But when the storm diminished to a mere flurry, she took her TIE fighter down. She flew over a ruined city flooded with silt and glimpsed specks in the mud that might have been bricks or corpses (impossible to know from so far away). She drifted into the marshes and landed. "Engine trouble," she reported to the *Pursuer*. "I'll make repairs from here."

She stripped off her helmet, climbed out of her fighter, waded into the silt, and stared into the wind as the colorful mud slashed at her cheeks and painted her face.

*Just for a minute,* she promised herself. Then she would return to her squadron and the *Pursuer* and her duty.

She'd had every intention of keeping that promise. But she didn't.

"I couldn't," she told Adan. "I'd turned a planet into a graveyard and I couldn't go back."

But that was a lie. It was a different lie from the one she'd told Adan the first time, but it was a lie nonetheless.

She stood in the silt as if transfixed until the second TIE landed barely fifty meters away. She straightened her back and raised her chin, wondering if she was to be arrested, executed, or merely scolded. She intended to meet her fate with dignity, regardless, and she watched the other pilot descend into the muck and stride toward her.

"Major," she called, when she recognized him at last.

"Lieutenant Quell," Major Keize said, lifting off his helmet. The wind nearly vanquished his words. "You shouldn't be here."

"I reported in—" she began, but his eyes held on her, silenced her like an unseen force around her throat.

"You shouldn't be here," he repeated, and drew close enough to stop shouting. "You told me before—you told me everything I needed to know, but I didn't expect things to fall apart so quickly.

"You shouldn't be in the 204th."

She shuddered. Her neck and shoulders felt like ice. "I did my part," she said. "I know I shouldn't have landed but I did the job, I made sure it happened after Captain Nosteen—"

Keize stepped forward and dug his fingers into her shoulder. The black fabric of her flight suit, now stained with color, bunched together. "You were extraordinary today. I don't doubt your dedication or your loyalty. No one ever should. But Lieutenant—Yrica—" His hand slid off her shoulder and he wiped the silt on his hip. "You've been sick. You've grown sicker with every mission against the rebels. You *told* me that."

"I didn't say anything like that," she said, though she had. "You told me I had to keep fighting. For the unit, for my comrades."

"That was before we lost the war."

She couldn't breathe. They didn't talk about *losing the war* aboard the *Pursuer*. They talked about setbacks, about the assassination of the Emperor, about what would come next. Never about losing.

"The Empire's not going to pull together and there's not going to be another Emperor," he said. "That was clear a day after Endor, and since then we've all just been in mourning. But it's time we accepted it. Time you moved on, because—" His eyes flashed, his face suddenly full of controlled fury.

"If you would do *this*," he went on, and swept his hand, gesturing to the corpse of Nacronis, "then there's nothing that will drive you out. You'll stay with the 204th out of honor and duty. You'll stay until the sickness leaves you empty and either it kills you or the rebels do. But there's no *point* to it anymore. There's no *need* for the unit, no use dying for brothers and sisters who don't have to die at all."

She couldn't deny any of it. She would stay with Shadow Wing forever, and it would kill her. And she knew that her mentor was being kind when he said that it was honor and duty that would keep her there when in fact it was fear—fear of being wrong and fear of her own guilt and complicity. All of it was clear in her mind, crystallized by the mortal terror she felt at his words.

"What am I supposed to do?" she asked.

"Do what you wanted from the beginning. Join the rebels. Join their New Republic. You have the nature of a soldier, and the need for— well. Trust me when I say I see the need."

She couldn't feel her limbs. The chill ran too deep. Her face felt blasted by the grit in the wind. "Are you ordering me to do this?" she asked, voice rising in a challenge.

"Yes," he said.

Her challenge met and defeated, her voice fell again. She felt a wash of shame at resisting so little and asked, "What about you? You're still here. You tell me to leave, but you're still here."

"I don't have your sickness," he said, "and I still have work to do."

"What kind of work?"

"*Most* don't have your sickness. But most aren't blind, either. I'll do what I can, but I will leave, and very soon. Best to set an example."

"And you'll join—"

"No."

She licked yellow sand from her lips and spat it out. Keize's voice was the voice of a major to his subordinate—clear and confident and uninterested in explanation.

"They'll accept you," he said.

"After this?" she asked.

"We'll make sure of it."

And they had. Major Keize had returned to his fighter and, without a wasted shot or a wasted moment, destroyed Quell's own craft. The blast had left her injured, and though she doubted that had been part of Keize's plan she was sure he didn't regret it. The wounds would make her defection all the more plausible.

She'd waited there for days, sheltering in the wreckage of her TIE, until the New Republic had found her. By then, she'd had plenty of time to practice the story of how she'd tried and failed to thwart Operation Cinder.

"Someone helped me on Nacronis," she told Caern Adan, as she faced him across the dusty plain of Pandem Nai. "He advised me to leave. He destroyed my fighter. You know what happened next."

Her arm trembled and nearly buckled. It was all that held her up against the ruined cockpit of her X-wing, and she knew her position made her appear fragile. (She *was* fragile, always had been, and she didn't know how much of her body was broken.) Adan hadn't spoken, hadn't asked a single question, and she aimed the last of her words like weapons: "I'm with the New Republic now. I have been since Traitor's Remorse and I've done everything you've asked. I'm here and I'm loyal."

"You destroyed a world," Adan said. There was no emotion in his voice. It wasn't a question, so she didn't answer it.

"You almost did it again today," he said.

She had no defense against that.

"What are you going to do?" she asked.

Adan expelled a soft, breathy sound that became a chuckle, then a boisterous laugh that stretched to the embers in the sky. He raised his arms and declared, "Nothing! I'm going to do nothing."

She stared. He dropped his arms and the laughter disappeared like oil combusting into flame. "You're going to keep leading your squadron," he said. "You're going to keep working for me, and you're not going to question or disobey because I know the truth and I know you don't deserve the chance you've gotten."

"Keep leading Alphabet Squadron," she said, trying out the words as if they were in another language. "Why?"

"Because you're not done. You promised me Shadow Wing and you failed to deliver."

"They—" Her brain wasn't functioning right. She wanted to slap herself. She had too many thoughts and they were all forming too slowly. *What happened up there?*

"They're gone. We confirmed Grandmother's death, and we're still tallying the TIE kills, but we know the bulk of them escaped during the chaos. I put that on you, Lieutenant—your plan, your mistakes, and your decision to abandon the mission halfway through to shoot down garbage."

*I saved Induchron,* she thought. Or maybe she said it aloud, too soft for him to hear. She wondered if it was even true—the distant city lights told her she hadn't utterly failed, but maybe she was too quick to claim that small triumph.

Then she heard Adan's words echo in her broken skull, bouncing between shards of bone. *They're gone.* Her comrades had escaped Pandem Nai. She forced herself to play soldier, to guess at the consequences, and said in a slurred, droning voice: "If Grandmother's gone, they won't be the threat they were. They won't have her. They won't have Major Keize. They won't have anywhere to go . . ."

"Then you won't have to work for me much longer," Adan said. "But they *are* still dangerous, even without a leader. Are you going to tell me they're not?"

She shook her head. It hurt, but it hurt less than trying to talk.

Adan scoffed and glanced toward the fires above. "You should know New Republic High Command considers this operation a success. Pandem Nai is free, a vital strategic resource is out of Imperial hands, and no matter how close we came, we *didn't* wipe out an entire planet's population. If General Syndulla weren't already a war hero, they'd call her one now. I expect a commendation along with a reprimand for carelessness." He gave Quell a final, pointed look before turning away. "Enjoy the victory, Lieutenant. It might be a while before you get another."

A victory, then. That was the New Republic's verdict.

She thought about it as she was being half carried to the U-wing by someone she couldn't see. She wondered if she agreed as she lay in the cargo netting with the torture droid floating above her administering sonic treatments and pumping her full of anesthetics. *Victory.* It didn't seem right, yet Quell decided she could accept it.

She didn't have another choice.

# CHAPTER 22

# CELEBRATION FOR HEROES

I

The victory party was aboard the *Lodestar,* and though a handful of officers had tried to forestall it—*there's still cleanup to be done,* they said; *Pandem Nai may contain pockets of Imperial resistance,* they said—they'd been unable to halt the eruption of exuberant forces from the Krayt Hut all the way to the hangar. For one delicate moment, when the *Lodestar*'s captain had marched snarling through the corridors, it had appeared possible that the party might be snuffed out; but then someone yelled, "The general says she'll allow it!" (a shout that was answered with "General Syndulla has surrendered!"), and the celebration had become unstoppable.

Wyl Lark always enjoyed a party, and he felt buoyed by the joy of the others on the battleship. He passed through the crowd, embracing strangers and toasting mechanics seated happily in the tight corridors of the vessel. He heard a roar come from the direction of the turbolift and someone yelling, "To the heroes of Pandem Nai!" and he smiled as he caught a glimpse of the New Republic special forces team that had planted the explosives on the orbital station.

The specforce troops marched past him and he pressed his back against the wall to allow them passage. They were nearly gone when one—a yellow, leathery-skinned humanoid with twice Wyl's body mass—turned back and grabbed Wyl by the shoulders, grinning a wild grin. "Chass's buddy!" the man cried. "Alphabet boy!"

"Alphabet boy," Wyl agreed with a smile. The man's breath was noxious, and he was leaning against Wyl as much as embracing him. Yet he exuded pure delight, and for that moment Wyl loved him.

"You all did good out there," the man said. "And hey—hey! You keep it up like that, and maybe someday they'll let you back in the starfighter corps! Get you out of Intelligence and let you work for a living—"

Wyl gave the trooper the gentlest of shoves, which sent him sprawling back into the arms of his brethren. The yellow-skinned man laughed in delight, and Wyl spent the next hour being bodily dragged by the specforce troops around the *Lodestar*, alternately mocked and praised.

He didn't mind. The troops had earned their accolades, and all of it felt familiar. It reminded Wyl of Riot Squadron and the days after the Battle of Endor—and if it troubled him that the most joyous times he could remember were among warriors instead of the people of Home, he had a thousand distractions in front of him to carry his thoughts elsewhere.

The celebration showed no sign of stopping by the time he slipped away on his own again. He was hunting now, scanning the crowds for familiar faces he'd barely seen since the chaos and aftermath of the battle. It was foolish, he knew, to worry—nothing had changed since he'd landed his burning, rattling ship in the hangar—but it felt like a loss to be without his squadron.

The sound found him before the sight: an electronic squeal and a series of loud pings. He spun around in the hangar and crouched almost in the same motion in front of the antique C-series droid. "Hey!" Wyl called in delight, and the droid hobbled forward. It smelled like smoke, and much of its paint had turned black. "You doing okay? You got a little singed, huh?"

"What've I told you about talking to the droid?" a voice asked.

Wyl rubbed a fingertip through the charred paint, dislodging flakes. "It never ends well," he said. "How are you, Nath?"

Nath Tensent, like his droid, had been burned—the red-and-white lattice of a fresh scar ran up his neck and to the right side of his chin. The mark was bold and angry now, but Wyl suspected it would fade with time and medical bacta. "I'm all right," Nath said. "Got off easy next to everyone but you."

"I was luckiest," Wyl agreed. The warmth in his smile didn't reach his voice.

"Nah," Nath said. "You're blasted *good*, is what you are." He clapped Wyl's shoulder with a heavy paw.

They drifted through the hangar, discussing their comrades. Quell, Wyl had heard, had been evacuated to the medical frigate, while Nath had seen Chass's electrical burns being tended aboard the *Lodestar*. Kairos was alive and unhurt (so far as Wyl could tell)—Wyl had seen her in passing, but didn't expect to encounter her at the celebration. The only fatality of the squadron was, perhaps, Quell's astromech unit. "No way the ship can be salvaged, from what I hear," Nath said. "Maybe there's enough left of the droid to rebuild. Memory cores are durable."

"That droid was smart," Wyl said. "It could've found a way to preserve itself."

"Could've."

"It must've helped her, too. It must've known what she was doing over Induchron—"

Nath laughed. Wyl cocked his head and then understood as the larger man smiled apologetically. "Could've died a hero," Nath said. "When we know for sure, if the news is bad? We'll drink to the tin box then."

*You're more sentimental than you pretend,* Wyl thought, though he said nothing of the sort.

When conversation about their colleagues faltered, they turned to talking about their ships; then to discussing the other celebrants, swapping rumors about romances among the ground crews and rivalries among the specforce operatives; then, finally, to stories of older battles and older celebrations. Wyl spoke of Jiruus, and what should have been his last night with Riot Squadron. Nath spoke of the day he was accepted to the Imperial flight academy.

They found their way to a seat atop one of the maintenance cranes. Their legs dangled off the crane's arm, six meters above one of Meteor Squadron's X-wings, and—out of earshot of the other celebrants at last—Wyl broached the subject that had been on his mind since finding T5. "You went off comms out there for a while," he said. "Even before the station started burning. You tried to make it look like you didn't, but you did."

He expected Nath to say: *There was a lot of interference.* Or maybe: *What are you blathering about? I was talking, same as you.*

But instead Nath rocked his head forward in a slow nod and didn't answer.

"Whatever happened out there—" Wyl paused and tried to meet Nath's gaze, but Nath was staring out at the hangar doors. "—you should've trusted me. I was your wingmate. You need someone besides Tee-five to watch your back."

Nath grunted, abruptly glanced Wyl's way, and asked, "How'd you know?"

Wyl smiled wryly. He thought of the bombing runs they'd made together—Nath's disappearance from his scanner and his intermittent silence. "You're a good liar, Nath. But you have to at least *try.*"

Nath laughed loudly, and the sound echoed through the massive room. "Fair, on both counts. But you? You'll get yourself killed one of these days. Next time wait for me before running off to save lives, huh?"

"Just be there when I call," Wyl said.

Nath clapped him on the back. Wyl nearly fell from the crane. "So what's that mean for you?" Nath asked. "You were on your way out when this whole thing—Shadow Wing and all—started. *Hellion's Dare* caught wind of Pandem Nai and now we've got the planet. You think you're done?"

"Shadow Wing's still around," Wyl said.

"Not much to it, though."

Wyl shrugged. "I don't know if Adan will see it that way. I'm pretty sure Quell won't."

"Probably not."

Wyl tapped at the metal of the crane, looking out at the crowd. "If the squadron isn't disbanded—if Adan and Quell and the others stay—" *If you and Chass stay.* "—then yes, I think I'll stick around. There's lots to do, isn't there?"

Nath nodded somberly. Wyl regretted his words like they were lies.

The mission of the *Hellion's Dare* was over. Riot Squadron's mission was over. Shadow Wing was still out there, but Wyl had never much cared for revenge.

Yet he'd been too long with his new comrades, now. He saw the greed and cruelty in Nath—his *friend* Nath—and how likely they were to get the man killed. He saw the desperation in Chass and the obsession in Quell. Even Kairos, for all her mystery, didn't seem to be a *healthy* woman.

How could he leave them, if Alphabet Squadron went on? What would become of them?

He'd been waiting to go Home for a long time. For their sake, he could wait awhile longer.

## II

"What's next for you, then?" Chass na Chadic asked, taking a swig of her ale.

By way of response, the woman sitting across from her in the cramped closet of Ranjiy's Krayt Hut pushed six cards onto the table. Chass looked from the cards to the woman's gloved hands and up to her helmeted face before grunting irritably. "Better answer than I expected," she admitted, and tossed her own cards down. Kairos had won the round.

Chass had run into the U-wing pilot while wandering through the celebration and asked her to play when two Vanguard Squadron fly-boys had slipped away from the card table. Chass hadn't really expected Kairos to agree, let alone be invested enough to win.

Yet for the first time, she found Kairos's presence soothing. The cryptic creature who murdered stormtroopers with obscene intensity brought a calm to the chaos of the party.

Chass dealt more cards. She scratched the bandages wrapped around her right arm. They played another round. Kairos won again. Chass could hear the conversations of thirty soldiers around her, but they mixed together into noise. In the absence of words, unwanted thoughts crept from the dark in the back of her brain toward the front. She tried to drown them in ale, to no avail.

"How did we survive out there?" she asked. It wasn't the question she wanted to ask, but it was close. "I mean, we shouldn't have, should we? There were five of us, and we went up against all of Shadow Wing. Hound Squadron and Riot Squadron *both* got killed."

Hound Squadron had died. The Cavern Angels had died. Before that, far away from Chass, Jyn Erso had died.

But Chass na Chadic kept living.

Kairos took the deck of cards, sorted and arranged them, then placed the deck in front of Chass.

"You going to tell my fortune with a sabacc deck?" Chass asked.

Kairos pushed the deck closer to Chass. Chass laughed throatily and leaned back in her chair, lifting the front legs off the floor and feeling her scalp touch the wall behind her. "Trick question," she said, "because I don't *have* a damn fortune."

Jyn Erso had died stopping the Death Star. Hound Squadron had died protecting the *Hellion's Dare*.

Chass na Chadic kept living. But never to do anything *useful*.

She took another swallow of her drink. "You know Wyl was at Endor? With Skywalker and all of them. He treats it like it was nothing and I just—" She flicked her fingers, sending drops of condensation onto Kairos's visor. Her lips worked, her mouth opening and closing.

She wanted to confess. She wanted to dredge the words from her skull and look at them in the soft, still light of Kairos's silence, expose them for what they were.

But she couldn't, and she slapped the bottom of the ale bottle onto the table instead.

They sat like that awhile. Chass absently shuffled the deck until Kairos tapped Chass's wrist with a gloved finger and pointed upward.

"What?" Chass asked.

Kairos, predictably, did not answer. Chass screwed up her face, trying to understand. She began to process the noise of nearby conversation and behind it—loud but barely audible under the din—the sound of music. Another moment passed before she recognized it as the deva pop she'd played while the world had fallen apart. The song she'd blasted through the comm as she, Wyl, Kairos, and Shadow Wing had fought together to cut away the tanker's gas pods.

"Is this mine?" she asked. Had she left the datachips in the cockpit? Had the ground crew been digging through her stuff?

Kairos sat implacably. The music kept playing—the awful, upbeat, sentimental song that had carried her through her final battle over Pandem Nai. The stillness was gone, and the desperation and despair crawled back to their nest behind Chass's brain. She could feel them, but the song suppressed their life.

The crowd shifted as someone pushed his way toward the closet and the card table. Wyl Lark emerged, boyish as ever and unmarked by the battle. He called Chass's name, and she smirked before rising to embrace him.

"I'll kill you if you stole my music," she murmured in his ear.

"Blame one of the ground crew," Wyl said, pretending not to study the bandages around her arm.

"Come on," Chass said. "Stay with us. Be our human buddy. We're going to celebrate like we saved the galaxy."

Maybe her heart wasn't in it. But for the moment, it was the best option she had.

## III

Nath could've spent the night mingling, polishing his reputation until the last of the tarnish was gone. He could've ingratiated himself with the specforce troops and bought a few favors for down the line. Instead he stayed close to Wyl and Chass and Kairos. He watched them dance—Wyl and Chass separately at first, then Wyl and Chass together, and finally, to his bemusement, Chass and Kairos. He bought the drinks when they dropped into their seats sweating and dehydrated, and watched a video feed of the celebrations taking place on Pandem Nai. *At least the locals are grateful,* Nath thought, though he supposed the Imperial loyalists were staying quiet.

When General Syndulla found her way to the Krayt Hut, Nath invited her over and bought her a drink, too. "You turned a disaster into a victory," she told them. "That's what you should remember about this day." Nath wasn't sure he believed it—he wasn't sure *she* believed it—but he appreciated her effort.

The five of them bickered and joked. He was surprised by how much he enjoyed the company of his squadron mates and Syndulla. Surprised he forgot *why* he was trading war stories with a hero of the New Republic and surprised by how natural it all felt.

He saw Chass weep at one point as she returned from the bathroom. He saw a faraway cast to Wyl's gaze as General Syndulla spoke about her youth on Ryloth; her accent slipped into something less refined and more provincial as she worried over what would become of her homeworld in the new galactic order.

They talked late into the night. Kairos was the first to depart. Not long after, Wyl and Chass rose to escort an intoxicated specforce trooper back to her bunk, and Nath was left alone with the general. He watched his comrades go, then asked, "So what do you really think?"

"About?" Syndulla asked.

"The fight today. *Turned a disaster into a victory* is fine for them, but don't tell me that's really the lesson you're taking away."

Syndulla shook her head, her head-tails swaying. "You're a suspicious man, Nath Tensent. Almost as bad as your commanding officer."

Nath grinned broadly. "How *is* Adan? Haven't had a chance to chat with him since landing."

That was true, although Nath had noticed Adan's transfer of credits into Nath's account. Payment for digging up dirt on Quell. So far as Nath was concerned, that meant his days working for the spy were over.

Unless Adan made him another offer, of course. He still needed to make a living.

"I know he went out to rescue Lieutenant Quell himself," Syndulla said. "Since then, my guess is he's been in contact with New Republic Intelligence and watching for whatever happens next. One of the perils of spy work—it's always busiest before and after the big fight."

Nath nodded. *He went out to rescue Lieutenant Quell himself.* He felt a twinge of—if not guilt—sympathy pain. From what he'd seen in Quell's file, he didn't imagine that encounter had been friendly. Adan had everything he needed to put a knife to Quell's throat.

Nath didn't much like Yrica Quell, but she hadn't killed his crew and she'd fulfilled her promise: helped him reach Shadow Wing and helped him murder Colonel Shakara Nuress. He didn't owe Quell. He didn't care to see her hurt, either.

*Not your problem,* he told himself. *Can't worry about all of them.*

He shook the thoughts away. "You didn't answer my question."

"About today's lesson?" Syndulla sat back, unfazed by Nath's persistence. Nath nodded and she wrinkled her nose before answering, "We're still learning. Not about Pandem Nai, but about all of it."

Nath waited. General Syndulla glanced surreptitiously to either side, checking to see if anyone was paying attention.

"I've been fighting this war for a long time," she said. "A lot of us have. And we know how to fight an impossible battle, but this . . . ?" General Syndulla sighed and looked past Nath, as if staring through the *Lodestar's* bulkhead into the scorched clouds of Pandem Nai. "We're old hands at losing. We're still learning how to win."

Nath considered the debts he'd accrued and the debts he'd paid off. He thought of Reeka and his old crew; of Adan, Quell, and his new squadron.

"I'll drink to that," he said.

He had no idea what he would do next.

# IV

Yrica Quell arrived aboard the *Lodestar* thirty minutes after midnight, fresh from the bacta tanks of the medical frigate. She stank of antiseptic washes and prickled like her whole body was waking from paralysis. The deck felt unsteady beneath her soles. She shouldn't have been on her feet at all—her medical droid had assured her of that, even as it had authorized her departure—but beds and bacta were in short supply aboard the *No Harm,* where the grim logic of computerized triage ruled.

The *Lodestar*'s hangar was aroar with New Republic soldiers and support crew, none of whom seemed to notice Quell or the other shuttle passengers. She drifted around the clusters of partygoers, catching snippets of conversation about Pandem Nai and Shadow Wing and Alphabet Squadron. It didn't seem right to be celebrating, but Quell didn't have the strength for outrage. Besides, it was the first time anyone had indulged since Argai Minor. The troops had been waiting a long while.

She'd intended to go directly from the shuttle to her bunk, but instead followed the path of least resistance. The currents of the crowd led her out of the hangar and down a series of corridors, and she was impressed to see that the celebration extended to multiple compartments of the battleship. She tried to think back to any victory party so sprawling aboard the *Pursuer,* and failed.

Just once, through a curtain of bodies, she spotted Chass na Chadic squeezing into a side room. Quell felt an urge to go to her and pushed it down.

*If your squadron is celebrating, let them do it by themselves.*

She was resting against a wall out of the flow of traffic when she heard a humming and a low voice. "You're looking well, Lieutenant Quell. I'm pleased you're recovering so rapidly."

"I look like garbage," she said. She turned to the torture droid, who bobbed in the air like a branch in a light breeze. Its presence sent her mind back to Pandem Nai and Adan, but she forced herself past those thoughts. "Thank you for treating me aboard the U-wing."

"It was my pleasure. I rarely get to exercise those skills."

She wanted to say: *More used to cutting open than sewing shut?* But it seemed ungrateful.

"The others aren't far," the droid said. "If you wish to join them, I can show you the way."

"Not tonight."

"I'm sure they'd welcome you."

"They're enjoying themselves."

The droid reached a full stop, as motionless as if it had been pinned to the air. Its red photoreceptor dilated. "Then join me awhile. Adan is occupied, and it seems a pity to attend the party alone."

Quell met the photoreceptor's stare. "I'm too tired for therapy."

"As am I. But if General Syndulla can walk among her troops as a fellow combatant, I can enjoy your company as a friend."

Quell laughed hoarsely. "Are we friends?"

"Would anyone else consider spending the victory party with a torture droid?" The droid's voice was mischievous, but Quell caught the note of self-pity. She wondered if it was intentional—a trick to elicit sympathy.

"All right," she said. "One night, we're friends."

The droid led them down the corridor, away from the noise and the bustle. Quell expected it to bring up her confession, but instead it told her about the signals from the ground on Pandem Nai: offers of surrender, broadcasts of crowds cheering in town squares, and messages from local officials pledging cooperation. "Pandem Nai, as surely as any other occupied world, desired freedom. It has that, thanks to you."

"That's not why we came," Quell said. "Do we have casualty numbers yet? From the civilian orbital stations? From the ground?"

"We do not. But you prevented—"

"Don't," she snapped. She paused to rest a hand on the piping lining the corridor, catching her balance. Then she resumed walking, still clutching the pipe. "I almost killed all of them."

The droid's humming scaled to a higher pitch. For an instant Quell thought her ears would split. Then the frequency changed again, and she could *feel* it more than hear it. The hum was almost calming.

"Don't," she said again. "I don't need it."

The humming stopped.

They turned a corner and arrived at a point defense station. Past a reinforced viewport, a turbolaser battery extended from the *Lodestar's* hull, and beyond the barrels of the cannons the shrouded orb of Pandem Nai spanned the horizon. Scarlet clouds concealed the continents and cities; only a few dark specks hinted at the orbital stations remaining.

"I almost ruined this," she said. Her voice was soft and passionless. "I decided to smash in the face of a defeated enemy and I thought I was being *heroic* because I was using rebel tactics.

"But I'm not a rebel. None of us are."

"The plan wasn't your responsibility. Caern Adan, General Syndulla, and her superiors all approved it."

"It was *my* plan. And I'm the one who should've known better."

Quell had experienced what it meant to have a dominant fleet behind her. She had hunted down determined warriors forced to flee to the far corners of the galaxy. She knew exactly the sort of carnage that resulted from applying massive pressure against a smaller force.

"You once asked me," the droid said, "why the Emperor ordered Operation Cinder."

She nodded, lowering herself into the defense station gunnery seat. "I remember. You said 'I couldn't say' and asked what *I* thought."

"And do you have an answer?"

Quell said nothing.

"Did he seek to save lives? To redeem himself? Was his motivation as pure as yours when you planned the attack on Pandem Nai?"

Her motivation hadn't been pure. But it hadn't been hateful, either.

She thought about the Emperor and Cinder and what had happened on Nacronis. "Maybe it was a sorting mechanism," she said. "A way to separate the people who would commit—who would obey that kind of command from the people who wouldn't."

"Perhaps. Can I offer my theory?" the droid asked.

"As a friend?"

"A proper therapist would let you figure it out yourself," the droid said. "But I'm ignoring boundaries tonight—so yes, as a friend."

Quell managed a strained smile and nodded. "What's your theory?"

"The answer," the torture droid said, "is simple: The Emperor who ordered Operation Cinder, who built two Death Stars, who oversaw countless genocides and massacres and created an Empire where torture droids were in common use, was not a man of secret brilliance and foresight.

"He was a cruel man. Petty and spiteful in the most ordinary of ways; and spiteful men do spiteful things. Whatever else he intended, *that* is at the root of it all."

Quell's instinct was to argue—to defend the Emperor she'd pledged to serve. She swallowed the words, knowing they came from propaganda holos and drill sergeants rather than intellect or experience. Even Major Keize had never argued the Emperor was a good man.

"He ruled the galaxy for over twenty years," she said instead. Her voice sounded small. She stared into the clouds of Pandem Nai. "Everything we are is because of him. How do we get past that?"

"Yrica," the droid said, with a voice that should have been condescending but instead sounded like a promise, "that's what we're all here to find out."

She leaned back in the gunnery chair. Her eyes stung.

On the night after her victory over Pandem Nai, Yrica Quell laughed, and the torture droid laughed with her.

## CHAPTER 23

# UNFINISHED BUSINESS

I

The rain in Tinker-Town had been ceaseless but apathetic—constant, thin, spattering rain that a person could almost grow accustomed to. The rain of Vernid was different. The drops came swift and heavy, brutalizing bare skin and flooding every crack and crevice in the landscape. A person could drown in Vernid's rains before growing used to them.

Yet after a few short weeks, Devon had grown fond of the world. He could almost imagine calling it home.

The Harch had been wise to send him here, he thought, as he peeled off layers of waterproofing in the cantina's cloakroom. When he'd hung his belongings above the drain, he marched barefoot into the common area and approached a corner table where four large humanoids passed around a bowl of steaming sludge. "Devon!" a burly man cried, and the others jostled to make room.

The cantina was packed; the evening shift at the dig-rigs was over and, except at the height of harvest, the worm farmers always called it quits after nightfall. Devon joined his work crew with a murmured greeting and took a generous swallow of the sludge. It burned his throat and sent warm pulses down his spine. "Tyros not joining us?" he asked.

"Got a lad he fancies, next town over. Catches the shuttle once a week." The speaker was a topknotted man perhaps twice Devon's body mass—Klevin, the crew's hauler.

"Boy's going to miss check-in one of these mornings," a woman with a grid of facial scars muttered. This was Nanchia, the crew's rigs-woman. "I'm not going to cover for him."

"Only way he'll learn," Klevin agreed.

The bowl reached Devon a second time; then a third not much later. The drinking of mijura, he'd learned, was part of the culture of Vernid— not a ritual he embraced, but one he respected. Even if it meant he went home some nights with an aching head and a sway to his stride.

A waiter passed by the table. The work crew shouted requests. Somewhere in the back of the cantina, a platter slid off the bartop and onto the floor. Devon shouldn't have heard it in all the noise, but he did; then he realized that the noise had diminished.

"Lower it!" someone from the underside crew shouted, and the buzz of a cheap viewscreen grew louder as the display unfurled behind the bar. Through wavering scan lines, Devon could barely make out the image of roaring flames.

Klevin was saying something but Devon ignored him, trying to hear the viewscreen's audio. Something about a New Republic victory off the Skangravi-Mestun Regional Hyperlane. A world called Pandem Nai and massive destruction leading to an Imperial defeat. Devon squinted at pictures of orbital mining facilities and TIE fighter squadrons and a half-repaired Star Destroyer bound up in scaffolding.

"Another one down," Nanchia muttered.

Devon shook his head briskly. Klevin was replying. Again, the picture of the flames. The broadcast cut to a New Republic senator asserting her pride over the operation's success and her concern over the careless and brutal tactics of the Empire.

"Bastards," Devon said, though he knew he shouldn't have.

"What's that?" said the man across from Devon. His eyes were wide and his beard of tendrils was festooned with gold rings. This was Vi'i'che, the crew's cranksman.

"They're bastards," Devon repeated. Some portion of his brain warned him, knew better than to allow the words, but he ignored it. "The New Republic comes sweeping in with a fleet—enough firepower to destroy any garrison—and has the audacity to act surprised when there's collateral damage."

"Maybe the Imperials should've surrendered, if they didn't want *damage*," Nanchia spat.

"You think they had the chance?" Devon asked. He smiled coldly, even as his mind raged at him. "You think the New Republic declared their presence and tried to negotiate a surrender? Or did they use guerrilla tactics, like they were still a bunch of terrorists without laws of war or rules of engagement to worry over?"

Devon was not a man prone to outbursts. Even now, he kept his voice level. He saw what was occurring, understood exactly why, and couldn't stop it. The sludge had shaken the words loose, but it hadn't given them form. He could blame only himself for that.

"Anything they did to the Imps counts as justice, far as I'm concerned," Klevin said. "You disagree?"

"I do," Devon said. "I thought the word *bastards* covered it."

Klevin rose fast enough to topple his chair. Devon watched the motion and saw, at the same time, other forms approaching him from across the room. He sensed the wariness from Nanchia, the concern from Vi'i'che and the nearby waiter.

"Maybe you've had too much mijura," Vi'i'che said.

"Maybe so," Devon agreed. He rose from his seat as well, slower than Klevin and with his hands on the tabletop. "Maybe best if I head home early tonight."

His heart was beating rapidly. His body was ready to fight. But he bore these people no ill will, and striking them wouldn't change anything shown on the viewscreen.

He felt bodies closing in, heard someone a pace behind him. But

Klevin stepped aside as Devon walked back toward the cloakroom. He was alone inside, and pulled on layer after layer, forcing his adrenaline-suffused limbs to move slowly, calmly, precisely.

He walked the bridges back home—metal catwalks suspended a meter above the muck. It was a longer path than slogging directly through the mud, but it gave him a chance to wear himself down. The rain slapped at him and beat at his hood and shoulders.

He liked the people of Vernid. They were hard workers, bitter and strong and loyal, and he'd felt at ease among them the first day he'd arrived—the day the Harch's contact, the dig-rig overseer, had offered him a position on the crew. He admired Klevin's protectiveness and Nanchia's devotion to her hounds and the emotion Vi'i'che instilled in his work songs.

He was getting tired of wandering. He feared he had only himself to blame.

No one spoke about the incident in the cantina as Devon checked in for work the next morning. Klevin kept his distance, and Devon partnered with Tyros on the rig's south side. Tyros was the youngest of the group, and he adjusted cranks as Devon pulled levers and flashed signal lamps at the other crews. Against the noise of the rain and under the gloom of the cloud cover, light made for more reliable communications than sound.

"True there was trouble last night?" Tyros asked, an hour into the shift.

"No trouble," Devon answered, grunting as he pushed an argumentative lever into position. "Could've been, but there wasn't."

"Sounds like trouble to me," Tyros said, and laughed.

Devon didn't hold it against the boy. But he wasn't keen on the notion that word was spreading.

As the day continued, he watched Klevin, Nanchia, and Vi'i'che whenever they were near. He kept alert for anyone else—he took care not to position himself with his back to a doorway, avoided the isolated corners of the rig, and checked his surroundings before leaning over the railings—but it was those three who knew him best and who had reacted most strongly. If trouble *was* coming, odds were decent one of them would be the source.

He didn't avoid his comrades. He did his duty and said nothing to indicate his wariness. But he hadn't survived as long as he had—aboard the *Whitedrift Exchange,* in Tinker-Town, and during an era in his life that now seemed distant—by ignoring potential threats.

During his meal break, he drained a pouch of nutrient broth and checked the shuttle schedules. If he had to leave the planet, he wouldn't find transport on any of the public lines for at least five days. His best bet was to find work aboard a freighter—assuming one passed through Vernid's single spaceport before a shuttle came—or, if necessary, to stow away on any departing vessel he could find. None of the options were pleasing, though he wasn't particularly *worried*. In a worst-case scenario, he could disappear into the mud plains awhile.

Devon was a survivor. Survival was exhausting.

When evening came and the shift ended, the crew trickled out to the turbolifts leading off the rig. Devon remained to double-check Tyros's work (the boy had a habit of leaving equipment in the water, justifiably irritating the night crew) and scanned the status displays on the wet console. He heard footsteps ring on the metal walkway and made no motion to turn.

"Hey!" Klevin called. "You coming tonight?"

"I thought I'd skip it," Devon said. He kept his focus on the displays. "Stomach isn't sitting well today."

Klevin laughed harshly, then spat into the rain. "That how you settle things in the Core Worlds? Crawl and hide out of sight?"

Devon had never claimed to be from the Core Worlds, but he supposed almost any world was closer to the Galactic Core than Vernid.

"Just trying to avoid trouble," he said. He turned at last and saw Klevin three meters away. The man showed his teeth, grinning brightly. "I came to Vernid looking for quiet," Devon continued. "If I can't find it—if I'm the one who makes too much noise—say the word and I'll move on."

The offer was genuine. Klevin was a brute when he wanted to be, but his mind was sharp and he was representative of his community. If Klevin didn't believe there was a place for Devon on Vernid, he was probably right.

"You serious?" Klevin swore and squinted at Devon. "You've got more spine than that. I saw you half drown hauling Grahamos out of the mucking pit. Why pretend you're a coward?"

Devon met Klevin's gaze and said nothing.

Klevin laughed and spat again. This time the noise was sudden and his whole body shook, as if he'd been struck by a revelation. "This about your *politics*? Hell, you know where you are?"

Again, Devon didn't reply. He forced his shoulders to relax; avoided any posture that would invite aggression.

"No one cares about your politics, Devon. You're a decent man and a decent worker. Stay as long as you want. Leave if you want. Just don't whine about it, huh?"

Klevin guffawed again, striding past Devon and smacking him with a wet hand. Devon let himself smile, and a few minutes later followed Klevin out of the dig-rig.

He didn't allow himself to feel comforted by Klevin's words. His instincts for survival—his hard-earned paranoia—were too strong. But he went to the cantina that night and found that nothing seemed to have changed. No one watched him. Nanchia joked about keeping him away from the screen. They drank mijura together and pooled their credits to bet on the Cantonica podraces.

His instincts wouldn't fade. But he allowed himself to hope.

The next day was the Red Moon Festival, when the clouds parted and Vernid's second satellite hung like a lantern over the world. The rain didn't stop but it lessened enough to be bearable, and in the evening the dig-rig workers rode out to Bakerstown for the celebration. Under a tin roof singing to the beat of raindrops, three dozen stalls offered up food and drink and games. It was, Devon thought, a small and sorry event even compared with what he'd seen aboard the *Whitedrift Exchange*.

But it was a place of joy on a world that didn't see much in the way of festivals—and the joy was real, even if the machine-spun stringfruit candies weren't. He spent most of the night observing, but when Vi'i'che tried to coax him into the knife-throwing competition, Devon relented; and when Tyros urged Devon to come, in Tyros's words, "Talk to my friends about the work and make me look good," Devon laughed and went along.

"You ever need something from me—you get eyes for one of the pretty folk here—you let me know, all right?" Tyros murmured to him when Devon excused himself after half an hour of boosting Tyros's reputation. "I know everyone. Plenty of them would like you."

"Maybe someday," Devon answered, and was surprised to realize he meant it.

Shortly before midnight, Devon decided he'd seen enough and exited the cover of the festival grounds. The public speeder was at the edge of Bakerstown, a few minutes away down the labyrinth of bridges. Devon tugged at his gloves and adjusted his hood as he returned to the rain.

He'd been gone no more than a minute when he heard someone shout his name. Three figures were rapidly strolling his way from the direction of the festival. Klevin stood in the lead, recognizable beneath his rain gear only by his burly physique. His two comrades were poorly dressed for Vernid—they wore ordinary jackets and looked soaked to the bone. They were a man and a woman, both human, the former young and the latter, perhaps, close to Devon's own age. Each wore a blaster on his or her hip.

"These strangers wanted to meet you," Klevin said as they stopped a short distance away. His face looked weary and grim. "Didn't really make it a choice."

"It's all right," Devon said. He looked to the woman and waited.

"Devon Lhent?" the woman asked.

"Yes," Devon said. "I left my scandocs at home."

"We're with New Republic Intelligence. We know who you are."

The man spoke next. "Why don't you come with us?"

Devon nodded slowly, as if this was the introduction he'd expected.

He watched their eyes. He watched their hands. "I'm not your problem anymore," he said. "If you found me, you must realize that. Leave Vernid now, and you won't ever have cause to regret it."

"That's not how this works," the woman said. "You know that."

"No one will come to harm," Devon said.

"Would that excuse have worked under the Empire?"

"I thought you were supposed to be *better* than the Empire," Devon said.

He knew it was imprudent to bait them. He also suspected, from the spies' expressions, that nothing he could say would matter.

The woman reached for her weapon first. Devon determined that on the rain-slick bridge, he wouldn't be able to reach her before she fired. Instead of charging, he turned and leapt in a single motion, diving off the side of the bridge and splashing into the muck below. Crimson flashed and lit the catwalks.

*Shooting to kill, not to stun,* he thought.

He ducked beneath the bridge as the male spy dropped down on the opposite side. Devon grappled with him before the man could find his footing, wrenching the man's arm and turning his blaster away from Devon, inward toward his chest. The man's finger was already on the trigger. Confounded by the mud and darkness, muscles straining in Devon's grasp, the man squeezed his weapon and shot himself dead. The stench of burnt flesh mixed with the reek of the mud.

Devon dropped the body and spun as he heard a shout. The woman had fallen off the bridge, entangled with Klevin. Klevin's advantage in strength, however, was not an advantage in skill. The woman slipped from his grasp, blaster still in hand as she struggled to rise.

Devon snatched away the weapon in one swift move. The woman was too disoriented to stop him, but she was repositioning to sweep her leg beneath him and knock him to the ground.

She didn't have the chance. He aimed the blaster he'd taken from her. At such close range, he couldn't miss. He didn't.

He drew in a long breath as he looked to the two corpses, confirming his kills. Then he looked over to Klevin, who stood unhurt beside him.

"I saw it," Klevin said. "They pulled first."

Devon nodded. He worked back through his memory, considering what his assailants had said. Studying the words. Examining the implications.

"Don't you worry," Klevin said. He was shaking, but his voice was certain. "Plenty of places two strangers could've disappeared on Vernid. We'll have some work to do, maybe even need to tell the overseer, but he'll back you. Same as we will."

It should have been comforting. But Klevin's words were buzzing in the back of Devon's thoughts. His hands were trembling, too, now—shaking with anger that rose as it had in the cantina. Anger that had been growing since Tinker-Town.

"No," Devon said.

"You're one of ours."

"No." His thin lips worked into a snarl as he disassembled the blaster, tossing barrel and gas chamber and power pack into the mud. It was the motion of an anxious child tearing up blades of grass. "No. Someone always catches up with me. One side or the other, it's always *someone,* and they're not going to stop."

"It's like I told you," Klevin said. "No one here cares about your politics."

But it wasn't politics, Devon thought. It was his past. His life, and the lives of people he'd left behind.

"Go home. Wait three hours. Then go to the overseer," Devon said. "Tell him I murdered the New Republic officers—with or without provocation, I don't care. After that, proceed as you like, but know that you can't help me and that I'll be leaving Vernid forever."

Klevin opened his mouth to say something. Devon stared at the man and let fury show in his eyes. Klevin clambered back up onto the bridge and Devon heard him running.

He thought of Rikton, the boy who'd nearly gone to Traitor's Remorse to blow himself up. He thought of Vryant, the Imperial Army officer who'd abandoned his post to join the gangs of Mrinzebon. He thought of Yrica Quell, who'd defected, and he thought of Shakara Nuress and Jothal Gablerone and Teso Broosh, who hadn't.

He hadn't expected all of them to follow Quell's path. But he'd expected some of them to follow his.

He'd been a fool, and they had been wise.

They'd known that the galaxy would not be kind to the soldiers of a defeated Empire. That there would be no place—not in the New Republic or the outlying worlds—for people like them. For people like Devon.

How had he not seen? How could he have deluded himself and asked others to follow him into fantasy?

Nuress and Gablerone and Broosh and all the rest had seen the new era with clear eyes and chosen to stay in the only home remaining to them. They'd held fast to their comrades, their family. Now the New Republic was slaughtering them for it.

The night of the incident in the cantina, he'd checked every public report he could find. Colonel Nuress—Grandmother—was gone. The others had fled. He knew what he had to do now.

He walked away from the dead spies. He left Devon with them.

His name was Major Soran Keize, of the 204th Imperial Fighter Wing. He had been among the Empire's finest pilots, and he would be again.

It was time he returned to Shadow Wing. Time he set things right.

## ACKNOWLEDGMENTS

Taking on this project was madness, but it was madness abetted by dear and supportive friends and colleagues. You told me I should do it (except one of you, who worried over me; and that, too, was appreciated), and I made it through this first book, at least. I've missed the lot of you, and I fear I'll forget someone if I start naming names. But you know who you are, and you mean the world to me.

My additional thanks to Charles Boyd, Susan Robinson, and Jeffrey Visgaitis, who all offered valuable feedback at various points and improved the story in important ways. I'm grateful to my colleagues at Fogbank Entertainment, as well, for trusting that I could juggle it all. Apologies to my derby brothers, who are doing just fine without me, but who I wish I could have supported better.

Thanks, too, to my editor, Elizabeth Schaefer, for putting such faith in me, and Jennifer Heddle and the Lucasfilm crew for doing the same. Much appreciation to Jody Houser for taking on the *TIE Fighter* comics project under tricky circumstances and bringing Shadow Wing to life in that medium, and for being a game collaborative partner in this endeavor.

One down. Two to go . . .

## ABOUT THE AUTHOR

ALEXANDER FREED is the author of *Star Wars: Battlefront: Twilight Company* and *Star Wars: Rogue One* and has written many short stories, comic books, and videogames. Born near Philadelphia, he currently resides in San Francisco, California. He enjoys the city's culture, history, and secrets, but he misses snow.

alexanderfreed.com
Twitter: @AlexanderMFreed

## ABOUT THE TYPE

This book was set in Minion, a 1990 Adobe Originals typeface by Robert Slimbach (b. 1956). Minion is inspired by classical, old-style typefaces of the late Renaissance, a period of elegant, beautiful, and highly readable type designs. Created primarily for text setting, Minion combines the aesthetic and functional qualities that make text type highly readable with the versatility of digital technology.